FALLEN FROM BABEL

FALLEN FROM BABEL

T. L. HIGLEY

REALMS
A STRANG COMPANY

Most Strang Communications/Charisma House/Siloam/Realms products are available at special quantity discounts for bulk purchase for sales promotions, premiums, fund-raising, and educational needs. For details, write Strang Communications/Charisma House/Siloam/Realms, 600 Rinehart Road, Lake Mary, Florida 32746, or telephone (407) 333-0600.

Fallen From Babel by T. L. Higley
Published by Realms
A Strang Company
600 Rinehart Road
Lake Mary, Florida 32746
www.realmsfiction.com

This is a work of fiction. Names, characters, places, and incidents are products of the author's imagination or are used fictitiously. Any similarity to actual people, organizations, and/or events is purely coincidental.

Cover design by studiogearbox.com
Cover illustration by Dave Seeley

Published in association with the literary agency of Janet Kobobel Grant, Books & Such, 4788 Carissa Ave., Santa Rosa, CA 95405.

Library of Congress Cataloging-in-Publication Data
Higley, T. L.
Fallen from Babel / T.L. Higley.
p. cm.
ISBN 1-59185-807-0 (pbk. : alk. paper)
1. Babylon (Extinct city)--Fiction. 2. Jesus Christ--Fiction. 3. Time travel--Fiction. I. Title.
PS3608.I375F35 2005
813'.6--dc22

2005016336

First Edition

05 06 07 08 09 — 87654321
Printed in the United States of America

To Rachel, Sarah, Jacob, and Noah—
My four wonderful, wacky, smart, and silly kids.
You make life a joy.

Acknowledgments

IT'S TAKEN SEVERAL years for this book to find its way to print, a slower path than my other titles. It was written before I'd been published at all, and early works often need much encouragement and refining. Thank you to each person who read some or all of the manuscript and encouraged me to keep going. Thank you to my wonderful friends Michelle King, Kelly Shennett, and Bette Jo Smith, who read the early version and still liked it (and me!). Randy Ingermanson and John Olson, you were the first two "real writers" I ever had the courage to share my work with. You have always been an encouragement, and I'm privileged to now call you friends.

To my agent, Janet Grant, thanks once again for your wisdom and guidance. Editor Jeff Gerke, I don't think I can write a book without you! Thank you for opening up this opportunity and investing yourself in my work. You are extraordinary.

I am so thankful to the Lord for my terrific family, who make it not only possible, but a priority, to give me time and space to write. All five of you are the best part of my day, and I love you more than I can say.

Prologue

AM I BACK? Dear God, am I back?

The same blinding headache. The same odd taste of sulfur.

A blessed absence of heat jolted his senses. How long since he had stood in a climate-controlled room? What day was it? What *year?*

Dear God, am I back? he whispered again into the silence, wondering if God Himself might answer.

He still held the blue glazed terra-cotta vase in his hand. It took willpower not to send the thing crashing to the floor. He glanced around the tiny room. He was alone. The naked bulb suspended above the vase cast an iridescent sheen on the centuries-old glaze. He stared at the markings on the side.

Underneath. I must look underneath.

He tilted it backward. There it was, the simple mark scratched into the surface.

Shaking, he returned the vase to the table and backed away.

Kaida. Oh, Kaida. I'm so sorry. I had no choice. If I could have made you understand, you would have agreed. I had no choice.

He fumbled for the door. Tears blurred his eyes. Not bothering to lock it behind him, he stepped into the cavernous hall that held the museum's Babylonian collection. An exit sign across the unlit room spilled a red trail across the floor. His footsteps thudded across the empty hall.

He barely had a conscious thought for the three flights down to the street exit of the museum. He unlocked a side door and stumbled into the alley. The city slept under a blanket of fresh snow. Where had he left his Buick?

The cold cut through his rented tux, and he wondered what three thousand years of late charges would amount to. No, he seemed to have returned to the moment he left. Time must have remained fixed here in Boston. And yet he knew...

Five weeks had passed since the night of the university's annual fund-raising gala, the night he had stepped into the museum to see the vase.

Chapter 1

THE MUTED BUZZ of conversation and clinking of silver and stemware in the banquet hall quieted as a wiry man stepped to the podium and adjusted the microphone. Peter looked up from his smoked salmon to give Hugh Rohner a half smile. He knew Hugh hated these affairs almost as much as he did.

The hotel's banquet hall held close to five hundred of the university's vital donors. *And lots of jewelry*, thought Peter. The ornate chandeliers seemed to bounce their light off a thousand gold-studded cuff links and glittering diamonds. He glanced over the room from his place at the head table, the faces merging into sameness. Blue hair and blue blood. Come to give away some money and make themselves feel crucial to the cause of research and education. Correction. *We* will make them feel crucial.

Hugh cleared his throat. "Ladies and gentlemen," he began. "We are honored by your presence here this evening. I trust you are enjoying your meal."

As Hugh droned on with his opening comments, Peter's mind wandered. Was it possible that only yesterday he had scaled the face of Mt. Shasta? His trip to California seemed a century removed from tonight. He wished he were hanging by his fingertips right now instead of checking the order of his speech cards. But it was an important night. In just a few days the announcement he'd waited his whole career for would be made public, and Peter would be named as the new president of the university. Tonight was all about impressing the alumni. He took a deep breath. Hugh would be escaping from the podium any moment now.

"... his classes are among the most sought-after here at the university," Hugh was saying, "and his research into ancient Near Eastern mythology has put our humble institution on the map."

The crowd tittered obligingly at Hugh's modesty.

"He has been a professor in the Religious Studies Department here at the university for the last fifteen years, making him slightly younger than myself." Again the polite laughter. "Like me, he spends all his time poring over crumbling artifacts, searching for information about dead religions. Perhaps that's the reason he's still a bachelor!"

Peter smiled. *What would you think, Hugh, if you knew that yesterday I was hanging from a cliff?*

Hugh was archeology and Peter was religion, but Hugh knew people didn't give away money merely to let someone else dig up broken pots. They wanted to know what good it brought humanity *now*. That was why Peter was here.

"So let me step aside and give you the man you came to hear. Ladies and gentlemen, Dr. Peter Thornton."

Peter grabbed his cards and checked his watch as the crowd applauded. Hugh had given him twenty minutes to impress the room with the fascinating research going on and the dire need for more funds. But he knew his audience. They didn't want twenty minutes of dull facts. He had to give them something to hang on to, something for the starched old ladies to repeat to their friends tomorrow at the country club luncheon.

"Good evening," he began. He patted the pocket of his tuxedo. Where were his glasses? His notes were swimming across the cards in front of him. He found the glasses and settled the gold wire rims down to the end of his nose so he could peer over them at the crowd. The ladies loved that, he knew. The whole Indiana Jones thing.

"We stand poised on the edge of a new era, ladies and gentlemen. Current research into the past gives us new direction for the future as we synthesize the myth of yesterday with the faith of today."

He delivered that last line with drama. He had their attention.

"The study of ancient mythology has taught us one thing: that all myth is essentially the same. It has a certain oneness that unifies it. Centuries of study—accelerating in our modern era—have revealed to the attentive student that there is no 'correct' religion. We must look within, ladies and gentlemen, to the divinity of our own consciousness."

He was losing them. He could see the glazed looks even from here. *Simplify, Peter, simplify.*

"One day even our modern Judeo-Christian beliefs will be relegated to the category of 'myth.'"

There. That woke up the old ladies who directed their church bazaars. He saw the raised eyebrows and smiled.

"Let me explain. Christianity is part of the whole, as all myths have been. But no doubt you have seen—this is a new era. People everywhere are embracing all types of spirituality, tapping into the power of the universe. The marriage of yesterday's myth and today's faith has given birth to a new doctrine, what some writers are calling the Doctrine of Divine Man."

From the dimly lit room full of tables, a shout rose up. "They have changed the truth of God into a lie! They have worshiped and served the creature more than the Creator!"

Peter paused and squinted into the murmuring audience. Where had that come from? Hecklers were not uncommon when he spoke on campus, but usually the people at these events had better manners.

Peter continued. "Ladies and gentlemen, it is chiefly the study of ancient peoples that brings us this new perspective. Your generous funding—"

"For the wrath of God will be revealed from heaven against all ungodliness and unrighteousness of men!"

The crowd's displeasure with the interruption was louder this time. Peter looked up from his note cards and removed his glasses. Two men from the physical education department were approaching a table in the center of the room.

A tall man with a shock of wild blond hair stood and pointed at Peter. "Once the gates are open, the demons will come pouring in!" The two physical education guys each took one of the man's arms. He twisted away. "You will see! There is no power that is amoral. There is only good and evil, and you invite evil! Your invitation will bring the old gods upon us, and they will not rest until we are destroyed!"

Yikes. Peter debated quickly: address the crazy guy, or ignore him? Security guards arrived and made his decision for him. They pulled the doomsayer from the table but couldn't keep him quiet. His last prediction, delivered as they yanked him from the room, echoed across the tables of shocked alumni. "It is already happening! The old gods are rising! And they will enslave us!"

Peter took a moment to readjust his glasses and let the room settle. When they were quiet, he opened his mouth to continue. *"Têtê malkuthach. Nehwê tzevjânach."*

Peter swallowed. *What did I just say?* The quizzical look on the faces below him proved he had not imagined it. What language was that? Aramaic? Maybe it was something he'd overheard in a recorded speech in Hugh's office in recent days.

He gave a half smile. "Ladies and gentlemen, we have so much to learn from the cultures of the past. And it is irrational fear, such as we have just witnessed, that we are here to eradicate.

There will always be those who fear the future, but I assure you, with your help, there will be no end to what we can achieve."

He went on for exactly twenty minutes. Peter was always punctual.

A half-hour later, while the donors were milling around and writing checks, Peter spotted Hugh's head over the sea of benefactors.

Hugh pulled him into a little group clustered near the bar, drinks in hand. "Peter, come meet Mrs. Weaver."

Peter pasted on a smile and nodded at the older woman with shocking red lipstick and jangling earrings.

"Oh, Dr. Thornton, I just loved your little talk. Very inspiring. I heard you speak two years ago at commencement. Just wonderful. And where is that lovely woman you had by your side that evening?"

Hugh rescued him. "Ah... Mrs. Weaver, tell Peter about your work with the children."

Peter smiled and nodded as the woman chattered. He forced himself to watch her eyes and not the thin, red lines of her mouth.

He had to get out of here. Small talk was not his strength. Besides, he was anxious to get over to the museum to see Hugh's latest artifact. "Unbelievable," was all Hugh would say when Peter had pressed him for details.

Hugh pulled him away from the group minutes later. "Lauren is around here somewhere," he murmured, searching over the tops of heads. "I wanted you to say hello to her. She's just started her graduate work. You've met my daughter, haven't you?"

"I think maybe once or twice." Peter remembered braces and giggles. Graduate work already? He was getting old.

"Never mind," Hugh shrugged. "She must have left."

"I hope she got out before the nutcase started his tirade," Peter said.

Hugh said nothing.

"Oh, come on, Hugh. I know you're a traditional monotheist, but you don't go along with that loon, do you?"

"The man obviously has some problems, Peter. But I wouldn't be so quick to dismiss what he says. You know that your fascination with power outside of God has always concerned me."

"Hugh, it's not power outside of God; it's—"

"Let's not argue tonight, Peter. Besides," Hugh smiled knowingly, "shouldn't you be working the room in preparation for Wednesday's big announcement?"

Peter sighed and looked around. He made eye contact with someone and was rewarded with an enthusiastic wave.

"Dr. Thornton!" Another jangling woman on the arm of a gray-haired tuxedo. Hugh abandoned Peter this time, moving on to network with the deep pockets. Peter glanced at his watch. One more hour.

Precisely one hour later Peter stepped from the hotel lobby into the city street. It was late, but the museum was only four blocks away. And it was worth the extra time to see Hugh's newest treasure. Peter jogged along the deserted street and pulled his overcoat against his chest to counteract the sudden chill.

His thoughts drifted back to Mrs. Weaver's earlier question about the woman she'd seen on his arm at commencement. Where *was* Julia? He wondered that himself. Married by now? Probably. She had been the only woman who had ever understood him. She saw right into his soul, or so he thought. Since then not another woman had given him a second look. Not that he blamed them. Hugh was right about how he spent his time, the occasional rock-climbing trip notwithstanding. Some of his best friends had been dead for centuries. Not exactly an attractive trait.

So much the better. He had important work to do. Research and teaching were companions enough. He spent his vacations alone, counteracting the tedium of university life with rock climbing whenever he got the chance, though his colleagues didn't believe he had a life outside the classroom walls. But all that was about to change. The university-sponsored Ultimate Success Seminar a few years ago had started him down the road of self-discovery, tapping into his own divinity. Now he was about to be named university president.

He got out the MP3 player in his jacket pocket to finish listening to the motivational sessions from another success seminar. Certain phrases stuck out as he listened.

Everything you need to change your life lies within you at this moment. Unlocking the power within yourself is the key to ultimate success.

The power within himself. Where could it take him? What extraordinary things were possible for him if he could unlock it?

The moon slid behind a thin line of smoky clouds and left the street in shadows as Peter reached the side entrance of the museum. He resisted a panicked look over his shoulder. He visited the museum at night frequently. There had never been a problem.

His key slid into the side door, and he locked it again behind him. The three-flight climb felt good after the heavy meal, but he couldn't shake the chill that had gripped him in the street. The empty building creaked and whispered tonight. He put his MP3 player away.

Pushing open the door at the top of the steps, he entered his home away from home. He paused a moment, thinking he might have heard the side entrance open again below him.

Had someone followed him? When he heard nothing more, he entered the dark hall, knowing the room well enough to navigate by the red glow of the exit sign. Unlocking another door, he entered Hugh's private sanctuary. One bare bulb flooded the room with light that glared off the piles of unimportant finds and stacks of yellow legal paper.

There it was, on the table. Had to be Hugh's prize. A blue glazed terra-cotta vase. Neo-Babylonian, Hugh had said. Circa 600 BCE, during the reign of the Chaldean Nebuchadnezzar II.

Peter loved pottery. It was firmly linked with his love for archaeology—for what was that science, he often joked to Hugh, but the study of old pots? He loved to study pottery, and he loved to create it on the wheel he kept in his apartment.

This piece across the room was striking. Eighteen inches high, rounded out wide in the middle, and tapering to a narrow neck. But what was so unbelievable that Hugh had urged him to check it out tonight? He took out his glasses again, planning to examine the markings around the side. An odd sensation flitted at the edge of his consciousness. He felt powerfully drawn to this piece, as though he were connected to it somehow. It was the oddest feeling. He felt as though he understood where it came from, understood the man who had created it. Stepping to the table, he reached out a tentative hand to tip the vase backward.

The moment he touched it a deafening roar *whooshed* through his head. He saw the vase, saw his hand on it, but it had receded from him, as if he looked at it through binoculars held backwards. Hot pain seared across his brain.

Was he having a stroke? He had only a moment to wonder before the vase, the room, and the museum disappeared as if they had been part of a dream.

Heat. Unbelievable heat. Pain in his head, pain in his side. The slight taste of sulfur. His eyes finally focused.

He stood in a large room, the walls a buff-colored mud brick, the high ceiling made of wood planks covered with reeds. Judging by the light filtering through a terra-cotta grid of holes in the wall it seemed to be dusk.

One of his hands was wrapped around the center shaft of a tall gold lampstand of some kind. The metal was burning hot. He yanked his hand from the shaft. It crashed to the ground, splashing oil onto the baked-brick floor.

And then he saw the man: lying a few feet from him, an obsidian-handled knife buried to the hilt in his chest. Blood everywhere. On the floor. On himself. He looked down to the pain in his side. Was that his blood? He looked through a jagged tear in his tunic and found a two-inch-long knife wound.

His *tunic?* Where was his tuxedo?

Movement behind him. He whirled around. A woman backed away from him, beautiful, but terrified. She rubbed at her hand as if it were injured. Her back brushed the wall, and she put her hands behind her to steady herself. The look of panic on her face no doubt matched his own. Her lips moved but without sound.

He spun back to the man on the floor. The first aid course he'd taken before he began rock climbing would be of no help. The stillness of death had fallen over the man's features. Peter turned back to the woman. She had blood on her, too. Had she stabbed the dead man? Had she stabbed Peter? He glanced at her face again, this time defensive. The gash in his side throbbed.

She shook her head, as if to keep him away.

What had happened? Where was the vase, the museum? Why was he in costume? The dead man, the gash in his own side—these were not movie props, but every part of his mind screamed at him that there was a rational answer.

To his left, the door opened to a hallway leading to a courtyard. Peter could see another man running toward him across the courtyard.

"My lord!" the man called. "He knows you have it! He is coming here!" The man ran into the room, his eyes taking in the dead man at once. "What have you done, Rim-Sin?" he whispered to Peter.

"I—I didn't do it!" Peter stammered. He looked at the woman behind him. She shook her head again.

"What has happened?" the man asked again.

Peter stared at him. Was that English the man spoke? It must be. He knew it was not, but he understood him perfectly. Impossible. *Impossible!*

"You must get out of here, my lord. The *rab alani* is not far behind me. You will be on trial for murder before the day is out!" He looked at the woman. "Perhaps you should take her with you—she is covered with blood."

Once more, the woman shook her head. Peter recognized the glassy look of someone slipping into shock. He swung around the room one last time, then pushed past the man and ran into the courtyard.

He had expected to be outdoors, but he was not. All around the sides of the courtyard other hallways led to other rooms. He circled like a caged animal, realizing he was trapped in the center of the house. Which way was out?

Choosing a hall, he flung himself through it and landed in the kitchen. A man glanced up from a cooking hearth, then bowed his head respectfully when he saw Peter. Peter backed up, returned to the courtyard, and chose another hallway.

This place is like a maze! Another startled servant was in this room, but Peter could sense that the door across the room led to the street. He scrambled past the doorkeeper, through the door, and up the five steps that led to street level.

The sight pulled him up short. *A dream. It must be a dream.* He stood in the center of a paved road lined with palm trees. Houses like the one he had escaped bordered both sides of the road. The heat! He could taste the gritty heat of the desert.

The street was in chaos, even though the sun was setting. Crowds pushed and pressed past him with no regard for his injury. Why were all these people in costume? Was he on a movie set for some biblical epic? His eyes traveled down the length of the street. And then his heart dropped into the pit of his stomach.

A pyramid-like structure overhung the horizon a half-mile in the distance.

He recognized the 300-foot, stepped ziggurat immediately. Seven levels of unadorned stone towered above the city, as though a giant child had stacked all his wooden blocks in a pyramid, then shouted, "Look what I made!"

Etemenanki. The House of the Platform of Heaven and Earth. Commonly believed to be the biblical Tower of Babel.

Peter stood rooted in the center of the street, jostled by the passing crowd. As he stared at the tower only one thought thrashed its way into his mind.

I am in ancient Babylon.

A yell from behind startled Peter into action. A turbaned man on a camel shouted to clear the way. Peter stepped to the wall of the house a moment before the camel crushed past him. The wall was cut into a saw-toothed pattern, and Peter pressed himself into one of the shadows.

He glanced in both directions. Several hundred feet down the street, three men strode toward him, cloaks flapping behind them, a cloud of sand swirling at their feet. Somehow Peter sensed they were coming for him.

He lurched away from the wall and ran down the road dodging animals, children, and merchants. He ran through the city streets with no idea where he was going. The ziggurat always loomed over the buildings, giving him a sense of direction, but he knew of no place to hide.

Trial. Murder. The words pounded in his ears as he ran. Behind him, he heard shouts. The men had seen him. They were chasing him. Maybe he should stop and explain that he didn't know what had happened. *Sure, Peter, they'll believe the old "I'm in a time warp" defense.* Better to run. He tried to sprint, but the jagged cut in his side tortured him. He put his hand over it, blood seeping through his fingers as he ran.

Finally, when darkness hid the streets, he could no longer run. He stumbled through the nearest doorway and fell at the feet of an astonished man who held a blazing reed torch.

"Get out!" the man screamed, punctuating his command with a kick to Peter's stomach.

Chapter 2

THE DUSTY NIGHT wind shrieked across the summit of Etemenanki, snatching at Qurdi-Marduk-lamur's outer cloak and tangling it around his bare legs. The priest lifted his shaved head to the sultry air and filled his lungs. A young lamb dangled by its neck from his left hand, kicking and bleating.

The gods of the night were dazzling this evening. He felt their presence as he closed his eyes and let them look down on him in their pleasure. He raised his right hand and began the sacred *su-ila.*

> May the great gods of the night,
> Shining Fire-star,
> Heroic Erra,
> Bow-star, Yoke-star,
> Orion, Dragon-star,
> Wagon, Goat-star
> Bison-star, Serpent-star,
> Stand by and
> Put a propitious sign
> In the lamb
> I am blessing now
> For the haruspicy I will perform at dawn.

The lamb kicked more after the Lifting-of-the-Hand. Perhaps it suspected what its fate would be in the morning.

Qurdi laughed. He tilted his head, and a shivering slave hurried over to take the lamb from him. If the gods were gracious, the lamb would provide an answer tomorrow.

And where was Rim-Sin? News from the *rab alani* had reached him already. Rim-Sin had escaped from his home where a dead Jew had been found. Where would he go? Certainly not to the Esagila complex. He would know the *rab alani* would search for him there.

Qurdi smiled at the stars above his head and spread his arms wide enough to embrace them. He would find Rim-Sin. He had no doubt. And when he did, Rim would give him the answer, if he had discovered it. Was it an incantation? An amulet? There was no way of knowing what Rim had found, but it had to have been awful in its power. No matter. Qurdi had worked too long to rise in the king's court. He would not let Rim-Sin take the place of chief advisor—that place rightly belonged to *him.* He laughed again. Prying open secrets was a diviner-priest's joy, and Qurdi knew special ways to extract information from those who thought to climb above him. Once he knew Rim's secret, he would escort him to the king for justice himself.

The Temple of Ishtar lay two hundred *qanu* from the outer enclosure around Etemenanki. It took Qurdi-Marduk-lamur only minutes to walk there, but he cursed himself for spending so long on the Platform. The goddess was demanding, and she would not favor him for arriving late, especially since he'd been delayed because he'd been offering the *su-ila* to her rival gods.

Temple slaves had lit the torches inside before he arrived, and from the courtyard he could see straight through the antechamber and into the oblong chapel where the statue of Ishtar stood centered against the back wall. He strode through the temple and into the chapel, pressing the back of his hand to his nose before the goddess, hoping she forgave him for his appeal to her fellow gods of the night sky.

She was so beautiful—sculpted from gold, clothed in the finest linen Babylon could produce. He prostrated himself before her, his heart calming in her presence. Standing, he studied her position. Had someone impure pushed against her? No, he was imagining it.

It was growing late. Soon the city streets beyond the courtyard would fill with people headed for the festival.

Qurdi clapped several times. "Bring the meal!" he shouted.

There was no response. He stalked to the temple kitchen where slaves still arranged pomegranates on an elaborate table.

"Fools!" he shrieked, smacking the nearest slave's face with the back of his hand. "It is the Day-of-Lying-Down! The festival begins soon!"

Four slaves rushed out behind him through the antechamber. They carried the tables for the evening meal, laden with beverages and trays of lamb, duck, eggs, and ripe fruit. The slaves placed the tables in the center of the chapel, and another slave brought the water for washing in a golden bowl, placing it beside the food.

All the slaves bore the eight-pointed star of Ishtar on the backs of their hands, branding them as dedicated to the goddess. To Qurdi, almost all his slaves were identical. They could be Hittites, Assyrians, Cassites, or Jews brought from any number of vassal countries. Thanks to the brilliant military strategies of King Nabu-kudurri-usur, Babylon had become a thoroughly mongrel city.

When the food was placed, all of them except two hurried back to the kitchen. Qurdi would recognize these two young slaves anywhere. They lingered behind, watching Qurdi for any further instruction.

"Go," Qurdi commanded, but gave a slight smile and nod to one as the fine-looking boy walked back through the chapel.

Qurdi presented the tables to the goddess. His stomach

rumbled at the sight of the food, but he would not eat yet. Not until the goddess had been served. He drew the linen curtain around the statue and tables of food, protecting his lady's privacy.

He clapped again.

More slaves danced in, banging drums and cymbals. They spun for Ishtar, their red robes snaking around them like a blood-red river. Qurdi watched in satisfaction as the ritual fumigation was performed for the goddess. After the meal, the slaves opened the curtain, removed the tables, and placed water before the goddess. They again drew the curtain so she could wash.

When all was complete, Qurdi followed the slaves to the temple kitchen. He had been eyeing the mutton since the tables had been brought. Now it was his turn. After he finished, the slow-moving slaves would need to be disciplined. Qurdi always enjoyed that.

And in the morning, when the sun's first rays streaked across the city, Qurdi would slit the lamb's throat and find Rim-Sin.

Pinpricks of torchlight danced across Peter's vision. He had only a vague sense of the man above him who had kicked him. Loss of blood, the heat, and the shocking strangeness of it all combined to leave him only half-conscious on the floor of the stranger's house.

"What is it?" a woman's voice called from within.

"Nothing! Go back into the courtyard!" the man yelled.

"But the festival! It is about to begin!"

"I said go back!"

Peter reached a bloody hand to the man's ankle. "Please."

"Get out." The man glared down at him.

"I need help." The pain blurred Peter's vision.

"I cannot help you. A bleeding man is an evil omen, especially today. Even the moon god Sin is dead tonight! I have no protection against your evil. Find the *asu* if you need healing. Now get out!"

Peter stumbled out of the house before the kick to the stomach could be repeated.

Which way? The sun had set, but the heat was still unrelenting. Hundreds of burning torches marched through the streets in every direction. High-pitched singing floated to him on a hot breeze. He could barely see the faces behind the flames of the torches. Pressing himself flat against a wall again, he waited for a cluster of people to jingle past him. The jewelry on their colorful tunics and cloaks glinted in the firelight.

Mrs. Weaver's absurd earrings. The fund-raising gala. *I was there only minutes ago. What is happening to me?*

A break in the crowd gave him the chance to cross the street. On the other side, he collapsed to his knees beside a roadside shrine, gripping the only solid thing he'd found in the waves of confusion. A mournful chant began in the street, and others behind picked it up.

The scholar in Peter struggled to race through all the learning of his life on the subject of Babylon. Into which part of the city's two thousand years had he stumbled? Impossible to say. Who was on the throne now? The scattered roadside shrines, the streets full of moon worshipers of all races, the tower rising above the buildings—all these things had remained the same in Babylon for centuries.

Forget that. Did he care what year it was? He had to get home. But how? How had he gotten here? Was this a dream? Could he wake himself up?

Reality is no more real than your dreams. Perhaps we are dreaming even when we believe we are awake.

The words came to him unlooked for. They were from that

success seminar. He closed his eyes and lowered his body to the sandy soil. He wouldn't have thought the words were so embedded in his mind. Playing them again and again had paid off. He had internalized the truths.

If you truly believed in this different reality, you could do impossible things when you are awake. There is a higher reality, and in it nothing is real but your own spirit. All the spirits are one—we have created boundaries between ourselves unnecessarily.

Had he created this impossible thing? This impossible place? Was it a lesson, a test? Was he in control of it?

He lifted his head, leaning against the stone shrine for support. Where should he go? The three-foot monument along the road hid him well, but if this were not a dream, he would soon bleed to death.

The angry man across the street was right. He must find the *asu.*

Peter fell in with the wave of worshipers, and the current sucked him into its rush toward the temple. He had no plan, but he would never find help if he didn't move. The procession streamed up and down streets, carrying him like a piece of driftwood until he was completely disoriented. He cursed his terrible sense of direction. Was it only a few hours ago he had gotten lost on the way to the hotel for the gala?

The bobbing torches began to blur, and the chants became muted. He was losing consciousness. He stumbled once, twice, and was certain he would soon be trampled, but then a hand shot into the fray and plucked him out. He collapsed against the brawny chest of a bearded man as the throng rushed past.

"Rim-Sin!" the young man shouted into his ear.

Oh, no, not again. Peter shook his head.

"Come," the man insisted, yanking him toward an open door.

Once in the coolness inside, Peter closed his eyes. Nothing mattered now but sleep.

"Stay awake, Rim."

A gentle slap on his face. Then darkness.

Cosam lifted Rim-Sin, tall as the injured man was, and carried him through his courtyard and into his central living room, setting him down on a wide palm-wood chair padded with palm fibers.

A woman gripped the back of another chair, her eyes darting back and forth between Rim-Sin and Cosam.

"I know, Kaida," Cosam said, in answer to her look. "I know who he is. But we cannot leave him in the street to die."

She said nothing.

"We must keep it quiet that he is here, however. Giving aid to the king's diviner would not be looked upon with favor by the elders. It will take Rebekah a few moments to get back with the *asu.* Once he is well enough to walk, I will send him home again, I promise."

Cosam bent over Rim-Sin and ripped at his tunic, exposing the wound. "Bring water," he said to Kaida, but she remained motionless, staring at Cosam.

"Kaida, you should sit down also. You look almost as bad as he does." Cosam pointed to the chair she held onto, and the woman sank into it as into the arms of a friend.

Ten minutes later a dark-haired girl glided into the room, graceful in spite of her protruding belly. She was even younger than Kaida. Cosam put an arm around her and kissed her forehead.

She smiled at his affection. "No Hebrew would come out when the Sabbath is beginning, Cosam," she told him.

"Then we must thank the Most High the *asu* is not a Hebrew."

Rebekah looked at Kaida, and her smile faded. "Cosam says he found you wandering the streets as well, Kaida. What has happened? Where did this blood on you come from?"

Kaida's eyes widened, then closed. Rebekah went to her and

touched her arm, but movement in the doorway caused them all to turn.

A man crept into the room, dark braids swinging against his purple tunic. With one squinted eye on the patient, he pulled a knife from a leather bag, laid it on a nearby table, and lit a small torch.

Hugh?

Peter blinked several times, trying to focus. What a bizarre dream! That would be the last time he would have tiramisu for dessert!

He started to speak, but a searing pain in his side tore a yelp from him instead.

"Hold him down!" a voice shouted in the blurred distance. "I must finish the cauterization!"

Waves of nausea washed over him, and then darkness again.

The dreaming returned.

Peter stood at the base of the Platform of Etemenanki. Before him knelt hundreds of tuxedoed and gowned university alumni, their faces downturned to the sandy ground. At the center of the crowd, one man stood and studied him.

Hugh! Peter reached out, unable to speak.

"Chief Thornton!" Hugh's voice carried across the heads of those that bowed to him.

Chief?

"Hugh, get me out of here!"

"It is not time, Peter. You are not finished."

Peter shook his head. "Finished?"

Hugh pointed to Peter's right. Bare-chested slaves pushed carts of bricks toward them.

"What are they doing?" Peter asked Hugh. He turned back to his friend. Hugh was gone.

A woman in the crowd in front of him looked up from her place on her knees. He had seen her somewhere before. At the fund-raiser?

She pointed at the sweating slaves. "They are finishing the tower!" Her voice raised to a shriek. "We must finish the tower!"

The crowd jumped to its feet. Peter backed away. They surged toward him, hands out, shouting, "Finish the tower! Finish the tower!"

Peter pushed them away, ducked through the crowd, and ran into the streets. They paid no attention, each of them instead picking up all the bricks he or she could carry and staggering up the first set of steps cut into the side of the tower.

Peter watched for a moment. A voice behind him set his heart pounding again. "You must tear it down."

Hugh.

"What is happening to me?"

"It is a test. You must tear it down."

"I don't understand!"

Hugh smiled. "He was trying to tear it down, but you killed him. Now you must finish the work."

"Who? How?" Peter grabbed Hugh's arm. "Help me, Hugh!"

Hugh shook his head. "There is a larger work to be done, but not until you finish his first task. You are not ready." Hugh disengaged from Peter's grasp. "There is much to learn, Peter. You've only begun."

Shouting arose behind him. Peter turned to the crowd he'd escaped. They still marched in succession up the stairs, each carrying bricks. But a common shout had united them.

"Rim-Sin-Thorn-ton! Rim-Sin-Thorn-ton!"

Peter sank to the sand, buried his head between his knees, and let the murky darkness cover him.

When he awoke, the room came into focus as though he had found his glasses. Sunlight poked through a terra-cotta grid mounted in the wall. He lay on a wide cot with a mattress of woven reeds. Across the room, a beautiful woman poured water from a yellow glazed pitcher into a matching bowl.

He shifted his weight, and the woman startled like a lovely, frightened rabbit. She watched him without speaking.

He had seen her before. Waist-length black hair and the pale, terrified face. She had been there with the dead man. Spattered with blood.

The bearded man from the street entered. "Ah, you are awake, finally. The *asu* has repaired you well, I believe."

Peter took a deep breath. The pain in his side had lessened. A dim memory of a man with braids floated through his mind. But he felt hot, very hot.

"Kaida told me what happened in your home, Rim-Sin. You are safe here until you can explain. I will not tell the authorities where you are."

Peter looked at the girl through narrowed eyes. What had she told this man? Had Peter somehow stabbed the dead man? Or had she done it herself and blamed him?

"One thing I must insist upon, however," the man continued. "Though we've newly become captives in this city, this is still my house. While you are my guest, you will treat my sister with respect. Under this roof she is not your slave, and she is not your—your—she is not yours to do with as you please."

Peter suddenly understood the girl's fear. Whoever this Rim-Sin was, the pretty girl across the room was his concubine.

Peter alternated between sleep and fevered wakefulness. Judging by the dark and light he had seen in the home when he woke, he knew that several days had passed uninterrupted. When he was awake, only Cosam visited him, but sometimes he would snap open his eyes and find Kaida bending over him or setting food beside the bed. He didn't trust her. What was she doing? Would she poison him?

Once, her dark hair fell across his face as his eyelids fluttered. He shut them again before she noticed he was awake. He fell asleep and dreamed again, this time of Julia.

A graduate student, three years ago. Fifteen years younger than him. Peter had had no intention of getting involved with her, no more than with any of the female students who found reasons to stop at his office door. They all liked to talk about his classes, and he didn't mind. There would be no one to talk to at home, after all. His colleagues invited him out for dinner or drinks every few weeks, but he was never himself around them.

Julia was different. She seemed to see the real Peter. Though the buttoned-down exterior fooled the others, he could never be fake with her.

She had hounded him about the slate-colored rock he kept on his desk until he admitted that he brought it down from El Capitan, the highest wall he'd ever scaled. He was shocked when she insisted on going with him the next time he climbed.

That climb began a year that chipped away at his cold heart, until he would have done anything she asked.

And then she was gone. A job offer in London. Nothing really to keep her here, she said. A great opportunity. He drove her to the airport, walked her to the security gate, kissed her good-bye, and went home to his empty apartment.

That had been two years ago, and not another person had entered his apartment, or his heart, since.

But today, in his dream, she was there. Climbing with him again, laughing at the way he almost slipped on loose rocks, calling him an old man. Except today, instead of blonde hair, she had long, black waves that the wind kept blowing across his face.

"Rim, wake up." A hand shook his arm.

"What is it?" Peter said, raising himself from the bed in the early morning light.

"The *rab alani* has discovered you. He is on his way. You must leave quickly!"

Peter jumped up, wincing as the wound on his side pulled.

"Slowly, slowly."

"You said quickly!"

Cosam smiled.

In his moments of wakefulness in the week he had been here, Peter had allowed himself to trust this big man, who was probably ten years his junior. Cosam could have turned him in—or killed him—if he'd wanted to. Peter marveled at the kind way in which Cosam had treated him, even though he believed Peter to be his sister's slave-master. Even so, Cosam had kept Kaida safely hidden from him most of the time.

Peter had wrestled with whether to tell Cosam everything. But he'd decided that mistaken identity was better than being believed to be insane. Instead, he had tried to gain as much information as he could about this time and place.

"The *rab alani* must not find you here," Cosam said. "Where will you go?"

Good question. What are my choices?

"Perhaps your fellow diviners will hide you," Cosam suggested. "At Esagila, or even in the palace."

Diviner. The textbook definition typed itself across the screen of his mind: specialists who solicited omens and interpreted signs from the gods. Esagila was the god Marduk's temple, he remembered. Could he find it?

It sounded far-fetched, but it was something to go on. Or should he face the *rab alani* and try to explain? Explain what? No, it would be better to stay out of sight until he figured out how to get back.

Kaida slid into the room, her eyes on Peter. "The *rab alani* is on the next street."

"Then you must go." Cosam gave Peter a cloak and took him to the outer doorway. With a wave, he disappeared into the house, leaving Peter alone in the street.

Chapter 3

BABYLON.

She could trace her lineage back to the earliest civilizations, a hybrid of every ancient people that had made their homes on the sand-strewn plain of Shinar. She had stood for ages as all manner of races had swept in from every direction and scattered through her streets. First the Amorites, then the Hittites, the Assyrians, the Aramaeans, and most recently the Chaldeans. She was a city of sand and blood, and although those who infused the city were from conquered lands, she was, in a sense, welcoming them home again. For it was out of the heart of Babylon that every race and culture had flowed through the East. She was their root, their source. And her heart was the Tower of Etemenanki.

She had smiled as the ancient tower had first risen above the plain. Man had decided to make himself equal with God. He baked bricks, he collected bitumen tar, and the tower rose. Before it was ever completed, the project was abandoned, victim to the sudden confusion of language. The people called their tower "Babel." It meant "Gate of God," but it sounded very much like "confusion."

Now, centuries later, the tower was partially restored, and Babylon honored her gods there. Around the tower, Babylon flourished in the desert sand, drinking in the Euphrates River, which flowed through the center of her, dividing the Old City and the New. She was beautiful, from the Southern Palace to the Hanging Gardens. She was protected from invaders by double walls, sentry towers, and a surrounding moat. And inside her walls, her people dedicated themselves to the search for exhilaration.

Babylon offered her citizens excitement in many forms. Revelry, drunkenness, and carousing whetted their appetites. They devoured prostitution and idol worship and then glutted themselves on uncontrolled immorality and violence. Witchcraft and sorcery inebriated them until their lives were completely given over to the endless search for stimulation.

Babylon was diseased. Rotting from the inside. But in her sated stupor of excess, she had no idea.

In the western courtyard of the royal palace, Qurdi-Marduk-lamur waited with an assembly of slaves, charioteers, astrologers, and diviners mingling in the blistering heat as they prepared for the hunt. The astrologers had informed the king that the day was an auspicious one for the kill, and he was only too eager to show his people the favor of the gods. As on all occasions, Qurdi would attempt to use the events of the day to manipulate the king's favor away from anyone but himself, the high priest of Ishtar.

Sunlight reflected off the buff-colored palace walls, blinding the eyes and tightening everyone's nerves. Even the horses were jumpy.

Conversation hushed as the king strode out into the courtyard, spear in hand. Here was Nabu-kudurri-usur, son of Nabopolassar, descended from the gods, war chief of the Chaldeans, son of the morning, conqueror of all nations.

His shoulder-length hair and square-cut beard were dyed black, and the ends of his hair had been curled before he'd made his appearance. His skin was lighter than most of his Persian subjects. The courtiers said it was a mark of honor to be thus protected from the killing sun, but Qurdi had heard rumors of a questionable lineage. The king had dressed for the hunt in a Tyrian purple belted tunic with straps running diagonally across his chest. A slave jogged beside him, carrying his cloak. The young king vaulted into a two-wheeled chariot and signaled a charioteer in a plumed helmet to depart. The man snapped the reins over the horses' backs.

"Halt!" the king demanded when they had just begun. "I want to speak to Belteshazzar."

A young man dressed in a plain brown tunic broke away from the enclave of wise men and approached the chariot with a smile. His wavy dark hair was worn defiantly shorter than Babylonian fashion, a feature that seemed only to endear him to the ladies of the court. Qurdi had heard women praise his dark eyes and strong build as well. Apparently, the king was only one of many enamored of the handsome foreigner, though Qurdi understood nothing of their admiration.

The king leaned down to him. "What does your God tell you about the hunt today, Belteshazzar?"

"He has told me nothing, O King."

The king grunted. "Do you have an incantation for a successful kill, then?"

"O King, live forever, I will gladly pray to God for your safety."

"So be it." The king waited for the recitation, but the young man before him only bowed his head.

"Jews," the king said, shaking his head as though the whole lot of them were a puzzlement. He flicked a wrist at the charioteer once more, and the horses headed for the courtyard gate. The rest followed on foot, their destination an arena surrounding the Tower of Etemenanki.

Qurdi dropped back from the crowd, and several of his colleagues slowed to join him.

"He consults the Israelite, even after we have spoken," Qurdi said, more to himself than to the others.

"He does not trust us as he once did, Qurdi," an astrologer said.

Qurdi tilted his head. "The young Jew has the king's ear in all matters these days."

"Something must be done!" a diviner said.

Something would be done, Qurdi vowed. Something would be done. The current chief of magicians held to none of the Chaldean's ways, yet still the king relied on the boy. Last week Belteshazzar had not even attended the festival dedicated to the monthly death of the moon god. Still insisting there was only one God, the Jews' Yahweh, he would not serve the created lights of the sky. The Day-of-Lying-Down was only one of three lunar festivals each month, and Belteshazzar intentionally spent each of them in his palace quarters. He was clearly a heretic. Why couldn't the king see it?

The procession reached the park in front of the tower where the hunt would take place. Etemenanki loomed over the arena. Hundreds of palm trees towering over the waist-high walls barely stirred in the morning heat. The king's chariot made a wide circle at one end of the arena, turning to face the opposite side where a lion paced in a wooden cage, hungry for a meal. A line of spearsmen stood inside the wall, protection against misread omens.

In his chariot, the king played to his audience, who leaned over the walls to reach for him. With his arms outstretched, he turned a circle in the chariot, inviting their praise.

Qurdi did not blink as the gold medallion at the king's waist shot an arrow of sunlight into his eyes. The golden light chilled in his eyes, and pure hatred reflected back. The king's father had been a son of the gods, worthy of service. Nabu-kudurri-usur was only a man.

"Prepare the lion!" the king charged.

Two slaves stood beside the cage. "The lion is ready!"

With a dramatic flourish, the king dropped his arm. The servants raised the door, and the lion roared out, shaking its mane.

The animal padded back and forth several times, saliva dripping from its jagged teeth, its eyes never leaving the king's chariot. The crowd cheered, anxious for action.

Another signal from the king brought vicious dogs snarling out of other cages, along with the beaters.

The dogs circled the lion, who bared its teeth and hunched its back. These dogs had been bred to attack, and they did not disappoint. Two of them lunged, and the crowd let out another yell. The lion had to choose, and one dog soon lay twitching in the sand.

The beaters rushed in then. They struck with their long sticks and drove the lion toward the king's chariot, where he waited with his spear.

Qurdi glanced across the crowd at Belteshazzar. The Jew still stood with his head bowed. Qurdi allowed himself the brief pleasure of imagining a spear driven into him.

Belteshazzar surprised him at that moment by lifting his head and returning Qurdi's stare. Qurdi watched him, wondering if the young Israelite diviner could read his thoughts. He certainly had power none of them possessed. Belteshazzar approached him, and Qurdi looked away.

"The heat incenses the lion today," Belteshazzar said.

Qurdi lowered his chin, his eyes on the hunt.

Belteshazzar seemed to stare through him again. "The king will no doubt be successful."

"Oh?" Qurdi said. "Does your *one God* speak to you now?"

Belteshazzar looked away. "You show your chief disrespect, Qurdi. Sometimes there is wisdom in silence."

Qurdi moved away with thinly disguised loathing. These captives from Israel had first come eight years ago. Nabu-kudurri-usur had brought royalty, soldiers, craftsmen, and artisans—all the best people of their land—to assure that the vassal nation would not rebel. Belteshazzar was among them, practically a child then. He had joined the *kasdim*, and before any of the wise men knew what had happened, the usurper had interpreted one of the king's dreams, been promoted to chief of magicians, and been given a Babylonian name, which he refused to use since he would not acknowledge Bel as god. Daniel, he insisted upon calling himself. Since then, he had not bowed his head to any Babylonian god. He worshiped only his one God. Hatred for the Jews was the only thing Qurdi and the king's chief diviner, Rim-Sin, shared.

A shout went up from the people. One of the beaters had drawn too close. He thrust with his stick in defense, but the lion swiped at it with a massive paw and sent it flying. With the gracefulness of a house cat the beast pounced on the slave. The people screamed in a mixture of horror and delight.

Ah, well. That is what slaves are for. All the more honor for the king when he kills the lion.

The beast approached the chariot now. The king stood poised with his spear held aloft. The animal bared its teeth only once before Nabu-kudurri-usur heaved the spear toward its chest. The shaft sank into the fur, blood spurting. The spear angered the lion, however, and it charged the chariot where the king had begun to seek victory acclaim from the crowd.

With his back to the lion, the king mistook their screams for praise. The lion moved closer, the spear jutting from its hide. When the spearsmen ran in, the king turned back toward his foe. He raised an arm to stay the spears and pulled an arrow from a quiver in the chariot, putting it to the bow. He took careful aim at the approaching beast, and then let the arrow fly. The lion dropped.

The people were half-crazed with devotion to their king. The gods favored him, and so would they.

The king stepped down from his chariot and raised a golden cup high. More cheers. He ran a hand through his hair, damp with sweat. Then with an arm across his chest and fist over his heart, he spilled a few drops from the cup over the dead lion, atoning for the harm he had caused it and appeasing its angry spirit. Even from this distance, Qurdi could hear his mighty voice recite the devotional speech thanking his patron goddess for the day's success.

Belteshazzar moved away, and Qurdi's colleagues surrounded him. "What did Belteshazzar say?" one asked.

"The dog never says anything of importance," Qurdi said. "Come. It is time to return to the palace. We must consult the omens. I believe there will soon be an unfavorable report to give the king about his chief of magicians."

In the home of Cosam, Rebekah's time had come.

Cosam waved off Kaida's attempts to calm him as he paced through the small courtyard, trying with his thoughts to speed the midwife to his home. Rebekah emerged from their main living chamber, one hand on the doorframe.

"What are you doing?" Cosam steered her away from the chamber. "Go back to your bed!"

"I have done this before, husband," she laughed. "It is better to walk."

Cosam shook his head, looking toward the street door once again. "Where is the midwife?"

"Perhaps the midwife would be here if you had called for a Jewish woman instead of a Babylonian."

"Rebekah, you know I had no choice. The Babylonian priests will not allow a temple goldsmith like me to contaminate his home with a Hebrew midwife. They would consider all my gold work to be impure."

Rebekah frowned. "This would not happen in Jerusalem."

"We are not in Jerusalem. We are in Babylon now, and we will stay here until the Lord God's judgment is finished!" Cosam's concern spilled over into irritation. He regretted it instantly and went to put his arms around the woman he loved more than life.

Rebekah doubled over, clutching the back of a chair as her face whitened.

"Back to our room, Rebekah!" Cosam cupped her elbow and pulled her toward the doorway.

"Kaida!" Cosam looked over his shoulder. "Come help Rebekah."

"She will be fine, Cosam, do not worry." Kaida led the laboring woman to her bed. The room had been darkened and was slightly cooler than the courtyard. Rebekah stretched out on the bed, and Kaida fanned her face with a palm branch.

Cosam's brow furrowed as he watched his younger sister help Rebekah onto the woven-reed bed. "You are so different since we arrived in Babylon, Kaida. That man has made you angry."

Kaida scowled. "I will not be his concubine!"

"Kaida!" Rebekah shook her head. "You must not think of running away!"

"Perhaps Kaida will one day buy her freedom, Rebekah," Cosam said.

Kaida's head snapped toward him. "How would I do that?"

"I have been saving scraps of silver when I can, but someday it will add up to something."

"Someday," Kaida said, as though the day were only a speck on the horizon.

Cosam pitied her. They'd been in Babylon less than a month, but already she'd been given to Rim-Sin. Even if she could buy her freedom, who would marry her?

Rebekah moaned in pain. "Where is the midwife?"

"What is wrong, Rebekah?" Cosam was by her side in a moment.

"I do not know. Something seems different this time."

Cosam bounded to the courtyard.

A little girl wandered into the bedroom, a five-year-old version of her dark-haired mother. Her glossy black hair was hidden by the ever-present linen head covering, but an errant curl strayed across her eye. She looked up at Kaida with a crooked-toothed smile.

Kaida put her arm around the girl's shoulders. "This is no place for you now, Hannah," she said, turning her toward the doorway. "Go now; play with your doll."

"What's wrong with Mama?"

"She's having a baby," Kaida said. "Sometimes it hurts. Run along now."

She watched the child skip away, then turned to Rebekah. "What name will you give this child?"

"I do not know. Cosam would like to name him Elmadam, after his father. But I want to call him Addi."

"And are you so certain it will be a boy?"

"I have prayed so, for Cosam's sake."

Another contraction gripped her, and she closed her eyes. "Something is wrong, Kaida. I can feel it. Don't tell Cosam. But pray for the midwife."

Peter tried to blend in with the noisy crowd as it moved toward the palace. The king's chariot, draped with the body of the lion, headed the procession. The throng that followed seemed a good place to get lost. He held to the back of the crowd, hoping any palace officials who might recognize him as Rim-Sin would occupy positions of honor near the front.

A whisper at his ear contradicted his hope. "Rim-Sin, where have you been?"

Peter glanced at the young man beside him, then continued toward the palace.

The younger man fell in beside him. He wore a purple robe, embroidered with gold stars. Gold bracelets encircled both wrists. "Word of the killing has reached the king's ear. He has mentioned you in court."

Peter shrugged. "I am trying to remain unseen for a time."

"You missed our meeting two nights ago. You were to teach me the new ritual."

Peter sensed disappointment in the man's voice. Rim-Sin's protégé? "I am sorry," he said. "It could not be avoided." The palace loomed before them. Peter nodded toward it. "I wish to remain hidden. Do you think there is a place in the palace where I will be safe?"

The younger man laughed. "The palace has more rooms than a honeycomb, Rim. You know that." He touched Peter's arm. "Stay behind me and keep your head down. In those clothes you will be mistaken for my slave. I will lead you in."

Peter followed the man and studied the embroidered stars that twinkled in the sunlight. He looked like a sorcerer's apprentice, all right. Peter wished for a closer look at the outside of the palace, but the young man ushered him through the arch and into a corridor. A door opened on his right, and Rim-Sin's young friend pushed him in. It was a bedchamber, sparse but clean, with a raised bed and a small table beside the window.

The man closed the door behind them. "You're safe here for a time, Rim-Sin. But the palace has sharp ears and a wagging tongue. It won't be long before you are found."

"Thank you."

"And what of the New Year Festival?"

Peter raised his eyebrows.

"It is your year! If you do not come forward to perform the

New Year sacrifice for the king, you will be hunted and killed!" He grabbed Peter's arms and studied him with piercing eyes. "If the gods do not kill you first."

Peter swallowed, then shook off the younger man's arms. "The New Year Festival."

"It will not be long. You must clear up this business about the dead man very soon, Rim! The king will not stand for your absence."

Which king would that be? Peter needed more information and decided on a risk. He turned his back toward the other man and picked up a golden bowl from the small table. "What do you call this king?"

"Call?"

"Has he given you his private name yet, or do you still refer to him as . . ."

He swiveled back to the younger man and tried to read the confusion on his face.

"I call him Nabu-kudurri-usur, as every other diviner in the court calls him."

Nebuchadnezzar II.

"Ah. Well, it is still early in his reign, is it not?"

"The seventh year. That is not so early."

Babylonians never counted the first year, "the year of accession," Peter remembered. Nebuchadnezzar had taken the throne in 605 BCE, after his father had died unexpectedly. Peter calculated. That put the current date at 597 BCE.

What was happening at that time? He plowed through facts and dates in his mind. The second deportation of Jews from Israel took place in that year. Babylon would destroy Jerusalem eventually, but not for another eleven years, in 586. The first deportation, eight years ago, had supposedly brought important biblical characters, including Daniel. The second deportation this year had brought King Jehoiachin and the royal family, the prophet

Ezekiel, and most of the temple's gold articles that Solomon had commissioned.

"Rim-Sin?" The younger man studied Peter. "You do not seem well."

"I am fine." Peter waved off his concern. "Perhaps you should go. I don't want you to have trouble on my account."

The other man nodded. "Take care, Rim-Sin. And do not forget the New Year Festival. The king's sacrifice must be performed by you, or every man and god in Babylon will be hunting your head."

With that dire prediction the man spun and left the room, his purple robe floating behind him.

Peter returned to his thoughts of ancient history. He felt grounded in time now. But this was not a university lecture—he was actually in Babylon! He had long ago given up the idea that he was dreaming. He would have wakened himself by now if he could have. He sat on the bed, the now familiar dizziness sweeping over him. Perhaps he was actually lying in a coma somewhere. Scraps of *Star Trek* and every time-travel film he'd ever seen flitted through his mind. The reality was incomprehensible. It pressed in on him, walls of irrationality threatening to crush him. But still, there must be a reason for his presence here.

The realization that he did not bring himself here nagged at him, and he struggled to resolve it. He remembered his speech at the fund-raiser a few nights ago: "The divinity of our own consciousness." Right. He took a deep breath. It was time for his divinity to kick into high gear and explain how he got here. Better yet, explain how to get home.

If he knew he could control this situation and go back to the twenty-first century whenever he wanted, he might think about staying here awhile. It was the ultimate research project, wasn't it? There was a world of unanswered questions in his time. What answers could he take back with him? He could make his fortune as an expert in daily life in ancient Babylon. But the most important answer he needed right now was how to find his way out of here alive. Besides, the thing he really wanted already awaited him at home: the position of university president. What had they done in his absence? Who would believe where he'd been?

But until he learned how to return, he would play the part of Rim-Sin, king's diviner. How much did he know about divination? It was a branch of sorcery, he knew that. The kings relied upon it. Diviners read chicken entrails and so forth, looking for signs of what the future held. Could he fake it if he needed to?

While many of his colleagues had drifted toward the more mystical techniques of self-transformation, Peter had tried to stay in the mainstream, choosing to concentrate on health issues, success training, and education. But admittedly, he had always been drawn toward mysticism. It was merely a lower form of understanding, really. Getting in touch with your subconscious was the first step toward godhood, but personal subconscious was merely your own local area of the greater collective subconscious. In the collective, there were archetypes, which some people called gods. Some sought to activate the forces of these gods through ritual, but they were merely symbols, Peter knew. Which rituals did this primitive society employ to call on the gods?

A sudden thought occurred to him. Perhaps he *had* brought himself here, however unconsciously. Perhaps he had been chosen by the collective subconscious to help move this society from its polytheism toward a broader understanding of their own oneness with divinity. What could be accomplished if humanity began to recognize these basic truths earlier in its existence? Could the harm already done to Earth be avoided?

A knock at the door roused him from the bed. His side throbbed again as he climbed off. He opened the door and beheld a stunning woman with fire-red hair and an emerald green dress. Her beauty was breathtaking.

"Rim." The word was soft and her smile slow, like a cat who'd found a treat.

Peter arched an eyebrow and said nothing.

"Aren't you going to let me come in?" Her lips formed a tiny pout.

He opened the door wider and she glided in, jewels tinkling from her ears, wrists, and ankles. Her eyes were painted in green and white with the care of an artist. She smelled like jasmine at night.

She turned and smiled. "You look like a slave. Where have you been?"

"I have been—occupied."

"Hmm. I see. The last time we spoke you were headed for the palace treasury, looking for some Jewish spoils of war, I believe. Were you successful?" She reached a jeweled hand to his shoulder to smooth a wrinkle from his tunic.

Peter took a step backward. "What have you been doing?"

She turned away, sighing. "The same thing I do every day. Waiting for my turn with the king. Trying to keep the foreign harlots from taking my place. You should hear what one of them told my slave girl."

Peter listened to her whining tirade about the other palace women. As he remained silent she continued to speak, revealing much. Assyria had been her home, she said. Royalty once, but one of the king's wives now. Her main goal seemed to be rising to the top of the other wives in the palace complex.

"I am tired," he finally said, hoping to stem the tide of her petty jealousy.

She pursed her lips in another baby-like pout. "You're not asking me to go?" She ran a red-nailed finger across his jaw line, leaned close, and smiled. "So soon?" Her hand slipped around to the back of his neck and felt hot against his skin. Her smile widened.

Tempting. But the king's wife? He was in enough trouble already. "Another time."

Her fingernails dug into his neck like tiny biting ants. She whispered into his ear, "Now."

He pulled her hand down. "Another time."

He closed the door behind her as she left, and the sound echoed through the empty corridor. It was ridiculous to be thinking of staying here for research purposes. He had no idea of how to exist in this world. He must get home. He had been Rim-Sin long enough.

Who was this Rim-Sin? Where had he gone? And how had Peter come to be walking around in his body? He had already figured out that he at least looked similar to his usual self. He could feel his disproportionate height, and his body looked the same to him—minus the glasses. Strange, he could see clearly without them now.

How could this be? Why did everyone think he was Rim-Sin when he was obviously still himself? How did they understand him when he didn't speak a word of Aramaic? It was as if everything about him—his appearance, his speech—all transformed before they reached the eyes and ears of those around him. He wished vaguely for his handheld tape recorder. It would have been good to get his thoughts down to organize later.

He lay on the bed again, his mind reverting to earlier questions. He had stumbled into a fascinating place and time, that was certain. He remembered another line from his speech: "The myth of yesterday, synthesized with the faith of today." Well, today *was* yesterday. Babylon was a case in point for his thesis. He was in the center of one of the most pagan, polytheistic societies that had ever existed. And with Cosam and his family it was juxtaposed with Judaism, the root of Christianity. What better place to prove that all myth, all religion, is part of the whole? Here in Babylon rival cultures lived and worshiped with little difference between them—proof that all truth is relative, that truth shifts as cultures rise and fall.

The success seminar tapes played in his mind again.

Question dogma. Question ideology. Question all outside authority that claims to be truth. Break free from the prison of social conditioning.

Peter spent the night in the palace trying to adjust to his new surroundings. Late the next morning, his door opened again and the red-haired woman appeared.

"Rim." Her voice was a whisper. "You must not stay in the palace. I have heard that Qurdi-Marduk-lamur plots against Belteshazzar. He plans to assure his own place as chief of magicians. There are some that say you are also in his way, and he would like to see you dead!"

Peter put a hand to his head. The *rab alani*—apparently the Babylonian equivalent of the town cop—was already chasing him. Now some crazy man named Qurdi-Mardi-llama, or something? Was all of Babylon trying to put an end to Rim-Sin? No wonder he had disappeared. Peter suddenly longed desperately to be back in his cramped, dusty, university office.

Instead, he followed the clinking woman into the deserted palace hall, wondering how long he could avoid the powers that sought his life.

Qurdi bent over the bloody entrails of a freshly killed goat, searching for an answer to his question. Would he rise to chief of magicians? He studied the details of the haruspicy as though his future lay in the bloody mess. Each discoloration, each unusual mark or deformation, was noted with interest. Some of these signs were well known; for others he checked the handbook to be certain of their answers.

But this time the answer was ambiguous. Even after he consulted his handbook there was no way to make the signs read one way or another today.

It does not matter, he thought. *The omens will say something else soon—a message for the king about his Israelite pet, Belteshazzar.*

A door whispered open behind him, and the single flame in the darkened room flickered. His two favorites entered. Qurdi said nothing, only turned to fix his empty eyes on the slave boys.

"Rim-Sin was seen in the palace," one of them said.

Qurdi straightened. "Where is he?"

"He is gone already," the other said. "The woman Ilushu entered his room to speak with him."

"Speak with him?" Qurdi's lips tightened. "I doubt that." His eyes narrowed as an idea formed. "An advisor with a royal wife. If the king were to know about Rim-Sin and Ilushu..."

The slaves bent their heads to the floor. The punishment for *any* palace official consorting with a royal concubine was a severe beating, possibly worse.

"No." Qurdi shook his head. "That would not suit my purpose. However..." He laid down the knife he had used to probe the entrails. "Perhaps someone else has been seen with Ilushu."

"I do not think so, my lord," the second slave said.

Qurdi's smile was almost tender. He laid a blood-spattered hand on the arm of the young man. "No? I believe you may have seen *Belteshazzar* with one of the royal wives, did you not?"

The slaves looked at the floor again, and Qurdi turned back to his bloody work. "But first the omens. I feel sure the omens will warn the king to expect treason from his favorite diviner."

Peter didn't know where else to go. He knew the *rab alani* had already been to Cosam's house and might come back any time, but besides the palace—where Qurdi-Whoever-He-Was waited for him—where else could he go?

He wandered the city for awhile and finally found Cosam's home by chance late in the day. Cosam had no doorkeeper, and Peter slipped into the house unnoticed. He let his eyes adjust to the dim light for a moment. A sudden scream from within the house startled him, and he jogged toward the sound. He found Cosam and Kaida in one of the bedrooms, hovering over Rebekah, who lay back on her bed, sweating and crying.

"What is it?" he asked.

"Rim!" Cosam's face was etched with worry. "The baby will not come! Something is wrong!"

"Where is the midwife!" Rebekah screamed.

Peter looked from Kaida to Cosam. What could he do? He ran back out to the street, searching in both directions. A portly woman toddled down the street, a black bag slung over her shoulder. Peter ran to her.

"Are you the midwife?" he asked.

"Your wife will be fine." She smiled and patted his arm.

"She is not my wife," Peter said.

"Your concubine, then. Do not fear." She continued at her unhurried pace.

"Please, you must come quickly! Her husband says that something is wrong!"

The woman smiled again, nodding her head.

Peter dragged her the remaining distance to the house as though she were a runaway dog.

She went inside and finally began examining Rebekah. She turned to them with a grim look. "The baby is turned. It will not come."

A breech birth. Did Babylonian midwives know what to do in these situations? Peter certainly didn't.

He caught Kaida's eye. Would she have any knowledge he did not? He raised his eyebrows at her, but her face revealed only hatred, mixed with fear.

"You must chew this," the midwife said, pushing a piece of tree bark into Rebekah's mouth.

"Cosam, please!" Rebekah twisted her head away from the woman's pudgy hands.

"Do as she says, Rebekah." Cosam was near tears. He turned to Kaida. "What else can we do but follow her instructions?"

"Pray, Cosam," Kaida said.

The midwife bared Rebekah's belly and began massaging it with ointment. Peter backed away to leave the family in privacy.

"Stay, Rim," Cosam said as Peter reached the doorway. "I do not believe your gods can help, but I want you to stay."

"I can do nothing here, Cosam."

Kaida stared at him, the lines around her mouth deepening.

"Stay," Cosam said, pulling Peter to his side.

The midwife wiped her hands and pulled what looked like a small rolling pin from her pouch.

Rebekah moaned and spit the tree bark from her mouth. "Cosam, these pagan rituals will do nothing! Make her stop!"

Cosam shook his head, the tears flowing now. "I cannot lose you, Rebekah. I cannot. I don't know what else to do."

The midwife placed something around Rebekah's neck. Peter leaned in closer to see it. It was a leather cord, with a carved image strung on it. Peter recognized the image of the demon Pazuzu from the pages of some old textbook he had studied. The god's canine face, scaly body, and talons were unmistakable.

"Pazuzu will protect you." The midwife touched the image. "The evil of the demon Lamashtu cannot touch you when Pazuzu protects."

Lamashtu, Peter repeated to himself. Female demon who caused miscarriages and stillborns. Lion's head and donkey's teeth. Not much uglier than Pazuzu, really. But apparently Pazuzu was able to counteract Lamashtu's evil.

Sad, he thought. *I know more about these people's foolish beliefs in demons than I do about modern childbirth. Rebekah could die, along with their child, and I am as helpless with all my education as they are in their religious ignorance.*

He was surprised by a rising wave of anger toward the midwife, now torturing Rebekah by using her rolling pin of "magic wood" over the suffering woman's stomach.

Kaida moved around to stand behind Peter, apparently frustrated by the midwife's useless ritual as well. "She might as well go home."

Peter agreed. "No magic wood will help here." Kaida studied him with narrowed eyes. Peter realized his mistake too late. He was supposed to be a diviner! Magic wood was probably a major part of his life.

"You spoke correctly a moment ago," she said. "You are worthless here."

Peter's ego flared. Who was this slave girl to call him worthless? "And I suppose you're going to help in some way?"

"I pray to the God who hears," she answered with the same sarcasm.

Peter responded without thinking. "There is no god but that which you create."

"Appropriate words from a man who spends his days and nights groveling before statues." Kaida's voice was bitter. Peter knew her animosity must have been directed toward Rim-Sin, but he felt it himself as well.

Rebekah screamed in pain. The midwife put away her rolling pin. "The baby does not come. She grows too tired to deliver. We must take her to the mortuary and recite the incantations."

Cosam put his hands over his face. "God, forgive me. I do not know what to do."

Peter shook his head. The poor man's torture over the conflict with his Judaism was pitiable, especially since neither Yahweh nor Pazuzu could be of any help here. A competent obstetrician was what they needed right now.

The midwife did not wait for Cosam to make a decision. "Pick her up," she ordered Peter. He dared not refuse, considering his supposed vocation.

The midwife set the pace as they marched out into the streets. Night was falling. Cosam and Kaida followed the midwife with Peter trailing behind and carrying Rebekah. She twisted and moaned in his arms, her head buried in his shoulder. They reached the mortuary in only a few minutes. Small shrines littered the field, and the midwife led them into a building. Peter glanced around him, taking in the bas-relief images of demons and gods on the walls.

"Lay her down." The midwife pointed toward the floor.

Peter laid Rebekah on the bricks and stepped back.

"I submit to your power, Rim-Sin." The midwife nodded in his direction.

Peter swallowed. Did she expect him to do something?

He panicked, his eyes flicking back and forth between Kaida and Cosam, who stared at him. Rebekah moaned again in the darkness at his feet.

Now what?

Chapter 4

PETER'S HEART POUNDED like a beating drum. Cosam and Kaida stared at him, waiting for him to do something to help Rebekah deliver the baby. The midwife stood in the corner of the room, head bowed.

Peter Thornton had never been without a plan, and he was always in control. What had happened to him? He shook his head, saying the first thing that occurred to him. "No. Cosam does not believe. I will not recite the incantation for one who does not believe."

Cosam looked angry for a moment, then ashamed again. "I do not know why I even consented to this. I never should have brought her here."

The midwife was all elbows, shoving everyone aside. "I will do it myself!"

She stepped to Rebekah, straddling her width where she lay on the floor. The other three stepped aside, backs against the cool wall, eyes wide. Peter could feel the images of the demons claw his back in the darkness.

The midwife swayed and moaned. "The baby is held fast," she said at last. "She who is creating a child is shrouded in the dust of death. Her eyes fail, she cannot see. Her lips are sealed, she cannot open them." The midwife looked down at Rebekah. "Finish the incantation," she said.

"I will not!" Rebekah cried. "I would rather die than repeat your evil words!"

Rebekah's cry echoed back into the dark chamber. Or was that some other sound Peter heard? A chill snaked up his spine in spite of the heat. A far-off keening came from the deeper recesses of the mortuary.

"I will say your words myself, then!" the midwife raged. "But do not blame me if you die along with this child!" She began to sway again like a séance medium. "Stand by me, O merciful Marduk! Now am I surrounded with trouble. Reach out to me! Bring forth the sealed-up one, a creature of the gods; as a human creature, let him come forth. Let him see the light!" Another wail from somewhere in the darkness.

Rebekah screamed again in terror and pain, her cry lingering in the stale air.

"Get out!" Cosam yelled at the midwife, as though he had suddenly awakened.

Kaida knelt beside Rebekah on the floor, touching her face. Cosam dragged the midwife to the door and heaved her out.

"O God, let her live!" Kaida sobbed.

Cosam buried his face in his hands. "Forgive me, Lord God! Let her live!"

Rebekah screamed again, a sound that shook Peter to the core. He collapsed against the wall, scratching at the bricks behind his back in frustration. Kaida rocked back and forth on her knees.

"Let her live," Peter repeated, his eyes searching the high ceiling above him.

Desires can be carried out merely by correct thinking. When you have a desire and send it into the universal oneness, you are really talking to yourself, but in a different form.

"The baby comes!" Rebekah's voice was clear and certain. Cosam rushed to her side.

Kaida scrambled to Rebekah's feet. "The baby has turned, Rebekah!" she said. "You must push!"

Cosam wiped her forehead, smoothing back her hair and holding her eyes in his gaze. "I love you, I love you."

Peter watched in amazement from his place at the wall. Within a few excruciating minutes, Kaida held a flailing bundle in her hands.

"A boy, Rebekah! A boy!"

Cosam laughed and cried all at once, falling over his wife, covering her face with kisses.

"His name is Addi," Rebekah moaned.

"Addi," Cosam nodded.

Peter crept out of the mortuary, feeling Kaida's stare on his back. He waited in the darkness. In the distance, torches flared on the Platform of Etemenanki.

Babylon graciously allowed her citizens to indulge their need for worship. If they chose to give themselves to carved idols, what was that to her? As long as they kept reaching, kept climbing, remained unsatisfied.

The gods and goddesses ruled Babylon, or so her people thought. Marduk, sometimes called Bel, was her patron god. He was god of the storm and had been worshiped for nearly as long as Babylon had stood in the desert. Just like all the gods, he had been known by many names through history.

Nabu, Sin, Gula, Ninurta, Adad, Aku—their temples and shrines flecked the city like grains of sand. But Babylon's favorite goddess was Ishtar, the goddess of love and fertility. She had been Inanna once. She had been Asherah. Today, as on all days, Babylon urged her citizens to offer themselves to Ishtar, to focus on pleasure and their unquenchable thirst for satisfaction.

Babylon loved her *kasdim,* the ancient sect of wise men who served the gods. She had divided them into classes. The magicians and diviners were scholars, well versed in the rituals and incantations and able to divine the messages of the omens. The astrologers studied the stars to predict the future. And then there were the priests. They served the gods and the king, sometimes in the temples and sometimes in the palace. Most of them were Chaldeans, like the king, and given special rank in the city because of their pure ancestral lineage. Babylon paid special attention to her *kasdim*. The kings were governed by the omens, and the omens were governed by the *kasdim*. The fate of the empire rested in their hands.

Usually Babylon was quite pleased by the men she had in these positions. Until the day one young Hebrew rose above the rank of captive and threatened to destroy the balance she had so carefully created.

Akkad lit another torch and placed it in a socket jutting from the outside wall of the High Temple. The flames danced in reflection from the gold-embroidered stars on his purple cloak. Torch lighting was work a slave should have been summoned to do, but Akkad was still embarrassed to demand help with simple tasks, even after months of being considered one of the *kasdim*.

Perhaps one day, when the older wise men no longer regarded him with contempt, he would summon slaves to do his bidding as though he belonged here on the Platform. If Rim-Sin continued to teach him, that time would come soon. He could always use for his benefit the fact that the high priest of Ishtar, Qurdi-Marduk-lamur, was his uncle. But Akkad wanted to advance because of his own skills, not because of the unfair advantage of a lucky birth.

"Lighting torches will not unravel the mysteries of the stars, Akkad," a sarcastic voice behind him said.

"I merely needed more light to see the charts," Akkad said,

but the older man had passed by, taking his own chart to the edge of the Platform to join several others.

Akkad debated. Should he remain here or take a place at the wall with them? After a moment, he sauntered to the left side of the group, keeping a little distance between himself and them.

The men were silent, except for the scratching of their pens on papyrus. Heads bobbed as they each pursued their own calculations and observations of the dome of night above them.

Akkad had been making a few notations of his own, but he had been spending the majority of his time on the Platform contemplating one question. Did he dare broach it to the others?

He cleared his throat enough to receive a few disapproving stares of attention. "I—I have been thinking," he said. Five heads turned his direction, frowns upon each face. "We spend much time studying the patterns of their movements." He pointed upward. "Yet no one has undertaken to discover *why* they move. What *causes* the lights of the sky to journey across the dome each night?"

The older men turned away as though he were an interrupting child. For a moment, Akkad wondered if anyone would even bother to answer him. But then Shamash spoke.

"The gods of the sky have their own reasons, Akkad. It is not for us to question."

"But why?" Akkad said, daring much. "We question everything else. We have discovered the pathway of the sun, we gain knowledge from the messages of the stars, why can we not also learn the reasons behind all of this?"

The five magicians shot impatient looks at each other.

"Akkad, you will learn," Shamash said. "But perhaps the youngest member of the *kasdim* should learn his most important lesson first—the lesson of silence when one is ignorant."

Akkad was grateful for the heavy darkness of the moonless

night. He turned back to his charts to hide his flaming cheeks. It was not merely embarrassment he felt. Akkad was angry.

Hours after Addi's birth, Peter took cover in the courtyard of Cosam's house. The warning he had received in the palace about his responsibilities at the New Year Festival worried him. He had to find a way home before then. If he could get a chance to think, perhaps he could meditate his way out of here. But he was so tired.

Little Hannah had been put to bed after greeting her new brother with squeals of delight. Peter had stayed in the background. Hannah had already proven that even in this time and place, small children were frightened of him. Now, Rebekah slept in her bed in one of the rooms branching from the yard, and Cosam waited beside her, cradling his new son.

Peter had felt a tiny pang watching Cosam carry his son home. They would have many precious years together, he knew.

In his mind Peter was seven years old again, walking between his parents through a carnival that had sprung up in a vacant field in town. "Can we ride the Ferris wheel, Father?" he asked.

Father scowled. "A ridiculous waste of time."

Peter eyed the massive wheel, carrying children whose parents smiled and laughed as they rode beside them. Down the lanes of carnival booths, he watched children throw darts at balloons and shoot down moving ducks with squirt guns. "But Father—"

"Oh, let him ride it, George," Mother sighed. "He'll never quiet down until you do."

In the end, Father had hailed a teenage girl and paid her to take Peter on the Ferris wheel. His face still grew hot at the memory. He could still see his parents far below the ride, involved in their own conversation as the wheel carried him above the colors and lights of the carnival field. He had waved once. They weren't watching.

Peter shook his head to knock the image loose. A tray of food had been placed near his chair in Cosam's courtyard, and he took the time to savor every bite. Apples, pears, figs, and some other fruit. Was it quince? He was so thirsty. He sipped from a cup of date wine and bit into some mild-flavored cheese.

The intensity of Rebekah's delivery had given way to quiet hours at home. Peter leaned back in the chair, studying the night sky. It was good to rest, if only for a few moments.

A footstep fell on the brick floor near the door to the courtyard. Peter half-opened one eye. Kaida. She pulled back when she saw him, as though she had stepped into a snake pit.

Courtesy forced him to acknowledge her. "Come in. Eat something." He picked up another piece of cheese and pointed with it toward the tray.

Her face was like silent stone.

"It is only food," he said. She still just stared. "I need to ask you a question, Kaida." He'd been planning his words since he left the palace. "The dead man whose blood was on you and me that night—who was he?"

Her eyes narrowed. "I don't know. But I wouldn't tell you if I did."

He nodded. "Right."

"I will not go with you when you leave." She spit the words out like some distasteful thing. "I will not be your…I will not be with you."

"Who asked you to?"

"If you force me, I will run."

Peter threw the cheese back onto the platter. "You don't know me, Kaida." He allowed a note of harshness in his voice.

A flicker of fear, perhaps confusion, crossed her face. "I know what you are," she said.

"And what am I?"

"A fool. A fool who prays to images after he carves them. Who thinks the stars will give him answers, rather than seeking the Maker of the stars."

"You are wrong." Peter knew it was foolish to argue religion with this girl, but his pride was wounded. Besides, she was a Jewish slave. What trouble could she cause? For calling him a fool he could probably have her hung by her thumbs or something.

The divine consciousness within you sees and knows everything. This cannot be proven; you must trust this to be true. But once you have found your true consciousness, all else will follow.

"Marduk and Bel are no more real than your Yahweh," he said. "The only truth is what we create for ourselves."

Kaida laughed, a mocking little sound that infuriated him. "The fool says in his heart, there is no God."

"Believe in your God if you like," Peter spoke through clenched teeth. "But your definition of the divine is narrow-minded, and it always will be as long as you insist on personifying it!"

Peter rose, intending to leave, but Cosam appeared at the doorway to the courtyard.

"Where are you going?" Cosam pulled Peter back to his chair. "You must stay. Tell me, did the *rab alani* ever find you?"

"No." Peter sat again. Cosam pulled the tray of food closer to him, and he shook his head. "I went to the palace for awhile. But there I heard that Qurdi-Marduk-lamur also seeks me."

He had pronounced the name carefully. Had he gotten it right? All the names here were so complicated, combinations of given names and the names of their patron gods. Even his own supposed name, Rim-Sin, paid homage to Sin, the moon god.

"You have fallen out of favor with the palace and with the law, Rim-Sin," Cosam said. "And this means you have fallen *into* favor with me. You will stay here. The *rab alani* has been here once and is satisfied. I do not think he will be back, but you play a dangerous game. Your group of magicians and diviners are a pack of wolves, looking to devour each other at the first opportunity. I am not surprised that Qurdi seeks you. He is no doubt trying to take the place of Daniel, and you are in his way."

"How can I be in the way when I'm trying to disapp—" He stopped himself. *Wait a minute. Daniel? As in Daniel in the lions' den? The biblical myth—a reality?* Hearing the name in such a casual, familiar way startled him. He shook his head, still trying to absorb this incredible development.

"You can remain here," Cosam was saying. "At least until you are fully healed. They will not look for you here again so soon, I would not think. Although when the New Year Festival comes, everyone will be searching for you."

"I am to perform the king's sacrifice," Peter said, hoping for more information.

Cosam nodded. "Disgusting practice. I don't know how you can justify it."

"Why do you say that?"

"It amazes me that you even need to ask. An innocent person, ritually killed as the king's substitute to protect the king from any wrath the gods may feel for him? It is a cowardly act. They say that the diviner who plunges the knife into the innocent every year is doubly blessed by the gods. I suppose that is why you are willing to do it."

Peter swallowed. He needed to get out of this place. "The New Year Festival. I've lost track of time since I've been ill. How far off—"

"One month."

Peter exhaled. Could he figure out how to get home in one month? "Thank you, Cosam, for allowing me to stay here." He would hide in Cosam's house until he found his way home. He glanced at Kaida. She showed no emotion.

Cosam saw the look and misinterpreted it. "What I told you before—about Kaida—I must still insist upon that."

Peter nodded again. "I understand."

"My only concern is having enough food to feed you," Cosam said. "I earn only three *siqlu* of silver each day at the temple."

"I will pay," Peter said. "What work can I do?"

Cosam laughed. "You must tell me that. Are you skilled at anything other than looking at the sky and reading the intestines of sheep?"

Peter searched his mind. "Pottery," he said. "I can make pottery."

He saw Kaida's eyebrows lift. He must be a riddle to her these days. She knew the old Rim-Sin, and Peter was willing to bet the palace diviner wasn't often sweating away at the potter's wheel.

"Good!" Cosam clapped his hands once. "We have a wheel. You will show me tomorrow what you can do. But for tonight, I return to my wife and son."

Peter's eyes followed Cosam as he left the room, but when he met Kaida's cold stare his gaze grew hard. He would not be a welcome house guest, of that he was sure.

Faram-Enlil, the *rab alani* of the New City Jewish district of Babylon, crossed his arms over his chest as he listened to the complaint before the judges. A man and a woman, the two opposing parties, stood before the judges. Waves of heat vibrated the morning air between them.

"The plot of land is mine," a man complained. "Her mother took possession of a larger plot than the one my father sold her, and now she has inherited the land and insists the entire plot is hers!"

One of the judges frowned. "She is a priestess, as was her mother. Are you certain you want to make the claim of land-theft against her?"

The man lifted his chin. "She has stolen my land."

"When was the land purchased from your father?" another judge asked.

"Fifty-two years ago."

"And your father has been invited by his god?"

"Yes," he nodded. "He has been gone three years now."

The judge turned to the priestess Naram-tani. "Your mother has also been invited?"

The woman nodded.

"Is the tablet of sale present?"

The priestess brought it forward, and Faram-Enlil leaned forward. In his years as *rab alani*, Faram had seen many tablets tampered with. They were simple to forge. But this one had been protected. Another piece of clay had been used as a sealed envelope. The terms were written on the outside, and both parties had rolled their cylinder seals over it. This envelope could have been tampered with, but the original inside could not be touched without breaking the envelope.

The judges broke the envelope now and read the contract.

"It is clear that the plot of land the priestess claims as her own is the same size as the plot of land originally sold by your father," one of the judges reported. "She has won the argument. We will hear the next plea."

Faram smiled. A simple decision. They were not always so easy. This city could produce a lifetime of judges' decisions over violence and greed.

But the defeated plaintiff was not so easily dismissed. He ran toward the departing priestess as if to attack her.

"Seize him!" one of the judges yelled. Faram jumped sideways, into the man's path, and wrapped his two massive hands around the man's upper arms. Faram stared him down, whispering, "Think before you dig a deeper hole for yourself, my friend!"

The man's shoulders relaxed, and he nodded. Faram escorted him from the courtyard and then returned. He had come to make his report to the judges about the murdered Jewish captive he had found in the home of the king's diviner.

"Faram." One of the judges motioned to him. "Have you yet found Rim-Sin to inquire about the situation?"

"Not yet."

"And the dead man, who was he?"

"He was an Israelite slave, a man the king had been using to register the palace treasure brought from the Israelite invasion."

The judge waved his hand as if batting away an insect. "It is of little consequence. I am certain Rim-Sin will explain all once he is found."

Faram masked his anger at the judge's nonchalance and turned away. "Because the dead man was only a Jew," he added to himself. "No one cares about one dead Jew." He moved to the side of the temple courtyard. He might be called upon again regarding another case.

Faram was a Chaldean, but he had been the *rab alani* of the Jewish district for six years. Perhaps it was his daily interaction with these captive people that made him angry with the judge. His wife said he was far too soft on these Jews. Perhaps he was. But he had seen the way they worshiped their God, the morality their God commanded, the way they treated one another. Something was different about these people.

Two others stepped forward to face the judges. This was not a trial, but a public ceremony and legal transaction, validated before the judges. One was clearly a slave. He brought forward a pestle, placing it on the ground before him. His master stood on the other side. The "crossing of the pestle" was a symbol of willing servitude. This slave must have been set free in some way, but he was here, choosing to remain with his master. He stepped over the pestle now, to signify his devotion to his master, and recited the formula. "I make my choice to remain with you."

Faram was anxious to resume his search for Rim-Sin, although he had no doubt that "all would be explained," as the judge had said. He would find Rim, but the diviner would have some explanation to pacify the judges. That was not justice. Faram smiled tightly. Perhaps justice would have to be satisfied when *Faram* found Rim-Sin. Faram was not a harsh man, but he believed in justice. If the diviner refused to be brought before the judges, Faram would have no choice but to kill him.

Cosam lowered his thickset frame to sit on the ground among his people. In this small clearing among the exiles' tiny houses, the grass was brown and crackling, too far from the canal and losing its war with the dry season's sun. Mishael smiled and stood before them, waiting for the crowd to quiet before he began.

Cosam looked around at the faces of friends and family who had arrived with him from Israel just a few weeks earlier. Many of them were joining family already brought in the first deportation. Some of these faces were familiar to him, having grown up with him in the streets of Jerusalem. Others he did not know. But all of them wore the common expression of anger and hostility. Cosam had come to this meeting of exiled Jews to learn the ways of his people in this land, to make the best of their captivity. But the air was charged with anger. His countrymen did not seem as accepting of their fate.

"Welcome to Babylon, my brothers," Mishael said.

The group hissed.

Mishael nodded. "I understand. Perhaps after the first group had left our nation, you believed you would remain at home. Now the king of Babylon has brought you here, and you do not wish to be in captivity. But that is what God has decreed for you, and I want to help you adjust in any way that I can."

Someone yelled from behind Cosam. "You can let us go back to Israel!"

"I do not keep you here, my brother. It is the hand of the Most High, through His servant Nebuchadnezzar."

Another voice came from the front of the crowd. "How can you call that man the Lord's servant?"

Mishael smiled. "Because that is what the prophet Jeremiah has told us from the Lord. Nebuchadnezzar fulfills the Lord God's plan for Israel at this time."

"Jeremiah is a prophet of doom!" someone called. "He prophesies that our captivity will go on for seventy years!"

Cosam had remained silent, but he tore up small bits of brown grass from under his crossed legs. The people were fools. He had watched them in Israel, throwing themselves before foreign gods, burning incense and worshiping at Asherah poles on every high place and under every spreading tree in the land, mocking the Most High and His inaction. Now God's judgment on their own actions had finally befallen them, and they would not see it.

"The Lord has spoken," Mishael said, but the people hissed again. They would not be humbled. Not yet.

When the meeting had ended and the people had melted away to their homes, Cosam approached Mishael. He was near Cosam's age, though he had been here eight years already. He had been only a youth when brought here with Daniel. Cosam had heard the stories back in Israel about how Daniel and his three friends had been propelled into prominence in Babylon. While Daniel had become chief of magicians, Hananiah, Azariah, and Mishael had been placed as governors over districts of the city. Those were their Hebrew names. Among their friends and family, none of them used the Babylonian names they had been given. Mishael's name had been changed to Mi-sha-Aku, meaning, "Who is like Aku?", but the young man had no desire to acknowledge the Babylonian god, especially with his name.

"Ah, Cosam, is it not?" Mishael asked.

"Yes."

"I trust you have found the house assigned to you to be satisfactory."

Cosam nodded. "It is fine, but I am surprised by the attitudes I have seen here among my people. They still do not recognize what their sin has cost them."

Mishael smiled, a fatherly smile in spite of his youth. "You are all newly arrived, Cosam. Give this place time to have its effect. You will not be so discouraged when you meet others who have been here for eight years." He led the way out of the courtyard.

"Then the people turn back to the Law?"

"Remember what Jeremiah has said, Cosam. The Lord has promised to give them a heart to know Him. They will return to Him with their whole heart. And some do already. Living in the midst of the Babylonians has given our people a new perspective on the worship of idols. They turn back to the Most High, seeking His forgiveness."

"I pray it will be so, Mishael. The situation in Israel only worsens."

"I am afraid it will grow much worse, my brother. Much worse."

Cosam lingered awhile in the streets before returning home. As he entered the twilight courtyard, Rebekah rose to her feet and hurried toward him.

"Peace, my dear." Cosam smiled.

"I am anxious to hear all that was said!"

The two huddled together in the courtyard, and Cosam told her the details of the assembly.

She dropped her chin when he had finished. "I weep for our people who still will not bow their heads under the Lord of Hosts. What more will He need to bring about to make them understand? Already we are captive in a foreign land, forced to do evil work."

"The work is not evil, Rebekah."

"Cosam, you are one of the finest goldsmiths in the land of Israel. Now they make you fashion gold jewelry for their false gods to wear!"

"Perhaps they do not want their own people to do it." He chuckled. "They might begin to suspect that their gods were not real if they had to fashion them with their own hands."

"As we have seen the people in Israel realize, Cosam?" She frowned.

His smile faded. "Our people are fools, Rebekah. Fools."

"And this is what our foolishness has come to." Rebekah hung her head.

Cosam leaned back in his chair, nodding. "The word of the Lord through Jeremiah," he said. "'As you have forsaken Me and served foreign gods in your own land, so you shall serve strangers in a land that is not yours.'"

"Cosam, I have heard that the prophets Zedekiah and Ahab here in Babylon prophesy that we will be home within two years. Could this be true?" Rebekah's eyes searched her husband's with hope.

"No, my wife. They are false prophets, I am certain. Jeremiah has said it will be seventy years. That is what I believe."

"Seventy years," Rebekah said, as though she could see the years stretch out across the desert. "Then we will live the rest of our lives here in this foreign city. We will never again see our homeland." Her voice shook.

Cosam wrapped his big arms around his wife, as though his love alone could protect her from this city. "But we will be true to the Law, Rebekah. We will be true to the Law."

Akkad sat in the evening cool beside a stream cascading through the Hanging Gardens, letting the water run over his fingers. He shouldn't be here. The moon had risen hours ago, and the other diviners would be expecting him on the Platform. But this evening he wished to be alone with the gods of the night sky, if only for a short time.

From his position on the uppermost of the seven tiers of the garden, Akkad could look across the city to the matching seven-tiered ziggurat of Etemenanki, or down upon the entire verdant wonder sprawling below him. Each tier of the Hanging Gardens was taller than a man, built from baked bricks and cultivated with every delightful flower and shrub known to its meticulous gardeners.

Water was pumped to the top of the garden through mysterious means Akkad did not understand. Then the water flowed down each successive tier, collecting in shallow pools, trickling into thirsty roots, and spilling over the stone ledges to tiers below. In the scorching heat of day, the palm trees rooted deeply in the upper tiers cast stripes of shade over the rest of the garden. In blossom-scented nights as this one, the garden was like a floating paradise, hung above the city by the gods themselves.

Akkad raised his eyes to the glorious dome of the heavens. What did she hide from him tonight? What answers? What questions? He scanned the eastern lip of the sky. Pisces had risen already. It was getting late. He should leave soon. The others would not be pleased at his absence.

The conversation several nights ago returned to him, along with the anger. He would use the anger, though, to drive him to the answers. Then they would stop laughing when he left a room. Perhaps he was one of the youngest of Nabu-kudurri-usur's trusted advisors, but there was a reason he had come so far at such a young age. The gods had given him gifts, and he intended to use them.

A muffled voice below near the entrance to the Gardens caught his attention. The light from Sin's crescent was barely enough to see the figure that wandered among the stone paths. Akkad remained still and silent, hoping to go unnoticed.

By the gods, she was beautiful! Akkad forced his breathing to slow when the young woman looked up at the sky and the moonlight caught her features.

Who was she? Why had he never seen her before? To be allowed in the Gardens, she would have to have some prominence in the palace. Or was she a slave, stealing precious minutes of solitude in a forbidden haven?

She was coming up here! Akkad looked down at his charts. She would certainly see him, but perhaps she would think he had not seen her.

He sensed her coming closer, but he did not look up. He heard footfalls on the tier below him, and then she stopped.

He looked up. "Greetings." He whispered the word, unwilling to break the enchantment of the place.

Her face broke into a relieved smile. Had she been afraid he would chastise her for being in the Gardens? She was not a kitchen slave; her clothes made that plain. Perhaps a servant to one of the royal wives? "Greetings."

"It is beautiful at night, is it not?" Akkad asked.

The woman looked around without answering, her smile agreeing.

"I am Akkad," he said.

She nodded, as if this were not unknown to her. "Abigail."

Akkad whispered her name, committing it to memory. "You are Jewish?"

She nodded, the smile evaporating.

Akkad smiled to reassure her again. "Will you sit with me awhile?"

Her eyes widened. "I cannot!"

"I am studying the sky." He pointed. "Charting the stars. Perhaps you can help."

"Why do you chart the stars?"

"To gain wisdom."

"Wisdom concerning what?"

"Concerning everything. The fate of men and kings, and of the land." He lifted his head to the night. "When you look up there, you only see small lights thrown against the blackness of the dome. But there are wondrous patterns to be discovered, and the gods have written their messages in the patterns of the sky."

Abigail tilted her head as though contemplating his declaration. "Perhaps," she said. "But why not merely ask God Himself?"

Akkad laughed with her. He had forgotten for a moment the peculiar thinking of the Jews with their one God. But he had no desire to speak of his philosophy with Abigail. Moonlight and flowers gave him thoughts of other things. "Won't you sit with me?" he asked again.

"I must go."

"Why? Will you be missed?"

She laughed again. "That is not likely."

And then she was gone.

Qurdi-Marduk-lamur swept through the city in anger once more, his two temple slaves scurrying at his heels. Though he had searched through every house he'd come upon, he had not found Rim-Sin again after the crafty fool had left the palace. And he still had no answers. He had killed a lamb every morning, picking apart its liver, searching for a word. He had fallen before the goddess every evening, but Ishtar remained silent.

There was one answer he had received. Something extreme

would happen in the palace hierarchy of diviners before the New Year Festival. He would make certain Belteshazzar was executed by then. And if he could find Rim-Sin, he would assure his own place as chief of magicians.

Rim-Sin had found a key to unknown power, Qurdi was certain of it. That was why he had disappeared, and it must be connected to the man he had killed. That knowledge would make Rim-Sin the indisputable choice for chief of magicians. And now Rim-Sin was making furtive appearances again. What was he planning? What was his power? Qurdi knew he must learn the secret and eliminate Rim-Sin—and the omens declared it must be before the New Year Festival.

The priest pushed his way into another house. An outraged doorkeeper leapt to his feet, but Qurdi rapped his face with the back of his hand. "Where is Rim-Sin, the diviner?"

The doorkeeper trembled under his gaze. "I—I have not seen him, my lord!"

Qurdi grabbed the man's throat and brought his face down, level with the doorkeeper's.

"Where is he?" He tightened his grip.

"Please, my lord!" The doorkeeper choked. "I have not seen him."

Qurdi released his grip and whirled, stumbling over his slaves. "Get out of my way!"

Hours later, in the Jewish district, he was more successful. The home of Cosam the Jew had no doorkeeper, so it was Cosam himself whose throat Qurdi seized.

Qurdi hated the Jews. They had no respect for the goddess, mocked her even, and he hated them for it. If he could have wiped out the entire nation of them in one killing blow, he would have done it. Buried deep inside him was a fear that one day these Jews and their one God would supplant everything he had worked so hard to achieve for the goddess. Though he and

Rim-Sin were rivals for the king's favor and the favor of Ishtar, they at least agreed that the Jews must be destroyed before they destroyed others.

Cosam said nothing when Qurdi questioned him. He only stared back into Qurdi's eyes. A child spoke from the doorway.

"Let him go! We will tell you where he is."

Chapter 5

QURDI TURNED TO Hannah. "You have seen Rim-Sin?" He released Cosam's neck.

"Hannah, go inside to your mother," Cosam said with authority.

Qurdi grabbed the little girl's arm. "Tell me!"

Her eyes filled with tears. "He was here before. He was hurt."

Cosam pulled the child from Qurdi's grasp.

Through clenched teeth, Qurdi repeated his question. "Where is he?"

Cosam pushed her behind him. "He has gone. I don't know where."

Qurdi took another step toward him, but Cosam put a hand out. Qurdi backed down. The younger man looked as though he could crack Qurdi's skull if he wanted to, and Qurdi hadn't brought any temple guards. No matter. Qurdi knew several rituals he could perform later that would repay this Jew if he was holding back information.

"If you see him again, send someone for me at the Temple of Ishtar," he said, his eyes locking onto Cosam's.

Cosam only stared back.

When Qurdi had left, Cosam exhaled loudly.

Kaida moved to the doorway. "Why do you protect him? We should have told the priest that Rim-Sin is here."

Cosam shook his head. "I can't explain it, except to say that I feel we must let Rim-Sin remain here." He studied her. "Though I am not the only one behaving strangely."

Kaida looked at her hands. "It is different here. We are all different."

Cosam frowned. "We should tell him of Qurdi-Marduk-lamur's visit."

They walked together through the courtyard, but Rebekah called out from one of the bedrooms before they reached the storeroom where Rim worked.

"Go to her," Kaida said. "I will tell him."

The storerooms branched from the courtyard like all the rooms of the house, but Kaida had to descend several steps to reach the lower, cooler level. Low shelves of baked brick held rows of storage containers. Rim-Sin worked at a pottery wheel in the center of the windowless room, an oil lamp on a table beside him giving the only light. His eyes were closed, however, and his lips moved silently even as the clay spun in his hands.

He looked up as Kaida entered.

"A friend of yours was here looking for you," she said, sitting on one of the storage ledges.

He frowned. "Who?"

"Qurdi-Marduk-lamur."

The vase spinning beneath his fingers suddenly crumpled. "What did you tell him?"

"Cosam told him that you were gone. He said he did not know where you were."

"Thank you, Kaida." He went back to spinning, pulling the soft clay back up between his fingers.

"It was Cosam's decision."

Rim-Sin nodded. "He is a good man."

Kaida sneered at the diviner. Is that all he would say? Didn't he realize Cosam had just risked his life to protect him? She sat in a chair near the corner. "You are afraid of the priest." She intentionally allowed her tone be accusatory.

"Should I be?"

She tried to provoke him. "He serves the gods."

"That does not frighten me."

"Because you serve the gods yourself?"

Rim glared at her. "I serve no gods. The gods are merely symbols."

Kaida frowned. "Symbols of what?"

He stopped spinning, turning to her as though he would patiently instruct her. "They put us in touch with something that transcends us, Kaida. A force, a consciousness. You could call it 'spirit.' It lies within each of us. People who have not yet recognized their inner spirit still insist on personifying it as outside themselves as a 'god.' That is acceptable for now. But one day people will see that spirit is beyond personification. That the whole universe is part of it."

Kaida laughed. "Perhaps one day they will. But they will still be fools like you, Rim."

His nostrils flared, which made her laugh again.

"All you need to do is look outside," she said. "That tower stands as a monument to the fact that man has been reaching for God since the beginning. It is the great Tower of Babel, standing for hundreds of years as a symbol of man's failed attempt to become God. Why is that? Why do all peoples, at all times, reach for God?"

Rim shook his head in condescension, returning to his pottery. "The tower shows us that man has always recognized his own divinity. I will not presume to criticize your Judaism,

Kaida. Especially as a guest here. You hold on to it if it makes you feel good."

"Makes me feel good?" She stood. "How could the Hebrew Law, which I am completely unable to keep, make me feel good? It makes me feel only shame. How do you explain why the Jews hold on to their faith in spite of that?" She found her chair again, annoyed with herself for letting him frustrate her.

"I don't actually know why you insist on making yourselves feel guilty," he said. "It's unnecessary. There is no absolute. Your world can be what you make it. There is no good or evil. They are two facets of a single reality."

Kaida tried to wither him with her look. "Are you completely certain of that?"

"Completely."

"Absolutely?"

He didn't answer.

"You see, don't you?" She smiled. "You cannot say you are certain of anything. The mere statement that *there is no truth* makes it impossible for you to say for certain that there is no truth. If *there is no right answer*, then you yourself cannot be sure *that* is the right answer. You have no base to stand on. Your logic is as circular as the pot you are spinning." As she stood again, she looked down at the wheel and laughed. "Definitely more circular than your pot!"

As she turned to leave, she saw him smash the clay down again.

Kaida hurried through the Jewish district of the Old City, keeping the Tower of Etemenanki on her right. She carried two of Rim's larger pottery jars in her hands. Despite his wickedness, he did make decent clay jars. Rebekah had asked her to bring fish home for the evening.

The streets were confusing. Where was the river? She should

have reached it by now. The tower was before her, on the right. Reaching the end of the street, she saw a canal running from behind the houses. The canals all ran to the river. She felt this had to be the right way. Kaida feared being lost in the streets. The city could swallow a person.

She hated this city, hated every minute she had spent here. But she did believe that her God had allowed her to be brought here for a reason. And she had come to believe that Rim-Sin was the reason. Him and others like him. She was here to show them the futility of their beliefs. She recalled her conversation with Rim-Sin. Had she gone too far today? She was, after all, supposedly his slave.

She reached the Street of Purchases in a few minutes. It was an open-air market that lined the river. The crowds jostled and bumped each other in their struggle for bargains. A shouted argument slowed her walk through the tables. "You cannot carry wine in that ship!" A merchant jabbed a meaty finger toward a cargo ship in the water.

The ship's captain shook his fist. "I will carry anything I wish."

The merchant looked around, grabbed Kaida by the wrist as she passed, and pulled her to a row of pottery jars lined up beside the captain. "Smell this!" he said, pointing to the first jar.

She sniffed. It smelled like tar.

"Does that smell like a fine grape wine from the north?"

Kaida shook her head.

"No!" He turned to the captain. "It smells of bitumen, which is all you are accustomed to trading! How can I sell wine that smells of bitumen?"

The argument continued, but Kaida escaped, making her way to the river's edge, where water licked at the sandy bank. The bridge lay to her left, the Processional Way leading over it. The huge bridge rested on five piers, squares of bricks bonded with tar, ten *qanu* wide, and pointed at one end to cut down resistance to the current. They were spaced more widely toward the western shore to allow for the passage of ships.

A woman brushed past her, nearly knocking a jar from Kaida's hands. She tightened her grip on the pieces. Though Rim-Sin had made them quickly, firing them and glazing them within two days, she had to admit his red and blue geometric designs were lovely. He would do better to forget about being a diviner and become a potter, she thought. She realized her neck muscles had tightened just thinking of Rim-Sin. In spite of her bold talk, she feared him more than she'd ever feared anyone. What would it take for her to be free of him?

Cosam had told her to trade the jars for six of the best fish she could find. She wandered among the food and trinket-laden tables, watching the river. Boats carried ingots of copper shipped up from the sea or loads of alum down from Carchemish. Slaves were loading a ship with sesame to be taken to a temple in a city downstream. Babylon was the center of the world.

Her shopping was interrupted by the sudden blast of a horn. Other instruments accompanied it. All around her slaves and citizens alike fell to the ground facing the Platform of Etemenanki. After a moment's hesitation, she also dropped to the gravel, careful of the pots she carried. She could hear recitations from those around her, but she kept silent. In a few moments the horn was blown again, and the people rose as one, continuing their business as if there had been no interruption.

She looked for the fish now. There was no time to waste.

In Cosam's storeroom, Peter couldn't tell how late it had grown. He had lost himself as his thoughts swirled around the pottery wheel. Three pots lined the shelf, ready for firing. Cosam had given him a daily quota to pay for his food. And, Peter realized, to pay for Kaida's food as well. As her master he was responsible for her.

He chafed at the unanswered questions about finding a way home—questions he could not now pursue. But it was either make pots in Cosam's storeroom or hide in the streets and scavenge for food. He had only a few weeks until he was expected to perform the dreadful deed at the New Year Festival, and he still had no clue who the dead man was or how he could get home.

Again he wondered if he should explain his presence to Cosam and Kaida and ask for their help. But the chances were too great that Cosam would throw him to the mercy of Qurdi or the law if they thought he was crazy. Besides, what help could two ancients offer him for traveling forward in time? Better to crank out pots as fast as possible to meet his quota, and then pursue a way home. His attempts at meditating his way out of here had so far been unsuccessful.

Tonight his thoughts strayed toward Kaida. The girl was a puzzle. Half the time she seemed frightened and nervous, but then at other times she met his look boldly, daring him to take her on. Her mocking questions disturbed him. It was absurd, really. He was a professor of religion caught in a philosophical discussion with a Jewish slave girl three thousand years in the past. Worse, she could hold her own against him! Something about her challenge to his glib answers about there being no absolute truth had touched a nerve. It wasn't as if he'd never heard that argument before. But for some reason, coming from her, he found himself paying attention to it now. He had always struggled with the idea that if truth were impossible to establish, how could he be sure of that very thing, that truth was impossible to establish? She was right. It was circular.

But one thing he had become convinced of: he was here for a cosmic purpose, to teach and enlighten. His guess was that the karma of the collective subconscious would not let him return home until he had made a difference here. And Kaida was his first student. He knew Kaida's Jewish beliefs would be difficult to overcome. He had begun to introduce the concept of duality to her today. If she were ever to transform, she would have to shed the burden of classifying things as good or bad, right or wrong.

The divine consciousness is beyond the opposites of good and evil. Innocence is our natural state. It has become buried in layers of guilt and shame placed on us from childhood by our parents. We spend our whole lives trying to return to the state of total self-acceptance we were born with. Release these negative energies of shame, and realize that you are free.

Those ideas weren't from the success tapes. That was another teacher, an Indian guru who leaned more toward the supernatural but whose books had been very helpful in giving Peter a sense of where his own transformation could take him. At first he had resisted the more metaphysical aspects of this teacher's wisdom, not wanting to find himself chanting in a forest somewhere or holding crystals to his forehead. But what he said made so much sense. When Peter read his books, it was as if the guru knew Peter from the inside out. The things that he promised would come to those that had reached self-realization were all the things Peter had searched for from the beginning. Transformation, peace, pure love, no fear of death. All of these could be his if he could complete the process of becoming.

He thought of his dream the night he had arrived here. It had been bizarre, yet he did feel a sense of calling as Hugh had said in the dream, as though there was a task he needed to finish. His interest in the spiritual nature was the thing that had led him to study religion. He truly believed that a better age had come, one that moved away from the secular humanism of the late twentieth century. Humanism had taught him that there was no god, only the science of humanity. Now he and others realized that there was something beyond science: there was *spirit.* And each person's spirit was god. He was helping to lead people into a future that would enhance their own spirit.

Back before his transportation to this time and place, he had listened patiently to Hugh, his friend and colleague, preach about Jesus, but it was all so foolish. Of course Jesus was divine. We all are. Peter would admit that Jesus probably exhibited a higher form of the "Christ-consciousness" than most. But it was something to aspire to, not something to worship. Peter felt sorry for Hugh, trapped in his bondage to a nonexistent God.

He removed a pipe lamp shaped like a small shoe from the wheel. He had fashioned it after the one he used for light, but added detailed ornamentation that would be pleasing when painted and glazed. He looked for a place to put his personal mark, the symbol Cosam had taught him all potters inscribed as a signature of sorts. He used an ivory pin to carve a small lion's head on the bottom. Around the lion he carved a shield. He chuckled at the rough imitation of his university's logo. The lamp was ready for firing, and he was satisfied with it. It was quite good. Perhaps he would give it to Kaida when it was finished.

No. He would give it to Rebekah.

Enough thoughts about the girl. Kaida was probably twenty years younger than him, anyway. *Twenty years younger? Try three thousand years older.*

The pottery was an enjoyable diversion, but Peter knew he must get back to important business. Surely he had somehow fallen into this time as a sort of "missionary" for a new world order. Would success here be the key to getting home? Or was there something else he should be figuring out? It couldn't be long before Qurdi-Marduk-lamur located him. What then? He couldn't forget the *rab alani.* And the dead man in Rim-Sin's home.

Home. He had not been back to Rim-Sin's house since he had

arrived. Would there be any answers there? It was definitely the place to begin.

He rinsed his hands in the basin of water at his side, dried them on a rag, and rubbed his eyes. It must be growing late. Had Kaida returned?

Down at the quay, Qurdi paced, waiting for the expected ship to dock. His two personal slaves trotted beside him like twin shadows. The hordes of purchasers crowded and jostled Qurdi, and he shoved them aside. The ship was late. He had other things to do. The goddess would be waiting for her meal. He hoped she would understand, since he had been detained while attending to her estate.

She was wealthy, his Ishtar. One of the richest of the Babylonian gods. She owned several *musaru* of farming property in the suburbs outside the city wall. There, farmers cultivated cereal grains and fruit trees, as well as sheep and goats. Her trading was always profitable, Qurdi saw to that. Her income supported her temple buildings and staff and purchased the fine clothing, food, and jewelry she demanded.

A shopper knocked against him, and he instinctively raised the back of his hand to the man, arresting it in midair when he realized it was a palace courtier.

"Be careful, Qurdi-Marduk-lamur," the courtier said. "I am not one of your slaves."

"And you are not my equal, either!"

The courtier lowered his head and moved away. Qurdi studied his back as he disappeared into the crowd. He would remember that one when he became chief. He would remember each of those who had dared to show him disrespect.

But first, Rim-Sin. Could he be somewhere in this crowd? Qurdi scanned the faces. Where had the diviner disappeared to this time? Qurdi feared the worst. They had both been searching for the key to ultimate power for so long, each determined to make the discovery first. Had Rim-Sin found an answer? Had he gone into hiding to prepare his attack?

As he looked through the faces, the crowd melted to the ground before him. A long blast on the horn called them to worship. He fell to his knees with them, stretching out his arms on the ground before him, facing the tower.

As the musicians danced through the streets with their strings and cymbals, Qurdi whispered to Marduk, patron god of this great city and the god for whom he had been named.

> Marduk, king of heaven and earth, judge above and
> below,
> Light of the gods, guide of mankind,
> I turn to you, seek you out.
> Command among the gods life for me.
> May the gods who are with you speak favorably of me.
> Let me sound your praises!

He lifted a loving eye to Etemenanki, House of the Platform of Heaven and Earth, and pressed the back of his hand to his nose.

As he rose, a tiny woman with dark, wavy hair caught his attention. Rim-Sin's concubine!

Kaida traded the jars for six fish and turned toward Cosam's home. She pushed through the crowds, their faces identical to her. The city grew more raucous as dusk approached.

She had not gone far when she glanced back and saw the bald head of Qurdi-Marduk-lamur towering above the crowd. She'd seen his face when he'd threatened Cosam in his home and hadn't forgotten it. She realized immediately that he was following her.

She quickened her pace, ducking through the throng. The fish felt slimy in her hands, even through the cotton that held them. The crowd thinned, and she glanced behind her. There was no sign of him.

Turning back, she ran straight into his black-cloaked chest.

"What do you want?" she said.

"You are out on the streets very late, child." He grabbed her around the waist, his voice quiet and still. "Have you come to join the celebrations?"

She yanked his arm away. "I am going home."

"Home to Rim-Sin?"

"He is not there."

"Tell me, why has Rim left his favorite concubine behind, wherever he has gone?"

"You will have to ask him that when you find him."

Qurdi put an arm around her again, this time gripping her too firmly for her to escape. "Perhaps if I have you, he will find me."

The package of fish slipped from Kaida's hands as he dragged her back into the crowd. She screamed and tried to pull away. No one bothered to notice.

Since the night in the Hanging Gardens, Akkad had not been able to forget Abigail. This evening he strung another shell onto the cord of wool and tried to concentrate on the work. He counted the shells once again. It must be perfect. The king's amulet had been lost—a very unlucky omen—and Akkad had been summoned to create another. He studied the instructions in the handbook, but then a thought struck him. The astrologers had been constructing this same amulet for hundreds of years. Could he perhaps make a more powerful amulet? One that would nearly guarantee success for the wearer?

He glanced around the dusky courtyard. There was no one about, no one to see what might be a traitorous act. Did he dare?

Before his courage left him, he slipped two shells off the cord. He dug through his small box of shells, selecting two others. No, that would not be correct. He pulled other shells from the cord and the box, changing the order as he restrung them, knotting each tightly into the cord. When it was finished, he studied the pattern he had created.

Yes, it might work. The king would never notice the difference in the design, but he might notice the effects—it was a powerful combination for success with one's wives. To his knowledge, it had not been used before. But he could see no reason why it would not have tremendous power for the king. And if it did, the royal wives would soon bear evidence of his success. When the time was right, Akkad would mention his new combination to the king. The crucial thing would be to keep it from the other wise men until that time. If any of them saw it, they might think he had changed the pattern to bring harm to the king. Any of them except Belteshazzar, that is. He wouldn't know an amulet from an apple.

No, Belteshazzar seemed to gain his wisdom in other ways. Akkad thought again of his brief meeting with Abigail the other night and her probing question, "Why not merely ask God Himself?" Did Belteshazzar truly have privileged communication with his God? And if he did, was this Yahweh the only God, as the Jews insisted? Where would that leave Akkad and his fellow astrologers? He thought of the times he had heard Shamash and the others slanting the signs they read in the omens so that the king would not be unduly distressed. At times they would pretend to receive a sign when there had been none. Was the whole thing a fraud?

He shook his head. No, the wisdom was there. It could not be denied. The patterns, the omens, they so often spoke the truth. And there were even times when Akkad felt the presence of the gods, felt them perhaps wanting to speak to him personally. He had never dared voice any of this to the others. Not yet. But someday, when he had gained their respect, they would envy him for his own special connection with the gods.

Akkad put the amulet in his shell box and gathered his robes around him, tightening the turban he wore wrapped around his head. It was time to get to the Platform, to let the amulet draw its power from the stars.

As he approached the courtyard doorway, a figure he had seen repeatedly in his mind's eye appeared.

"Abigail!"

"Greetings, Akkad," she smiled.

Akkad's eyes darted around the courtyard again. It was still empty. He turned back to Abigail. He could think of nothing to say.

"You seem to be in a hurry." She stepped aside to let him pass.

"No—I mean, I was going to the Platform. Yes, I suppose I must go." He cursed himself silently. He sounded like a child.

Abigail searched his eyes and smiled again. "Good night, then."

"Yes. Good night."

Akkad arrived at the High Temple on Etemenanki late again. The older men raised their eyebrows but said nothing.

"I am sorry," he said, taking his place at the wall.

"Have you fashioned the king's new amulet yet, Akkad?" Nadin-Aku asked.

Akkad thought he detected a note of jealousy in Nadin's voice. "Not yet." The lie was necessary. He could take no chances of them wanting to see it.

"Perhaps you would rather one of us do it?" Nadin said.

"No! No, I will finish it at the proper time."

"And was it your work on the amulet that caused you to be late this evening?"

Akkad floundered. "No. I—I was speaking with someone at the palace." He saw a chance to steer the subject away from the amulet. "A palace servant, I believe. She is very beautiful. Jewish."

The men laughed. "Could it be that our young Akkad is thinking of taking a woman?" Shamash asked around the group. But then he sobered. "Use your mind before anything else, Akkad," he said. "A Jewish slave is not the sort of woman your position requires."

Akkad nodded, angry with himself again for giving them a reason to ridicule him. "I only commented that she was desirable."

When Aries had risen in the east, Akkad descended the Platform with the others and returned to the palace. But as soon as they had parted ways within the palace halls, Akkad jogged back to the tower.

He reached the top perspiring and out of breath. Pulling the amulet from his shell box, he laid it carefully on the altar beside the High Temple. It would take the remainder of the night to draw its power from the stars, but it must be tonight for his new arrangement to be blessed, since Venus was in her exaltation sign.

When the amulet was properly arranged, Akkad sighed and leaned against the altar, watching the sky. He wished for a moment that Abigail were here with him, but Shamash's words echoed in his mind. Perhaps it was time for him to think of taking a woman, but a Jewish slave would not be the one, even if she was a servant to a royal wife, as he felt Abigail must be. No, he would find someone else.

But he couldn't let that issue distract him from more important thoughts. If this new amulet worked, he would finally achieve recognition among his colleagues. If it did not, he would need another way. In that case he would find Rim-Sin and beg for more instruction. And if the gods were willing to favor him with knowledge, he promised to have no more doubts about their authority.

Chapter 6

BABYLON FLAUNTED HER beauty tonight. She seduced and beguiled, charming her people into selling their souls. She crooned to them on the night breeze, and her melody coaxed them to more and more and more. *Excess is a virtue*, she whispered. *Reach higher. Be like the gods.*

Beyond her walls, on the plain of Dura, torches blazed around slaves at work. A timber framework surrounded a platform, and from the platform rose the lower half of an enormous golden body of a man. When finished, it would stand ten *qanu* high, a monument to the king who had given her more than any other in her history. She was pleased. Nabu-kudurri-usur was her child, her guardian, her savior.

Inside the city, around Etemenanki, the people celebrated with music and dancing. There was nothing special to celebrate tonight, but they did it anyway. They danced around the base of the tower; they beat their drums up and down the criss-crossing staircases that led to each successive tier. On the flat-topped roofs, they whirled and spun around the temple. They loved to climb her tower. They loved to reach the top and lift their hands to the gods of the night.

They fed themselves to Babylon, and she swallowed them gladly.

Kaida struggled in the grasp of Qurdi-Marduk-lamur as he dragged her through the Street of Purchases. "Where are you taking me?"

Qurdi ignored her, but she saw a smile play around his mouth.

She watched the faces of those he dragged her past, her eyes imploring them for help. But Qurdi was well recognized even here. There were few who would dare to intervene.

Ahead, a wild pig darted out from the crowd into their path, startling a woman and overturning a cart. Kaida saw her chance. As the pig squealed past Qurdi's feet, Kaida shoved against him, knocking him off balance long enough to twist out of his grip. She plunged into the crowd that swarmed through the street. She heard him scream behind her.

Kaida pulled her tunic above her knees and fled through the streets. Behind her, she could hear the priest shrieking as he chased her. She pumped harder, her heart slamming against her chest. She had always been a good runner. She wove through the textile district and into the glassmakers' area. Finally, she slowed to a stop and bent over, her hands on her knees.

She looked behind her, waiting for the bald head and black cloak to appear. There were only the curious stares of the neighborhood. She had lost him.

She spun a few times, trying to get her bearings. The city still confused her. Tower on her left, almost behind her. She moved through the dark streets, more confident now. Could she find Cosam's home?

A suffocating arm wrapped around her waist and snatched her backward. Kaida twisted her own arm up and behind her, and her hand slapped against smooth skin. She curled her fingers and dug her nails into the flesh.

A moment later her hands were pinned painfully behind her back. A voice hissed in her ear. "I wasn't finished with you."

Kaida inhaled forcefully against Qurdi's grip. "Let me go, and I will tell you what you want to know."

Peter rested in a reed chair in the courtyard of Cosam's home, nearly asleep. He should go to bed, but Kaida had not yet returned. He admitted to himself that he would not like to see her hurt because of him. Because of Rim-Sin, that is. Tomorrow he would go to Rim's house to see what he could learn.

Power lies in the ability to command your own personal kingdom—your thoughts and then your behaviors—so that you are able to accomplish exactly what you desire.

Heavy breathing at the doorway startled him, and he jumped from the chair. Kaida. "What's wrong?" he said.

Kaida stifled a scream. She had not seen him.

A figure appeared in the twilight behind her. Peter stood.

The man's shaved head towered above Kaida. Cold eyes took in the courtyard and locked on Peter. Two red lines were scraped across his cheek. "Rim-Sin, did you think you would remain hidden forever?"

Was it the *rab alani* or the sorcerer? Either way, he wanted out. Peter measured the space between himself and the door. Not a chance.

Kaida backed up and tried to slip away.

"Where are you going?" The black-cloaked man stepped to his left and blocked Kaida's exit. He touched two fingers to his injured cheek. "You still need to pay for this." He smiled at Peter. "Even though you kept your word and led me to him."

Kaida glanced at Peter, then away.

This must be Qurdi-Marduk-lamur. Part of Peter felt a sense of relief at finally seeing the faceless man he'd been avoiding since he arrived here.

"What do you want?" he asked.

"Why, justice, of course." Qurdi smiled again. "You must answer for the murder of a man in your own home." Qurdi slipped his fingers around Kaida's elbow and held her tightly. He took several steps closer to Peter. "But first, you are going to give me whatever you have found."

Peter watched that hand on Kaida. "I don't know what you're talking about."

Qurdi laughed. "That will not work, Rim-Sin. I know this murder means you have found something important. What is the secret you have uncovered?"

Peter shook his head. "I have found nothing."

Qurdi jerked Kaida toward him. She nearly lost her footing, but still didn't meet Peter's eyes. Qurdi's face was only inches from his own now.

"Listen to me, Rim-Sin. I will not allow you to steal the position I have worked so long to gain. Whatever power you have found, I will kill you before I let you use it to defeat me."

Peter leaned backward, trying to break the hold those eyes seemed to have on him.

Behind Qurdi, movement caused them both to turn.

Two soldiers entered the courtyard. They carried swords strapped to their waists and leather helmets that fit down over the sides of their faces. "We will take care of the matter now, priest," one of them said.

Qurdi turned back to Peter. "I have not finished with him."

The soldier who had spoken stepped close to them. "I said, we will take care of the matter now." His expression held no fear of Qurdi.

"Do you know who I am?" Qurdi's voice was a mere hiss in the darkening room.

"Our orders are to apprehend Rim-Sin, the diviner. We do not take our orders from priests. The king himself seeks the diviner."

Qurdi snorted. "Very well. And what of her?" He twisted Kaida around to face the soldiers.

"We have instructions only for him."

Qurdi pointed to his face. "She dared to strike me while fighting to hide the truth from me."

The soldier shrugged. "We will take her as well, if it suits you. The king and the court can decide the matter."

Qurdi dropped Kaida's arm and backed away. The two soldiers moved in, grabbed them both, and dragged them outside.

The streets were beginning to fill as the heat of the sun drained into the desert. Curious townspeople stared and pointed at the diviner and his concubine being herded down the street.

"Where are you taking us?" Peter asked.

The soldiers said nothing. If they didn't answer to Qurdi, outlawed diviners were apparently even lower on their list.

Kaida tried to pry the soldier's fingers from her shoulder. "You're hurting me!"

Will they take us directly to an execution? Peter wondered. He doubted a trial by jury was in his future. He watched Kaida, who still refused to look at him. "You told him where to find me?"

"He would have killed me." Finally, she raised her eyes to his. "And why should I protect you?"

Good question.

The palace again. Only this time instead of sneaking in, Peter was being escorted through the front arch and into the courtyard, for everyone's entertainment, perhaps. He raised his head and attempted to look innocently accused and dangerous at the same time.

A contingent of guards waited inside the first lush courtyard. The two soldiers pulled Peter and Kaida up to a man who stepped from their ranks with the bearing of an officer.

"Rim-Sin, the diviner accused of murder," the soldier reported. "The girl is his concubine. She attacked Qurdi-Marduk-lamur."

The captain gave a brief nod. "Put them in a room in the east wing." He motioned to two others within his ranks. "Guards at the door at all times."

From behind them, a voice called across the courtyard. "They should be imprisoned, not given a room!"

Peter twisted in the soldier's grasp to see that the voice belonged to Qurdi. He must have followed them here.

The captain straightened and faced Qurdi. "I understand that you were attacked, High Priest. But these captives are mine to deal with. And the king would not be pleased to hear that one of his favorite diviners had been thrown in a cell for the questionable offense of killing a Jew."

Peter shot a look at Kaida. Her eyes had widened at the word "Jew." Was she reacting to the insult to her race, or had she not known the murdered man was Jewish?

"He has yet to explain his actions," Qurdi said. "Until then, he should be kept in a cell!"

The captain's chin raised slightly. "He will be guarded under my watch, High Priest. When his time comes to explain his actions to the king, then and only then will it be decided where he should remain."

Qurdi spun and stalked from the courtyard. The captain signaled the guards with another curt nod, and the two moved forward to take Peter and Kaida.

They were led through a mazelike series of corridors to what must have been the east wing. Peter had long since lost track of where this room lay in relation to the room he had already spent a night in during his first visit to the palace. But when the guards pushed the two of them into the room and shut the door, he found that it was very similar to his first experience.

Tapestries hung on the walls and covered the floor. An oil lamp burned on a table beside the bed, which was narrow and low and situated in the center of the room.

Peter surveyed the room, his eyes coming to rest on the bed. When he looked at Kaida, he saw that she too was studying the bed. He saw a look of terror cross her face.

"How long will they keep us here?" Peter wondered aloud. He paced the room where they had been left, unable to remain still.

Kaida sat against the wall, her legs drawn up against her chest, her arms wrapped tightly around them. "The guard said you would go before the king to explain the killing."

Peter stopped and faced her. "I will be executed," he said. "And it will be your fault!"

She hugged her knees more tightly and scowled at him. "I did nothing you wouldn't have done yourself, Rim-Sin! And my fate is tied to yours. If you are executed, I will probably be right beside you!"

Peter turned away and began his pacing again. He wanted to be angry with her, but he understood why she'd led Qurdi to him.

The silence between them lengthened. The evening dragged on, and no one came to haul them before the king. No one brought food, either. When the moon rose enough to appear through the terra-cotta grid in the wall, Peter admitted that their court appearance was not likely to be immediate.

He eyed the bed again. "I am going to sleep," he announced to Kaida. Perhaps that would allay her fear of him somewhat. But from the look in her eyes, it hadn't seemed to help.

He understood. She was Rim-Sin's concubine, and obviously a very unwilling one. They hadn't been alone since Peter had arrived here. What horrors must she have faced with Rim-Sin?

"Take the bed, Kaida. You can sleep there."

She looked at the bed, looked at him. "I will stay here."

He pitied her. She was so beautiful, it was not surprising that she would be fearful of men in this culture. He wished he could assure her that she didn't need to fear him.

There are no wrong desires. You have a right to pursue whatever will make you happy.

Well, yeah, but not that. Obviously he wasn't going to force himself on someone against her will. He could never feel right about something like that.

There are no wrong desires. You have a right to pursue whatever will make you happy.

He admitted that it was tempting to take advantage of the power he had over her here. The culture and society had deemed it acceptable for him to have an unwilling concubine, and since all morality was merely a construct of society, it would not even be "wrong." And yet he just felt in his gut that it wouldn't be right, either.

He became aware of Kaida watching his philosophical struggle. He went to her, lowered himself to the floor beside her. She shifted away from him slightly. "Kaida, listen." He touched her arm, waited for her to meet his eyes. "I know I have mistreated you in the past. But that is not going to happen here. You are safe in this room with me. I promise I will not hurt you."

She licked her lips and swallowed. She opened her mouth as if to speak, but then closed it again and looked away.

"Get some sleep, Kaida. Please."

"What about you?"

He shook his head and pushed up to a standing position. "I can't afford to sleep. I need to figure out what I'm going to do."

"Why did you kill that man?"

He looked down at her. Why indeed. "You were there. You must know what happened."

Her forehead wrinkled. "I came in just as you stabbed him, Rim. You know that."

"Yes. Of course." He was fishing now, but he had to find answers. "But you know why he was there."

She shifted against the wall. "How would I know my *master's* business? You do not inform me when you plan to kill someone."

He clenched his teeth at her sarcasm. "And I don't need to explain myself to you now." He turned away. "My explanation would not satisfy the king anyway. I must think of something else."

Easier said than done. What possible story could he concoct that would get him off the hook when he didn't even know what was considered legal here?

The door swung open.

Peter wished for more light in the room. A series of creepy-looking guys in robes and turbans filed into the room. One by one, they nodded and repeated his name. When the last of the ten of them had filled the room, they watched him with seeming expectation.

Peter was at a total loss.

Finally, the tallest of them spoke. "Your actions cast suspicion on all of us, Rim-Sin. We deserve an explanation."

Peter wondered if they could hear his heart pounding. There was an oppressive feeling in the room.

"Shamash is right, Rim-Sin," another robed man said. "The king could sweep us all out of the palace with you. You must convince him that this killing was justified."

Peter nodded, ready to bluff. "When the time comes for me to speak to the king, all will be understood."

A slightly built man emerged from the back of the group. Peter recognized him as the diviner he had spoken with when last in the palace, Rim-Sin's protégé.

"What of the New Year Festival, Rim? If you are imprisoned—or worse—you will not be able to fulfill your responsibility. You anger the gods and risk the well-being of the entire city with your actions!"

The group of men seemed to advance on him. Peter wondered if they would decide to exact justice right then. Kaida hovered in the back corner of the room.

"Have you lost the favor of your goddess already, Rim-Sin?"

Peter shook his head. "Not at all. You will see. The goddess will show herself through me when the time is right."

Another diviner spoke out, and Peter was surprised to see the beginning of a smile on his face. "You know what happens to diviners who have lost the power of the gods, Rim-Sin."

The smile seemed to pass from man to man, and Peter suddenly understood. These fellow diviners were not here out of concern for him. They were hoping he would go down. In their quest to each be the most favored by the king, they would rejoice at the downfall of any competition, especially one at the front of the pack. It was the reason that Qurdi was so anxious to see him arrested.

"We will look forward to hearing this explanation, Rim-Sin. And the reason you claim you are so highly favored by Ishtar."

Peter watched them file out of the room and wondered how he was going to convince a group of ancient magicians that he had the favor of the gods.

Hours later, Peter still paced the room, sometimes gazing out at the night sky. Kaida had fallen asleep at last. She had agreed to take the bed finally, though Peter was certain she slept with one eye still on him.

A quiet knock at the door surprised him. He turned from the window, and the door slid open. A handsome young man slipped in. Peter had never seen him before. He was robed and turbaned like the diviners had been, but his robes had none of the symbolic ornamentation of the others.

"Hello, Rim-Sin."

Peter squared off against the man, ready for anything. "What do you want?"

The man silently watched him for a moment. "You are different."

Peter's heart stuttered. He glanced at Kaida, still sleeping, and drew himself up to his full height. "Why have you come?"

"I have a message for you from the Most High God."

OK, so not a diviner. Jewish, obviously. Peter exhaled some of the tension. From what he'd seen so far, the Jews didn't have much power in Babylon.

The younger man still studied him, and a quizzical look passed across his face. "You have dreamed."

Peter waited, unwilling to comment.

The man came forward, touched Peter's arm, and closed his eyes. Almost to himself, he said, "I do not know why the Lord God speaks in dreams to pagan men or why He sends me to tell them the meaning. I only obey."

A light bulb went on for Peter. "You are Daniel."

The man pulled his hand away, his eyes wide. "Now I know that you are different. No Babylonian has ever addressed me by my Hebrew name."

Peter fought the urge to sink into the nearest chair. Good grief, he was talking to the biblical prophet Daniel in the middle of ancient Babylon! Could this actually be real?

"The call of the Most High is upon you," Daniel said. "You are fighting it."

Peter regained his voice. "I'm fighting nothing, except a murder accusation."

Daniel closed his eyes again. "It is not time. You are not finished."

Peter inhaled sharply. Those had been Hugh's exact words in Peter's freaky dream just after he'd arrived in this place. "What does that mean?"

"Do you wish to know the interpretation of your dream?" Daniel asked.

Peter looked away. Was he really going to fall for this? He didn't believe this guy could interpret dreams any more than Peter could call down power from Ishtar. Daniel—like the entire Bible—was a myth. This man was some trickster who happened to bear the same name.

Daniel moved slightly, positioning himself in Peter's line of sight again. "You dreamed of the tower."

Peter gave him his full attention.

"Of people trying to build the tower higher, trying to finish the tower."

Peter wiped sweaty palms against his tunic. Right so far.

"And you must tear it down."

Again with the tearing down. "I don't understand."

Daniel fixed his gaze on Peter. When he spoke, it was with a clear voice, full of the conviction of a man who believed he spoke from God. "You have been called to fight against evil. Not here. In a different time and place. But first you must prepare and learn. And you will do that by finishing the work of the man you killed. Only then will you be able to go home, and only then will you be ready to fulfill your calling. And it must be before the New Year Festival."

Peter felt light-headed. It was as if this man could read his very soul. "But who was the dead man? What was he trying to do? How can I complete his work when I don't know anything about him?"

Daniel's shoulders relaxed and his features softened. "That is all I have been given to know. But it is weighty, Rim-Sin. A call on your life from the Lord of Hosts is no small thing."

Peter crossed his arms. It would be crazy to try to fight his way out of this time by finishing any job being done by the man Rim-Sin had killed. How could that possibly get him home?

"You doubt," Daniel said.

Peter didn't know how to answer. His doubts would not

have been Rim-Sin's doubts, but even Rim-Sin wouldn't have bowed to Daniel's God, would he? "Your God is not my God," he said.

"Yet He is the one true God. All others have no power, or else they have a lesser power that is not of Him."

"Your knowledge is impressive, Daniel. But I am not ready to acknowledge that God speaks to you directly."

"And yet you claim that your gods speak to you."

Peter turned away. He had already heard what happened to diviners who lost their connection with the gods. He wasn't about to tell the chief of magicians that the gods didn't speak to him at all.

"Peter."

At the whispered word, Peter spun back to Daniel. "What did you say?"

Daniel only watched him.

"Say it again! What did you call me?"

Daniel smiled. A slow, knowing smile. "You are called by God, *Peter.* Finish the man's task. It is the only way home."

Peter watched as the young man backed away, slipped through the door into the palace hall, and was gone.

Finish his task.

A shaft of sunlight found its way through the terra-cotta grid in the palace bedroom wall. It cut into the room with the precision of a laser and found Peter where he slept on the floor. He opened his eyes, blinked, and rolled away from the light with a groan.

The night had been long, and the bedroom floor hard on his joints. Kaida still slept in the bed.

She gets the floor if we're here another night.

The door opened unannounced, and Peter jumped to his feet. But this time it was only a slave carrying breakfast. He nodded to Peter, placed a wooden tray of apricots and cheeses on a low table by the door, and backed out of the room.

Just like room service at the Ritz. Without the tip.

Kaida stirred and pushed her dark hair away from her face.

"Breakfast is here," Peter said.

"Hmmm." She stretched like a cat and yawned.

Peter watched until she turned to him. He went to the tray of food. "How long do you think I have before the king summons me?"

She shrugged. "What will you tell him?"

Peter chewed an apricot. "I don't know. I need more answers myself before I can give any to the king."

The morning passed slowly. Peter poked his head out of the door once to see if there was any way to get out unnoticed, but two soldiers on either side of the door quickly convinced him there was not.

The room was comfortable enough, if plain. It even had its own bathroom, a small closet with a chamber pot to the right of the door.

Kaida had found a tapestry unraveling on the floor and had busied herself by attempting to reweave the piece with her fingers. Peter paced some more, trying to think of a good story for the king. If only he knew the truth about why Rim-Sin had killed the Jewish man. Perhaps there was a good explanation, one that would satisfy the king.

He grew tired of pacing and flopped next to Kaida on the floor. She stopped her weaving and watched him.

"What?" he asked.

She shrugged. "Why don't you ever treat me like a concubine?"

Wow, this girl could be direct. What could he say to that question? "How do I treat you?"

"Like a child, usually."

He grunted, "You are a child."

"Am I? I am twenty-four years old."

So young. For a moment he wished he were ten or twelve years younger himself. He looked across at her. "Do you... want me to treat you... that way?"

Her eyes were like daggers. "What do you think?"

Stupid question. Very stupid. He almost took her arm, but then let his hand drop. "I won't, Kaida. I never will. You have my word."

She studied him, and her eyes softened. Had he ever noticed her eyes?

Behind them, a voice said, "Isn't this a lovely domestic scene."

Peter looked over his shoulder and stood. "Qurdi!"

The high priest smiled. "It's time, Rim-Sin."

"You're here to take me to the king?" Already? He hadn't thought of a plan yet!

Qurdi barked a laugh. "No, Rim-Sin. Not time for your execution yet. You will not take the road to your forefathers until you tell me what you have found."

Peter inhaled deeply and blew the air out. "Qurdi, I have told you—"

"Stop! You have told me lies! Are you waiting until you are before the king to display your newfound power? Do you think you can make fools of all of us? We will not let you succeed so easily!" Qurdi took a few steps toward him, and Peter stepped in front of Kaida.

The high priest smiled. "She is important to you?" He stepped closer to Peter. "Listen to me, diviner. I will lay her on an altar and split her open to the gods if that is what it takes. You will not be chief of magicians!" He reached for Kaida's arm.

Peter heard Kaida's sharp intake of air. For the first time in his life, he wished for a knife. Peter took the only action he could think of. "Guards!"

The door swung open, and the two soldiers posted outside his door ran in.

Peter pulled Kaida away from Qurdi. "The high priest has threatened to kill us before we are given audience before the king, in spite of the king's request to hear my explanation."

One of the guards, young and lean like a wrestler, stepped forward. "High Priest, it is time to leave." He spoke with respect, yet with the firmness of a man expecting to be obeyed.

Qurdi's eyes bore into Peter's. "I will be back."

The young guard pushed between the two of them. "There will be no more visits until the diviner is taken before the king."

Qurdi scowled at the guard. "And I will say a prayer to Ishtar on *your* behalf before the day is over."

The guard's face whitened, but he held his ground. Qurdi left the room without a backward glance.

When the guards had repositioned themselves outside the door, Peter turned to Kaida. Her face was pale, and the shadows under her dark eyes seemed intensified. "It's not going to happen, Kaida. I'm not going to let him hurt you."

She let her breath out, then sucked it in again. Peter realized she was panting her way to hyperventilating.

"Kaida!" He shook her arms, then pulled her to himself. "Stop! I will not let that evil man touch you!"

Her breathing slowed against his chest, but when she pulled away it was with doubt in her eyes. "And what do you know of evil?"

At midday, the slave returned with more food. Peter stopped him before his silent exit. "Have you heard how long before the king will require my presence in the throne room?"

The slave shook his head.

"Do you know if he has spoken of me?"

Again, the head shaking.

"Speak, man! Tell me anything you know."

The slave swallowed hard. "My lord, the kitchen staff is saying that tomorrow will be an entertaining day in the throne room."

Peter exhaled. Tomorrow. "What have you heard about why Rim—why I killed the Jew?"

"I have heard nothing, my lord. Diviners do not confide in slaves. They have each other for that."

Peter nodded. He looked at the tray of meats. "What is your name?" he asked the slave.

"Sabar."

"Have you had enough to eat today, Sabar?"

The boy shrugged, his eyebrows knit together.

Peter pointed to the tray. "Have some meat." The slave didn't move. "Eat."

The boy tentatively reached a hand for a thick piece. Peter nodded. He popped it into his mouth.

"There is another diviner, Sabar. A young man whom I have taken a special interest in. Do you know his name?"

Sabar nodded, chewing. "Akkad."

"I need you to bring him to me. Can you do that?"

Sabar shrugged. "I will see if I can find him."

Peter squeezed the boy's shoulder. "It is important, Sabar. I am trusting you."

Sabar swallowed. "I will find him."

"Good." Peter handed him another piece of meat. "Quickly."

When Sabar had gone, Peter looked at Kaida and pointed to the tray.

"Why do you need Akkad?" she asked.

Peter shook his head. "I don't know yet. But he may be the only friend I have here."

Kaida looked at the floor, then through the window. "I'm not hungry."

Peter thought hard as he ate. He was to be called before the king tomorrow. He still had no explanation to give as to why he had killed the Jewish man. Neither the truth nor any fiction that he was certain would get him off the hook. But something Qurdi had said replayed in his mind. Qurdi was expecting Rim-Sin to perform some act of power before the king tomorrow, thereby impressing the court and getting himself released. Was it possible that power was all that truly mattered in this place? Perhaps a show of power, proving that he was favored by the gods, was all it would take. Did anyone in the palace care about one dead Jew if Rim-Sin could prove that the gods were on his side?

He flew through ideas that would impress the king, trashing them one by one as impossible or not impressive enough.

What I need is a good solar eclipse to predict. No such luck.

It seemed insane that a man from the twenty-first century wouldn't have something that would blow them away in the throne room. But any knowledge he had of the future could not be proven immediately and wouldn't impress anyone. He didn't have any skills at pulling rabbits from hats. Card tricks, mind reading, disappearing doves. He'd never had one of those "Astonish your friends" kits as a kid.

He could tell them the earth was round, but how could he prove it? He could teach them about what was happening right then in China, but again he wouldn't be able to prove it. The more he frantically discarded ideas, the more he realized that for all his centuries of learning, he had nothing to offer without the aid of technology.

Kaida cleared her throat from the other side of the room. "You're quiet."

He sighed. "I'm thinking. Thinking about how hopeless all of this is."

"Why don't you tell the king the truth? Perhaps it will be enough."

Peter went to the window and looked out. The room was situated at the outside of the palace, facing the tower. Everywhere Peter had been in this city that tower seemed to be in the center.

Suddenly a plan took root and began to grow.

Chapter 7

PETER POUNDED A fist against the table. "When will he come?" He had been waiting all afternoon, hoping that the slave Sabar would have gotten his message to the diviner Akkad. It was crucial that Akkad help him. He couldn't do this alone.

"I don't see how Akkad can help you now," Kaida said.

Peter studied the tower through the grid window again. The seven-tiered pyramid was built like a square layered wedding cake, with each successively smaller tier stacked on top of the one below. Staircases zigzagged back and forth along the sides, leading from one level to the next. One long staircase ran from the center of the courtyard directly up to the fourth level. Was it the original Tower of Babel described in the Bible? Scholars were uncertain, but many believed that it was. Could he do it?

A voice came from behind him. "You wanted to see me, Rim-Sin?"

Peter turned. "Akkad, thank you for coming." He took a deep breath. This was going to be tricky.

"The guards have given me only a few moments."

"Akkad, I am determined to meet my responsibility at the New Year Festival. I will not harm the city by my rash actions. But I need your help."

The younger man bowed his head. "Whatever I can do, Rim-Sin."

"I need an incantation."

Akkad looked up. "An incantation?"

"Something powerful. Something that will call down the power of Ishtar upon me, that will show that the goddess favors me." A vague consciousness ran behind Peter's words, a wonder at the words that poured so easily from him.

Akkad shook his head. "I have heard you recite many incantations, Rim. Why do you need me?"

Peter inhaled and glanced at Kaida. It was critical that neither of them suspect that he had lost any of his powers or connection to the gods. If word got out that he was a has-been, it would be the end of Rim-Sin.

"This must be different, Akkad. New. And very powerful. Consider it a test of your own development. The gods intend to show themselves through me in a very special way. Can you help me?"

Akkad nodded. "I will try to find something."

"Quickly, Akkad. I do not have much time."

The diviner bowed to Peter once more. "I will return."

Some time later the evening meal arrived. Peter placed the tray in the center of the bed. He and Kaida sat on the bed, facing each other. The melon and pork Peter recognized, but a bowlful of something green in the center of the tray looked like some kind of science experiment. Peter handed Kaida a wooden spoon for the green slop.

She took the spoon and looked at him. "Thank you."

He smiled. "My pleasure."

She touched the spoon to the sticky green mush, then lifted it to her nose and sniffed. The look of disgust on her face overcame Peter's resolve not to laugh.

She lowered the spoon, trying not to smile. "I believe this delicacy was intended for you, Rim-Sin. I would not want to deprive you." She tried to give him the spoon.

Peter pushed it away. "Your kindness surprises me, Kaida. I

could almost believe you are starting to care for me. But I insist you take it."

She laughed now. "You have grown so much kinder, Rim-Sin. But perhaps we could feed it to the guards and make our escape while they gag."

It was the first time Peter had seen her laugh. He didn't want the moment to end. In spite of being displaced in this primitive culture and about to face certain execution by the king, Peter wished he could remain right here.

The door opened, and Peter turned. "Akkad?"

But it was not Akkad who entered. Peter rose from the bed and faced yet another magician, this time a Hebrew hated by almost everyone.

"Rim-Sin," Daniel said, "the Lord God has sent me to tell you that the king will require your presence in the morning."

Peter raised his eyebrows. "Yahweh is using the chief of magicians as His errand boy now?"

Kaida rose from the bed behind him. "Chief of magicians?" Her voice was a whisper. "Daniel?"

"Yes." He peered around Peter. "Who is this woman, Rim?"

"She is—my concubine," Peter said, swallowing hard.

Kaida moved to Daniel. "My name is Kaida."

He smiled. "You are Jewish."

"Yes."

He touched her arm. "I have so little contact with our people," Daniel said. "Tell me of life out there with them."

Kaida pointed to the floor, and the two sat against the wall. Peter watched their conversation with arms crossed over his chest.

Daniel and Kaida looked to be about the same age, and Peter suddenly felt very old. And boorish. Peter remembered the Bible stories. Daniel was one of Israel's finest, brought during the first deportation. How had he been described? Perfectly featured, amazingly brilliant. Something like that. He certainly seemed to be dazzling Kaida. And the two of them together looked as if they could have stepped from an ancient version of *People* magazine's 50 Most Beautiful People issue.

He interrupted their conversation. "Aren't you worried about being seen here with me, Daniel?"

Daniel smiled. "There are some benefits to being the chief, Rim-Sin. I have the favor of the king. It is only the other diviners who hate me."

Kaida frowned. "They hate you simply because you are a Hebrew."

Daniel shook his head. "My youth and my race do not please the palace diviners, but they hate me most because I serve the God of Israel instead of their carved images."

"Rim says he does not serve any god," Kaida said. "He believes the gods are only symbols of something higher that has no personality, something that lies within all of us."

Peter frowned. He had said too much to Kaida, clearly. He couldn't have her thinking that he didn't believe in the gods. Especially with his fate hanging on his performance tomorrow. "Daniel is not interested in my beliefs, Kaida."

Daniel smiled. "I think you know that I am very interested, Rim-Sin." His eyes had a knowing look. "And so is the Lord. He is waiting and watching to see you finish the task He has given."

"Well . . . I have to get free of this situation before I can take on any other tasks, Daniel."

Daniel nodded and stood. "Then I will leave you to your rest."

Kaida clutched Daniel's arm. "Can't you stay? I have so many things I'd like to speak with you about."

Daniel turned to Kaida, then impulsively embraced her. "Another time, dear girl."

Peter frowned and held the door open for Daniel.

Akkad arrived a short time later. He pushed a piece of papyrus into Peter's hands, then disappeared without a word. Peter sensed fear in the man and didn't hold him.

The papyrus contained an incantation.

Kaida looked at it over his shoulder, then backed away. "I don't even want to read it," she said.

The prayer was long, and the time was short.

Peter turned to her. "You're going to have to. I need you to help me memorize it."

They worked late into the night. Kaida sat on the bed while Peter paced and repeated the words. Eventually she lay on the bed, and when Peter finished the recitation of one section, he realized she had fallen asleep.

He took the opportunity to do a few sets of push-ups on the floor. It was dangerous enough to have Kaida in the know about the incantation. He wasn't about to let her see him preparing physically.

When his arms grew fatigued, he went to the window and watched the night sky. The stars seemed close and friendly tonight. He thought of Akkad and the other diviners, able to read the stars like any modern astronomer. The knowledge born in this culture would extend more than twenty centuries into the future. Amazing.

Peter whispered the incantation once more, the prayer for power from Ishtar flowing easily from his lips now.

You will succeed.

The words were a whisper behind him. Peter turned and smiled at Kaida, but she was asleep. He leaned his back against the window, frowning.

You are favored. The whisper was behind him again, outside the window. He peered through the grid, but saw no one. A strange sensation tingled up the length of his spine. He had prayed to Rim-Sin's patron goddess.

And now someone was answering.

Akkad's new amulet had drawn down the power of the stars, and it now resided around the king's neck. To thank Akkad for his skill, Nabu-kudurri-usur had included Akkad on the guest list for the evening meal. It was an honor he had not received since joining the *kasdim*.

Akkad dressed with care, twisting the traditional red turban around his dark hair and fastening it with a gold star-shaped pin that matched the gold stars embroidered into his blue robes.

He left his chamber and joined the flow toward the banquet hall. He was not so naïve as to think he was the only honored guest this evening, but still the blood pounded in his veins.

In the banquet hall, he watched and waited for the right moment to be seated. Too soon and he would have no control over who sat nearby at his table. Too late and there would be no good spots left. Every other wise man played the game, too.

When he finally chose a seat with several of the wise men of other circles, he was delighted to see Belteshazzar and his three Hebrew friends, now governors in the city, join the table. Akkad studied the chief of magicians. Belteshazzar's hair was shorter than the Babylonian style, his complexion lighter than his Persian counterparts. Piercing eyes took in each person at the table. Truly, this was the high point of Akkad's career to this moment.

Belteshazzar's gaze rested momentarily on Akkad, a question in his expression. "A new colleague joins us this evening?"

"I am Akkad," he bowed his head in respect.

"We are pleased to have you at our table, Akkad," Belteshazzar offered.

A diviner at the end of the long table, whom Akkad had never met, called down to the Jews. "Your table? Have the Hebrews now taken over the banquet hall as well?"

Belteshazzar's Hebrew friend, Shadur-Aku, leaned forward and turned toward the diviner. "Do not fear, magician, we will never take over your temples and high places!"

The circle of wise men at the table chuckled and exchanged glances. Akkad joined the laughter carefully. He was unsure if Shadur-Aku's comment was very humorous. The laughter seemed a bit strained to him. One of the other Hebrews, a slightly built young man Akkad knew as Mi-sha-Aku, quietly touched Shadur-Aku's arm. The bigger man looked at his companion, smiled slightly, and ducked his head. Belteshazzar's third friend seemed unconcerned about diplomacy, however.

"Oh, I don't know," Abed-Nabu said. "Perhaps we *will* take them over and turn them into places of worship to the Mighty One of Israel." Abed-Nabu did not smile.

There was no laughter now. More looks were passed around the table, raised eyebrows, tightened lips.

The food arrived, and Akkad breathed out in relief.

The meal was excessive, as all palace meals must be, and Akkad ate well. When he finally pushed away from the table, he took the time to survey the room. The king reclined at a table across the banquet hall with Amyitis, his favorite wife, at his side. Other royal wives and their servants lined a table that lay at a right angle to the king's.

Akkad scanned the faces of the women, until his eyes locked onto one familiar face. He gripped the table edge for a moment. Abigail!

She was laughing at something the woman next to her had said. Akkad already loved the way she laughed. His ridiculous thoughts of finding a more suitable woman were forgotten. He puzzled instead over how he could see her again.

When the king had dismissed the company, Akkad approached Abigail.

"Akkad, what are you doing here?" She glanced around at the women who streamed around them through the hallway.

"A reward for a favor to the king." He dismissed it with a wave of his hand. "I want to see you again." He gripped her hands. "Where can we meet?"

She cast fearful looks around her again, pulling her hands from his and whispering, "Akkad, please!"

"Tell me where I can meet you!"

She allowed her eyes to rest on his face for only a moment, but he was surprised to see tears. "I cannot, Akkad!" She pushed past him and ran through the hall.

Akkad watched her go. Moments later he spotted Belteshazzar as he passed. "Belteshazzar, may I ask you a question?"

"Certainly, Akkad."

"That woman, there." He pointed to her fleeing figure. "I believe she is a Jewess."

"Yes. Abigail," Belteshazzar nodded.

"Is she servant to a royal wife?" he asked.

Belteshazzar smiled. "No, my friend. She *is* a royal wife."

Kaida stirred in the early morning light. She rolled over in the bed and bumped against something. She opened her eyes. Rim-Sin! He lay in the bed next to her, his mouth half-open in a deep sleep.

She slid off the reed mattress to the floor and made her way to the corner washing room.

The last thing she remembered was Rim reciting that awful incantation for the hundredth time. She must have fallen asleep, and then he must have joined her. She couldn't blame him. She already felt guilty about him sleeping on the ground.

Guilty? She poured water from a white-glazed pitcher over her hands and rubbed her face with wet hands. Was it possible she cared whether Rim-Sin slept comfortably or not? Tears welled in her eyes. What was she thinking? The last few days had seriously undermined her hatred of Rim-Sin and almost completely wiped out her fear of him. She wasn't sure how well she was doing in her attempts to point him to her God. Was she failing in the task she'd been given? In spite of his pagan beliefs, she was drawn to him. He was so . . . alone. Somehow she could see so clearly that no one had ever truly loved this man. He had covered himself in a protective shell to keep from feeling the pain. But it was still there.

She emerged from the washroom and watched Rim-Sin sleep. Daniel's face appeared in her memory, and she compared the two. The beautiful, God-fearing Daniel, and the angry, pagan Rim-Sin. And there was no question which way her heart was drawn.

Crazy girl.

The door burst open, and two helmeted soldiers stepped into the room.

"Rim-Sin!"

Peter bolted upright from the bed. Kaida's hand was warm on his shoulder, her face close. He had allowed himself to fall asleep beside her last night, watching that perfect face. But this morning it was etched with fear.

"It's time," she said.

"What?"

Two soldiers appeared above her. "The king has requested your appearance in the throne room, Rim-Sin," one said.

So soon? It couldn't be later than eight o'clock. He had fallen asleep late, trying not to think about the whispers he had heard in response to his prayer. Peter took a deep breath and rubbed his eyes. "Can you give me a few moments?" he said the guards. They nodded, retreated to the inside of the doorway, and waited with hands on their belted swords.

Peter tried to smile at Kaida. He saw the fear in her eyes. He stood and touched her face. "Don't worry."

He spent a few minutes in the bathroom, and then emerged ready, if not truly prepared.

"Will you come?" he asked Kaida.

She looked at the guards. "I will follow wherever they will allow."

Peter nodded. "Don't stay too close, though. If this doesn't go well, I don't want you swept along with me."

She gripped his forearms. "Rim—"

He pulled her gently away from him. "Don't worry."

The guards approached. It was time.

The guards pushed Peter and Kaida ahead of them through the halls.

Part of him knew this was probably the end of his adventure in Babylon, yet Peter still felt a tiny thrill. He was about to enter Nebuchadnezzar's throne room and address one of the most famous ancient men of all time—and to be personally respected in that room by crowds of people.

The palace seemed constructed to lead a person to the throne room whether he liked it or not. Peter took a deep breath at the entrance. Nebuchadnezzar was holding court. The morning heat had already built up in the room, and a partially clad male slave stood beside the king, fanning him with two large palm branches. The walls of the throne room were brightly painted from floor to lofty ceiling. Columns and lions were painted in yellow, white, and red on a vivid blue background. It was amazing.

The guard pulled them into the back of the room. A dozen pairs of eyes traveled in their direction, including the king's.

"Ah, the missing Rim-Sin." The king held a hand out to Peter and smiled sarcastically. "We are so honored you have found your way back to us."

Peter began to approach, but the king held up a hand. "Stand aside, Rim-Sin. I will deal with you presently."

What did that mean—deal with? Kaida stood beside him as he waited in the back of the room. The red and yellow lions on the imperial wall behind him seemed ready to devour him. It was apparently another diviner's turn before the king.

"You told me that yesterday would be an auspicious day for the hunt," the king said.

"Yes, O King. But the liver was difficult to read and—"

"The ostrich evaded me all day." The king's voice was taut.

"Yes, O King."

Nebuchadnezzar reclined on his throne and flicked his hand toward a guard. "Execute him," he said, then turned his attention elsewhere.

Guards took the diviner away, and another official bowed before the throne.

"O King, live forever," he said. "There is a problem with the Jewish district of the Old City. Several men stir up the people to contradict the king."

"Go on," Nebuchadnezzar said.

"There are several who continue to tell the Jews that their God will soon conquer you and bring them home. And there are others who encourage the people to reject Marduk and Ishtar and all the gods who have favored the king."

Nebuchadnezzar yawned. "Put them in the prison and await my instruction." As the official moved away, the king seemed to notice Peter again. "Come forward, Rim."

Peter stepped toward the platform that held the throne. "O

King, live forever." It was a pathetic attempt, but he felt he should say something.

"The king is not pleased when his diviners are accused of murder, Rim-Sin."

What worked best here? Groveling? Honesty? "The incident in my home, O King, I have been attempting to amend it."

The king only nodded, his face rigid.

Peter took a deep breath. "O King, live forever." He repeated the words he'd heard a few minutes earlier, apparently the customary way to begin addressing the king. "The Hebrew in my home, O King, he came there to attack me. He spoke of the Hebrew God and said that his God had told him to kill me. I was able to subdue him, but he continued to abuse our gods, O King. I warned him to show respect, but when he went on to speak ill of the king, I could restrain myself no longer. I am afraid I was enraged, O King, and I flew at him with a knife, killing him before taking any thought of my actions. I had only the king's honor in mind."

There. It was the best he had. A manslaughter defense. Perhaps even justified, depending on how highly the king valued his own honor. Peter waited.

The king studied him, his face unreadable.

From the back of the room, another voice called out. "O King, live forever, I have heard the truth in this matter, and Rim-Sin does not speak the truth."

The king held out a hand. "Approach, Qurdi-Marduk-lamur."

Peter studied the floor as Qurdi walked past him to stand before the throne.

"O King, it is said that Rim-Sin sought the Jewish man for his knowledge of the God Yahweh. Rim-Sin has come to believe that Yahweh is the more powerful God, and he plans to gain the favor of this new God to replace Belteshazzar as chief of magicians."

The king snorted. "You priests and diviners. All of you so anxious to become chief." He waved a hand. "There are days that I desire to dispose of the entire lot of you." His eyes narrowed. "But Belteshazzar has proven that he is more powerful than any of you." He turned to Peter. "If you have forsaken your goddess, Rim-Sin, in favor of the Hebrew God, then you are a man without power. For I do not believe that the Hebrew God will ever favor you. And if you are a diviner without power, than you are of no use to me at all." He leaned back against the throne and turned his eyes to a pair of guards nearby.

Peter drew himself up and took a deep breath. Time for Plan B.

He raised his voice. "I have been given greater power from the gods than any diviner, O King!"

The throne room stilled at his shouted claim. The king turned back to Rim slowly and watched him without speaking.

The silence in the room lengthened. Finally the king spoke. "You make a bold claim, Rim-Sin. Are you saying that you have more power than even Belteshazzar?"

Say it. Say yes. Say yes. "Yes, O King." There. It was done. He'd committed himself now, and there was no going back. Prove himself or die.

The king smiled and looked around the throne room at the diviners, slaves, and petitioners. "It would seem that we are to be given a special display of power today, my people." He chuckled and held out both hands, palms upward, to Peter. "Watch and be amazed."

Peter put his hands on his waist and turned a slow circle in the center of the room, making eye contact with as many as he could. To a person, they backed away, widening the space around him until he stood like an island in the center of a human sea. Kaida was somewhere in the crowd, but he didn't see her.

Then he acted as if he sensed something he didn't like. He

turned to the king. "Not here!" he shouted. "The gods wish to display power through me outside of the palace."

The king raised his eyebrows.

"The Platform of Etemenanki, O King," Peter said. "It stands as a symbol of the slow and difficult way in which we must please the gods. To reach the summit is arduous, a difficult path upward that shows us there is no easy way to gain the favor of the gods."

Peter felt the riveted attention of the room on his words. "But the goddess has granted me special favor. She allows me direct access to her, like no other diviner has received. And to prove this, she allows me to ascend to the Platform directly, without using the steps that all others must climb to reach the gods."

Snatches of murmured conversation rippled through the room as people reacted to Peter's claim.

Nebuchadnezzar laughed. "Not even Belteshazzar has made such a ridiculous claim, Rim-Sin. We will go to the tower, and you will show us this favor of the goddess you insist upon." The court erupted in cheers, and the king stood. "And if you cannot do as you claim, we will have no further use for your life."

The flood of people poured from the throne room. With four guards surrounding him, Peter was swept into the courtyard and then out into the city street where his fate awaited him at the Tower of Babel.

As the crowd approached the tower, Peter came as close to a real prayer as he had ever come in his life. From his room under house arrest in the palace there was one thing he had been unable to determine, and it was the one thing that would determine his success or failure today.

Did the tower have any toeholds at all?

He had scaled plenty of challenging rock faces in the United

States and other countries. And he had climbed man-made rock walls manufactured to provide challenging but adequate spots for fingers and toes. But he had never scaled a man-made edifice that was not created to be climbed.

And he wouldn't know if it was possible until he either made it to the top or died trying.

There was a party atmosphere among the crowd that followed him to the tower. The king had quickly been hoisted into a litter while still in the palace courtyard, and now six bare-chested slaves carried him through the throng. Excitement buzzed through the people, and Peter was reminded of Fenway Park before a big game. The people were ripe for a show, and Peter knew it didn't much matter to them whether he succeeded or failed. They would be entertained either way.

He caught sight of long, dark hair through the crowd. Kaida!

She was unguarded. It looked like the excitement of his claim had caused Qurdi's threat against her to be forgotten. Peter was thankful for that, at least. He tried to catch her attention through the people that kept coming between them.

A rough prod from behind urged him on. "Keep moving, diviner."

They reached the tower far too soon. The day had grown hot already, and Peter sweated under his tunic. His palms were clammy. He wished for his chalk bag and nearly laughed. He was about to climb sheer rock without gloves, climbing shoes, a rope, a carabiner, or a belay brake. He had no anchor, no harness, and no one spotting him. Missing chalk was the least of his problems.

I've got to get out of here. In this crowd, I might have a chance at disappearing.

And then what? How was he supposed to remain unseen long enough to finish the dead guy's job, whatever it was? He stepped to the base of the tower and ran a quick glance over the surface. Tiny ledges cropped out at various levels.

Thank you, God. Or goddess. Or somebody. He nearly laughed again. Hysteria, no doubt.

Peter closed his eyes for one quick moment of preparation, stooped to rub his hands in the sandy clay at his feet, and then turned his back to the tower. He held his arms high above his head and waited for the crowd to quiet. The silence began in front of him and spread through the throng until the city itself seemed to hold its breath.

"The goddess favors me with direct access to herself!" he shouted. "I can ascend into her presence through her aid. I have no need of steps!"

They waited as one. Peter saw the king rise from the litter and focus his gaze on Peter. He sensed Kaida pushing through the crowd at his right, trying to get a better position.

Peter threw back his head, closed his eyes, and began the incantation he had so carefully practiced.

"O heroic one, Ishtar; the immaculate one of the goddesses, torch of heaven and earth, radiance of the continents..."

The incantation went on, line after line. Peter had a moment of doubt. Was it too long? Was he losing them? But the crowd was still silent. He delivered the last line as loudly as he could. "Lengthen my days, bestow life! Let me live, let me be well, let me proclaim your divinity. Let me achieve what I desire!"

And then he turned to the tower. He unstrapped his sandals and studied the wall.

The first foothold was easy to find. He boosted himself up and found a crack for the fingers of his right hand. He kept his hands close to his head and his feet directly under his hands. The footholds were small here, but he was able to use an edging technique, pushing the inside of his foot onto the small ledges that cropped out from the rock. He used a cling grip on most of the handholds, trying to pull his thumb up beside his four fingers and force them into the tiny cracks he spotted. His progress was slow at first, and he sensed the need to go faster if he were going to impress them. He scrabbled for another handhold, using a pinch grip on this one.

A murmur was beginning to spread through the crowd, now about ten feet below him. He was counting on convincing them by the time he reached that first platform, about forty feet up. He could hear the excitement in the crowd. Were they impressed or not?

Sweat trickled from his forehead and stung his eyes. He couldn't spare a hand to wipe it away, and he couldn't close his eyes when the next hand and footholds were still to be found.

His arms began to tire. There was no rope to relax against. The still-healing wound in his side pulled and threatened to reopen.

His fingers grew bloody. The next handhold was too slim. His fingers slipped. The crowd gasped.

Can't let that happen again, he told himself. *Need to do more than make it. Needs to look easy.*

His tunic was soaked with sweat now. Clay dust drifted off the tower and lodged in his throat, turning his mouth into a desert.

He risked a look upward. He had to be halfway there by now. He was, but just barely.

His arms and legs began to tremble with fatigue.

Let me live, let me be well… Let me achieve what I desire.

A sudden cooling breeze drifted across his forehead, drying the perspiration. He took a deep breath and found new energy in his arms and legs. A force seemed to steady him, to guide his hands and feet to the next holds. The climb grew easier, even as an irrational fear grew inside Peter.

Not Ishtar. My own divinity. I've found it. I've tapped it. I knew it! Keep going.

He felt as if he nearly soared up the last few feet, like a

superhero from his childhood comic books. Below him the crowd picked up a chant, and it echoed through the city.

"Rim-Sin! Rim-Sin! Rim-Sin!"

He reached the landing, climbed onto it, and jumped to his feet. He turned to the city and raised his arms once again. The throng below him exploded into cheers. Peter had never felt such euphoria.

And into the raucous cheers that lifted from the city street, a whisper found its way into Peter's ear.

You are mine now.

Chapter 8

A QUICK JOG DOWN the tower's steps, and Peter was escorted to the king's litter. The king motioned to the slaves to lower him to the ground, and he stepped out to face Peter.

"I have never seen such a thing, Rim-Sin." He squinted up at the tower. "The gods have favored you, indeed. Even the king can see that."

Peter bowed his head, attempting to show humility before the king.

Nebuchadnezzar held up an arm and addressed the crowd. "Rim-Sin has proven himself this day! Ishtar favors him! Let all of Babylon show him honor!"

The crowd cheered once more, people surged around him, hands touching him. Peter noticed the absence of any other diviners he recognized. There would be no congratulations from them.

The people began to move back into the city. The king ascended to his litter again and was carried back to the palace.

Fatigue began to overwhelm Peter. *I've got to get out of here.* But where to go?

Go home. Of course. Rim-Sin's home. Where else would he go?

People still swirled around him, touching him and bowing.

Peter caught sight of Kaida, watching from about twenty feet away. She took a hesitant step toward him and then stopped.

He motioned to her, and she came forward. He grabbed her hand and squeezed it, felt her return the pressure.

"I must leave," he called to the crowd. "The goddess calls for my presence alone."

The crowd parted at these words, and Peter grabbed his sandals and walked through the people, pulling Kaida with him.

When they had left the people behind, Kaida took her hand from Peter's but still walked beside him. Peter let out a sigh that felt like he'd been holding his breath for the past hour.

"That was amazing, Rim-Sin," Kaida said.

Peter said nothing. It had occurred to him that he did not know how to find Rim-Sin's house. The night he arrived here, he had run from the house in a panic. There was no way he would ever find his way back.

"I am exhausted, however," Peter said. "Perhaps we should go to Cosam's house to rest."

Kaida looked sideways at him.

"And I wish to thank him for his help."

Kaida said nothing.

"I am not sure I remember the way, however. You lead."

They walked in silence through the city, twisting through streets and alleys lined with two- and three-story houses and their gardens. Was she leading him in circles? Hadn't they been past that shop before? He studied her reaction at the next crossroad. She hesitated, as if unsure which way to go. Didn't she know the route to her brother's home? She seemed to choose a street, and in a few minutes they arrived at the doorway of the home that had been his only refuge since he stumbled into this city.

Rebekah met them in the courtyard inside the home. She held baby Addi in her arms. "Kaida! Rim-Sin!"

Kaida smiled. "Rim-Sin has been released, Rebekah."

The sisters-in-law embraced. Rebekah eyed Peter. "I cannot

say I care much about Rim-Sin, but I am so relieved to have you back, Kaida!"

"I came to thank Cosam," Peter said.

Rebekah shifted the baby to her other shoulder. "He has gone to work."

Of course. The three stood in silence for a moment. It became clear that Rebekah didn't intend to extend an invitation for him to stay.

He bowed his head to her quickly. "I will return to my own home, then. I do thank you for your help and ask that you pass my thanks to Cosam."

Rebekah nodded.

Peter looked at Kaida. Rim-Sin would take her with him. And Peter wanted to as well. "Shall we go?"

She bit her lip but followed him back to the street.

Outside, Peter subtly shifted positions to allow Kaida to take the lead again.

She seemed preoccupied and only after several minutes of walking did she speak. "Rim-Sin, do you really believe that you have been given direct access to the gods?"

"It is the power of all the universe, Kaida. All of it is available for each of us, if we will only open ourselves up to it, connect with it."

Kaida slowed and looked at him. "But there was a moment when you were climbing, when I felt—something."

Peter watched her.

"I felt a presence. I almost believed that the prayer you had uttered to Ishtar was working."

Peter debated only a moment. "I felt it, too, Kaida." He watched her expression turn from curiosity to fear as he spoke. "There is power out there. And I think it has been given to me."

They reached Rim-Sin's house through another winding route. Kaida explained that she was so new to the city it sometimes confused her. All the streets looked so similar. Peter had to agree.

Kaida had been silent since he had spoken of power. They entered the house together. Peter's only thought was of the rest he desperately needed. He would make a plan to follow through on Daniel's instructions for getting home after he had recovered from the events of the morning.

The house was cooler than the street. He let his eyes adjust to the dim light and take in the surroundings. The doorkeeper's lodge. But no doorkeeper. He walked through into the central courtyard. His home was larger and more elaborately furnished than Cosam's. But of course it would be. He was a palace diviner, and Cosam was only a captive goldsmith.

No, you're Peter Thornton, he reminded himself. If he stayed in this city much longer, he might lose his mind.

Kaida disappeared from behind him, going to her own quarters, he assumed, and Peter wandered farther into the house. Small flower gardens flanked his courtyard, and a few palm trees provided spotty shade. He crossed through into the kitchen and found a slave cutting green stalks. He asked about the other slave, the one he had seen the night he arrived in Babylon, and was told that Elam was working in another room.

He found Elam hunched over a wooden table working on something. Peter could see a neat pile of wood shavings on the table beside him. He approached from the back and watched the slave work for a few moments. He was carving a block of soft wood. The top of the block had already begun to take the form of a muscular horse. The work was intricate and skilled.

"You have talent," Peter said.

Elam jumped. He dropped the carving on the table, stood,

and faced Peter. "My lord, I did not know when you would return. I—I was only . . . "

Peter held up a hand to stop his defense. "Your work is beautiful."

The slave looked at his feet. "Thank you, my lord."

Peter picked up the half-carved horse, ran his fingers over the flowing mane. "What will you do with it?"

Elam still looked at the floor. He answered slowly. "I would send it back to my beloved homeland if I could. But that is impossible."

"Your homeland? You are from Israel, correct?"

Elam looked up. "Yes, my lord. A land I will never see again."

Peter set the horse back on the table. "Was it truly so much better than Babylon, Elam?"

The slave studied him, and when he spoke, his voice was soft. "It was home."

Peter swallowed the sudden lump in his throat. Home. Yes, he understood. He pointed to the horse. "But surely you could sell such a fine piece."

Elam picked it up and held it close to his chest. "It would have been a gift for . . . a young boy I know. But as that can never be, I will keep it for him myself." His voice was still low, and Peter watched his eyes cloud with sorrow.

"A little boy?"

Elam looked away. "My son. He is still in Israel with my wife. I have not seen them for eight years. And I know I never shall again."

Peter exhaled. He could think of nothing to say.

Elam wiped at his eyes with the back of his hand. "Will you excuse me, my lord?"

Peter nodded. The man bowed briefly and fled the room.

In spite of his fatigue, Peter searched for Kaida. Five minutes later he had been through every room in the house and had his gut feeling confirmed.

Kaida was gone.

Cosam made his way toward the great temple of Esagila and entered one of the offices within the precincts of the temple. He still had not grown accustomed to the pagan nature of his work. He worried that the Lord would be displeased. Should he refuse and be sentenced to death?

The temple authority on duty issued him his quantity of gold and gave him instructions for the day. "You are to make rings and bangles for the adornment of a new statue of Marduk," he told Cosam. Along with the gold, the authority gave him a strip of silver, payment in advance for his work. It was a much smaller sum than usual. The tablets were drawn up, specifying the weights of gold and silver and the work to be done. Cosam took them and went his way.

He stopped on the way to the goldsmith's bazaar at the house of a merchant to buy a *gur* sack of barley. He snipped off and weighed out a piece from his strip of silver, and the merchant kicked the sack over to him. He hefted it onto his back and turned toward the bazaar. He was sweating by the time he reached the furnace.

The goldsmith's bazaar was longer than Cosam's house and two more besides, and it was walled to prevent travelers from wandering through. No roof covered the bazaar, as the heat from the small stone furnaces scattered throughout the sandy yard would have been too great for those that toiled over them. Heat rose from the entire enclosure in waves that smelled of the dung cakes used to fuel the fires.

One of Cosam's fellow goldsmiths used a small bellows to blow life into the furnace they would use this morning to turn the silver to liquid.

"Good morning, Cosam," Jacob said. "Any word on your sister?"

Cosam shook his head. "She is still being held with the diviner. I am afraid she will only be saved if Rim-Sin is able to clear himself of accusation." He slapped a palm against the side of the furnace. "Why does God allow this? Is it not enough that we are captives in this terrible place?"

Jacob patted his shoulder. "From what Jeremiah's letters have said, we will soon be thanking Him for the rich life we lead here, compared to what our brothers in the Land will suffer."

Cosam nodded, but pointed to the metal that heated in the furnace. "But do we compromise, Jacob? To be spared?"

Jacob shook his head. "We must do what the Lord gives us to do."

Cosam smiled. Jacob was a good man. He kept the Law as closely as he could, leading his wife and daughter in the way of the Lord. Cosam was glad to have a friend who shared his devotion to the Law.

He placed the gold he had received earlier in a terra-cotta crucible and nudged the crucible into the hottest part of the furnace. Jacob put the blowpipe to his mouth and soon had the charcoal around the crucible blazing. Cosam lifted the appropriate molds from the terra-cotta box in which he kept his tools. He set them in a bowl of sand before putting them and the bowl into the heat, so that the molten metal would not crack the molds. When the gold in the crucible had melted, Cosam took tongs and lifted out the crucible, pouring its molten contents into the molds.

While the molds cooled, Cosam and Jacob talked more. "Zedekiah and Ahab are still prophesying that the Lord will break the yoke of Nebuchadnezzar soon," Cosam said.

Jacob grunted. "They do not want to admit that we are here because of our sin, and so it is easier to say we will soon be delivered."

"I encourage our people to turn from idolatry and repent before God whenever I have an opportunity."

"I know. But you should be careful, Cosam. In one breath you tell the people to bend their necks under the rule of Nebuchadnezzar, and in the next you condemn his gods. The king may grow angry. Life is not valued here in Babylon. We are all subject to the whims of the king. His anger could be your destruction."

"I will not keep silent out of fear, Jacob."

"No, but perhaps you should consider what would happen to your wife and children if you were executed by the king."

Cosam had no answer for that.

When the ornaments were cooled enough to be taken from the molds, they began the intricate work of the day, using files and chisels with gold and silver wire. Cosam applied solder and heat with the blowpipe, converting the cast gold into embossed and engraved ornamentation and filigree work.

"The king is not the only one you should fear, Cosam," Jacob said. "You aggravate our people by nagging them to leave their idol worship."

"I must tell the truth, Jacob. Only through the Law can we be saved, and the Law says that we must have no other gods besides the God of Israel."

"You do not have to convince me, brother," Jacob said as they worked. "But some of the others… My friend, I hear what is said about you among the elders. Some do not appreciate a younger man's chastisement."

Cosam looked up from his work. "As I said, I will not keep silent out of fear."

"Be careful, that is all I am saying," Jacob warned.

When he had finished enough work for the morning, Cosam snipped another small piece from his strip of silver. The tiny piece melted into a small puddle and Cosam poured the molten liquid into a small mold.

"What is that you are making, Cosam?" Jacob asked.

"It will be a necklace when it is finished. For Rebekah." Cosam took some beads from his terra-cotta chest. He had fashioned them with intricate detailing despite his meaty hands. The tiny beads were perfectly formed and engraved.

Cosam shook his head, a small smile playing on his lips. "But at this rate it may take me until the end of the seventy years of captivity!"

Peter slept in Rim-Sin's house through the remainder of the day and into the night. He awakened in the darkness and thought of Kaida. She had returned to Cosam's house, he was sure. Their fragile connection while in the palace had been broken by his claim to have accessed some kind of power. He regretted his honesty now. He knew he could go and force Kaida to return to this house with him, but what would be the point? He tossed on the reed bed through the rest of the night and was grateful when the sun rose. After finding food in the kitchen and wondering why there were no slaves or servants in the house, Peter sat again under the palm tree in his courtyard.

Daniel's words came back to him. "You must finish the task of the man you killed. Only then will you be able to go home."

Did he believe it? Daniel had been convincing in his knowledge. Peter could see that the man had also connected with whatever power was available in the universe. He'd called him *Peter,* for crying out loud. If Daniel insisted on calling the power "Yahweh," it made no difference. And Peter would have to accept that this task given to him, whatever it was, was the only way to get home. He had lost days already, and the New Year Festival grew closer, now only a little more than three weeks away. He needed answers, beginning with the identity of the dead Hebrew, whose job he was supposed to do if he ever wanted to claim his new title as university president.

It was time to start asking questions.

Outside, a feeling of exhilaration hit him. He was alone in the ancient city of Babylon, immersed in the most intense research project of his life! It was a scholar's dream come true. What mysteries did this city hold? What could she teach him today? His main objective was to find out who the dead man was. What was he doing in Rim's home? Who killed him? Why?

The Jewish district of the Old City lay to the east of Etemenanki. He took careful note of his position this time, wanting to be sure he could find Rim's house again. He then wandered down the street, wanting to get a feel for the city before he branched out and began asking questions. Always the great tower loomed over all.

During his previous forays into the city he had been trying to remain unseen, guarded by soldiers, or too tired and ill to care. But now he had the time to appreciate the city. The architecture of this place amazed him. The saw-toothed pattern of the walls of many houses was obviously designed to throw stripes of shade onto the walls, keeping the heat down. Ventilation grids kept sand to a minimum while allowing air to move through. Every room of every house opened to a central courtyard, providing air circulation but retaining privacy. Canals chased each other along streets and behind houses in every direction, feeding the flourishing gardens and mocking the fact that this city stood in the center of a desert.

The Processional Way beckoned him. His special interest in archeology had led him to discover the aerial photographs of Robert Koldewey's work in the ruins of Babylon during the early 1900s. Only fragments of the Processional Way remained when Koldewey began excavation, though huge portions of the Ishtar Gate had been uncovered by the archeologist. But to see it in person and in its prime!

He found the road easily. He was beginning to understand the city's layout. The streets ran north and south, roughly parallel to the river, with small streets crossing them at right angles, terminating in the eight great bronze gates at the city wall.

The Processional Way. He moved out to the center of the road in awe. The center of the broad avenue was paved with huge flags of limestone. On either side were slabs of red breccia veined with white. Peter remembered that the edge of each great paving stone was inscribed with Nebuchadnezzar's dedication to the gods. Once laid, only the gods could see it.

On both sides of the wide road, walls climbed over thirty feet above him. From top to bottom the walls were glazed in a vivid blue. Sixty roaring lions of molded brick, symbols of Ishtar, ornamented each side, white and yellow with red manes. It was breathtaking, even to Peter's jaded eyes.

The Processional Way led through the Ishtar Gate, the main gate of Babylon. The gate connected the inner and outer fortification walls. It was also glazed in blue, with some 150 yellow and white bulls and dragons, symbols of Adad and Marduk. An archway towered in the center of the gate. Molded brick rosettes and intricate patterns of multicolored bricks bordered the arch and ran along the base of the gate.

Peter laid his hand on the gate and took a deep breath. What an amazing city. What *could* it be like if the people were not trapped by their gods into denying their own higher place in the cosmos?

The words of his success seminar tapes returned to him.

Realize the power that exists within you to turn the inferior qualities of shame, fear, and ignorance into love and fulfillment.

He turned back after a few minutes. With his back to the gate, the wall on his right was actually the eastern wall of the palace. He studied it without fear this time. Above the wall Peter could see a massive tiered garden, with palm trees jutting into the sky. The Hanging Gardens of Babylon. One of the Seven Wonders of the Ancient World. Though built into the upper part of the palace, he hadn't seen them up close. Definitely on the "must-see" list.

It was all incredible, yet he didn't feel the rush of adrenaline he would have expected to feel. He'd always been searching for something indefinable and just out of reach. Was this it? He had tasted it briefly in the way the sunlight edged a storm cloud or a distant mountain ridge traced a misty line across a sunset. Sometimes it felt like a longing to travel to that elusive place, and so he climbed. He climbed all the mountains he was able to, hoping to reach a distant ridge and discover that unnamed desire. He had not yet found it. At the top of every mountain he climbed he waited for that moment of fulfillment. Instead, it felt like every other moment of his life—filled with only thoughts of what the next moment would be like. And the thing he sought seemed to have fled from him.

Since high school he had studied one religion after another, waiting to find one that addressed his search. It wasn't until he found that the desire was not to travel to another place but to travel within himself that he began to think he had found answers. Perhaps everything he ever wanted had been inside him all along.

Finding the voids in your own heart and filling them with being is the only way to have perfect love.

He had not seen nearly enough, but it was time to move on. He was here for answers, after all. Back in the Jewish district Peter approached a woman dumping garbage into the street. He tried to project a warm smile and ignore the foul smell.

She acknowledged him, but only with a nod of her head.

"How are you this morning?" he said. How did one make small talk in ancient Babylon?

She gaped at him.

Apparently not like that. *Get to the point.* "Did you hear about the man who was killed several nights ago?"

She looked up now, the garbage pot on her hip. "Do you mean the man you killed?"

Peter swallowed hard. Ah. Of course she recognized him. Still, he had to take a chance. "Who was he?"

A wild dog ran to her feet, scavenging for his morning meal. Fear was in her eyes as she turned and went into her house without replying.

This was not going to work. He needed someone to convince these people to give him answers.

Kaida. Would she help him willingly?

How would he get back to Cosam's house? Could he be lost again? If he ever got home, he should write a book, *Lost in Babylon.* He was getting very good at it. Even with Etemenanki always overshadowing, it was difficult to get his bearings. Perhaps because all the houses were so similar and loomed so close to the street.

The houses thinned until they ended at the edge of a tan building, twice as high as any of the houses in the area, a grassy courtyard in front of it. The center of the building stood even higher, with a dome sculpted into the bricks. The walls of the building were painted in alternating yellow and blue squares, from the ground level to higher than a man. Two statues stood guard at the entrance to the landscaped courtyard, where gravel paths crisscrossed the grass at right angles.

The large courtyard was filled with people, mostly men. Peter neared the edge, keeping his head down and hoping he would not be recognized. Through gaps in the crowd, he could see into the building. Consecutive doorways led from the outer chamber into a back room. Centered along the back wall was a gold statue of a goddess. The Temple of Ishtar.

Peter's heart beat faster. One more incredible piece of history that he was witnessing firsthand. Rim-Sin's patron was the fertility goddess, known throughout all ancient cultures by many names. She had been Asherah before this time. She would go on to be known as Aphrodite and Venus in Greece and Rome. Goddess of love. She was fed and clothed as though she were a living being, and she even had her own estate.

What was happening in her courtyard? Peter searched the crowd for an answer. He had been wrong in assuming the crowd was made up of men. Now he could see that women sat all around the courtyard with wreaths of string around their heads. Running through the crowd of women were passages marked off in all directions. The men walked along these passages, each seeming to choose a woman.

Peter was suddenly shoved from behind, forced to enter the courtyard. He tried to fall back, but others behind him kept pushing forward. As he walked through the rows of women, he could see that they were of many different classes.

A weasel of a man before him threw money into the lap of one woman. "I call you by Ishtar," he said.

The woman's face was a mask of repulsion. She stood, holding the money as though it were poison and followed the little man to the side of the shrine. Peter watched them until he realized what they were doing, and then looked away in embarrassment.

He remembered now. The Greek historian Herodotus had recorded temple prostitution in detail. Every woman was required to give herself to a stranger once in the shrine of Ishtar. She could refuse no one. As he watched, he noticed that the beautiful women were able to fulfill their duty without delay. The ugly ones looked as if they'd been waiting a long time. He looked around him at the women still sitting on the ground and pitied them. How terrible for them.

But then again…

All expressions of love should be honored, even if they are distorted.

Maybe he would choose that good-looking woman over against the pillar. When in Babylon . . . , and all that.

Peter looked up to see a man with a shaven head staring at him from the temple doorway. Qurdi-Marduk-lamur. His throat tightened. He considered running, but he held his ground.

Qurdi-Marduk-lamur watched the courtyard from inside the antechamber of Ishtar's temple. The morning light was behind the temple, throwing the courtyard into shade, making it a cool respite from the heat. He loved the days of the fertility ceremonies. All those women giving themselves to the goddess. The pleasure-seeking men, celebrating their passions. Qurdi felt the goddess increase in power each time she was honored in this way. It almost made him forget Rim-Sin's victory at the tower this morning.

He would never approach one of these women himself. He had no interest in them. But he would encourage them all, the wealthy and the poor citizens along with the regular temple prostitutes who served any man who desired to honor the goddess on other days of the year as well.

Qurdi watched as the men chose women from the crowd and pulled them to various spots around the shrine. Sometimes he tried to predict which woman a man would choose. His eyes fell on one man who seemed more interested in the crowd than in the women. Qurdi clutched the doorframe of the temple. It was Rim-Sin! He approached the diviner, hatred seething through every part of him.

Rim-Sin glanced around, as though considering running, but then faced Qurdi, resolve in his eyes.

"Rim-Sin." Qurdi acknowledged him with an exaggerated bow.

"Qurdi."

"Do you come to gloat?"

"I came…I came to warn you. The goddess has shown her favor. You would be wise to respect it."

Qurdi clenched a fist at his side. "We will see, Rim-Sin. We will see."

Chapter 9

Ahab and Zedekiah stood before the people in the courtyard where they'd been holding their gatherings. Cosam listened in anger as they "prophesied" what the people wanted to hear.

"Be patient," Ahab said. "In only a short time the Lord God of Israel will bring this pagan people to their knees. We will see them humbled before us, and we will be restored to our land!"

Cosam tried to remain silent. But he could not. "The return from captivity has been promised by Jeremiah," he said, "but only when seventy years have been accomplished, and not before."

"Why should we believe this weeping prophet?" an elder said. "He gives us nothing but bad news."

"And it is what we deserve!" Cosam said.

Many eyes turned toward him in disgust. "Why should we deserve to be held captive in a foreign land?" a man beside him asked.

Cosam stood, taking in the crowd with his eyes. Their meetings in the sun-baked courtyard had become customary. But it seemed to him that his people were still no closer to humbling themselves under God's hand.

"How can you ask why? Your temples and altars to Baal litter our country. You erect sacred stones, put up Asherah poles, burn incense to other gods. Even here you make idols and worship the stars. Has Israel's captivity not been enough?

When will you heed the Lord and return to His Law?"

"We worship the Lord!" someone said.

"Yes," Cosam said, "beside altars built to Baal! How long did you expect Him to be patient?"

One of the elders called to him. "You condemn us, Cosam? When you make idols for pagan worship yourself?"

Cosam turned and faced his accuser. "I am forced to fashion them with my hands," he called back, lifting his head. "But I will never chase after them with my heart!"

An uneasy silence fell on the crowd. Cosam turned his back in disgust and headed for home.

Peter left the Temple of Ishtar, both relieved that he had avoided physical danger from Qurdi and even more resolved to find a way out of this place. He was getting sick of the intrigue. He would find Kaida, and she would help him get answers. He managed to find his way to Cosam's home this time. He entered the courtyard and found the family all at home. Kaida was not with them.

Cosam rose. "Rim-Sin!"

Peter waved a hand. "Please, sit." He nodded to Rebekah. "I've come for Kaida." Peter realized too late how his words sounded. Cosam's face hardened. Peter tried to undo it. "I mean, I need her help. I am trying to learn more about the Jewish man that—was killed."

Cosam lowered himself to his seat beside Rebekah. "It is no secret any longer who he was, Rim."

What's this? Peter sat beside Cosam and leaned forward. "Tell me."

Cosam appeared confused, but shrugged. "His name was Reuben. He lived across the bridge, in the New City. He had been ordered by the king to catalogue the articles stolen from the temple in Jerusalem and brought here by the Babylonian army."

Peter sat back. Was that all? Daniel had said he was to finish the dead man's task. But Reuben was only a pencil pusher for the king. Was he supposed to finish Reuben's paperwork? There had to be more. A memory surfaced. Something the red-haired woman in the palace had said when he had been there last, something about Jewish spoils of war. He needed to find that woman again. But to get close to a royal wife? He was still going to need some help.

Peter found Kaida in the kitchen, pounding some sort of legume with a stone mortar and pestle. Seeing her again seemed to knock the wind out of him. He leaned against the doorframe to catch his breath. Kaida didn't appear to notice him. He watched her hands for a moment, watched how she breathed heavily with the effort.

"Did you come to take me back?" she asked, not lifting her eyes from her work.

"No. I need your help."

"I am busy."

Peter swallowed. What was the use of having a slave if she never did what he told her to do? He couldn't figure her out. When he had first arrived here, she had been so terrified of him. But now there was no fear. She knew Rim-Sin perhaps better than anyone else. Did she suspect that her master was...gone? That a gawky university professor who didn't know the first thing about owning a slave had taken his place?

He tried a different approach. "Please, Kaida. Please help me."

She kept grinding, but looked at him. "What do I have to do?"

"I need to go back to the palace for some information, and I need you to help me get it."

She hesitated, then shrugged. "Fine."

A damp wave of hair fell in front of her dark eyes, and Peter had the sudden urge to step closer and smooth it back. He straightened his back instead. "Good. We will go tomorrow."

She returned to her mortar and pestle. "Yes, *master*."

Qurdi-Marduk-lamur paused at the entrance of the throne room to appreciate his surroundings. It had taken many years to achieve his status in this room. Years of scraping as a *mushkenum*, a citizen of second-class nature, until he had been recognized for his wisdom and granted the full rights of *awilum*. Even still, there were those among the palace advisors who only grudgingly paid him the respect he had earned.

He was far from giving up on his quest to be chief of magicians. He had failed to rid himself of Rim-Sin for now, but there would be another opportunity, he was certain. In the meantime he would return to concentrating on the main obstacle between himself and the position he coveted.

Yes, he belonged here in this beautiful room. As he entered, he skimmed the glazed brick frieze on the walls with his hand. The yellow, white, and red lions marched across the blue walls in perfect symmetry. The room was ornate, ostentatious even, but he loved every part of it.

Nabu-kudurri-usur sat on his throne, holding morning court. The morning banquet would soon begin, but the king still attended to small matters of state. Anything truly important would be postponed until court convened after the meal.

Qurdi glided up to the throne and nodded to Amyitis. The king often allowed his favorite wife to remain in the presence of officials when all the other harem women had been chased to their quarters by their overseeing eunuch. Amyitis was a Mede, the product of an arranged marriage to seal a treaty between Nabu-kudurri-usur's father and her grandfather, the Median king. In spite of the prearrangement, the king was devoted to her.

It was no secret that the rest of the royal wives hated her for the silky black hair she flaunted, the dazzling smile she shone on anyone she wanted to win over, and the graceful height that made her a perfect match for the king.

Now she draped herself over the arm of the throne and leaned against him. Her purple and gold linen dress fit her figure as though she were sculpted of amethyst and gold, and rubies and emeralds glittered from her ears and around her neck, wrists, and ankles.

Qurdi waited with head lowered while the king finished speaking with an ambassador from Carchemish.

"O King, live forever," Qurdi said when the ambassador was through. "I must speak with you." He raised his eyes, but the king was looking over him. Qurdi turned. Belteshazzar had entered the throne room.

"Approach," the king waved to Belteshazzar over Qurdi's head. Qurdi stepped away, his fists clenched at his sides.

"Is the king feeling better this morning?" Belteshazzar asked.

"Yes," the king said. "The headache has left me. What was the potion you gave me? Was there an incantation with it?"

The young Belteshazzar laughed. "No incantation, O King. Only a remedy my mother in Judah prepared for me when my head ached."

The king laughed with him and glanced at Qurdi. "All the wisest men of Babylon at my disposal, and I am indebted to a Jewish mother in Israel!"

"O King, live forever—" Qurdi started.

The king waved him away. "Not now, Qurdi. I am not in the mood to hear from you."

Qurdi nodded and backed away, his dark eyes trained on Belteshazzar.

Amyitis whispered something in the king's ear. He smiled at her and pulled her mouth down to his. After an extended kiss, he turned again to Belteshazzar, grinning. "Tell me, young Jew, can you divine my thoughts now?"

Belteshazzar smiled. "It would not take a wise man to determine that, O King."

The king threw back his head and laughed. "You are right again, my young chief. But it is time for the meal."

Qurdi took a hesitant step toward the king.

"Qurdi," the king acknowledged. "Go to the feast hall and make certain that all is ready for the morning meal."

The priest lowered his head in respect and hurried back out of the throne room. He clutched the edge of his black robe between stiff fingers. "I'll be reduced to a *wardum* if that Jew has his way."

He was one of the first to arrive in the feast hall. He took a chance and stood beside a seat near the king's chair. He was determined to speak with the king before the day was over. It must be today. Everything had been arranged for tomorrow, but it would all be wasted if Qurdi could not tell the king tonight what the omens had predicted.

Of course Qurdi had arranged the haruspicy to give him the desired message. Only this once. The gods would not fault him. Sometimes they spoke to him. Whispered to him in the cool of the night, pounded their messages into him during the heat of the day. He was to be chief of magicians. Belteshazzar must be destroyed. And then when he was chief, he would turn on all the Jews who infested their city. They must all be destroyed, each one. He would kill them all himself, he thought. He would wander through the city, picking them out, killing each one of them. The gods had made it clear. He knew what Belteshazzar's plan was. The Israelite wanted to get rid of all the other diviners. Ever since the scheming boy had interpreted the king's dream, he had been plotting against the palace advisors. *And I am probably his first target.*

The king entered the hall, followed by Amyitis and Belteshazzar. He took his seat at the table, and Qurdi sat beside him. Qurdi noted with satisfaction that Belteshazzar was seated much farther down the table.

The king hosted over fifty people at the morning meal, including a group of visiting dignitaries.

The first course was brought out by the palace slaves, mainly food returned from the sanctuary. Trays piled with peas, beans, cucumbers, and gherkins were placed between the guests. Their cups were filled with filtered beer. Between bites, Qurdi tried to gain the king's attention. Nabu-kudurri-usur was interested only in Amyitis this morning.

When the second course of beef and partridge had been served, the king clapped for entertainment, ignoring Qurdi's attempts.

Qurdi barely tasted his partridge. It must be tonight. It must be.

Slave girls streamed in from the corridors, their dresses jingling with tiny bells. They jumped into a frenzied dance, accompanied by tambourines and pipe flutes.

Over the commotion, Qurdi tried again. "O King, live forever! May I speak with you?"

"What is it, Qurdi?" the king said, leaning past Amyitis to see him.

"I must have a private word with you this evening concerning the omens."

"Oh?"

The king looked concerned, and Qurdi suppressed a smile. "I have received a disturbing message, O King."

Nabu-kudurri-usur nodded. "We shall speak later."

Qurdi relished the third course of pomegranates and pastry as though he were a king himself.

Akkad smiled at his ingenuity as the royal wives filed out of the palace past him, followed by the representative of the harem. The man in charge of the palace women was by necessity a eunuch, as were others placed in positions of prominence, though the palace diviners had escaped this fate, thankfully. Akkad observed the representative's watchful eye and knew that he and Abigail would not be completely on their own. But if Akkad could manage to separate her from the others, perhaps he would have a few minutes alone with her.

Learning that she was Nabu-kudurri-usur's newest wife, brought from Israel only a few weeks ago, had done nothing to extinguish the flame he felt every time he looked at her. Instead, he had used the opportunity of the king's attention over the new amulet to suggest a ritual river wash for the women. To honor the gods properly, it would need to have the oversight of a diviner. Akkad had solemnly volunteered.

The women had responded with an enthusiastic plan of their own, seeking to make their rare excursion out of the palace into a holiday.

Akkad sought Abigail's eyes as she passed him in the entrance to the palace, but she would not give him the pleasure. He thought he detected anger in her expression. Or was it fear?

The sun beat down on them as the representative of the harem pushed his way to the front of the crowd. The eunuch seemed to believe the women could not find the river without his direction. It was another ruthlessly hot day. Akkad dropped to the back of the group and was pleased when Abigail did the same moments later. She kept several paces in front of him.

"Why did you not tell me who you were?" he whispered to her back.

"What difference would it have made?" she responded, throwing the answer over her shoulder.

She was right. Slave or royal wife, she was as unattainable as the stars.

Several women had glanced behind them at the whispered voices. Akkad thought it best to keep silent for now. When they reached the chosen place, the women fanned out in the shade on the banks of the Euphrates, lying on blankets spread for them by slaves.

Akkad kept a close eye on the eunuch and dropped to the ground a few *ammatu* from Abigail, who had found a shady patch of grass away from the other women. If everyone would stay where they were for the afternoon hours of rest, his plan would be a success.

Abigail lay on her side, her back to the rest of the group. Akkad stared at the river, but felt her eyes on him.

"You should not have done this," she said.

"I know."

"Why did you?" Her voice was soft.

He allowed himself to look at her, and for a moment wished for an amulet of his own.

The amulet! Why had he not thought of the power he had given it since finding out who Abigail was? A knife of jealousy stabbed at his heart. His very own amulet would cause the king to have great success with his wives. With *all* his wives.

"I had to see you again," he said.

Her fingers drifted through the hardy grass beside her blanket.

Akkad returned his gaze to the river. "Tell me about yourself," he said.

She was silent for a moment. "I am here because of God's judgment."

It was an odd start, but once she had begun, the story of her life flowed from her like warm olive oil spilling from a jar.

Peter and Kaida left for the palace at the hottest part of the day, and he was instantly sorry when they stepped out of the house. But Cosam had said that Reuben was cataloguing the temple articles, and the palace was the one place that held answers—in the form of one red-haired royal wife. Peter glanced at Kaida. "Thank you for coming with me. I appreciate it."

She slowed and looked at him fully.

He stopped. "What?"

"Sometimes you surprise me, Rim-Sin."

Peter hoped that was a good thing.

They retraced their steps from their previous outing. As they passed a five-foot-wide alley between the windowless walls of two houses, Peter noticed a soft bleating coming from a narrow doorway about ten feet from the street where they stood. He peered into the shaded alley, which was silent and empty except for a pile of rags that had been dumped in the single doorway. "Did you hear that?"

She listened. "It is only a lamb."

Peter moved toward the pile of dirty rags. It moved, and he jumped back a little. "Kaida! Come here!" He knelt and pulled back a dirty rag to reveal a tiny face.

Kaida gasped. "A baby!"

The little thing gave another cry. The child was only hours old, perhaps minutes. What was it doing in the street? He was about to lift it when a pair of feet appeared in the doorway. Peter stood.

"Leave it," a man said.

"Is this your baby?" Peter asked.

"It belongs to the demons now," he said. "It is an evil omen. Deformed. It must be abandoned to the dogs while still in its water and blood."

You have got to be kidding! He looked again at the infant's face. Trusting blue eyes flickered open for a moment. Peter looked at

Kaida. Her eyes were wide, a look of horror on her face. "What is wrong with the child?" he asked.

The man pushed the rags aside with his foot, as if unwilling to even touch the baby. "Look at its leg. See how it turns inward. It is cursed."

The leg was indeed turned inward. Perhaps modern medicine could correct it with a brace. Without it, the child would certainly walk with a limp. But abandoned to the dogs? It was unthinkable!

"I see," Peter nodded. "The child is cursed."

"I have already sent for a priest to write out the preventative ritual," the man said.

"Good." Peter raised a hand in good-bye and wrapped his hand around Kaida's upper arm, towing her along.

She pulled back. "We cannot—"

Peter silenced her with his eyes and a slight shake of his head. When they had walked a few paces, the man disappeared into his home.

Peter jogged back, scooped up the baby in its rags, and turned from the house. When they reached the end of the street, they heard the man call from the doorway again.

"Qurdi-Marduk-lamur!" the man said. "I thought the purification priest would come to write out the incantation. But the high priest himself! I am honored. Please come in. You can see the child is already gone."

There was a buzz of excitement when Cosam arrived with the others from the Old City Jewish District. For now, their grievances against him had quieted. A letter from the prophet Jeremiah had arrived. Hananiah and Azariah, who had also risen to governorship under Nebuchadnezzar, had arrived to hear the reading. Jeremiah had been unpopular in Israel, but here in

Babylon his words from the Lord were hungrily devoured, every letter an event to treasure.

The three governors stood near the front of the crowd. Cosam elbowed through his fellow Jews, hoping for a chance to meet the other two of these well-respected men. He approached the three, and Mishael extended his hand.

"Cosam. Have you met Hananiah and Azariah? Please, do not call them Shadur-Aku and Abed-Nabu—not here!"

Cosam gripped the arms of the two men. "You give us assurance that the Lord still blesses the faithful, even in this place."

Hananiah, who was as large a man as Cosam, slapped Cosam's upper arm. "Welcome to Babylon, my brother, where the God of Israel still works wonders."

Azariah grinned. "A God who places His people where they can rub pagan noses in their own folly!"

Mishael sighed. "Azariah, one day your rash words are going to lead to trouble."

Azariah shrugged, still smiling. "Let it come."

The grassy area filled up with Hebrews, and Cosam took his place with the others on the ground.

Mishael raised a hand for silence and began to read. "Jeremiah's letter, men of Israel. 'This is what the Lord Almighty, the God of Israel, says to all those I carried into exile from Jerusalem to Babylon: "Build houses and settle down; plant gardens and eat what they produce. Marry and have sons and daughters; find wives for your sons and give your daughters in marriage, so that they too may have sons and daughters. Increase in number there; do not decrease. Also, seek the peace and prosperity of the city to which I have carried you into exile. Pray to the Lord for it, because if it prospers, you too will prosper."'"

There was some grumbling at this last instruction. Were they really to pray for the prosperity of the city of Babylon?

Mishael continued. "There is more. 'This is what the Lord

Almighty, the God of Israel, says: "Do not let the prophets and diviners among you deceive you. Do not listen to the dreams you encourage them to have. They are prophesying lies to you in my name. I have not sent them," declares the Lord.'"

Many heads turned toward Zedekiah and Ahab.

"'This is what the Lord says: "When seventy years are completed for Babylon, I will come to you and fulfill my gracious promise to bring you back to this place. For I know the plans I have for you," declares the Lord, "plans to prosper you and not to harm you, plans to give you hope and a future. Then you will call upon me and come and pray to me, and I will listen to you. You will seek me and find me when you seek me with all your heart. I will be found by you," declares the Lord, "and will bring you back from captivity. I will gather you from all the nations and places where I have banished you," declares the Lord, "and will bring you back to the place from which I carried you into exile."'"

At that point Zedekiah and Ahab left the assembly, a clear protest against Jeremiah's authority.

The letter continued, detailing the plague that would befall those Israelites still in the land of Israel. Cosam listened with sadness at the coming plight of his brothers.

Mishael continued, but slowed as he reached a portion he was apparently loath to read.

"'Therefore, hear the word of the Lord, all you exiles whom I have sent away from Jerusalem to Babylon. This is what the Lord Almighty, the God of Israel, says about Ahab son of Kolaiah and Zedekiah son of Maaseiah, who are prophesying lies to you in my name: "I will hand them over to Nebuchadnezzar king of Babylon, and he will put them to death before your very eyes. Because of them, all the exiles from Judah who are in Babylon will use this curse: 'The Lord treat you like Zedekiah and Ahab, whom the king of Babylon burned in the fire.'"'"

Not a person moved among the assembly. Mishael lowered his eyes in sorrow.

"Come." Peter pulled up the lower part of his outer cloak and swaddled the baby. They jogged to the next street, Peter hoping that Qurdi hadn't seen him or the baby.

Maybe he should change the name of his book, Peter thought as he trotted down the street. *Running in Babylon.*

"What are we going to do with this baby?" he said.

"Cosam and Rebekah will know what to do."

They were back in Cosam's house within minutes. The house was empty.

They both had the same thought: they moved through the courtyard and into the storeroom. Peter shoved aside his pottery wheel, laid the bundle down on the stone ledge as though it contained an ancient treasure, and knelt beside it. Kaida left for a moment and came back with an oil lamp as Peter unwrapped the rags.

"Get some water, Kaida." He looked up at her. "Please."

She rushed back a moment later with a basin of water and clean cloths. They both laughed as the baby bellowed out an angry cry when the cool water dripped onto his skin.

When Kaida had formed a makeshift diaper from the clean rags, Peter carefully tugged on the baby's leg. "He'll never walk correctly."

"No," she said, "but he will live." She smiled at Peter. A brief smile, but he saw it.

"What will we do with him?" Peter asked.

"Rebekah and Cosam will keep him. I know they will. Rebekah can nurse him, along with Addi. They would never abandon a child."

"But it will be impossible to protect a child like him in this city."

Kaida cradled the infant in her arms as if it were the most natural thing in the world and sat on the stone ledge. "They will do their best."

Peter trudged over to his stool beside the pottery wheel. He watched Kaida lean over the baby, stroking his head. For a moment, his heart pounded an irregular rhythm.

Kaida looked up. "We didn't reach the palace."

Peter shrugged as if the New Year Festival did not exist. "Perhaps tomorrow." He changed the subject. "I am so angry with that father I could strangle him."

Kaida observed him for a long moment.

"What?" he said.

"Why are you angry at the baby's father?"

"How can you ask that?"

"I am as outraged by it as you are, Rim. But I don't understand why *you* are outraged."

"Who wouldn't be?"

"That father, for one." She rocked the baby as he fussed a bit. "And most of this city. They don't see anything wrong with killing a deformed baby. It's common practice."

"It should be against the law."

"Why?"

Her questions grew annoying. "Because it's wrong! Why do you continue to challenge me about this if you agree?"

Kaida smiled again, that superior smile that said she had cornered him. "Once again, your reasoning is faulty, Rim. Haven't you told me there is no absolute, no certain truth? Although we never established how you can be certain of that. Now you are so certain that abandoning a baby in the street to the dogs is wrong. I ask you, on whose authority do you claim it is wrong? What basis is there for your morality?"

Peter spun the empty pottery wheel with the foot pedal and traced the outlines of it with his finger. How could he explain to her his moral outrage at this crime? How could he explain it to himself?

There is only one solution to evil. Don't struggle against it. Realize that it does not exist.

All his adult life he had asserted that since there was no absolute, evil did not exist. Morality and values arose from society, and laws could be based only on what society accepted as virtuous. Here he was in a different society, one that did not consider it immoral to leave a baby in the street or repugnant to force yourself on a woman. Theoretically, that should be enough for him. It should be proof of what he'd always argued for. The culture had not deemed it to be wrong; therefore, it was not wrong. Why couldn't he leave it at that?

Kaida seemed to sense his thoughts. "Perhaps we should give the baby back to the dogs on the street, since there is no reason to save him."

He swore at her under his breath. She didn't grasp his cross-cultural dilemma, but she knew she had him trapped. They both knew that justifying infanticide was inconceivable in any society. He spun the wheel faster. If enlightening her was part of his reason for being here, he was failing royally.

The opposite impulses of good and evil within us are both part of the whole of divine consciousness. Because you contain both sides, they cancel each other out. You are free.

"So where are we then?" Kaida asked. "You say that everything is relative, and yet that particular statement is the only thing that cannot be relative. You say there is nothing on which to base morality, and yet you clearly recognize immorality. How do you explain that? For a wise man, you are very confused, Rim."

It was not said unkindly. In fact, he almost felt she pitied him. Was this girl a slave or a philosophy student? He didn't need her pity.

"You go too far, Kaida," he said, standing. "You forget to whom you speak."

Coward. He'd always hated people who ended a losing argument by asserting their superiority and running away. Her cold eyes followed him as he left the storeroom.

In the evening Kaida took the baby into the courtyard to bed him down. Peter remained in Cosam's storeroom for hours, spinning pots. He didn't know if Qurdi had seen him with the baby or not. He had decided to stay here in case his protection was needed.

He worked at the wheel to distract himself, but he still fumed over Kaida's accusations of philosophical confusion. How could he make her understand? He taught his students that the ultimate reality manifests itself in both good and evil, and that once a person had reunited with oneness he would transcend good and evil. Passions were to be celebrated. Evil was only that which inhibited the actualization of a person's full potential. It had all made sense.

Until he'd held a discarded baby in his arms.

Our reactions of anger and fear whenever we encounter "evil" are really themselves the cause of evil. If we stop struggling against evil, it will cease to exist.

Images of the woman in the courtyard of the Temple of Ishtar flashed onto the pottery wheel as he spun. He recalled her disgusted expression as she got up to fulfill her duty to the goddess. And he remembered the man. One of the two celebrated his passion at the expense of the other. If the woman did not allow it, she would be inhibiting him. If he did not indulge himself, he would be inhibiting himself. The only way to avoid the evil of inhibition was for them both to willingly engage in temple prostitution. Yet the look on her face tortured Peter. It was not the face of a person actualizing her full potential. But if good and evil both originated from the ultimate reality, then there could be no distinction and no room for argument.

He was beginning to think there might be a flaw somewhere in his philosophy.

Kaida came into the storeroom with an unfinished weaving in her hands, apparently planning to stay awhile.

Peter snatched a cloth from his worktable and covered a small item he had been studying.

Kaida frowned. "What is that?"

Peter laid it aside, still covered. "Nothing."

"If it is nothing, why are you hiding it?"

"I'm not hiding it. It is nothing."

Kaida slid to the table, reaching out to the cloth and the shape under it.

Peter grabbed the item and stood.

"Come on," she said, taking a step toward him, "what is it?"

He backed away.

Kaida laughed softly. "You are making me so curious. Show me."

Peter held the cloth-covered item against his chest as Kaida stood only inches away. He looked over her head as she loosened his fingers, one at a time, from around it. Finally, he let the cloth fall into her hands.

"It is only a tiny vase!" She smiled. "Nothing mysterious at all." She studied the piece. "It is beautiful, Rim-Sin. It is so small, yet so detailed. Did you make it for someone?"

The lamplight reflected in her eyes as she looked up at him. He looked away. "I—I made it for you." He stepped away and sat at his table, throwing a lump of wet clay onto the wheel.

Kaida still stood behind him, silent. Finally she sat down, placing the vase beside her on a stone ledge as though it were a diamond.

Neither spoke for a while. The silence was awkward. It made Peter feel like he needed to say something entertaining. It reminded him of Sunday evenings as a child. For some reason—probably guilt, he assumed now—Mother always felt they should have one night each week where they all remained in the same room for an interminable amount of time, supposedly some sort of family bonding. In Peter's mind, the same evenings in his friends' houses were no doubt filled with board games and roasting marshmallows in front of the fireplace. But in his home they sat in uncomfortable silence. All these years later, Peter could still close his eyes and see in perfect detail the pattern of the unyielding upholstered couch. He had studied that pattern for many hours over the course of many Sunday evenings.

His sister Debra would always have something to say during those times. Her attempts at humor or entertainment were usually met with blank stares, as if Mother and Father could only communicate on some other, higher level, and Debra were speaking a foreign language. Why had it been that way? And why had Father always turned his head when Peter looked into his eyes?

Tonight, Kaida's presence made it difficult for Peter to concentrate on his pottery. In a few minutes he smashed the clay down once again when a small imperfection began to grow. He could feel her eyes on his hands.

"Can you show me how to do it?" she asked.

He nodded. "I suppose."

She stood beside the wheel. Peter indicated a bowl of water for her to dip her hands into, and then placed her hands on a large lump of clay. He worked the foot pedal to spin the wheel, keeping his hands on top of hers, applying just the right amount of pressure. Her skin was cool and pleasant.

"When it is ready," he said, "you put your fingers here." He pushed her fingers into the center, forming a small well in the lump of spinning clay.

They continued to work the clay together for some time, with Peter showing her how to draw it up by placing one hand inside and one hand on the outside of the piece. Before long, the vase was fully formed. Kaida washed her hands, stood back, and smiled. "Thank you."

Peter lifted the vase from the wheel and set it aside for firing. He grabbed more clay and flung it onto the wheel, not wanting the night to end. Kaida went back to her weaving, but he could not concentrate. The minutes stretched out.

"You have crushed that same piece four times now," Kaida finally said.

"I know that."

"Doesn't the clay get difficult to work with?"

"Yes."

"Why do you keep smashing it?"

"Because I keep making mistakes."

She studied him until he was forced to respond.

"What are you thinking?" he asked.

"I am thinking that there must be a standard outside the clay that determines if it's adequate. The potter is that standard, right?"

Peter shrugged. *Here we go again.*

"But none of your standards for your life come from outside of you."

Peter looked up. "You're right. I am both the potter and the clay."

She smiled and watched his hands on the spinning lump. "That must be challenging."

He crushed the clay again. *You don't know the half of it.*

Darkness crept over the High Temple on the Platform of Etemenanki. Qurdi-Marduk-lamur and the woman, High Priestess Warad-Sin, dragged their unconscious captive through the enclosure at the tower's base and over to the central stairs.

Warad-Sin kept forcing him to pause and rest. He sighed in impatience at her slight build and weak constitution. The close-cropped hair and intense black eyes of the high priestess might frighten the temple prostitutes, but Qurdi saw that she was clearly trying to compensate for her lack of strength, both physical and spiritual. He used her tonight only because it was a necessity.

They pulled the body up onto the stairs. The climb was almost vertical. The air grew cooler as they mounted, past the first platform, the second, the third. They pulled the almost naked slave between them by his arms, the lower half of his body jolting against the steps. Qurdi wished for more slaves to do the lifting, but he knew this was something the goddess required him to do himself.

Qurdi did not speak to the high priestess. She was not welcome at this ritual. He desired to perform it alone. But she had insisted on coming, and her authority was high enough that he could not prevent it.

They reached the wide upper platform of the High Temple as the last of the sun god's rays streaked across the city, lighting the tops of the temples like torches.

"Bring him to the altar," Qurdi instructed.

"I will perform the ritual myself," she answered.

Qurdi nearly raised the back of his hand to her. "No! This is not your ritual. It is mine! The gods will speak with me and me alone tonight!"

"Go your own way, then, priest." She dropped the arm she carried.

Qurdi wrapped his arms around the slave's bare chest and

yanked as though the man were a sack of barley. He managed to stagger backwards to the altar, where palm wood had already been laid. Torches stood ready.

He tried three times to heave the slave onto the altar.

"Do you need help?" Warad-Sin taunted.

He hated her. "Lift him up!"

Warad pulled the slave's lower body up onto the altar as Qurdi lifted him from above. When his bare chest lay across the needle-sharp wood, Qurdi unsheathed the knife.

It was risky, what he was about to do. Only the king could approve this ritual, and it was undertaken only in extreme situations. But Qurdi was desperate.

He was beginning to suspect he couldn't trust the goddess completely. She had been capricious lately. He hoped the ritual tonight in her honor would cause her to favor Qurdi with success tomorrow with the plan that would destroy Belteshazzar.

The slave on the altar suddenly jerked. They had been foolish not to tie him while he was unconscious. His eyes fluttered open, and he stared up into Qurdi's face, terror distorting his features as the wood on the altar pricked his bare skin.

Warad threw herself over the slave's upper body. "Do it, Qurdi!" she shouted.

Qurdi rushed through the incantation. "Great goddess, accept this sacrifice, made at this hour, made in your honor. Grant victory over our enemies; grant knowledge to make your name great."

Warad stepped back from the altar, and Qurdi plunged the knife into the slave's chest.

Akkad tossed on his bed, victim to spirits that prodded him to stay awake. Was it guilt over the warm afternoon spent beside Abigail on the banks of the river? No, Akkad never felt guilt anymore. Besides, the spirits he listened to rarely chastised him for anything.

Tonight it was doubts that chased sleep from him. Abigail's words echoed, telling him of the Lord God, of His justice and righteousness, of His love. This was a God unlike any that Akkad had ever worshiped. A God who created everything, she told him, including the stars. It was He who controlled their movements.

Akkad remembered his question to the other magi on the Platform. Who causes the lights of the sky to journey across the black void? Abigail had claimed to know Him. Could she be right?

A warm breeze seemed to blow through his bedchamber. *"No. . . "* it whispered. *"No. . . "*

"Is someone there?" Akkad's voice scratched in the silence.

"Do not deny. . . " the chanting voice faded into the darkness.

Akkad rolled to his side, staring through the ventilation grid in the wall, trying to catch a glimpse of the Ecliptic. He knew the Pathway of the Sun as well as he knew his own palm. The stars winked down on him like trusted advisors.

There, in the sky, all the answers could be found. Not in some conquered country full of strange people with strange beliefs. The wisdom of the ancients had been passed down in secrecy to Akkad and his kind, and he would preserve the secrets for the next generation. The answers of time and seasons had been given, and so many more answers were waiting to be revealed. Akkad raised a hand to the stars, doubts fleeing.

"Use me, gods of the sky. Use me to enlighten, to bring knowledge. I give myself wholly to you."

"Yes. . . " the stars whispered back.

In the palace, Qurdi whispered to the king of acts of treason. He had already convinced the king that the omens spoke ill of his most trusted advisor, the Israelite Belteshazzar. But the king knew that omens were not always certain. The gods could be appeased. He desired a preventative ritual to suspend any treachery that might be impending.

They were alone in the king's grand bedchamber. The size and opulence of the room did little to ward off the heavy darkness. One oil lamp sputtered at the king's bedside, struggling to conquer the silent blackness. Qurdi had brought his copper kettle-drum and now beat a slow, steady rhythm on the dark bull-hide. His eyes were closed, and he swayed as he spoke. The king's eyes never left Qurdi's hands.

Qurdi recited the oral formula. Nabu-kudurri-usur did not notice that Qurdi left out the most crucial section. When it was finished, he carried his drum to the door and turned to the king.

"Solicit another omen for me, Qurdi," the king said. "Ask the gods if anything has changed."

"I will perform the lecanomancy."

As Qurdi poured oil slowly over the surface of water in a glazed basin, the king asked, "What do you see?"

Qurdi positioned himself between the basin and the king to watch the pattern of the oil. "Will there be treachery among the diviners?" Qurdi asked the gods. He waited what seemed to be an appropriate interval, then spoke as if reading the omen. "Yes."

"Will the chief of magicians, Belteshazzar, be involved?" He watched the king from the corner of his eye. "Yes. Will he betray the king? Yes. Will someone else be part of the betrayal? Yes."

The king leaned forward on his bed. "Who?"

"Will it be another diviner?" The pause. "No. Will it be palace staff? No. Will it be one of the royal harem? Yes."

"Which one, Qurdi?" The king's face was grave. There was only one wife that mattered.

"Will it be Amyitis?" Qurdi paused again dramatically. "Yes."

The king fell back on his pillows. "Leave me, Qurdi."

The diviner retrieved his kettledrum, bowed, and backed out of the room with a smile.

Qurdi hurried into the palace courtyard as the morning sun beat through the archways. He had sent one of his staff to summon Belteshazzar, and now he caught a glimpse of him striding into the flower-decked courtyard. A uniformed palace official called out to the chief of magicians, and Belteshazzar stopped beside a waist-high stone fountain to answer his question.

Qurdi hurried into a tiny chamber off the corridor to hide. The room sometimes served as a meeting place, with a small table beside the wall and several chairs in the center. Qurdi occasionally used it for reading entrails when an omen was called for in the palace. Today he seated himself in the semidarkness of the room, the only light coming from a single oil lamp. The door opened a moment later.

"Qurdi?" Belteshazzar said.

"I am here."

Belteshazzar entered.

"Close the door behind you."

Belteshazzar glanced back through the door, then shut it. "What is it?"

"The king has dreamed a dream in the night. He has asked me to interpret it, but I am unable. He sends for you."

Belteshazzar nodded. "I will go immediately, though God has given me no message for my lord the king."

"Do not go now. The king goes to his morning meal. He desires to see you in his bedchamber afterwards. And he has instructed that you not speak of it until then."

"I understand. But why did the king not summon me first?"

Qurdi tilted his head off-center. "Perhaps you are not as favored as you once were."

Belteshazzar left. Qurdi waited several minutes before leaving the room. He found a slave and gave him a message for Amyitis. "Tell the woman that her king desires her company in his chambers immediately after the morning meal." He grabbed the slave's arm before he walked away. "And say nothing to the representative of the harem."

Qurdi stared at the departing slave's back. Everything was almost ready. He drifted to the dining hall to join the morning meal.

He found the spacious hall half-filled with diners. Belteshazzar had already arrived and was seated with his Hebrew friends. He had not been the only royal captive Jew to rise to a position of prominence. Shadur-Aku, Mi-sha-Aku, and Abed-Nabu had all been set over the affairs of various districts of Babylon. The four talked and laughed at the table, as if sharing some private knowledge that superseded anything Babylon could produce.

Qurdi was confident that after the morning meal the king would go to his audience hall where he would hold court. There were pressing matters of state this morning to attend to. No dreams had disturbed the king's sleep in the night, despite what he'd told Belteshazzar. Qurdi left the hall before the meal was complete, searching for the representative of the harem. He found the eunuch in the halls outside the women's quarters.

A quick word to him, and Qurdi hurried back to the dining hall. He arrived as Amyitis left and gave her an empty smile as she passed on her way to the king's chamber. Belteshazzar left the hall a moment later with his friends.

"A word, Belteshazzar," Qurdi said.

The Jew smiled at the other three. "Go along. I must meet with the king. I will find you afterward." He turned to Qurdi. "What is it?"

"It is about the king's dream."

"Yes?"

"It is a puzzling one. I have listened to him tell of it several times, but I cannot make anything out of it."

"I am not surprised."

Qurdi ignored the condescension. "I have consulted the Dream-Book and even spoken with the observer of the birds. Still, I have no answer."

Belteshazzar nodded and attempted to walk past him, but Qurdi laid a hand on his arm.

Belteshazzar jerked it away. "Perhaps if you would let me go to the king, an answer would be found."

"Of course, Belteshazzar," Qurdi bowed. "Of course."

Qurdi watched the Jew walk down the corridor. He was certain he had delayed him long enough for Amyitis to ready herself in the king's chamber.

Chapter 10

BABYLON AWAKENED THIS morning ready to greet the day. As the sun lit the edges of her city walls, she called to her midnight revelers to rise from their beds and find a new way to reach above themselves. Forget the gluttony of last night; there was more to be gained today. Her message to them was age-old. "Find your bliss."

The towering statue of her favored son neared completion, but she was not jealous. When they worshiped him, they worshiped her.

She was the glorious capital city of a far-flung empire, and she knew her power. Already this morning travelers from other cities approached the Ishtar Gate. She opened her mouth wide and welcomed them in, gulping them down the throat of the Processional Way. They would become part of her, if only for a short time. When she had gotten all she could from them, she would vomit them back out into the desert to return to their own cities.

And they would thank her for the privilege.

"Abigail!" Akkad whispered down the hall.

He had come out of his chamber on the way to the morning meal and spotted her at the end the hall. They were alone.

She turned and took several swift steps toward him before catching herself. "Akkad." Her voice broke as she said his name.

He ran to her, grasping her hands in his. She did not pull away. "What has happened?" he asked.

"Nothing. Nothing yet."

"What do you mean?"

Akkad's heart pounded. They had met several times since their afternoon by the river, sometimes by chance and other times by arrangement. Akkad was no closer to forgetting about her in exchange for someone more suitable. And her feelings toward him were continuing to grow.

"The king has sent for me," she said, leaving unspoken the full import of her words.

Akkad's eyes burned into hers. "No. You must not go."

She shook her head, tears springing to her eyes. "How can I refuse, Akkad? He has not sent for me since I arrived. We could not expect him to forget me forever."

Akkad dropped her hands, turning a circle in frustration. "Why you? Why does he want you?"

Abigail lowered her eyes to the floor.

He held her by the arms. "Of course, I know why he wants you, Abigail. You are— I only meant—"

She nodded, still studying the patterned tiles. "I understand."

"I will go to him!" Akkad said.

Abigail smiled sadly, as though she indulged a child. "And what will you say, Akkad? That he must not touch his own wife because you would have her instead?"

Akkad turned away again, this time pounding the wall with his fist. Several slaves entered the hall, passing by the couple with inquisitive glances. Abigail's eyes returned to the floor, and Akkad stared down the presumptuous slaves, daring them to comment on the forbidden dialogue.

"Are you going to him now?"

Abigail frowned. "Why are you angry with me? You know that in this I have no control, no control over my own life!" She wiped at her eyes as if embarrassed to find tears flowing.

Akkad softened. "I am not angry with you, only with him!"

"Stop, Akkad! You will get us both thrown in the furnace by speaking like that. If this is the will of the Most High for my life, there is nothing I can do to stop it. And I will accept His plan for me."

"The Most High! If your one God allows you to be used by a king who cares nothing for you, then he is not a God I wish to know."

Abigail's eyes reflected even more pain. "Do not say that, Akkad. You must learn of Him. You must not continue to follow your false gods. It will only lead to destruction."

"Then I will be destroyed! But I cannot allow Him to destroy you!" He grabbed her arm and pulled her down the hall.

Abigail pulled away. "Stop, Akkad! There is nothing we can do. He wishes for me to come to him tonight. The representative told me. I am to meet him in his chambers after the evening meal."

Peter and Kaida arrived at the palace as its inhabitants were leaving the hall after their breakfast. Peter led the way to an entrance in the eastern wall where the red-haired woman had let him out on his last visit. They slipped in unnoticed. Could he find her again? He did not dare approach her himself. He had brought Kaida for that.

The corridor led to the first palace courtyard, used mainly by the palace guard and other household staff, but still landscaped with dozens of flower beds and pots overflowing with red and yellow blooms nestled among clusters of palms. Kaida slowed to appreciate the display.

Peter looked around. How was he supposed to find that

woman? Maybe he should find a slave to bring her to him. But at the moment, there wasn't anyone around. He followed Kaida's gaze to the flowers. "I wish I could have seen the Hanging Gardens more closely."

"Haven't you seen it many times?" Kaida asked.

"With you, I mean. I'd like to show you."

Kaida touched his arm. "Could we?"

Peter did a quick mental calculation as to the position of the trees he'd seen high above the palace walls. He led Kaida toward the northeast corner of the palace, hoping for obvious stairs.

A wide set of steps rewarded his guess. They climbed.

At the top of the steps they passed through an archway to the rooftop, and the garden rose like an enormous wide staircase before them. His mother had landscaped the hill leading up to his childhood home this way, with several levels cut into the hill, shored up with timbers, and planted with perennials. This garden used the same principle, but on a scale worthy of the gods. Seven high tiers spilled over with ferns, shrubs, flowers, and trees. A flight of steps led from each tier to the next. Throughout the garden, stone fountains spurted, and a small stream ran through the center of each wide step, dropping to the level below in a miniature waterfall.

Kaida seemed delighted. She climbed to the third tier where a stone bench stayed cool under a knot of palm trees. All around her feet, flowers sprawled out in blue and white and purple. She rested on the bench for a moment, gazing at the lush landscape under the killing desert sun. Peter watched as she left her shady nook and ascended to the seventh tier to find the source of the water. She beckoned him up.

It was a wonder of engineering. Three stone shafts laced together and ran down into a cavernous well. Peter assumed a canal from the river had been dug under the palace to supply the well. An endless chain of buckets ran through the stone shafts, drawn up in continuous rotation, spilling out into the rooftop stream and descending for another liquid load. He could not tell what powered it. Perhaps the current of the river itself.

He suddenly wanted to stay in this place. His heart seemed to reach out to something here. Was this beauty what he had been searching for? Why was he still searching at all? If anything should have satisfied his hunger, it would have been this unbelievable journey into the past. How many times had he hunched over his books or stared out his office window dreaming of what it would be like to live in a time he had only ever studied?

Now he had climbed to the top of this "mountain." As always, he waited to feel contentment, but it was still a moment in time, and he was left wondering what else there might be. Would he ever arrive at the place he always felt himself longing for, the place he could never quite define?

"Let's rest here awhile," he said, pointing to the shade of a tree on the top level. It provided a good view of the Gardens, and they would be able to see if anyone approached. They sat together, and he studied the greenery below them. "Kaida, do you ever feel like you're looking for something you never find?"

She tucked her legs beneath her. "Rim, you insist you don't believe there is a God, yet you still reach for Him."

"No, Kaida, not God. This is different. It is beauty, or excitement, sometimes even fear. I can't describe it well, but it is a feeling, not a person."

"It is a longing for something to be real outside of *yourself.*"

Peter thought about that for a moment and had to agree.

"Rim, when you are hungry, your desire is to eat and be filled. That desire proves that food exists. This feeling you describe, the thing you are reaching for, it proves that something outside of yourself exists."

He shook his head. "Then it is the impersonal divine consciousness in all of us."

"If that is so, why haven't you found it, the thing you are looking for?"

"Because I have not yet transformed myself."

"Why?" she asked. "When will it happen? In this lifetime? A hundred lifetimes? A thousand? What if you live a thousand lifetimes and never find what you search for?"

Peter leaned back and closed his eyes.

Be glad that you seek for your entire life. Transformation is an ongoing process.

Then why did he always seem to be exactly the same person?

He stood up abruptly. "Let's go. I need to find the woman."

"What woman?"

"Come with me."

They left the Gardens and descended to the palace floor again. The place was alive and busy now with dozens of staff members, officials, and slaves crawling all over it. But there was only one person Peter wanted to see. The one person who might have answers about Reuben's mission, newly adopted by Peter.

Qurdi watched from the corner of the hall like a hungry cat waiting to pounce. He had followed Belteshazzar from a few paces behind, waiting in the shadows as the Hebrew entered the king's chamber. As if it had been rehearsed, the representative came along a moment later and stood at the door. It jerked open, and Belteshazzar faced the eunuch. Qurdi trotted over to stand beside the eunuch.

"What is happening here?" he asked. He peered past Belteshazzar into the king's bedchamber.

Amyitis stood beside the pillowed bed in the dim room, a linen sheet hastily wrapped around her obviously naked body.

"There has been a mistake," Belteshazzar said, scowling at Qurdi.

Qurdi glanced at the representative. The eunuch's face was purple with rage. He grabbed Belteshazzar by the neck and screamed for guards. Qurdi hid a smug smile and headed to the throne room to wait.

In the high-ceilinged throne room, Nabu-kudurri-usur held morning court. Officials and ambassadors lined the sides of the room waiting for their audience with the king. At the moment, he was listening to the details of a trade problem. A ship had been wrecked on the Euphrates, so that the grain it carried for the palace had had to be beached. What was to be done about the grain and the crew?

Qurdi would be needed soon to advise the king on weightier matters, but for now he would remain unnoticed, where he could watch and enjoy.

The representative of the harem stomped into the throne room, leaving a wake of officials, diviners, and townspeople shoved out of the way. He still held Belteshazzar in his grip.

"Approach," the king said to the eunuch. "What is it?"

"O King, live forever. There is a problem within the harem."

"What is this problem?"

The eunuch grimaced as if unwilling to deliver such dreadful news. He pushed Belteshazzar toward the throne. "I found the diviner, Belteshazzar, O King, with the king's wife in the king's bedchambers."

Nabu-kudurri-usur was stony-faced. "Which wife?"

"Amyitis, O King."

The king's nostrils flared, and his eyes pierced through Belteshazzar.

Belteshazzar lifted his chin. "O King, live forever—"

Guards entered, dragging Amyitis in her sheet. The king stood, the color washed from his face, and he breathed heavily.

Amyitis pulled against the guards. "My King—" she called.

"Silence!"

In the back of the room, Qurdi hid his smile. He had done his work well in preparing the king for this moment. The faked lecanomancy in the king's chambers had had its desired effect: the king had no wish to hear their defense. Instead he stood nose-to-nose with Belteshazzar.

"Take him to the prison," he said. "The woman is to be kept in her quarters."

"There has been a mistake!" Belteshazzar said as he resisted the two helmeted guards who had seized his arms. "It is not as it appears!" His eyes found Qurdi in the crowd. He pointed. "It was—"

One of the guards pulled a club from his belt and dealt a blow to the back of the Jew's neck. Belteshazzar's knees buckled, and the two guards dragged him from the throne room.

Peter and Kaida found their way to the wide palace wing where the harem was quartered. A commotion at the end of the hall forced them to step backward into a doorway.

"Let go of me!" The woman, who wore only a sheet, pulled her long arm from the grip of a palace official and rubbed the place where his fingers had dug into her.

Dozens of women streamed out of doorways up and down the hall, chattering like a flock of multicolored birds. Several of them circled the woman, pulling her into a room. The others milled around the doorway.

Among the wives and servants Peter spotted red hair and a familiar face. "That woman, there," he said to Kaida, pointing. "Blend into that crowd and tell her that I want to speak with her privately."

Kaida held out her tunic. "Have you looked at me? How

am I supposed to blend in with them?"

Peter shrugged and gave her a little shove toward the flock of women.

She slid into the group, observing for several moments. When the woman turned toward her, she whispered something in her ear. The woman raised her eyebrows and looked in Peter's direction. She glided over, with Kaida behind. She seemed reluctant to talk with him.

"Rim."

Kaida stood beside her. Peter noted with surprise that Kaida was at least eight inches shorter. Kaida's face was flushed. "Ilushu tells me that the last time you were in the palace, you left before she had finished with you."

Peter squirmed. "Can we speak privately?" he said to Ilushu.

The woman nodded. "That would be preferable, my love," she smiled. "In here." She pulled him through the doorway where the three stood, into someone's living quarters. Peter looked around to be sure they were alone.

"You act as though you'd never been in my room before, Rim."

Kaida stood by the door, as if refusing to be part of this. Ilushu turned a disdainful eye on her and spoke to Peter. "Can we get rid of the slave, my love?"

Kaida's eyes burned into Peter, but she backed out of the room. He caught her before she left. "Where can we meet?"

"I don't think you'll be needing me again."

Peter shook his head. There was no time to argue with her. "The Hanging Gardens. Go there. I'll meet you soon."

Kaida looked doubtful. Ilushu slithered to the door and closed it against Kaida with a triumphant smile.

Kaida returned to the bench in the Gardens, closed her eyes, and leaned back against a tree. She prayed no one would find her in this place where she didn't belong. She should probably take the opportunity to run from Rim-Sin. But she was too tired to run right now.

Why did Rim need to talk with that woman? He'd better just be *talking* to her. Kaida snorted at the memory of Ilushu's cloying smile. Royal wife or not, was that the kind of woman he wanted? She shook her head to clear her thoughts and looked around her.

Such a beautiful place. On the ground at her feet two caterpillars seemed to argue over a green leaf. She nudged one with her toe, almost wishing she could stay here forever. The sun rose higher in the sky, and even under this shade a hot breeze reached her. How long had it been? She was certain he could have gotten any information he needed by now. She knew she should leave while she had the chance. But she stayed. He might need her.

Why did she care? She was supposed to be convincing him of the error of his stupid beliefs. But ever since she had seen Rim with that baby, her heart had changed. What was she thinking? It was impossible.

Peter peeled Ilushu's hands off him again. She wasn't getting the message. "I need to talk to you," he said.

She pouted her painted red lips, flouncing over to a chair beside the wall. Crossing her legs, she tapped a sandaled foot in midair and examined her fingernails. "What is it?"

"When I was here before, you said I had been to the palace treasury looking for something. What was it?"

Ilushu came to him again. "Oh, I don't remember, love. It doesn't matter. You're here now."

He disentangled himself. Were all harem women like this? With her crimson red robe and snow-white skin, she could be the cover model for a magazine. *Babylon Glamour.* He nearly laughed. But was there a brain inside that head?

"Ilushu, please. This is important. What was I looking for?"

She pulled away, angry this time. "Some Jewish thing. I don't know."

"What Jewish thing?"

"A lamp. Or a lampstand. Something like that." Her hands returned to his chest.

That was all the information he was going to get, that much was clear. But it was something, at least. And he should go. "Good-bye, Ilushu."

"What?" She held him again. "Do not go," she said. "Please. You know there is no one here who cares for me."

Peter studied her face, misery etched into fine lines around her eyes. He pitied her, wished he could change her circumstances or at least make her feel better for a time.

She wrapped cool hands around his neck and brought his face to hers. Peter's thoughts of leaving flew. He had spent many days wanting a woman who would never be his. Why not spend some time with one who was not so resistant? He let himself be drawn into her kiss, waiting to see if this was really what he wanted. It was.

A flutter of guilt slowed him. Kaida was waiting for him. What would she think?

Guilt is merely a product of societal conditioning.

Ilushu's kisses grew more intense. She pulled his outer tunic from his shoulders.

Peter backed away. But why? Why should he feel any guilt at all? He could do anything he wanted, couldn't he?

Ilushu wrapped her arms around him again, and he brought her to him. They kissed.

Peter heard a gasp from behind him.

He turned, trying to keep Ilushu hidden by his body.

Another woman stood in the doorway, her mouth hanging open. Peter didn't recognize her. "Ilushu!"

Peter looked at his red-haired companion.

She smiled and shrugged one shoulder. "We may have a problem."

Akkad was going to spend the day poring over his handbooks in the privacy of his palace chambers. There would be no other opportunity to see Abigail today. And tonight she would be with the king.

He didn't wish to think of it. He would apply himself today to every spell and charm he could find to stop this disaster. In essence, he was looking for a counter-spell to release the king from the magic of the amulet that Akkad himself had created. Akkad had no time to appreciate the irony. He was wild to stop Nabu-kudurri-usur in his advances toward Abigail.

Since he had met her, Akkad had realized the emptiness in his life. His spells and star charts had consumed him for years, almost since he was old enough to recognize the lights in the sky. But Abigail had brought his eyes down from the dome, and now he saw only her. He spent his days torn between his desire to establish himself among the *kasdim* and his desire to win her for himself.

He knew that a public relationship was impossible. She was the king's wife, and Akkad could be executed for even looking inappropriately at her. He didn't care. He would go on this way, in secret, forever if she would allow it. But brief meetings in the halls and the Gardens had been all that Abigail had allowed thus far. Her devotion to her one God and His ludicrous morality kept her from more.

What did he hope to accomplish here? Did he expect to keep Abigail from the king forever? He knew in his heart that such a feat would be impossible, no matter how many spells he recited. The best he could hope for was to share her with the king, though he doubted she would ever agree to that. But he could not bear the thought of the king with her. Not yet. At least not until she had admitted that she loved Akkad alone.

The magic that Akkad consulted now was not of the common sort. Most spells, if they mentioned demons or malevolent powers at all, were invoked to turn away the evil they caused. Desperation had driven Akkad to the blacker arts. His only hope was to bring some evil upon the king himself, thus preventing his plans for this evening.

He found what he searched for in the *Surpu*. Hardly daring to think about the intended victim of the spell, he left his room to gather the supplies he would need.

Chapter 11

Cosam wiped the sweat from his brow and moved away from the furnace. He and Jacob were working again on the king's new statue of himself.

"I don't have all the answers, Cosam," Jacob said. "But Mishael speaks of the Messiah as not only our Deliverer but our Redeemer as well. One who will atone for our sin in a way the animal sacrifices never could."

Cosam ran a hand through his damp hair, unwilling to give voice to his confusion. "Nevertheless I am confident that the priests still sacrifice for us in the temple in Jerusalem, Jacob." He reached for the box where he kept his tools. "It is time to stop for the afternoon."

Cosam left the goldsmith bazaar as the sun climbed overhead. The day would soon grow unbearably hot, and he planned to be at home for his afternoon nap before it did. As he neared his home, he grew anxious to bathe. It was not only the sweat of the work he wanted to be rid of. He felt contaminated from the work of the morning.

He had grown almost accustomed to fashioning jewelry and accessories for the Babylonians' preposterous gods. At least with those articles he could pretend he was making them for a person. But the pagan nature of his latest work had been impossible to ignore. He had spent the morning staring into the eyes of an enormous golden head. It was the king's head, carved from wood, which Cosam, Jacob, and several others had been assigned to overlay with gold. The project had been a lengthy one. The statue was to be the greatest image ever erected in the Babylonian empire. Cosam had spent this morning carefully detailing the eyes. It was the knowledge that this thing would one day soon be worshiped that made him feel unclean as he entered his home.

He hurried directly to the bathroom. He couldn't help but stop once more to admire the design of Babylonian bathrooms. There had been nothing of this sort in Israel. The burnt brick floor of the small room was waterproofed with bitumen and slightly depressed in the center where a drainage hole would carry water out of the house. In the corner, a small seat had been built over another drainage hole. Beside the seat on a low platform was a water jar used for flushing. Cosam quickly disrobed and lifted another water jar above his head as he stood in the center of the room. He let the cool water run through his hair, over his shoulders, and down to the floor, hoping to wash away the impurity he felt.

After his bath he found Rebekah in their bedroom with Addi and the Babylonian baby, whom they had decided to name Isaac. It was a good name, Cosam had said. It meant "he laughs," and this boy would need a cheerful name as he faced his future.

Cosam lowered himself to the bed with a groan. Rebekah reclined against pillows beside him, holding the babies.

"You seem especially tired today," Rebekah said.

"Tired, aggravated, and confused," he answered, throwing an arm over his forehead.

Rebekah laughed. "Many emotions for only one day. I understand the fatigue, and your work for the temple always aggravates you, but why confused?"

"It is the conversation at the goldsmiths' bazaar as we work. While we labor over this abomination we are creating, we cannot help but speak of the Law and of all that the Lord God expects of us. But lately, Jacob has been spending more time with Mishael, and the things that he is learning puzzle me."

"Such as?"

Cosam smiled at his wife. Not many women he knew were interested in such things. "Mishael points toward the Messiah, as the prophets have always told us. The Messiah will rescue us from those who would oppress us, he says."

"You have always believed that, Cosam."

"Yes. Although many here have lost that faith. They feel betrayed, I suppose. They don't see that it is their own sin that has brought them here."

"So what is troubling you?"

"Mishael also says that the prophets tell us that the Messiah will do more than save us from tyranny. He will save us from sin. The sacrifices are not sufficient, Mishael says. They are only to point us to our own failure."

Rebekah nodded, thinking. "But Cosam," she said, "keeping the Law is one of the most important things in your life! How can it not be enough?"

Cosam closed his eyes. He needed to think.

Peter didn't stick around to find out who Ilushu's visitor was. He grabbed his cloak, pushed into the palace hallway, and headed for the front courtyard. He was nearly out of the palace before he thought of Kaida. He hesitated, then ran for the entrance to the Gardens and up the stairs. Below him he could hear shouting. Had word spread to the guards already?

The sun was high overhead when Peter reached the Hanging Gardens. He saw Kaida before she saw him. She lay on a stone bench on the tier above him, her eyes closed, her head on one arm. A white lily was tucked into her dark hair. He studied her outline for several moments.

She opened her eyes, saw him, and jerked upright. He took the small steps two at a time and jumped up to the third tier.

"I wasn't sure if you would come for me," she said in a chilly voice.

"I said I would."

"Did you enjoy your visit?"

He couldn't read her. Anger? Could it possibly be jealousy? "It was informative. That's all it needed to be. We need to go."

"Ilushu apparently wished for it to be more."

Peter shook his head. "She is nothing to me, Kaida."

"Ah," Kaida said, glaring at him. "But all women are nothing to you, aren't they?"

"No, not all of them." He meant to sound sincere, but it came out sounding sarcastic instead.

Kaida took the lily from her hair and tossed it to the ground.

"We need to go now, Kaida."

"What has happened?"

"Nothing. Come."

There was more shouting at the base of the stairs they had climbed. Peter pulled Kaida along the bottom tier of the Gardens, searching for another exit. At the other end of the Gardens he found a narrow corridor that ran along the eastern side of the palace. The steps he had used to reach the upper level lay at the end of the corridor. He hesitated a moment, then ran to the top of the steps.

Then he saw that someone was coming up from the bottom. He jerked back, and Kaida slammed into his back.

She pounded a fist against him. "What are you doing?"

"Shh!"

A quick look around made it clear there was nowhere to run. He turned back to the stairs and raised his head. Would he be recognized? Did everyone know he was a fugitive? Time for some good acting.

It was a palace slave. He walked with his head down. He reached the top of the stairs, his eyes studying a teetering tray of filled goblets.

Peter deliberately stepped into the center of the corridor.

The slave jumped when he saw feet on the floor ahead of him. One of the golden goblets rocked and then crashed to the stones, the red wine running in a stream toward Peter.

"Rim-Sin!" the slave quaked.

"Clean this up at once," Peter said.

"Yes, my lord." The slave bowed several times and moved aside, his back to the wall, to let Peter and Kaida pass.

Peter stomped past him, head still held high, and jogged down the steps. When they reached the bottom of the steps, Peter pulled back again. Another hall. This one wide and high and filled with people. The palace day was well underway, and staff members scrambled through the hall like members of an ant colony.

Peter couldn't tell if word of his . . . indiscretion . . . had spread or not.

There was no going around the crowd, so Peter plunged into it, hoping Kaida would not lose him. They weaved through the mass of people. Anyone who made eye contact bowed or nodded to Peter and ignored Kaida as though she were invisible.

Hundreds of doors seemed to open off the hall. Should he take any of them? Did any lead to an exit, or were they all living quarters?

Finally, the hallway spilled them out into the smallest of the courtyards. More palace staff filled the area, tending the flowerbeds or cleaning the brick walkways. Peter looked across the courtyard. The palace gate! Nearly out.

"Ready?" he asked Kaida.

She nodded.

You are Rim-Sin, he said to himself. With a purposeful stride, he set out across the courtyard. More bowing and scraping.

When they passed through the palace gate and out onto the Processional Way, Peter heard the shouts intensify behind them. Time to move faster. As usual, the street teemed with citizens. Peter clutched Kaida's hand, and they melted into the crowd.

He pulled Kaida through the high-walled chute of the Processional Way, pushing shoppers and travelers aside as they ran. They darted around loaded pack mules and their slow-moving guides. Peter tried to think.

People and animals blurred. Peter shot a look over his shoulder once or twice. He and Kaida were plowing a path through the indignant crowd, and he had no doubt that the palace guards were following hard. The street had narrowed since they'd left the palace in the distance.

Tumult up ahead slowed him down. A caravan of donkeys and loaded wagons had spread across the street, blocking pedestrian traffic. One wagon had overturned, spilling its load of red pomegranates onto the street. The angry shouts of travelers raised the fists of the merchants.

There was no way through, and Peter didn't want to wait. He dodged into the nearest side street, staying close to the jagged walls of the houses. After a few minutes, he slowed. They were alone in the narrow street, its houses pressing up close against the cracked paving stones that led down the center.

"What happened back there, Rim-Sin? What did you find out from that woman?"

"That I need to find a lampstand."

She nodded. "The one in your home."

In his home? Peter stopped and studied Kaida's face, lit by the sun. Why would Rim-Sin have a lampstand from the palace treasury in his home? His mind flashed back to the moment he had arrived in Babylon. The searing heat, the dead man, and something else. A gold lampstand in his hand. Hot. Crashing to the floor. Oil spilling.

He had been holding the lampstand when it had happened!

He leaned his back against the warm brick wall of a house. "Where would it be now?"

She shrugged. "Perhaps the *rab alani* took it when he removed the body."

Of course! It would be evidence, wouldn't it? Rim-Sin must have stolen the lampstand. What had Rim's slave said that day? "He knows you have it." *He* must have referred to the *rab alani.*

Peter moved forward into the street with resolve. "We must find it."

Chapter 12

PETER DIDN'T KNOW if the king knew about him and Ilushu. He didn't know where the lampstand was, and he didn't know how to find it. But one thing he did know—he needed to get out of this time and place, and the lampstand had to be the key to finishing what Reuben had started. Kaida said she knew nothing about it. So Peter would find the only other person who he knew might have answers.

The guards must have lost them in the street, so Peter and Kaida moved directly to Rim-Sin's home and entered. This had to be quick, because surely the guards would think to search here.

The slave Elam was in the courtyard. He jumped to his feet as they entered.

"Elam," Peter said, "I need some answers."

The slave stood silently before him.

"The night the Jew Reuben was killed—you saw what happened?"

"Yes, my lord."

"Why was Reuben here? Why did he have the lampstand?"

"My lord, you needn't worry that I will reveal your secret. Your threat to kill me to keep me quiet was sufficient."

Peter sensed the palace guards growing closer. "Tell me what you know, Elam!"

The slave said nothing.

Peter wished Kaida wasn't at his side. He had to get the information. He stepped to Elam, wrapped his hands around the man's throat, and squeezed.

"Rim-Sin!" Kaida took a step toward them.

He warned her away with his eyes. "Tell me everything you know, Elam!"

The slave gasped for air. Peter loosened his hold only slightly.

"He was cataloguing the temple articles," Elam said.

"Yes?"

"The lampstand. He—he took it from the treasury."

"Why?"

Elam tried to pull Peter's hands from around his throat.

In one movement, Peter swiped his leg behind Elam's and knocked the slave onto his back. Peter knelt on his chest and resumed his hold on the man's neck. "Why did he take it?"

Elam struggled for breath. Peter could feel the heat of Kaida's eyes on him.

"The lampstand is a symbol to our people. Important. Reuben could not bear for it to lie forgotten somewhere. He was trying to smuggle it back to Jerusalem."

Peter released his hold slightly. "Where is the lampstand now?"

"The *rab alani*, Faram-Enlil, took it after you killed Reuben."

"And where is Faram-Enlil now?"

"I do not know. He lives in the New City."

Peter let go of Elam's throat, removed his knee from the man's chest, and stood. The New City. "Let's go, Kaida."

There was disgust and fear on her face. She shook her head.

He had no intention of leaving her behind when he headed into new territory. She was coming, whether she liked it or not.

They headed back out into the city. "Kaida, listen. I would not have hurt him. You know that. I had to make him believe I would. I must find the lampstand."

Kaida stomped ahead of him and didn't turn. "Why? What is so important about the lampstand?"

"It's the key to everything."

They reached the stone bridge that crossed the Euphrates River, with its five huge tar-covered piers holding it above the water. The Processional Way led directly over the bridge. Peter and Kaida fused with the crowd pushing its way across and were soon in the New City, home to the Jewish captives, among others. "You must do the talking," Peter said. "Help me find Faram-Enlil."

Kaida began approaching people. "Where is the Jewish district?" she asked an old man leading a donkey.

He pointed, but said nothing. Strange that Kaida didn't know where the Jews lived on this side of the river. She kept asking as they walked, getting few answers.

Several streets running close together, with small mud-brick houses butted against each other, marked the beginning of the exiles' homes.

Faram-Enlil was the Babylonian *rab alani* of this area who had given chase to Peter that first night. Peter was hoping to find the lampstand without Faram finding them.

Kaida was still asking questions, this time about Faram's home.

"Why do you ask about Faram-Enlil?" a hawk-nosed woman questioned when Kaida spoke to her. She leveled a suspicious look at Peter.

Peter pulled Kaida away from the woman. "Perhaps we should try to find him without questions."

The woman behind them was speaking to her husband now. "There—those are the two." She pointed at them as her husband squinted in their direction.

"Let's keep moving," Peter said.

Kaida nodded. "They are suspicious of outsiders,"

"I can see that. I don't want them asking Faram-Enlil to examine their two newest arrivals."

In the streets of the Jewish district, the shouts and calls of tattered children playing games echoed off the walls of crumbling homes. Dogs scrounged for food among the garbage and chased a group of children kicking a ball made of dirty rags. Peter and Kaida moved through the streets studying the utilitarian little gardens that struggled to feed each house's inhabitants and trying not to breathe in air that reeked of inattention by the city's sanitation department.

At the end of one narrow street, they came upon an incongruous house, set apart from the others, several stories high, with a low wall surrounding a flourishing ornamental garden. A small statue of a god stood sentry at the gate.

"I would guess that this is it," Peter said.

They approached cautiously. A little boy played in front of the house inside the low stone wall.

"Hello." Kaida smiled and waved.

He smiled up at her, but his smile faded when he looked at Peter.

"Could you tell me if this is the home of Faram-Enlil?" Kaida said.

The little boy studied Kaida for a moment. "Father!" he yelled.

The day had exhausted Faram. He closed his eyes against the fire-hot sun as he walked toward his home.

They were a contentious people, these Jews, and difficult to govern. He had listened with waning patience as they had argued over everything from biting dogs to garbage in the garden. He was even less patient now. Rim-Sin's murder of Reuben had been all but forgotten in his grand display at the tower, and Faram chafed at the injustice. If he found the diviner, perhaps he would mete out fairness himself. Faram gave a tired smile to the little boys who played in the street as he walked. Right now, he only wanted to get home to his wife and son.

Peter and Kaida traded worried looks. When no one answered the boy's call, Peter breathed easier. The boy was afraid of him, so he backed away. He didn't fault the child. Towering over the charming little garden, he must have looked like an ogre.

"I know you are frightened of my—friend," Kaida said. "He is a little bit scary. But he won't hurt you."

The boy looked a little less tense.

"We need to know if your father is Faram-Enlil. Can you tell us that?"

The boy nodded, still very serious.

Kaida looked back at Peter as if to say "now what?" He gave her a little nod, urging her to probe further.

"Your father does very important work, doesn't he?"

The boy nodded again.

"Does he sometimes bring things home for you to look at?"

"Yes." He was warming to her now.

"Did your father ever bring home a gold lampstand?"

The boy screwed up his face as if concentrating. "Yes. But we only had it for a day. Then father said it must go back to the palace treasury."

"I see." She looked at Peter as if to say *You owe me.* "Thank you, young man. We must be leaving now."

"You don't have to leave. My father will be here any time now."

Peter pulled Kaida down the street toward the bridge.

Qurdi's plan for Belteshazzar and Amyitis had unfolded perfectly. In the gravel paths that interlaced the grassy courtyard of the Temple of Ishtar, he slit the neck of a goat, partly to thank the goddess for Belteshazzar's imprisonment, partly to seek her aid in finding Rim-Sin once again. Temple prostitutes sitting in the open sun looked away from the bloodletting. Qurdi reveled in it. In spite of his intentional misreading of the omens to indicate betrayal by a royal wife, it had actually happened—though not with the wife he had named. Rim-Sin and Ilushu had been caught together, and now once again Rim-Sin was sought by the king's men.

Qurdi brought the goat to the stone altar in the center of the courtyard, cut out the entrails and organs to consult in a few moments, and laid the bloody carcass before the goddess.

He served Ishtar well, with everything he had in him. Except for the part of him that needed to serve his own purposes. He hoped that one day she would see his devotion, realize that he had spent his lifetime loving her and serving her, and would favor him. Yes, there were the days when he wondered if she even knew him, but he quickly made a sacrifice to atone for those doubts, and he sought to better serve her. There was no one else, he knew, in all of Babylon who served her better. Surely if she chose to look with favor on someone, it would be him. He had just sacrificed a slave in her honor. What more could he do for her?

The courtyard was filled today. The New Year Festival approached, and the men sought the favor of the goddess of love. The temple prostitutes did their part, and the crowds came and went. Inside the temple, Qurdi lay before the only woman he loved, Ishtar.

A silent servant brought the tray of goat entrails into the chamber and placed it on a table beside the wall. Qurdi roused himself to go to the table and pull the organs and tissue apart, in search of a message written there for him by the gods.

When the liver lay still warm in the dish, Qurdi asked only one question: "Where is Rim-Sin right now?" He looked for the message and consulted the handbook.

There was no doubt. The answer written there was "West." He must be in the New City, perhaps something to do with the dead Jew? Qurdi would look there first. He clapped for his slaves to remove the liver. His two special ones came at once.

He would find Rim-Sin. And he would make sure he got Rim-Sin's knowledge before he killed him. It was time to go to the New City. It was only a short walk from the Temple of Ishtar to the bridge.

Faram-Enlil had never dreamed he would be so favored by the gods today. He had crossed the bridge back into the New City headed for home when he'd caught a glimpse of the Jewish girl Kaida. Now he stood on tiptoe and danced around the crowd, trying to get a look at the man she was with. The gods be praised: it was Rim-Sin! He nearly shouted.

Instead, he pushed his way through the mass of people, trying to remain unseen. It didn't work.

"Faram-Enlil!" someone shouted from the midst of a passionate argument. "It is the *rab alani!* Ask him!"

The concubine's head turned at his name, and she saw him. She grabbed Rim-Sin's arm and pulled him toward the bridge. Faram pushed harder through the crowd. They reached the bridge long before Faram did. They were running along the side where the crowd thinned while he still fought his way to the threshold.

Qurdi saw the sudden congestion at the bridge's rail up ahead. What was happening? When people began shouting, he pushed into the crowd.

Could it be? Qurdi nearly cursed the gods. For all his prayers, he had not once been prepared for his sudden encounters with Rim-Sin. Each time Qurdi had seen him, it had been only by chance, and the man had always seen him first.

Now the crowd on his end of the bridge had stopped, and he was snared in the middle of it. Had Rim-Sin and the woman seen him already? Why were they standing on the edge? He pushed forward, but the people pressed against him, threatening to trample him in their urge to be part of the excitement. He began smacking faces with the back of his hand, screaming curses at everyone around him.

"Rim-Sin, I think that is the *rab alani!*"

Kaida pointed at the man, and Peter saw the recognition on his face, saw the man push through the crowd. Part of him wanted to hold out his wrists and just surrender. He was so tired of running. But he couldn't give up now. He finally knew what he needed: he needed the lampstand, and he knew where to find it. He was so close to going home, back to the life of university president that awaited him. He had to get to the palace and find the treasury.

Halfway across the bridge, Kaida stopped short. Peter stumbled against her. She looked terrified. "What is it?"

"Look!" She pointed.

On the other side of the bridge, Qurdi-Marduk-lamur approached. The priest looked to be in a rage.

They were trapped.

Which way?

Better to take their chances with the *rab alani*. At least he wasn't some kind of crazed sorcerer. Peter pulled Kaida back, away from Qurdi.

"No," she said.

"We must!" The *rab alani* would at least protect them from Qurdi long enough to bring Peter to trial for the dead Jew's murder.

Kaida pulled him to the edge of the bridge. "We can jump!"

"What?"

"We can do it! Can you swim?"

Two-time all-state champion, he almost told her. But it was a long way down, and the high dive was not his event.

"You'll be hurt!" He pulled her away from the edge.

"Don't worry about me! I can do it if you can!"

She was amazing. He nodded, and they slung their legs over the wooden rail to stand on the outside of it. The foot traffic around them suddenly stopped as people watched in astonishment. Peter looked to Kaida, but she was looking down at the river. The river was dotted with boats and rafts. His fingers tightened on the rail.

Faram-Enlil struggled to get onto the bridge. The crowd was so anxious to make their way to the Old City today. He pushed and shoved, moving through the crowd like honey on a cold day. He kept to the side, as Rim-Sin and the girl had done, hoping to avoid the throngs.

A shout rose up ahead of him. Two figures climbed over the rail and perched on the edge of the bridge. Faram cursed. It was Rim-Sin and the woman.

He yelled at the people, hoping recognition would clear a path for him. What would he do if they jumped? If he went back to the river's edge, they would certainly try to swim to the Old City side, and he would only be farther away from them. He could wait in the center of the bridge to see which way they went, but then they might reverse their course. Besides, the current was swift. Faram doubted they could even make it to either side. They would probably be carried downstream and drowned before they reached the shore.

Perhaps justice would be served by the great river itself.

Peter stood nose to nose with Qurdi from his precarious hold on the outside of the rail. Despite the crowds, Qurdi had moved with amazing speed and brought his face to Peter's. Peter tried to look unafraid, but he felt himself falling into those vacant eyes. He pulled away, leaning out over the water. He really didn't want to jump.

"Rim-Sin," Qurdi said.

His voice made Peter's flesh crawl.

Qurdi placed his hands on Peter's chest, fingers spreading out across his tunic. With a long look into Peter's eyes again, he dug his fingers into the fabric, pulling Peter toward him.

A shadow seemed to pass over Qurdi's features. A voice spoke, a low voice that was not the priest's. *You are mine.* Peter's arms began to tremble. He knew that voice. It had spoken to him after he had climbed the tower.

In one smooth motion Peter brought his fists up between Qurdi's wrists and snapped his arms outward. As Qurdi's hands lost contact, Peter leaped backward. An instant later, Kaida jumped.

Peter hit the water hard. The water was shockingly cold despite the desert sun. He came up quickly and searched for Kaida. She surfaced about thirty feet from him. He had barely missed smashing onto a ship. Three other barges floated very close by, their oarsmen watching the swimmers in surprise.

Peter called out to Kaida, "Are you all right?"

She nodded. "Which way?"

Peter looked up to the bridge. Qurdi's movement through the crowd was obvious. On the other end, Peter could see nothing that indicated the *rab alani* was near. But he must be there.

Peter called out to one of the oarsmen on a nearby boat. "Help us onto your boat," he said.

The man responded by shoving an oar at him. "We will not interfere with the River Ordeal!"

Peter couldn't remember anything about a river ordeal from his study of Chaldean history, but if it was like other cultures, this could be considered a test of the gods to see if they were worthy to live. They would get no help in the river.

"How long do you think you can swim?" Peter called to Kaida.

She swam over to him. "Longer than you."

Even now she challenged him. He paddled hard against the current to stay in one place. She was obviously a strong swimmer, with a style to rival any twenty-first-century athlete. He made a note to research when the crawl stroke had appeared in history.

"We could swim north," he said, "toward the palace, and hope to lose them."

She shook her head. "That's against the current. You'd never make it."

"Downstream then. We'll let the current take us and get out when we don't see them."

She headed downstream without responding.

Boats of all types crowded the river. Peter ducked as a long oar swept over his head. It protruded from a flat-bottomed boat that looked like a floating basket made of braided rushes and covered with animal skins. Two men with oars navigated the river in it. All around him, rafts loaded with goods sailed by. Men propelled and steered them with poles. Peter and Kaida dodged and swam around the boats, staying with the current and moving away from the bridge.

The two alternately swam and floated in the Euphrates River for a long time. Their arms and the current carried them faster than their pursuers on the bank, and they soon gained separation from them. Kaida had been right about her swimming strength, but Peter would not be outdone.

Fortunately, his pride was saved by the appearance of a canal leading into the Old City. "Look." He pointed across the water. "Should we take it?"

Kaida nodded and began a faster swim toward the canal. Peter struggled to keep up. Once they reached the mouth of the canal, they let the current take them for a while.

"I need to rest," Kaida said. She crawled up on the riverbank as though she could not swim another foot.

Peter joined her, lying nearby on the bank. He eyed the street that ran parallel to the canal. The streets of Babylon would be empty at this time of the afternoon, with everyone escaping indoors from the heat. They appeared to be safe for now.

"I'm too tired to make it to the palace, Rim." Kaida stretched out on the bank. "I need to sleep."

"Sleep, Kaida. I'll watch for Qurdi."

His promise was hollow, however. With Kaida's eyes closed, Peter could watch nothing but her, the way her hair traced her cheekbone and fanned across the grass, the way her tunic outlined her body. Suddenly he thought about her tender hands holding the baby. There was a softness there, and she had let him see it. Would she ever be that tender toward him?

Qurdi had left the bridge immediately. He had been face-to-face with Rim-Sin again and yet had learned nothing of Rim-Sin's power. But the goddess had given him his prey and would surely end his life now. The River Ordeal was the discipline of the gods. No one could survive the river unless the gods chose to deliver him. And Qurdi was certain the gods would punish Rim-Sin for his actions with the king's wife. But there was always a chance…

He pulled three soldiers from the crowd in the marketplace, pointed to the river, and gave instructions. He knew they would follow through since they were looking for Rim-Sin anyway. It seemed all of Babylon had heard of Rim-Sin and Ilushu already.

Peter watched as Kaida finally awakened. She looked around and saw that the sun was low in the sky.

"I must go to the palace, Kaida. I need to find the lampstand."

"You have no right to it."

"I know. I can't explain, but I plan to send it back to Jerusalem, as Reuben intended."

Her hair was still damp, and he watched as she braided it and then loosened it again.

Kaida's brow furrowed, and she looked down the street. "I can't believe we got away from them."

"I must be doing something right." Peter picked a few blades of grass and twirled them between his fingers.

"What does that mean?"

"You know, when you do something right good things come back to you."

"Why?"

Peter sighed, wondering about the best way to explain karma to a woman from antiquity. "If you live a good life, Kaida, when you die your energy goes on at a higher level. There is a cause and effect. A circle. Eventually, your energy reaches a level at which you reunite with the one."

"So you think our only hope to go on to something better after death is based on our efforts at good living while we are here?"

"Right."

"That's foolishness, Rim! How can you know what is good living if you have no truth on which to base anything?"

He shook his head. "Do you do nothing but argue, Kaida? I liked it better when you were asleep."

She smiled that smug smile. "Perhaps you are not accustomed to being challenged. Perhaps you don't like being forced to think."

Forced to think? Who does she think she is? Peter found himself tongue-tied. The words of the success seminar came to his aid.

Your spirit merges with the spirit in everything when you have transformed your life and have shed all negative qualities.

There are no negative qualities.

Peter sighed. There it was again. How could both of those ideas be true? The whole essence of his philosophy was that he could not be judged. As part of the divine, good and bad did not exist for him. Yet the entire idea of karma was based solely on a judgment of a good or bad life. He hated to admit it, but the two were contradictory.

He threw down the grass he had been ripping into pieces. "Kaida, you push me to insanity!"

"Do I? I was hoping only to push you to think for a change!" Her tone took on that familiar sarcasm.

"Ha!"

"And one more thing. Why would you be rewarded for a good life by a force that is completely impersonal? Why does the divine consciousness care? Why would it give out rewards? By your own logic, it shouldn't matter how you'd lived, right? Right?"

"No more questions! No more! Didn't anyone ever teach you to keep your mouth shut?"

She stood, her back straight. "There is no need to be insulting, Rim. Good night. I'm going home." She marched away toward the city.

Peter shook his head. He would have liked to let her go, but he couldn't do it in good conscience.

He caught his own thoughts. In good *conscience?* What was that?

"Kaida, let's stay together. It's dangerous for you to be alone."

Peter allowed Kaida to walk thirty yards ahead of him on the dusty street. They both needed space. But he didn't intend to let her walk home alone. The sun hung low in the sky, and the city would soon be dark. He would follow her winding trek through the residential streets to Cosam's house and then drag himself back to the palace. The lampstand awaited him in the treasury, though he had no idea how he'd get it.

In the failing twilight he could still see—and enjoy—the way Kaida's braided hair swung at her back. Suddenly a voice behind him barked Rim-Sin's name.

He whirled and saw three soldiers approaching. Thinking he could bluff, he nodded gravely. "I am on my way to the temple to make a sacrifice," he said. "What is it you need?"

One of the leather-clad soldiers stepped nearer, leading with the point of his sword. "Do not move."

The other two circled him, as if unsure what tricks a fugitive diviner might conjure.

Peter glanced up the road and saw Kaida watching from the shadows of a building. He shook his head once, slowly. Did she see him? She didn't move. *Good girl.*

The two soldiers who flanked him each grabbed an arm.

"What is this about?" Peter asked.

"The king wants a word with you, diviner." The soldier flicked the point of his weapon down the street, and his escorts began to march him that direction.

"Where are you taking me?" Peter asked.

"To the palace."

Well, at least that explains how I'll get in.

Unfortunately, he'd be under guard once he got there.

You merely need to send an intention in the ultimate consciousness, and you will receive a response. Reality will become what you desire.

Oh, shut up.

The soldiers led Peter through the red vaulted archway of the palace, across the first courtyard, and to a staircase he had never seen before.

They pushed him down the steps, and the air grew musty and damp as they descended. Every ten feet a torch blazed, stuck into a hole in the wall. Somehow the darkness seemed to smother the light down here.

When they finally hit bottom, Peter could barely discern the low-ceilinged room in the darkness. The sound of dripping water echoed from somewhere far away. Clay jars of varying sizes lined the walls. It was apparently the kitchen storeroom.

They crossed the dark room, finding a small door on the other side that led to yet another room filled with stores. This wasn't the way to the throne room. Maybe he'd be spared until morning at least.

They worked their way through the storerooms, each one spilling into another. How did the slaves ever find their way out of this darkness? Would he?

The well-stocked storerooms gave way to empty stone caves, and the sound of dripping water grew louder. Peter held his breath against the fear of what might be to come. The clinking of metal stopped him cold. Ahead, the light of two torches in the walls on either side of a narrow stone passageway reflected in red and yellow splotches on the armor of a guard, standing at the end of the passage, spear in hand.

The two soldiers who held him thrust him forward into the passage. He dragged his feet over an uneven stone floor, as though the end of the journey would mean certain ruin. The heavy stones beneath, beside, and above him seemed to leech their weighty oppression into his soul. There was no chance to escape, nowhere to run in this stone dungeon. Their sandals clapped against the stones, but the sound was deadened, buried in the underground crypt.

The stone passageway widened, opening to a small room. In the torchlight Peter could see the iron bars of three different cells, shadowed and murky. Greenish mold grew on the walls of the room.

The man behind him spoke to the beefy young guard who barred their further entrance with his sword.

"The diviner, Rim-Sin. Wanted by the king."

The guard nodded once, a half-smile on his lips. "I think everyone must know why he's wanted by now."

The soldiers threw him onto the stones at the feet of the guard and left. Peter climbed to his feet.

The guard poked him with a stick. "Here's another one, Belteshazzar," he called behind him. "A friend of yours. And two in one day. The king must be furious."

Peter peered behind the guard. Belteshazzar? Was Daniel here?

A face appeared behind the iron bars and confirmed. "Rim-Sin!" Daniel said. "What has happened now?"

Peter said nothing. The guard unbarred a door in a cell next to Daniel's, shoved Peter through it, and secured it again.

Inside, Peter's eyes had to adjust to even dimmer light. Only a tiny oil lamp flickered on the side of the room. Peter felt tiny creatures scatter at his feet. Cockroaches. He shuddered.

"Get used to it," the guard said. "No doubt you'll be there awhile."

From his position in the cell beside Daniel's, he couldn't see the younger man, but Daniel's hand reached through the bars of his cage and gripped the iron bar at the side of Peter's.

Peter resisted the urge to clasp the man's hand. "What's happened to you, Daniel?"

"The king believes I was involved with one of his wives. Of course it's not true, but it's likely I will be executed nevertheless."

Peter closed his eyes and exhaled. A tickle on his neck roused him. He slapped at something black and hairy, and it flew to the floor.

"Rim-Sin—*Peter*—I had heard that your display at the Platform put the king in good favor toward you. What has happened?"

Peter leaned against the mud wall, feeling the dampness seep into his tunic. He felt strangely ashamed to admit the truth.

Abigail lingered in front of the bronze mirror. Her heart pounded in her chest. She was frightened, more frightened than she had been the day the Babylonian soldiers had poured into Jerusalem, claiming her for their king. That day she had been one of many taken to their new country, and she had been as glad to be taken as she would have been to be left behind. Jerusalem burned behind her. Most of her family had already been taken to Babylon eight years before. What was left for her?

But today she was no longer one of many. She had been

singled out by the king to do his bidding tonight.

When the guards had dragged Amyitis, the king's Median wife, to her quarters, Abigail had hurried to the hall with the other harem women to watch the unusual occurrence. The king's anger with his favorite wife only served to heighten her fear about meeting with him tonight. What if he were displeased with her? He could easily have her executed if she did not meet his expectations.

Abigail pushed shaking hands away from her table of cosmetics. There was only one thing that she was certain of in all this: the God of Israel had a plan for her life, and He would preserve her for as long as He wished. In response to this thought, she fell to her knees before her bed and laid her head on her arms. "Show me the way," she prayed. "Show me the way."

Thoughts of Akkad flooded unbidden into her mind. Akkad, so intense, so intelligent. She forced her attention away from him. How could she even allow herself to think of this man who served foreign gods? It was impossible for so many reasons. She would not be drawn into his life, no matter how much he begged her.

But there were moments, unguarded moments, when she saw him in the throne room before the king or eating in the banquet hall, when her heart told her that this was the man she had always dreamed of. And then one glance at the king would remind her of all her life had become.

She worried about Akkad with his spells and charts. So much reliance on wisdom outside of the true God. Was it truly wisdom that he listened to? Where did the answers that he found in the stars come from? Was it possible that the Lord spoke His messages through the stars as Akkad insisted his gods did?

It was too lofty for her to understand. But one thing she knew: since she had met him, she had seen Akkad surrender himself more and more fully to powers she did not trust. What would the result be?

Abigail's knees began to ache from kneeling on the floor, and she realized that her prayer had fled long ago because her mind had trailed off to follow Akkad.

"Forgive me, Lord God," she whispered. "I think of things I should not. Tonight I must think only of following Your plan for my life. I do not understand it. I must admit I do not like it. But I commit myself into Your hands, knowing that You will protect me wherever I go."

Abigail rose and headed for the door. The king would be waiting for her by now, and it was not healthy to keep the ruler of the Babylonian Empire waiting.

The representative waited for Abigail in the hall when she opened the door to leave her chambers. Was this the usual custom, or had he come to be certain that she would not fail in her new duty?

Abigail walked in front of him, conscious of his gaze on her back as the two of them drifted toward the king's chambers. Abigail was not in a hurry.

When they reached the door, the representative passed her and gave three sharp knocks. A muffled voice within beckoned, and the eunuch opened the door with the quietness of a spirit and stepped aside.

Abigail entered.

The king reclined on a raised bed, draped from above with purple linens embroidered in gold thread. He rested on a myriad of pillows, and an oil lamp beside the bed cast his face into shadows. "Enter."

Abigail took a step forward, and the door was pulled shut behind her like the door of a prison cell. She swallowed.

"Who is there?" the king asked, lifting his head only a fraction off the pillows.

"It is Abigail."

"Abigail?" The king looked confused. "Step closer."

Abigail willed her knees to stop shaking as she edged toward the bed and into the light.

"You are one of the harem."

She nodded.

"Where are you from?" Nabu-kudurri-usur asked.

"Israel, O King."

"Israel!" The king spat the word back at her. Abigail closed her eyes to the fury in his voice. "You are a Jew like Belteshazzar."

She nodded, eyes still closed, and prayed that the hot tears she felt pricking her eyelids would not spill out.

"And have you heard what your brother has done to me?" he said.

Abigail nodded again.

"The whole palace laughs at their king, I suspect." He threw his head back onto the pillows.

"No, my King," Abigail said. "No one is laughing." She spoke the truth. The palace residents feared the king's wrath too much to ridicule him, even in private.

Nabu-kudurri-usur raised his head again, studying her. "Good. That is good." He frowned again. "But still, your Jewish brother has betrayed me, and Amyitis is no longer mine."

Again, unbidden thoughts of Akkad came to her. What would the king say if he knew that another of his wives was consorting with another palace magician?

"Perhaps, O King, things are not as they appear."

"What do you mean?" The king was interested in her now, his eyes probing hers for more information. "What have you heard?"

"I have heard nothing, O King." Her voice shook, and she calmed it with her will. "But rumors seem as common as sand in the palace, and I would have expected to have heard rumors of Daniel—Belteshazzar—and Amyitis before now if they had been…"

"And there have been none of these whisperings?"

"No, O King. Belteshazzar has the utmost respect of your court. Even his enemies cannot deny his moral restraint. I have heard nothing until today when Amyitis was confined to her quarters."

The king swung his legs off the bed, bumping Abigail as he did and knocking her off-balance. She fell toward him as he stood, and he caught her against himself. He seemed to see her for the first time as he held her. Abigail looked up into the king's face, and her heart began to pound again.

Nabu-kudurri-usur pulled away but still held her by the arms. "You are beautiful for a Jewess," he said.

"Thank you," Abigail said, ignoring the embedded insult.

"Why have you not come to me before tonight?" he asked.

"The king has not asked for me until tonight."

"Foolishness on the king's part, then, was it not?"

Abigail didn't like the turn the conversation had taken. She'd been more comfortable when they'd been talking of Daniel. "Will the king question Belteshazzar about Amyitis?"

Her ploy worked. The king dropped her arms, pacing the room in his agitation. "What questions need be asked? The representative saw them together."

"I would not wish to see harm come to Amyitis because of a misunderstanding."

Nabu-kudurri-usur stopped his pacing and smirked at Abigail. "You are so concerned for another wife? That is most unusual. Or perhaps it is your precious 'Daniel' you seek to protect."

Abigail lowered her eyes in shame.

The king laughed. "You need not feel guilt. And perhaps you are right. Perhaps I should speak with them myself."

Abigail continued to study the floor, aware that the king was looking at her, but not at her face.

The day's excitement in the palace had gone unnoticed by Akkad, who had spent many hours in his chamber with the handbooks. When the first star-sign rose in the east, Akkad had already ascended to the Platform, needing time to himself before the others arrived. He waited with hands outstretched to the sky, his eyes closed, and all his power focused toward the gods. They must help him tonight.

The warm wind caressed his face as darkness fell. The sun god had descended below the earth. Night had come, and Akkad was ready. The breeze picked up. It carried a coolness and the scent of the river. He kept his hands raised toward the sky.

"Gods of the night," he whispered above him. "Hear my prayer."

Speak... they chanted back.

Akkad smiled. He was hearing their voices more often now, and it pleased him. "He must not have her."

Must not... the words echoed back to him.

Akkad took out the stones he had brought and spread them on the altar, arranging them into the sacred pattern known only to the wise men. As the stars began to appear one by one, Akkad recited the secret spells over the stones, his heart beating like a bull's-hide drum.

Night had fallen completely, and Akkad knew that Abigail was now with the king. He left the Platform and returned to the palace, but he could not remain in his chambers for long. Seeking the stars, he found his way to the Hanging Gardens, the place they had first met. He remembered the way the moonlight had lit up her face the first time he had seen her.

In his mind, he cursed the king and his many wives. He

cursed his own amulet, which even now betrayed him.

More power...

The voices were there again, beckoning him to listen to them. He didn't want to now. He wanted to think only of his anger.

You must have more power...

They were right. Only when he was the most powerful magician in the palace would he be able to gain what he wanted. If he couldn't have Abigail as his rightful wife, and if she would not consent to anything else, then he would use sorcery to gain her.

A tiny stab of guilt found its way to his heart, but he ignored it. He couldn't live without Abigail, and he couldn't live if she belonged to the king.

Abigail lay on her back on the bed, studying the ceiling above her. She couldn't sleep, though she'd returned from the king's chamber hours earlier.

She had been humiliated to open the door and find the representative standing beside it. Was that customary also? Did he always wait for the king to finish with his wives? As the eunuch walked behind her back to her chambers, she wondered if he was questioning the amount of time she had spent with the king.

She replayed the meeting in her mind for the hundredth time. Had she said or done anything that, when he had time for further reflection, would displease him? Would he summon her tomorrow, angry about the things she had dared to say?

When she had reached her own room, she had collapsed in weary relief onto her bed, tears flowing as she thanked the Lord for preserving her, at least for this night. The king's thoughts had been only of Amyitis tonight, and after Abigail's suggestions he had only wanted to be alone. He had sent her back to her chambers immediately after their conversation.

Akkad would be pleased, she knew. She tried to force her mind away from him. Why did everything always return to thoughts of him? She knew he wanted to keep her from the king, but only so she could be his, and that was something she would never allow, not as long as she was the king's wife. Still, she could not help but dream of a different life. One in which Akkad served the God of Israel, and she was free.

But that was not to be. And tomorrow, when Akkad found a way to see her, as she was certain he would, she would tell him so. They must not see each other again.

No one bothered Peter or Daniel for many hours. The guard shoved a meal through the bars, listened to their conversation with some interest, and occasionally threw in a coarse joke. Peter observed Daniel's easy way with the guard Kerkuk, almost a camaraderie, and marveled at how the most likable man he'd ever met seemed to be hated by nearly everyone in his life.

When Peter and Daniel talked, they spoke of the political intrigue of the court at first, but the conversation eventually moved to Peter's dream and Daniel's interpretation of it.

"So then you have not yet completed Reuben's task?" Daniel asked.

Peter sat in the muck, his back to the wall that adjoined Daniel's cell. He imagined the young Hebrew sitting in the same position on the other side of the wall.

"I'm very close. I know that Reuben intended to send the lampstand back to Jerusalem. I know that the lampstand is here in the palace treasury. But I don't know how to get out of here and finish what I must do to get home."

There was silence from the other cell for a few moments. "The Lord has not given me to know why Babylon is not home to you. But I see that you are eager to return home, and I understand that feeling."

Peter leaned his head against the wall. He had stopped caring about the dampness and filth hours ago. "I have a life waiting for me there. I am about to be given a position of honor."

"Ah, yes. Always the position of honor."

Peter swept a hand at an itch on his leg. It was too dark to see whether all the twitches and tickling feelings were real or imagined cockroaches, but he wasn't taking any chances. "Have your voices told you whether I'm going to get out of here alive, Daniel?"

"My voices—"

"I know, I know. Your God. Sorry."

"You still do not acknowledge His call on your life. But you must if you are to leave here prepared for the work He has for you to do once you are home."

Peter folded his arms. "I think I've jumped through enough hoops here. I don't have any intention of doing anything similar once I get home."

"If you simply complete Reuben's task but do not submit to God and defeat the powers arrayed against you, Peter, you will leave this place with something very important unfinished. Something you will regret."

More riddles. "I still don't even know how I will get home, Daniel. Do I just send the lampstand off to Jerusalem? Should I put it on the nearest camel headed that way? Or do I have to take it there myself?"

Daniel was silent, then said, "I will pray for wisdom on this matter."

Peter left him alone to say his prayers. And for once he hoped someone was listening.

Chapter 13

AKKAD MOVED THROUGH the hall where the harem was chambered. He knew which room was hers, though he had never entered. It was still the dark hours of early morning. He knocked quietly on the door and was relieved when Abigail opened it softly. At least she was here and not with the king.

Her eyes widened when she saw his face through the crack. "Akkad! What are you doing?"

"Let me in, Abigail."

She hesitated a moment, as if she wanted to refuse, but then she opened the door wider and allowed him to enter. As he turned back to her, she leaned her head out the door, scanning the hall in both directions. She nudged the door closed and turned to him.

"You should not be here!" she said.

He took her into his arms. She resisted only a moment.

"What happened last night?" he asked, bracing himself to hear the truth.

She shook her head. "Akkad, you must leave. You and I—we cannot be together. I am the king's wife. I cannot be yours."

"I don't care about the king!"

"You must care!" she said. Her features softened. "You must care, if only for me, Akkad. I don't want to see harm come to you."

"Harm will only come to me if I cannot have you!"

Abigail pulled away. "You speak foolishness, Akkad. You must think. You are one of the king's trusted advisors. You have intelligence, position, and respect. You cannot throw all of that away for something impossible."

"It doesn't have to be impossible, Abigail."

"No!" She faced him, eyes flashing. "I am telling you no, Akkad. We cannot be together. I will not betray the king, even if you are willing to do so."

Akkad turned away, fists clenched. "So then, he has won you. One night with him and he has won you."

"You hurt me, Akkad," she said. "You know how I feel about you. And about him."

He returned to her, embracing her again. "Tell me."

Abigail closed her eyes. "Stop, Akkad."

"Tell me."

A tiny cry escaped her lips before she dropped her head to his chest. "I love you," she said against the folds of his robes. "I love you. But it cannot be."

Akkad clutched her to himself, unwilling to hear anything but what he had wanted to hear for so long. He stroked her hair, glorying in the moment.

"He sent me back," she said, her face still buried against his chest. "He only spoke with me awhile. He never...we didn't...we only talked. And then he sent me back."

Akkad smiled over the top of her head, lifting a silent prayer of praise to the gods. They had heard him after all.

Akkad crept from Abigail's room, taking care not to be seen. Her confessions had lifted the weight from his heart. Akkad would not allow himself to be discouraged by her dedication to the laws of her God. His gods were as powerful, and now that he was certain she loved him, he would find a way to make her his own. He refused to acknowledge that he had taken on the king as an adversary. Perhaps he could not be the only one Abigail gave herself to, but he now knew he desired at least to be the first.

Later, in the courtyard outside his own chamber, the diviner Shamash caught up with him again. "The king is desirous to have all *kasdim* in the throne room this morning, Akkad."

Akkad nodded and changed course to follow Shamash.

When they arrived, Akkad looked around the spacious hall. Qurdi-Marduk-lamur leaned one shoulder against the wall at the side of the room, arms folded across his chest.

The king was on his throne, looking upset. "I wish to speak to the wise men," the king called out. "All others, leave the room."

Akkad waited as the officials and palace staff filed out, then took his place toward the back of the group of wise men standing before the awesome throne. Had the king dreamed a dream in the night that needed interpretation?

Nabu-kudurri-usur leaned back on his throne, crossed his arms, and scowled at the men who waited below him. "You have all heard by now of the difficulty with Amyitis, I am certain."

Heads bobbed.

"The omens warned of their treachery, but I wish to know why the counter-spells and sacrifices did nothing to defeat this evil."

Their eyes dropped to the floor. Several sorcerers shifted to look at each other, as if trying to find someone to blame.

The king hooked a finger into the amulet he wore around his neck, and Akkad swallowed hard. "This new amulet was to give me success with my wives. I do not consider a wife's betrayal a success."

Akkad's pulse quickened.

Nabu-kudurri-usur surveyed the group with disdain. "Who will explain to me why Amyitis has betrayed me with the Jew?"

Several astrologers turned to Akkad.

"Akkad made your amulet, O King," Shamash said. "He must explain the failure of his amulet."

Akkad narrowed his eyes at the older man. There was no loyalty, not even among their circle.

The king yanked the amulet from his neck and tossed it into the group of men. Shamash caught it and held it up for all to see.

"What is it?" a diviner asked. "What is the pattern there?"

"I have never seen this pattern," another said.

"Akkad, why did you not follow the handbook?"

Akkad sucked in air and looked at the king, who also waited for an explanation.

"It's a new charm," he said, "a better amulet for the king, to give him greater success with his wives."

The astrologers, diviners, and magicians broke into laughter at Akkad's claim.

"Can you make one for me, Akkad?" one sarcastic magician called out.

"Silence!" The king's shout echoed off the walls. Nabukudurri-usur stared at Akkad. "Akkad, what is the reason for this new amulet?"

"O King, I sought only to give you greater success. The pattern was suggested to me by the gods themselves, and I was certain that this was the amulet they desired you to wear."

The king seemed to contemplate this for a moment. "Give the amulet to Akkad," he said to Shamash. The older man flung it into Akkad's face. "Fix it," the king said simply.

"Yes, O King," Akkad said.

No one moved.

"Without delay!"

As Akkad hurried to his chambers for his box of shells, several of his circle caught up with him.

"You avoided the furnace this time, Akkad," they said. "Next time the gods will not spare you."

Akkad ignored them and hastened on. He closed the door behind him as though he could keep out the wolves, and for a few moments he simply breathed.

How could this have happened? He looked at the amulet in his hand. He had been so certain it would work. The dark words of the counter-spell drifted across his mind. Of course! He had cursed the amulet so that the king would not pursue Abigail. His spell had been so effective there had been implications with other wives as well!

A surge of secret pride swept through him. His colleague was right, he had been lucky to avoid the furnace, but he had also never felt so powerful. The voices that had spoken to him had truly given the power they had promised. His spoken word alone had brought havoc to the palace. Amyitis had betrayed the king with a Jew. Belteshazzar would not have long to live.

He laid the amulet on a small table and flexed his fingers. He had succeeded in becoming more powerful than he had imagined. The only problem was that all his colleagues, even the king himself, considered him an utter failure, and he couldn't explain the truth to them. What could be done about that?

He hesitated only a moment. He was finally learning where the source of his power lay. He gave his mind to the voices, laying his will at their feet and entreating them for wisdom.

Akkad sought the stars again. Questions about the power behind their movements no longer troubled him. The gods were out there; he had spoken with them himself. Perhaps they were the stars themselves. Perhaps they only pushed the stars along their courses, tracing their messages in the heavens. Either way, Akkad knew that they had smiled down upon him. He was a favored one among favored ones. He would soon have everything he sought.

He waited now at the uppermost tier of the Hanging Gardens. Abigail would be here any moment. She was the one person to whom he could reveal the truth about the amulet and the strength of his counter-spell. Surely she would see the power the gods had given him.

He spotted her tiny figure below long before she saw him. He watched her climb the tiers, knowing she would soon be his. When she was close enough, he whispered her name.

"Abigail."

Her eyes darted up to his hiding place. "Where are you?"

"Here." He emerged from behind a shrub.

"Akkad!" Her voice carried a mixture of fear and relief. She ran to him.

"I thought you would never arrive." Akkad smiled, taking her hand in his.

"I came as soon as I could. Akkad, I am worried about you."

"Why?"

"How can you ask that? Everyone is talking about the failure of the amulet you made the king. They are saying that you purposely changed it to bring harm upon him."

Akkad scowled. "They are not exactly correct."

"What have you done, Akkad?"

"The amulet is a powerful charm, so powerful that I feared for you."

"For me?"

"I did not want him to call for you, Abigail."

She looked away.

"I performed a counter-spell to release him from the magic of the amulet. It would appear that I performed my task so well that it worked on other wives as well."

"Oh, Akkad!"

"Do not fear, Abigail, I will make it right again."

She shook her head. "I don't fear what the king can do to you,

Akkad. I'm afraid of what you're becoming. You're so dedicated to the gods you serve, you don't see that they're false."

"How can you say that when you see the power they have given me, Abigail?"

"Any power you have received has only come from the evil one, Akkad. The true God does not work in spells and charms."

Evil one? Akkad grew frustrated with the conversation. Talk of the gods was not the reason he had wanted to meet her here tonight.

"Abigail, we must talk about what we are to do."

"About what?"

"About us. I cannot go on like this, having only a few stolen moments with you in hallways and here in the Gardens. We must find a way."

Abigail stood. "I've already told you, Akkad. And I won't change my mind. This is all we will ever have. Nothing more. And I don't feel that even these brief meetings should continue. It only makes it harder—for both of us. I am the king's wife, Akkad. I am the king's wife." She pulled away from him and hurried out of the Gardens.

Akkad raised his eyes back to the stars.

Qurdi enjoyed the relative solitude of the temple today as the barber carefully shaved his head with a long-handled knife. Warad-Sin was gone, the *naditum* priestesses served the goddess now, and the prostitutes were in their quarters. He had the goddess's estate business to attend to later, but for now he could think. The clinking of the barber's knife in the water basin echoed through the chamber.

No one had learned of Qurdi's sacrifice at the High Temple. The flames had completely consumed the slave's flesh, and he and Warad-Sin had scattered the bones in the street for the dogs.

It had been worth the risk. The goddess had favored him. Belteshazzar was imprisoned, where he could be dealt with before he had a chance to explain the situation with Amyitis. And although the River Ordeal hadn't killed him, Rim-Sin had been imprisoned for the very same crime. Truly Qurdi had been favored.

All that remained was to go to the palace prison, extract Rim-Sin's secret, and kill them both. He would be as powerful as Rim-Sin, and when both he and Belteshazzar were disposed of, Qurdi would be ready to take his deserved place as chief of magicians. He was very close.

Cosam patted Kaida's back and tried to think of something to say. They were sitting in Cosam's courtyard eating a light morning meal. The house was still cool. The girl had returned last night distraught over the arrest of Rim-Sin, and this morning was no happier. It made no sense to Cosam.

He didn't have long to puzzle over it. Just then two armed guards pushed their way into the family's courtyard and called his name.

Rebekah came into the courtyard holding the babies, with little Hannah following behind. Cosam spread his arms, keeping his small family behind him. "What is the reason for this intrusion?"

"The people of the city denounce you," one of the guards said. "You are being charged with speaking against the gods and the king."

"I haven't—"

"You have been seen in the company of the Jews Ahab and Zedekiah, shouting their prophecies against the king with them."

"No! I'm one of the only ones speaking *against* Ahab and Zed—"

"We care nothing for your defense, Jew. Speak to the king—if you are given opportunity."

The second guard circled Cosam and studied the babies in Rebekah's arms. "Twins?" he said. "Boys or girls?"

Cosam stepped between the guard and Rebekah. "Two boys."

"Perhaps you are innocent, then, if the gods favor you with two sons." He looked at the babies again and squinted. He pointed to the Babylonian baby they had named Isaac. "Although this one does not have the Jewish look about him."

Cosam took several quick steps away from Rebekah. "I will not be arrested like a common thief!" he shouted, acting as though he might run.

The two guards were on him at once. They grabbed his arms and hauled him toward the door. Cosam mouthed an "I love you" to Rebekah and was yanked into the bright morning.

The streets were busy with the morning foot traffic. The people made way for the guards and their captive, but beyond that they didn't seem to take notice. There was a haze hanging over the city. Smoke from cooking fires and very little wind. The top of the tower was indistinct from this distance.

At a crossroads they were joined by four more guards. They brought with them two other Jewish captives.

"Ahab! Zedekiah!" Cosam said.

The two men had been beaten. Purple bruises swelled Ahab's eye, and blood streamed down Zedekiah's face. Cosam remembered Jeremiah's prophecy about the two men. He had never imagined that he would be pulled in to face destruction with them.

Peter wished for a pen and paper. Daniel had prayed for wisdom about how Peter was supposed to complete Reuben's task. He must have received an answer, because right now he was spouting out specific instructions.

"You are to follow the way of our forefather Joseph," Daniel said, his voice animated, "but you must follow it from end to beginning. That is how the lampstand will be returned to our land. Reuben's task must be completed before the New Year Festival begins. You have only a few days. Before the Festival begins you must go to the king's Gardens. You must bring the object that brought you here. You must cleanse yourself of this place, and you must ask the God of Israel to return you to your home."

Daniel fell silent.

"Isn't there more?" Peter asked.

"That is all I was given to know."

The way of Joseph. The object that brought me here. Cleanse myself. For now, Peter concentrated only on remembering it. He would figure it out later—if he ever got out of this place.

"Well... thank you, Daniel. That's a lot more than I had." He struggled with the next words. "And... thank your God for me, I suppose."

Daniel's smile penetrated even the dark cell. "Why not thank Him yourself?"

Shouting filtered to them through the dim passageway. Peter got to his feet, curious. Kerkuk stood with his back to their cells, sword drawn.

Soldiers appeared, several men in tow. "More Jews," they said to the guard. "Where do you want them?"

Kerkuk sheathed his sword and glanced backward at Peter. "Put them with the other Jew," he said, and removed the bar from Daniel's cell.

The soldiers pushed forward and shoved their captives through the doorway of the cell.

Cosam! Peter gripped the bars of his cell but said nothing.

Cosam's eyes met his, though he did not appear as surprised to see Peter.

The soldiers went back the way they'd come. Kerkuk laughed and settled back down on the knee-high stone bench built into the side wall of his tiny chamber. "You can have yourselves a Jew party in there now," he said. He nodded at Peter. "I chose not to disrespect you, Rim-Sin, by putting them in your cell."

Peter nodded back and tried to smile in gratitude. He went to the front corner of his cell. "What has happened, Cosam?" he whispered.

"Ahab and Zedekiah are imprisoned for their words against the king. I have been seen speaking with them in public, and it is mistakenly believed that I share their views." Cosam's voice was very close. "Kaida is much concerned for you, Rim-Sin. Are you hurt?"

Peter tried to answer, but his voice caught. He cleared his throat. "I am well, Cosam."

Daniel spoke to his new cellmates. "What news is there of our people, brothers?"

Cosam turned from his place at the corner of the cell where he spoke to Rim-Sin and squinted into the darkness of the cell. "I am Cosam," he said, "son of Elmadam. What is your name?"

The man crawled forward, his features barely visible in the sputtering lamplight. "Brothers, it is I, Daniel!"

"Daniel!" Cosam gripped the younger man's arms as though he and the chief of magicians were dear friends.

"What have you said against the king, Cosam?" Daniel asked.

"I have not spoken against the king himself, only against his gods. In fact, I have agreed with Jeremiah that we should pray for the prosperity of the king and his city. But the people are still so quick to bow at the feet of the graven images. I challenge them to turn from their idolatry and return to the Law."

"Good, Cosam. This is good. I am glad to know that there are those who speak for God." He turned to Zedekiah and Ahab. "And you, do you also speak against the Chaldean gods?"

Zedekiah answered for both of them. "We care nothing for the gods. But we have prophesied to the people that the Lord will deliver us."

"Yes, He shall," Daniel said. "Blessed be His name."

Cosam interjected. "Daniel, they tell the people that our bondage to Nebuchadnezzar will be ended before two years are finished."

Daniel frowned at them. "Is this true?"

Zedekiah dabbed a rag at the wound to his forehead. "It is what the Most High has said to us."

Daniel's tone showed he disagreed. "Then you ignore the word of the Lord through the prophet Jeremiah, and you prophesy falsely, brothers."

Ahab clenched his fists.

"The Lord has given us seventy years of distress," Daniel said, "that we might be found again in Him. *This* is what the Most High has truly said."

The two looked away.

Cosam and Daniel discussed how best to keep the Law in the time of captivity. Cosam had heard nothing from Rim-Sin in some time, and he assumed the diviner slept. Though Daniel was not considered a prophet, it was well known that God had granted him great wisdom in the court of Nebuchadnezzar.

"You do well to adhere to the Law, Cosam," Daniel was saying. "But remember that no man is able to keep it fully. That is why the sacrifice is necessary."

"But some men come closer than others, Daniel!" Cosam said, laughing.

Daniel smiled with him. "Yes, some keep more of the Law, some keep less. But all are guilty before God."

Cosam frowned. "Then why keep the Law at all?"

"Ah, it is a good question. The Law is a lesson, Cosam. A lesson I fear we have not yet learned."

"What is this lesson?"

Daniel and Cosam had moved away from the two false prophets to speak alone. "The lesson of the Law, Cosam, is that God is holy. We have been set aside, our little nation, to learn among the heathens that the Lord our God is one God, and there are no others. We have yet to learn it, or else we would not be here. This exile is God's punishment for our nation's idolatry, Cosam. But we must also learn what the Law teaches us, that no man is able to satisfy the holiness of God, no matter how much of the Law he is able to keep."

Cosam nodded. "For this we have the sacrifice."

"For now. But one day the Redeemer will come to save us all, and the sacrifice will not be necessary."

"You speak of the Messiah?" Cosam asked. "Mishael spoke to me of this. It is not a thing I know much of."

"Messiah is coming, Cosam," Daniel said. "He alone will be able to fully atone for our sin."

"When will the Messiah come, Daniel?"

"No man knows that answer, my friend. But we must remain faithful, trusting that He will come."

Chapter 14

IT WAS FINISHED. The golden image of Babylon's favored son, towering outside her city walls, was finally complete. As tall as nearly twenty men, it looked down upon the city's inhabitants with regal arrogance, a perfect golden version of the king himself, with his square-cut beard and wavy shoulder-length hair. The image had been fashioned with one arm crossed over its chest, fist over heart. When the sun struck it at a certain angle, the statue could blind the eyes of its subjects, forcing them to duck their heads in obeisance.

Babylon opened her gates to pour her people out onto the plain where they could better see the dedication. Satraps, prefects, and governors had all assembled before the image, ready to pay honor to it when the signal was given. Every one of her officials was there, along with many of her ordinary citizens who had been anxious to join the celebration. Conspicuously absent were the Jews, excepting their governors, who were required to attend. It was just as well. She had tried relentlessly to absorb these Jews, to make them part of her, but they refused to be digested. One day, she would spit them out.

The people streamed down the sandy road out of her, pouring over the desert like barley from a sack and forming two fields on either side of the road. Their arms were raised, waving in unison like heads of grain in the breeze. Nabu-kudurri-usur came last, driven down the road in his royal chariot, his hand raised to her people.

She was satisfied.

Musicians carried their instruments through the noisy crowds, pushing their way to the platform. When they ringed three sides of the image, the king mounted the steps to the platform.

"My people!" he shouted. His voice carried in the gritty wind. "Behold, your king!" He raised a hand to the image.

A great shout went up from the people. Some of them fell prostrate already, anxious to please.

He lifted both hands to the sky, waiting until they quieted before him. "No longer must you be content with mere glimpses of your king, which can never satisfy!" He dropped his arms and lifted his face upward to the statue. "The likeness you see before you will be to you as I am. I will watch over you from its lofty height, will bless you even as I stand guard." He gazed down on the field of his people again. "When you worship this golden image of me, you are worshiping me. When you honor it, you honor me!" His voice rose to a shout. "When you fall before the image, you fall before me!"

The musicians raised their instruments.

"Each day," the king said, "when you hear the sound of the horn, flute, lyre, trigon, psaltery, bagpipe, and all kinds of music, you will fall and worship the golden image. For your king is a son of the gods!"

Another shout from the people. The king spread his arms to the musicians. One long blast of the horn, and then the symphony began. The people fell to their knees as though a sickle had hewn them down, arms outstretched in the sand before them, their chants rising in the wind and blowing back into the city.

At the edge of the crowd, three lone stalks of grain remained upright.

Akkad allowed himself to be pulled into the flow of worshipers who poured from the city out onto the plain before the giant statue. He searched the crowd for any sign of Abigail. She would not be here unless she had been forced to come, he knew, but there was a chance. The royal entourage had followed the king, and Akkad had scanned the faces of each person in the chariots, but hers was not among them.

When the wind carried the king's speech to his ears, Akkad raised his hands, along with those around him, but his eyes still searched for Abigail. The music began to play, and the people around him fell to the ground. Akkad fell with them, but his heart recited no prayers of honor to the king. While the people still prostrated themselves before the image, Akkad dared to raise his head.

The citizens of Babylon are sheep.

He wondered where that thought had come from. But the image lodged in his mind, and he saw the whole plain of people flocking around the idol like a herd of senseless animals, driven only by their basest instincts of self-indulgence.

Movement not far from him at the edge of the crowd caught his attention. Three men stood straight amidst the bowed crowd, and others around them attempted to pull them to their knees. The three had locked their eyes on the king, as if daring him to notice them.

Akkad recognized Belteshazzar's three Hebrew friends. They had wormed their way into palace government as Belteshazzar had. What were they thinking, defying the king's command like this? So far, though, the king did not seem to notice. Surely someone would tell him. Such secrets had a way of finding their way to the king's ears.

His eyes were pulled to the three young Hebrews. There was nothing of the mindless obedience in their faces that was in all the others who groveled around them. Instead, Akkad saw intelligence, hammered into raw courage by resolute faith.

Jealousy stabbed at him. Akkad turned his eyes away and refused to watch them through the rest of the ceremony. When it was over and the crowds turned back toward the city, Akkad walked alone.

The two guards returned to the underground prison. Cosam, Ahab, and Zedekiah were yanked from the cell, and Daniel was left behind. He lifted his hand in a silent farewell, and Cosam wondered if Daniel would die in the cell. He saw Rim-Sin watching with dark eyes through the bars of his cell, anger written on his face.

In the throne room, the three were dragged before the king. "Ah, the agitators," the king said. "Pity you were not at the dedication earlier. You would have been given a chance to show your repentance by worshiping your divine king alongside every other citizen of Babylon."

The guards pushed the three to their knees before the king's throne.

"I am told that you insist your God will deliver you Jews from my rule within months."

An official at the side of the throne room spoke up. "O King, live forever, only these two have said these things. The other tells the people not to worship the gods of the king."

Nebuchadnezzar looked down on Cosam. "Is this true?"

"O King," Cosam said, his insides quivering, "I do not tell my people to defy you as king. But I do tell them to worship the God of Israel alone."

The king pursed his lips, but then broke into a smile. "These Jews are funny, are they not?" He spoke to the throne room as a whole. Officials and advisors offered their laughter. "They insist on only one God. But I am of the mind that more is better, don't you think?"

Nods and agreements came from around the room.

"It does no harm, I suppose, to let them have their one God." The king's face darkened. "But I will not have them suggesting that their one God will bring about my downfall." He pointed to Zedekiah and Ahab. "Take these two to the furnace and execute them." He looked at Cosam. "Take him, too, and let him watch before he is released. Perhaps when the Hebrews hear how rebellion is dealt with they will not be so eager to talk amongst themselves."

The guards dragged out Zedekiah and Ahab, pulling Cosam along with them.

The largest of the city furnaces lay only a short distance from the palace, in a wide brick enclosure filled with slaves who had been charged with the loathsome task of brick-making. The furnaces themselves were built like small, flat-roofed brick homes scattered through the enclosure, each with a door and a small chimney. The fire inside the largest of these blazed white-hot from the charcoal the slaves fed into it. Around the furnace, slaves formed perfect mud bricks, lining them up on the platform above the furnace to be baked solid in the intense heat.

Cosam was dragged along to watch in horror as the guards forced Zedekiah and Ahab through the street and up to the furnace, and then without pause heaved them in.

Peter awoke with a jolt, feeling a strange heaviness in his chest. He didn't know how long he had dozed on the floor of his cell. Day and night had merged into sameness in the murky darkness, and he had lost track of the time. Days? Hours? How much time had passed since he had been brought here? How long until the New Year Festival? Was Cosam dead? Did Daniel still reside in the cell beside him?

He inhaled deeply, trying to remove the oppressive feeling in his chest. But it would not dissipate. He propped himself on his elbows and looked toward his ever-present guard.

In his place stood Qurdi-Marduk-lamur.

Peter pulled himself to his feet, grateful for the iron bars between them but wishing the guard's usual sword was trained on the high priest. There was a stirring in the cell beside him. Did Daniel feel the oppression, too?

Peter watched Qurdi's eyes flick toward Daniel's cell, watched the smirk grow on his face.

"Both of you together," he said. "My two rivals for the position I must have—in prison and at my mercy. Who can say that the goddess does not favor me above all others?"

Peter assumed that Daniel listened beside him, but the younger man did not speak.

A strange fire burned in Qurdi's eyes, one that frightened Peter. "I will begin with you, Rim-Sin." His eyes sought Daniel's. "But I will end with you."

Qurdi moved forward, and Peter took a step backward in his cell. As he did, he saw the guard lying prone on the floor at Qurdi's feet. He couldn't tell if the guard was dead or only unconscious.

"What do you want, Qurdi?" Peter knew he was not safe behind the bars. Qurdi had only to unlock the door, and there would be nothing between them. He calculated whether he could overpower the high priest with no weapon.

Qurdi was laughing. "Do not be a fool, Rim-Sin. Since the day you killed that Jew I have known that you found the object of power we both seek. Something that will allow you to outshine all other priests and diviners." He wrapped bony fingers around the bars of Peter's cell. "I want to know what it is."

"I've told you, Qurdi, I have found nothing." The lampstand? Was that what he wanted? Was that what Rim-Sin was after? There was no way Peter was going to give Qurdi the lampstand's location. It was his ticket home.

Qurdi raised his arms and threw back his head, surprising Peter. With his eyes closed, he began a muttered prayer.

"What are you doing?" Peter asked, hoping to break his concentration. It worked. Qurdi lowered his head to stare at Peter.

"You know the power of the prayer I recite, Rim-Sin. I ask the goddess to destroy you. To begin with your heart, your liver, your stomach. To turn everything inside you to mere blood and water, and to consume you for her pleasure." Qurdi's eyes sparked, and his head tilted backward again.

Peter found his breath coming in short gasps. His stomach roiled. The ridiculousness of the threat evaporated. The heaviness on his chest gave way to a weakness everywhere that threatened to bring him to his knees. He put a hand out to the wall.

"Qurdi!" The voice was a shout from the other cell.

Peter swallowed, wondering if Daniel was his only chance to survive.

A strange wind seemed to whistle through the underground prison. In the hollow of the wall behind him Peter's lamp flickered and went out. An oily smell filled the cage. Bile filled his throat.

Qurdi's arms were still raised above him, and now his words filled the room, a rhythmic chant that echoed in Peter's chest.

Daniel's voice rose above the chants. "Qurdi-Marduk-lamur!"

Qurdi lowered his head and looked at Daniel. Peter felt a sharp reprieve in the crushing weight on his chest.

"I will deal with you presently, Belteshazzar," Qurdi said. "First Rim-Sin. Then you."

"You have no power here except that which the Lord of Hosts

allows! And He will not allow you to harm this man!"

Qurdi's lips twisted into a feral snarl. His fingers curled as he clawed his own clothes. "Yaaaahh-weeehhh!" His voice was a guttural hiss, the same unnatural voice Peter had heard on the bridge.

Peter panted, feeling the pain in his chest again, the weakening inside of him. The fear came only partly from the physical pain he endured. A deeper terror prevailed. It was not Qurdi who spoke now from inside the body of the high priest. Peter knew that somehow he faced the goddess Ishtar herself. The knowledge proved too much for his numbing limbs. He sank to the mucky ground, fell on his face before Ishtar.

The goddess spoke again, her voice like a spreading poison in his mind. "Yahweh cannot take this one from me. He is mine. He has given himself to me!"

Peter burrowed his forehead into the mud, covered his head with his forearms.

Daniel shouted beside him. "He has given himself in ignorance! The God of Abraham, Isaac, and Jacob has not given him over to you! You may not have him!"

The walls of the cell seemed to shake with the echo of Daniel's pronouncement. Peter felt the conflict of powers in the air around him. Real personified powers, not some vague cosmic consciousness. Then with an almost audible *whoosh* he felt something leave the room as though a foul odor had been sucked out. He lifted his head to face Qurdi again. The high priest was frightening, though not as much as the presence that had just left.

Qurdi reached under his robes and pulled out a long dagger. "The two of you have cursed me long enough," he said. "It will end today." He took a step toward Peter's cell.

Peter jumped to his feet and backed away from the bars. From the cell beside him, a low sound began and then swelled. Daniel was singing.

Qurdi paused, his hand on the bar of Peter's cell. He watched Daniel. The song went on.

Daniel sang of Israel's God and His mighty acts in battle. Of His protection of His people. Of His great love and faithfulness.

Qurdi remained unmoving as the song grew and the words tumbled over one another in unending praise to Daniel's one God.

Peter's eyes grew misty. Hot tears spilled onto his cheeks. He ignored them, barely aware that he wept. Peter could almost believe that Qurdi wept, too. Tears for the love of a God that changes never, whose love endures. The song ended, its last notes fading into the darkness.

The knife clattered against the iron bars and fell into the mud.

Qurdi turned and fled.

Qurdi-Marduk-lamur had long been a mystery to Akkad, even though he was his mother's brother. He knew that the priest was intensely devoted to Ishtar, but the diviner's actions always seemed rooted in anger, as though he sought to control the world and could not understand why it had not been given to him. But that made him the person for Akkad to consult about his recent problems with spells and counter-spells, in spite of the priest's hatred for Akkad's mentor, Rim-Sin.

He found Qurdi in the temple.

The older diviner scowled at him. "I am indisposed, boy."

Qurdi seemed distraught, now that Akkad stopped to notice. His robes were askew, and he sat on the flagstones of the temple. His cheeks were flushed, too, and his voice sounded raw. He'd never seen his uncle this unhinged.

Finally Qurdi seemed to gather himself. He turned those black eyes onto Akkad. "What do you want?"

"I wish to consult with you, Uncle," Akkad said.

Qurdi smirked. "I wondered how long it would be until you came to me for more favors. I am not surprised it is now, after the king's disapproval. I only hope that he does not soon remember it was I who asked for you to be considered for the palace *kasdim*."

Akkad ignored the self-serving comment. "There is a problem I need your help with, Qurdi, but it demands secrecy."

Qurdi's lip curled into a sneer. "The young Akkad makes demands of me?"

Akkad's face fell. He had hoped to unburden himself to at least one person.

"What is it?" Qurdi asked.

But Akkad did not know if he should trust him, so he remained silent.

The older man seemed to reconsider. "Come, Akkad," he said. "Come to my chamber where we can speak privately. I am certain I can help with whatever problem you are having."

An hour later Qurdi watched Akkad leave the temple courtyard. Jealousy gripped him. Would this foolish boy be his next competitor? Qurdi had been surprised to hear of the power that had been given Akkad and his counter-spell. Qurdi had no respect for the boy, but the power... it could not be disregarded. He would use that power.

Qurdi refused to acknowledge even to himself that he had just sent a boy to do what he himself could not accomplish. Fear had driven him from the underground prison. The combined magic of Belteshazzar and Rim-Sin had been too much for him. He did not want to descend to that place again. Could Akkad's power prevail?

He had whispered secret things into the young astrologer's ear.

Ways to draw down more power until he could have anything he wanted. A more powerful spell, Akkad had said. He wanted to give the king success with Amyitis and his other wives, so that the amulet would not be suspected, but he wanted the king to refuse Abigail. A very specific spell, and it would take more power than he had thus far discovered to accomplish it. Qurdi knew of only one way. The voices that spoke to Qurdi as well had pointed fingers at the enemy. And enemies must be destroyed. Belteshazzar must die.

It was not only desire for the Jew's position that drove Qurdi against him. The voices had told him all along that all Jews were a threat to the very kingdom. They had come as conquered people, but one day they would raise up a ruler whose throne would encompass the world. That must not be allowed to happen. He'd had the false prophets burned and the chief of magicians caught with the favorite wife. Belteshazzar would soon be dead, but still more had to be done to destroy them.

The answer had fallen in his lap when one of his slaves had commented on the dedication ceremony for the image of the king. Apparently the king did not know of the three who had not bowed. But he would. Their own foolish worship of Yahweh would prove the doom of every Jew in Babylon. Qurdi smiled.

And if Akkad succeeded in his task, the way would lie open before Qurdi as never before.

Akkad crept through the underground storerooms, trying to keep his sense of direction as he searched for the cell where Belteshazzar was held. The slim knife he had sheathed under his tunic and robes felt as though it were burning through his leg. He prayed to the gods for courage.

When Qurdi had first suggested this method of drawing

down power, Akkad had resisted. He had never physically harmed anyone in pursuit of magic, and the prospect did not please him. But later, as he had lain on his bed and gazed out into the night, the voices had come again and assured him that the Jew was not worthy of life, and that they would be gratified to see him invited to his one God.

And so Akkad stumbled through the dank rooms, not knowing how he would accomplish the deed once he found the man.

A light flickering ahead gave him hope and dread at the same time. A few more paces, and the torch illuminated the guard posted outside the cell reserved for crimes against the king. The gods smiled on Akkad: the guard slept.

Akkad stepped to the prone man's side. The cell key lay beside him on the stone bench. Akkad reached across the guard's body for it and lifted it slowly.

The hem of his wide sleeve brushed the guard's face.

Akkad held his breath. The guard did not move. Only then did Akkad realize the sleep seemed an unnatural one. It covered the guard like a woolen blanket. Surely the work of the gods. Again, Akkad felt confirmed in his actions.

He glanced into the cell on his right. A man huddled asleep in the corner, his legs drawn up with his arms wrapped around them, feeble protection against the other living things that also made the cell their home. It was Rim-Sin, his mentor.

Akkad entered the other cell, hands trembling.

The chief of magicians stirred and looked up. "Akkad, isn't it?" Belteshazzar seemed uncertain. "Yes. The amulet. I remember." He leaned forward. "Has your amulet failed, Akkad? Is that why they have sent you on this errand?"

Akkad shook his head, his hand reaching under his robe. He could feel the knife, still strapped beneath his tunic. "I am here for other reasons, Belteshazzar." He turned his right side away from the seated man and drew the knife out unseen.

"I would offer you a seat, Akkad, but perhaps you would rather stand."

Akkad had not thought beyond this moment. How was he to accomplish this?

Belteshazzar made it easier by standing himself. "What is it, Akkad? I can see you are troubled. Please tell me what is on your mind. What drives you to the dungeon to seek out an imprisoned Jew?"

Akkad was not prepared for kindness. As he faced this man of his own age, he felt more in common with him than he cared to admit. They both had been admitted into a society of older men and were constantly being required to prove themselves worthy.

But now Belteshazzar's striving would come to an end.

Qurdi had timed his entrance to the throne room perfectly. Now that Belteshazzar was as good as removed, he needed only to solidify the king's hatred for the Jews. The king was still angry about Belteshazzar and Amyitis, and inclined to disfavor the captive people. Qurdi bowed as the king acknowledged him in his audience hall.

"What is it, Qurdi? New omens I must see?"

"O King, live forever! It is not for the sake of omens that I come before you today. You, O King, have made a decree that every man who hears the sound of the horn and all kinds of music is to fall down and worship the golden image. But whoever does not fall down and worship will be cast into the blazing fire of the city furnace."

"Yes, Qurdi." The king pulled one of his harem women toward himself, his attention focused there.

"I have heard there are certain Jews, O King, whom you have appointed over the administration of the province of Babylon, namely Shadur-Aku, Mi-sha-Aku, and Abed-Nabu. These men,

O King, have disregarded you. They do not serve your gods or worship the golden image which you have set up."

The king's boredom quickly turned to anger. "Jews again! Jews who will not honor the image of their king? Bring these men before me!"

Qurdi smiled and bowed, knowing that even if Akkad failed, Belteshazzar would not be left in prison long.

Things were not going well for Akkad. He had come to obey the voices and to do it quickly. Instead, Belteshazzar had drawn him into conversation and would not let him go.

"But your gods behave like men," Belteshazzar was saying. "What kind of gods are those? They have quarrels, they hate each other, and they try to destroy each other. Does that not sound like stories that only men have created? If there are gods, wouldn't they be unlike men?"

"*If* there are gods?" Akkad said. "There must be gods, Belteshazzar. Have you looked at the sky?"

Belteshazzar smiled. "I agree, Akkad. And I tell you that there is one God who paints the stars on the dome of the sky. If there are messages to be read there, it is He who places them there. They do not appear of themselves. And He is above us all in a way that none of the created images you worship can be. Those idols are only distorted pictures of men. The Lord God is not a man, not even a distorted one."

Akkad shook his head. The voices were speaking again, inside his mind, but he couldn't hear them. He struggled to make out what they were saying to him.

"Akkad," Belteshazzar said again.

"Be silent!" Akkad said, and the chief of magicians raised his eyebrows in surprise.

Akkad closed his eyes and concentrated. They did not want

him to listen to the lies of the Jew. They wanted the Jew dead.

Akkad readjusted the knife in his hand. The man was kind, it was true, but kindness did not matter. Only the voices mattered.

Akkad took a step closer to Belteshazzar. The Jew tilted his head as if trying to read Akkad's expression. He smiled slightly, as though he suddenly understood. "You are not the first to try, Akkad, and you will not be the last."

Without further thought, Akkad slipped the knife from behind his robes and thrust it up between Belteshazzar's ribs.

Akkad spread himself on his bed, his head toward the starry sky. The bloody knife lay on the table by the door. His thoughts raged within him.

Had he truly done it? He remembered the sickening feeling of the knife sliding into Belteshazzar's flesh, the warmth of the blood that rushed out over his own hand. Belteshazzar's eyes had widened, and then he had fallen to the ground at Akkad's feet. Akkad had fled past the guard and had not stopped running until he had reached his own chamber.

Now he lay on his bed and waited for the rush of power he was certain would be his. He had done what they asked. His thoughts drifted into the night, and he felt consciousness slip from him.

A pounding on his door roused him. He jumped to open it. A rush of guards and slaves bounded in. They dragged him from his room without explanation.

A moment later he was thrust into the dark throne room, where the king paced on the floor beneath the throne.

"What is this that I hear, Akkad?" the king said. "Have you attacked Belteshazzar?"

Akkad's mind raced. How had he been identified? "O King, live forever…"

"Yes?"

"I went to speak with the chief of magicians about the recent treachery in the palace. Belteshazzar was so arrogant about his own betrayal, O King, that I grew incensed." Akkad wondered at the lies that poured so easily from his mouth. "I could think of nothing but the king's honor, and I attacked the man before I could think more clearly. It was not my place. I am sorry, O King."

Nabu-kudurri-usur stopped his pacing and scowled. "It seems my honor has become quite important to my diviners of late. First Rim-Sin, and now you. Or perhaps it is merely a convenient excuse." He frowned at Akkad. "You puzzle me, boy. Everywhere I turn you are suddenly part of what is happening in this palace. I do not like the way you have taken over this matter. Belteshazzar's betrayal is mine to deal with. But in this matter and with my amulet I must commend you for your loyalty to your king. In the future, do not be so hasty with justice."

"Yes, O King. Thank you." Akkad bowed several times, waiting to be dismissed. The king flicked a hand at him, and he fled back to his room.

He had escaped again. Perhaps the power lay not in what he could accomplish of his own goals but in succeeding in the work he was given to do. But that was not enough. There was something he must have for himself as well.

Abigail.

In the throne room the next morning, Qurdi lingered as guards dragged Shadur-Aku, Mi-sha-Aku, and Abed-Nabu before the throne. Only days before they had dined at the king's table. Qurdi could not suppress a smile.

"Is it true," the king said, "that you do not serve my gods or worship the golden image that I have set up?"

Qurdi smiled again. The king was willing to let these Jews have their one God, even willing to let them go on calling themselves by their Hebrew names instead of the Babylonian names he had given them. But when they did not worship *him*, that was inexcusable.

"It was my decree, was it not, that when you hear the music, if you do not fall down and worship the image that I have made, you will immediately be cast into the furnace of blazing fire. What god is there who can deliver you out of my hands?"

Mi-sha-Aku spoke for the three. "O Nebuchadnezzar, we do not need to give you an answer concerning this matter. If He chooses to do so, our God whom we serve is able to deliver us from fire. *He* is the God who will deliver us out of your hand, O King."

The king stood, the veins on his neck bulging.

"But even if He does not," Mi-sha-Aku continued, "let it be known to you, O King, that we will not serve your gods or worship the golden image that you have set up."

The king's face was purple now. He shouted to the guards who bracketed the three Jews. "Heat the furnace seven times hotter!"

They ran ahead to do his bidding. Several soldiers rushed forward at his command and tied the three men with ropes.

"Take them now!" Nabu-kudurri-usur said. "I will attend this execution personally."

Minutes later, in the brick-making enclosure outside the palace, the largest furnace blazed with a heat so intense the mud bricks above it turned to ash. Slaves kept their distance, unable to get close enough even to add more coal. Word of the execution had traveled ahead of the royal party, and a mob of citizens ringed the enclosure, anxious to watch the destruction of three men foolish enough to defy the divine king. They pressed against the low wall, hushed voices hanging heavy in the unbearable heat.

A royal chair had been brought for the king, and he watched from a safe distance, but still, sweat dripped from his chin. Soldiers gripped the arms of the three rebels.

The king stood and waved an arm. "Throw them in!"

The three, still bound, were dragged to the mouth of the furnace and shoved inside.

The heat was so intense the soldiers fell dead beside the opening.

Akkad's opportunity to see Abigail came at a time he could not have foreseen. The sudden decision to execute Shadur-Aku, Misha-Aku, and Abed-Nabu took everyone in the throne room by surprise. As the palace staff, *kasdim* and slave alike, flooded out of the courtyard into the Processional Way to witness the fascinating event, Akkad merged into the harem crowd and found himself face-to-face with the woman who had occupied his mind like the stars never had.

He touched her arm as they moved through the street, but she pulled away without looking at him.

"Abigail, do not be angry," he said.

She turned to another of the wives and murmured something about the execution.

"Abigail," he began again.

"Akkad, there is nothing to say," she said, her anger flaring white-hot.

Akkad backed away. It was not the time to speak of his love for her. Her fellow Jews were about to be executed. Later, perhaps, when she had calmed and forgotten what they were about to see, he would try again to convince her that they could be together.

Akkad was not as confident as he once was. He was uncertain if he had pleased the gods sufficiently with his attack on Belteshazzar, and he still had no new wisdom about how to gain Abigail for himself. The only positive thing that was happening was the execution of the three Hebrews. Three fewer Hebrews in positions of prominence could only be considered a good thing.

When they reached the furnace, the heat was so extreme that most of the crowd stayed well away from it. The king drew closer than most, his royal chair placed close enough that he could see into the immense brick-making structure.

Akkad wanted to cheer as the soldiers dragged the three to the mouth of the furnace. But in case Abigail might be watching him, he resisted.

The men were thrown in, and a murmur swept the crowd at the fate of the soldiers who fell dead in the heat.

The spectacle seemed to be over. But instead of leaving, a strange hush fell over the witnesses, and no one moved. Akkad watched the people and felt with them a sense that something astonishing was about to happen.

Akkad looked back to the furnace in amazement. Were his eyes fooled by some trick of the heat?

The king saw it, too. He stood. "Was it not three men we cast bound into the fire?"

Near the king, Qurdi nodded. "Certainly, O King."

"Look!" The king pointed. "I see four men loose and walking around in the fire unharmed, and the fourth looks like a son of the gods!"

Akkad wiped away the sweat that had begun to run down from his turbaned head. The heat was unbelievable. He needed to walk away, but he couldn't. A bizarre desire welled up within him: a desire to join the men in the furnace. Something was in there; he could feel it. Something he had been searching for.

Another voice in his mind, unlike the ones he had come to know so well, whispered of Truth in the furnace.

Akkad shook his head to clear away the absurd thoughts, but they persisted. And then the other voices rushed in, thundering down the corridors of his mind like a pack of angry wolves, eager to devour the thoughts he had allowed to enter. He put his hands to his face.

His mind was being split apart, he knew. Still the furnace beckoned him. He felt as though he could run to the entrance and fling himself into it. A shout arose from the crowd. The king stood, his mouth open in shock. And then something happened that shattered Akkad's beliefs beyond repair.

Three Jews walked out of the fiery furnace.

Chapter 15

Abigail's anger had not abated when next she saw Akkad in the palace hall. Only one thing was on her mind, and she would speak it, not caring who heard.

"Is it true?" She jabbed a finger at his chest.

"Abigail." Akkad looked dazed, as if he had not even heard her question. He reached for her.

She yanked her hands away from his. She did not want him to touch her until she had an answer. "Is it true?" she said. "Did you attack Belteshazzar?"

Akkad's face fell. "It had to be done."

"Had to? Why?"

"The gods wished it. They wished him to be dead."

Abigail scowled in reply. "Then your gods must be disappointed with you, Akkad, for the Most High has healed His servant." She enjoyed the look of surprise on his face.

"He's not dead?" Akkad asked.

"He is not. I told you, the God of Israel controls all that happens in this world. Not you, and not your evil voices!"

She whirled away, leaving him in the hall. She would have nothing more to do with him, no matter what her heart kept telling her.

Kaida sat in Cosam's storeroom, slowly spinning the empty pottery wheel with one finger.

Her thoughts were scattered and seemed to keep coming full circle, like the wheel.

It would appear that she was free of Rim-Sin.

But she did not want to be free of Rim-Sin.

She should not care what happened to him.

But she could think of little else.

Cosam entered, leaned against the doorframe, and folded his arms.

She stopped her spinning. "Is there news?"

He shook his head. "You must stop this, Kaida."

"I know." She spun the wheel again. "But you saw how horrible a death the furnace was for Ahab and Zedekiah. Do you want that for him?"

"And yet God has also delivered men from the furnace."

"Do you think he will deliver Rim-Sin in the same way?" She asked the question sarcastically, knowing the answer.

"Kaida, he is not of our people."

"I know. Still—"

"No. That must be enough."

She stood and pushed her hair away from her face. "I only wish I knew what was happening to him. Perhaps I will go to the palace and see if I can learn something."

"No!" Cosam came to her and gripped her arms. "I don't want you to even be associated with him, Kaida. I'm afraid that harm may come to you if people know how much you care."

She sighed. "Don't worry about me, Cosam. I won't do anything foolish."

Akkad studied the stars through his chamber w
day he had witnessed the Hebrew God spare the
men thrown into a furnace and learned through
that Belteshazzar had survived Akkad's attack. He
admit that this was a more powerful magic than anyt
known. He must learn the truth.

He cracked open his door and put an eye to the sli
way was dark and silent. He slipped from his room
the stairs in the central courtyard by the light of Sin,
god. Ordinarily he would have thanked Sin for his
Tonight he whispered no prayers.

A different guard stood before Belteshazzar's cell,
barred the way with his sword when Akkad approached.

"I only want to speak with him," Akkad said. "Come
with me yourself."

He shook his head. "My orders are clear. If you want
with the prisoners, you do so from here. There will be no
attacks."

Belteshazzar slept in his cell with his back against the far
Akkad could see Rim-Sin, his mentor, watching Beltesha
from the next cell. The diviner didn't look well. Prison was
good for a man.

Akkad studied the dozing Belteshazzar, suddenly unsure
himself.

As though some force had awakened him, Belteshazzar opene
his eyes and focused them on Akkad with clarity of thought.
"Akkad."

"It is true," Akkad said. "You are still alive."

"Are you here to finish what you began?" Belteshazzar asked.

The guard stepped closer, and Belteshazzar held up a hand.
"It's all right, Kerkuk," Belteshazzar said. "The Lord God will
continue to preserve us from evil. We need not fear."

Akkad stepped closer to the cell. "When I . . . the reason I

ried . . . " He sighed. "The gods instructed me to do it, but I uspect you have a greater magic." He looked at the ground. "I am sorry, Belteshazzar."

"God has not finished His plan for me here, it would seem."

Akkad closed his eyes. "I wish you would tell me how to draw down the power of Yahweh."

Belteshazzar laughed. "Akkad, you are so far from the truth I wonder if you can ever find it. You seek to use power. But God's power is not to be used. It is to be served."

Akkad shook his head. "I do serve. That is why I did what I did."

"No, you attacked me for your own selfish gain, nothing more."

The truth silenced Akkad.

"Akkad, my God is so powerful He cannot be used, cannot be manipulated. But He is a God who loves you."

Akkad put his hands over his ears, but it was the voices screaming inside his mind that he wished to quell. They would not be still, would not give him up so easily.

Forget the Hebrews . . .

But Akkad couldn't forget. He couldn't forget the smiles on the faces of those men when they had emerged from the fire, couldn't forget the king's declaration afterward that the Hebrew God was not to be maligned.

The power he served had told him to destroy the Jews. But the power the Jews served had saved them. It was the greater power. But more importantly, it was a power that *saved* rather than destroyed. Akkad's heart was drawn toward it, but his mind clawed at his heart, dragging it back to the gods he had promised himself to.

"I have prayed that it will let you go," Belteshazzar said.

"What?" Akkad asked.

"The evil you have given yourself to."

Akkad ran his hands through his hair. Once again this was not the conversation he had come to have. He had come for a rational argument about the merits of their respective gods. Belteshazzar had, in one comment, made the entire conversation very personal.

"I control my own destiny, Belteshazzar."

The other man shook his head. "No."

Akkad bit his lip.

"What has happened to bring you here, Akkad?" Belteshazzar asked.

Akkad told him of the day's events at the furnace.

Belteshazzar's look of concern changed to amusement as the story went on. "The God of Israel is good," he laughed, clapping his hands in delight. He grew serious then. "But Akkad, these things are not merely to save His people. He acts to show Himself to all peoples through His display of power."

Akkad looked away. "I am a Chaldean," he said. "How could I ever serve the Hebrew God?"

"The Most High is the God of the Hebrews, it is true. But He is the one God, Akkad. There are no others. And that must mean that He is the God of *all* men, Chaldean or Israelite."

"I do not hear the voices now," Akkad said, mostly to himself.

Belteshazzar nodded. "I have asked God to silence them while we speak."

Akkad's eyes widened. "You have this power?"

"Not I. The God in heaven has power over all evil."

Akkad lowered his voice to a whisper. "What does He want with me, your one God?"

Belteshazzar smiled. "He wants you to serve Him. And Him alone."

The stars calmed Akkad tonight as he charted their positions from outside the High Temple on Etemenanki. The others of his circle worked nearby, but Akkad was content to remain silent.

Everything fell into place as he pored over his charts. It was all so predictable, so ordered. From these charts he and those before him had succeeded in creating the lunar calendar with its twelve months of twenty-nine or thirty days each, and then discerned how to insert the intercalendary month every second or third year to cause the lunar year to coincide with the solar year. They had divided the months into weeks, the weeks into days.

In the heavens above, they had discovered the Ecliptic, the pathway of the sun, and the twelve houses it passed through. Each of these they had given a sign, eleven animals and Libra, the balance. The zodiac, they called it. And then they had read the messages that appeared there. Messages about family, fortune, and friends, and everything else a man could wonder about.

All of this Akkad had been trained to read and understand since he was a child. He had been destined for the *kasdim* and had distinguished himself at a young age.

Tonight he tried to ignore the crumbling foundation of his beliefs, but Belteshazzar's words kept prodding him to verbalize his questions. He finally drifted closer to the other men. They were discussing the rise of Gemini in the path of the moon god tonight.

"What did you think of the deliverance of the three Hebrews?" Akkad asked.

Shamash scowled at the interruption. "What do we care about three more or three less Jews in the kingdom?"

"I should think the king's decree about Yahweh would concern all of us," Akkad said.

"Perhaps," Nadin-Aku said. "But he will soon forget his new attraction to the Israelites' one God. We will see to that."

Akkad quieted the roaring in his brain as he took a deep

breath. "Have you considered that their one God may be the true god and that there are no others?"

The entire circle swiveled their heads in Akkad's direction. The uneasy silence lengthened.

He held their gaze, but he felt his resolve crumbling. "I—I have only been thinking," he said. "This God has shown Himself to be more powerful than our gods . . ."

The mood broke as the circle began to chuckle. "You have no idea of true power, Akkad," Shamash said.

"I have seen and used more power than you know, Shamash!" Akkad said. The others stopped laughing.

Shamash turned to face Akkad squarely. "You are but a child."

"Even so, I know of power. I have seen enough of the Hebrew God to suspect this may be a power of a higher order. And as a man of wisdom, I open my mind to other possibilities."

The others turned away, and Akkad felt he had failed. He had ended up defending himself when his intention had been to convince the others.

He tried to begin again, but Nadin-Aku cut him off. "We must work on the birth chart for the king's new son," the astrologer said. "There is no time to talk of other things."

Words of the king's newest child brought thoughts of Abigail flooding into Akkad's mind. How long would it be until *she* carried the king's next son?

They worked over the birth chart long into the night. When they had assembled all the information, they stood in silence, each unwilling to discuss the dark omens they had read for this particular son. His life would be short and would end violently.

"The king will not be pleased," Nadin-Aku finally said. The others said nothing. "Now is not the most favorable time for us to bring bad news," he continued, "with the recent display of the Israelite God."

When the moon was advancing through Scorpio, Shamash finally spoke. "We do not have to tell him of the message."

The others looked to him as if he had said the words they had all wished for the courage to speak.

"We could alter the birth chart in this one respect."

They studied the stars as if the answer instead of the question were written there.

When they again looked at each other, nods traveled around the circle. Akkad said nothing, but his silence made him an accomplice.

It was all falling apart. Everything Akkad had believed. Yahweh worked miracles, but the *kasdim* worked deception. Ignoring his doubts had only led Akkad to violence. Facing them had led him to be ostracized by his circle. There was nothing left for him but a life of more deception, or certain execution for disloyalty to his gods. Akkad needed to speak with Abigail. She would bring sanity to his troubled spirit like no one else could.

He waited for an opportunity, but it did not come. She was always surrounded by other wives or closely guarded by the representative of the harem. So closely guarded that Akkad wondered if there had been suspicion of their affection. Even when he saw her across a courtyard or the banquet hall, she would not meet his eyes.

Since speaking with Daniel and then revealing his thoughts to his circle of magicians, Akkad had kept thoughts of Yahweh at arm's length. But his growing doubts had brought a change in his thoughts of Abigail, as well. The desire to conquer her faithfulness to her God had left him. He realized that her faith was part of the reason he loved her, and he would not take it from her.

Today he saw her again in the central courtyard. She talked

and laughed with other wives as he passed through on his way to the throne room.

She glanced up as he passed. He caught her eyes for a moment and read the pain in them. It gave him hope, but it broke his heart as well. These looks across the courtyards were all they would ever have. He would have to be content with only seeing her, perhaps occasionally speaking to her, but never more. He would leave her to the king. To do anything else would destroy her, and he loved her too much for that. He smiled at her before she looked away. He hoped his smile had shouted everything that was in his heart.

Akkad entered the throne room and felt the tension immediately. Qurdi-Marduk-lamur stood at the side of the room, his hands clenched behind his back. Before the throne, Belteshazzar waited, his head bowed.

"A misunderstanding, then?" the king asked.

"Yes, O King. I was mistaken that the king had summoned me to his chamber that morning."

"And the cause of this misunderstanding?"

Belteshazzar said nothing.

"Very well, Belteshazzar. You have served me with loyalty and wisdom for too long that I would not believe you about this incident. You may return to your position when you are recovered from your wound. But," the king said, leaning forward from the throne, "there will be no more misunderstandings."

"Yes, O King."

Akkad sensed the relief in Qurdi's change of posture. Did he have something to do with Belteshazzar's imprisonment? Why hadn't the Jew told the king if Qurdi had been involved?

Qurdi turned suddenly and saw Akkad, and his expression turned to hatred.

Akkad knew he had failed Qurdi by not killing Belteshazzar. He would bear Qurdi's wrath for it. But at the same time he was glad he had failed. In his brief encounters with the Israelite he had seen more good than he had discovered in a lifetime of knowing Qurdi.

Qurdi approached the throne. "O King, live forever. The diviner Rim-Sin is still in prison awaiting the king's judgment."

The king stroked his face. "I am in remembrance of Rim-Sin, Qurdi; do not fear. But I am reluctant to order his execution before the New Year Festival. It is his year to perform the sacrifice, and I would not want to anger the gods."

Qurdi bowed his head. "Then certainly the king will deliver justice soon after his task is complete."

The king nodded and sighed, as if the death of another diviner troubled him.

"If I may suggest, O King..." Qurdi waited.

"Yes?"

"The one sacrificed on the second day of the New Year Festival is to be someone close to the heart of the one who holds the knife. This is what gives it its power." Qurdi leaned forward. "It is well known that Rim-Sin is very fond of his new concubine. I believe the gods would be most honored if she were the one he offered."

The king waved a hand. "Let it be so. Thank you, Qurdi."

Akkad's uncle turned from the throne room with a sickening smile. On his way out, their eyes met. Akkad read the threat in them. He was not safe here, even from family.

If only Akkad could speak with Abigail one more time, he could tell her that he had changed his mind, that he would be content to love her from a distance. He could tell her that he was sorry about what he had done to Belteshazzar, that he was no longer certain that Yahweh was not the true God. But the anger he felt from her whenever he saw her prevented him from even approaching her. He longed to find her alone somewhere so that he would have a chance to speak to her.

That desire led him to her hall this night to watch from the doorway of an unoccupied room in hopes that she would leave her room alone.

The evening dragged on, and Akkad's legs grew tired and cramped. Several slaves passed by, but he had nothing to fear from their curious stares. Finally, his wait was rewarded as he saw her door glide open.

He took a step from his alcove, but pulled back when another form entered the other end of the hallway.

The representative of the harem! Akkad cursed his luck. But perhaps the representative would pass by before Abigail reentered her room. He nudged the door open behind him and slipped in so the eunuch would not see him as he passed. With his head against the door, Akkad watched the eunuch approach Abigail and speak with her. He could not hear what they said. She nodded. The eunuch turned back to leave the hall, and Akkad smiled. But his smile faded as Abigail closed her door behind her and followed the representative away from Akkad.

He crept from the room and followed them.

Where would she be going at this hour? And with the representative? Akkad tried to ignore the only possible answer that came to his mind, but when the two ahead of him turned into the hall where the king's bedchamber lay, there was no sense in continuing to deny it.

Akkad held back as the door opened and the representative stepped away. Nabu-kudurri-usur stood framed in the lamplight of the room. He held out his hands to Abigail, and she took them, smiling, and stepped into the room.

"Come in, Abigail," Nabu-kudurri-usur smiled.

Abigail entered, as nervous as she had been the first time she had been summoned here, but trying not to show it.

"Come, sit," the king said, as he sat on the royal bed.

Abigail sat beside him on the bed, not taking her eyes from his, as if afraid of some sudden move he might make.

"You have heard that Belteshazzar and Amyitis have explained the misunderstanding?" he asked. "And that they have both been freed?"

"Yes," Abigail nodded.

"It was you who first suggested that there might be some mistake," the king said.

"I only wanted you to be certain of the truth, O King."

"Yes. It took courage for you to say the things you did. I wanted to thank you."

"To thank me?" Abigail smiled. Thus far, this meeting had not been what she had imagined.

The king stood and went to a small table, pouring himself a crock of water with his back to her.

"I love her," he said.

Abigail studied his back.

He turned. "Amyitis. I love her."

She nodded. "I know."

"Do you not wonder at the size of my harem, then, little Jewish captive?"

"I understand that treaties are sometimes necessary, and that you feel captives in the palace assure that there will be no rebellion in your vassal countries."

"Ah, you are wise in the affairs of empires, then."

Abigail smiled.

"Do you fear me?" the king asked.

Abigail lowered her head. "I—I am not experienced in being the wife of a man I do not know. It was not what I expected for my life." She raised her head to look at him again. "But I will accept whatever plan the Lord God has for my life."

The king set his drink on the table and came to sit beside her again. "Stay with me, Abigail, and tell me more of your one God."

Akkad could wait as long as it took. As long as the representative could stand beside the door, Akkad could stand in the darkened recess around the corner where he could barely make out the edge of the eunuch's robe.

When Abigail emerged hours later, Akkad could not see her face before she turned to return to her chamber. The representative led her there and blocked Akkad's view as she closed her door.

He returned to his chambers for the night.

The next morning he saw her in the banquet hall. He could find no trace of sadness on her face. He'd expected her to look pained or crushed in some way, but she laughed and talked in her usual friendly way to all who sat with her.

He had slept little last night after returning to his chamber, and this morning he felt old and slow of thought. The anger that had ignited toward the king as he had waited in the hall last night was this morning transferred to Abigail. Why was she not broken and saddened? Had Akkad meant nothing to her that she could so enjoy her position as one of many wives of the king?

When she walked past him on her way from the hall, he waited for her eyes to fall on him. Surely she must have seen him while she ate. But she was engrossed in conversation and gave no notice of him at all. His anger burned hotter, and he tasted acid in his throat. Had she really given herself so willingly to the king that she would not even acknowledge him now?

Jealousy spoke so loudly in his ears as he left the banquet hall that he did not even notice that it spoke with the same voices he had grown accustomed to listening to.

Jews... it said. *They are all worthless...*

Akkad caught up with her in the courtyard outside the throne room. "Abigail!" he called, not caring who heard him.

She turned and stopped, holding her hand in front of her as if to block his advance. "No, Akkad." She shook her head as he approached. "I am the king's wife in every way. I will not allow you to interfere, no matter how you beg." She hurried away.

Akkad's anger flared. She had discarded her love for him like the carcass of a dead animal. And now she would treat him like an unwanted pet that begged for its master's attention? He stalked toward the throne room.

His circle was to present the birth chart this morning, so he took his place before the king's throne with the others. Shamash held the clay tablet, its lies carved into it, preserved for generations to come. Akkad wanted no part of it.

"The stars read favorably for the new son," Shamash smiled as he held the birth chart before him.

The king surveyed the group and noticed Akkad standing apart from them. "Akkad," he said, "have you done your part to read the stars?"

"I have done my part, O King."

The king nodded, a frown creasing his face. "I thought perhaps you had been too distracted lately. I have heard rumors from some in the palace about your—attachment—to one of my wives."

Akkad closed his eyes. It was as though his gods had abandoned him. There had been a time when he would have almost been willing for the king to know of his love for Abigail. But now? Now that she had rejected him in favor of the king, he was finally going to be disciplined for his imprudence? The anger toward Abigail had not abated. First she had lured him with her smiles and her fascinating talk of Yahweh, then she had cast him off. Because of her he had lost his standing among his circle of *kasdim*, and now he was in danger of losing his place before the king. His heart gave him the words to say before his mind had time to evaluate them.

"It is true, O King, that one of the royal wives has distracted me. The unwanted attention she has shown me has been a source of agitation for me. I have not wanted to speak ill of her before the king, but I am afraid I can keep silent no longer. She has obviously not learned the way of the harem yet, O King, and does not understand that she must be loyal only to you."

Daniel was gone, and Peter was sick to death of this cell, this city, this time, this life of the diviner Rim-Sin. He'd been scorned and hated, he'd been attacked, he'd been imprisoned. He knew the New Year Festival must be soon, when he'd be forced to kill some unfortunate victim. When Daniel had been taken away, Peter had sworn that he would get out of this cell and find the lampstand or die trying. Enough was enough. He *would* get out of this place, this time, and return to the university to claim his new title, if they hadn't given him up for dead by now.

Qurdi's attempt on his life had not been wasted. Peter now possessed the knife the priest had dropped as he'd fled the power of Yahweh. It was hidden in the dirt in a corner of Peter's cell. Peter chatted with Kerkuk, knowing that his best chance of escape lay with gaining his trust as Daniel had.

When soldiers brought a woman to the underground cells, Peter was ready. The soldiers were laughing as they roughly shoved the woman toward Kerkuk.

"Ishtar does not smile on the king this day, Kerkuk," one said, chuckling.

His companion elbowed him. "Quiet! Men have been killed for saying less!"

Kerkuk laughed along with them. "And who is this?"

"A royal wife. She is accused of being unfaithful to the king."

Kerkuk looked at Peter and raised his eyebrows. "It looks like your royal consort did not go unpunished after all."

Peter said nothing.

The guards corrected Kerkuk. "No, she wasn't with Rim-Sin. This one was amusing a different diviner!"

Kerkuk joined their laughter. "We will say nothing of the goddess of love and of the king," he said. "But perhaps we should say a prayer that the goddess will change her feelings before the entire harem and circle of magicians is under my guard!"

Kerkuk took the woman's arm.

The soldiers laughed cruelly. One of them, a muscle-bound brute with a neck like a tree trunk, came to Peter's cell and clanged the bars with his armored forearm. "Say, Rim-Sin, I don't suppose you're keeping up with the palace news down here, eh?" The men laughed. "Your consort, Ilushu, claims you attacked her. Says you were trying to have your way with her, but she screamed for help and some of us guards came running."

The other soldier came up beside him. This one was thinner and spoke through broken front teeth. "And here's how your concubine pays you back for all your deeds of kindness you've shown her. We hear she found you and Ilushu together, and she says that Ilushu was fighting you off." He spit into Peter's cell. "Where's the loyalty?"

The soldiers laughed and clanked away.

Peter sighed. Attempted rape. Great. But they couldn't do any worse than execute him, could they? He swallowed, thinking of every torture scene he'd ever seen on film. Perhaps they could.

He went to the bars of his cell and looked at the woman there. She was very pretty and young. Younger even than Kaida.

"What's your name?"

"Abigail."

"You are Jewish?"

"Yes."

Peter lifted an eyebrow and smiled at Kerkuk. The guard was putting Abigail into the next cell.

"My own concubine is Jewish," Peter said to him.

Kerkuk shrugged and gestured toward the direction the soldiers had just gone. "Guess that didn't work out too well for you, huh?"

"Oh, no," Peter said. "It's just because they're fiery. Jewish women are quite—worthwhile—if you know what I mean."

Kerkuk laughed and looked at Abigail. "She's pretty, I will say that."

"How long am I to be kept here?" Peter asked him.

The guard shrugged. "They don't tell me."

"It's a cruel to keep a man so long without the company of a woman, don't you think?"

Kerkuk laughed again. "You should be part of the royal guard."

"Put her in here with me, would you? Just for an hour or two."

The guard looked back and forth between the two cells, as if contemplating whether the entertainment factor was worth the possible trouble he might find himself in.

"Come on, Kerkuk. After that, you can have a turn with her. We'll keep each other's secret." Peter winked at the guard and smiled again.

Kerkuk sighed. "Just for a little while." He raised the bar on the outside of the Abigail's cell.

Peter was counting on the fact that Abigail would back away from Kerkuk. The guard disappeared into her cell. Peter took two quick steps backward to the stone he'd used as a marker on the floor. He scrabbled in the dirt, clutched Qurdi's knife, and turned back to the door of his cell just before the guard dragged Abigail from hers.

Putting the leering smile back on again, he waited beside the door, knife at his side, as Kerkuk raised the bar on his cell.

Kerkuk swung the door inward, pushed Abigail into the cell, and reached for the door again.

Peter slashed the knife down onto the guard's forearm.

"Aaahhh!" Kerkuk screamed and clutched at the bloody arm. His surprise gave way to defense immediately. He reached his uninjured right arm across his middle to grasp the hilt of his sword strapped to his left side. Peter took the opportunity to thrust the knife into the man's thigh.

He doubled over, reaching for the knife in his leg rather than his sword.

Peter grabbed him by the leather chest plate and shoved him to the floor of the cell. He pushed Abigail out, closed the cell door, and lowered the bar to secure it.

He turned to Abigail, knowing he'd done all he could for her. He could not allow her to slow him down at this point. "Run while you have the chance!" he said, then left the stunned woman behind and fled into the underground passageway.

Peter ran through the maze of storerooms, frantic to find a set of steps. When he finally found a way upward, he hesitated and took a deep breath. This was it. All that lay between him and going home, assuming Daniel's interpretation was correct, was finding the lampstand and getting it back to Jerusalem. Oh, and all that other stuff about going to the Hanging Gardens. But he couldn't think about that right now. First, the lampstand. He ascended the steps and tried to guess where the treasury would be.

At the top of the steps, the first of the palace's landscaped garden courtyards widened before him.

A hollow laugh drifted across the space. "So, the gods grant my desires to have you, Rim-Sin."

Before him stood Qurdi-Marduk-lamur, clutching Kaida around the neck, a knife at her throat. Four of his slaves stood behind him.

Kaida's eyes were wild with terror. Despite how she'd allegedly sold him out to save her own skin he found he could not be angry with her. He tried to calm her with his own eyes, but it wasn't working.

"Come, Rim," Qurdi said. "Join me over here, and retrieve your precious concubine."

Chapter 16

PETER HESITATED. QURDI tightened his hold on Kaida's throat, and she winced. Peter had no choice. He turned and ran.

Qurdi screamed as though surprised by his action. The priest wouldn't be able to hold Kaida and chase him at the same time. That would give Peter time to get away. As he ran through the middle palace courtyard, he could hear Qurdi screaming for his slaves to go after him.

Peter knew that if he had given himself up, Qurdi would have killed them both. Now he was gambling that Qurdi would keep Kaida safe so long as he could use her against him. It was a dangerous gamble. But if he could find the lampstand, it would pay off.

Where would the palace treasury be? He had been all over this level, he was certain. Up? Down? He would try going up first. He wasn't too crazy about what he had found below.

He swung into the first set of steps he encountered. In the tight passage at the top, he stood in one spot for a moment. Left? Right? Left. Away from the Hanging Gardens. He'd been that way already. The shouting of the slaves drifted up from the lower level. Or was it the sound of guards sent by the king?

Kaida was too frightened to even pull away from Qurdi this time. She had ignored Cosam's advice to stay away, and now she would bear the consequences. He dragged her through the first courtyard, into the second, and through a doorway leading off the open area. The room was someone's bedroom chamber.

"Sit," Qurdi said, and threw her against a chair. Her teeth bit into her lower lip as she hit. She tasted blood.

Qurdi drew up a chair in front of her and brought his face close to hers. He twisted a small knife between his fingers and took her hand in his hand. The light poked feeble fingers through the ventilation grid, just enough light to illuminate the oiled glow of Qurdi's smooth head.

"Now," the priest said, his dead eyes boring into hers, "you will tell me what Rim-Sin is doing here." He laid the edge of the knife against the top of her index finger and pressed gently. "Or I will begin cutting off your fingers."

The sound of pursuit was getting closer, and Peter ran down the passage in search of the treasury. This direction did not feel right. Everything felt too narrow, too confined. The treasury would be grand, impressive.

He searched for several minutes, opening and closing doors randomly. He must head down again. Had there been any stairs he'd missed? He couldn't recall any, except the staircase he had come up, which was at the far end of the palace. Would he have to go all the way back?

Kaida closed her eyes so she wouldn't see the knife.

Qurdi asked again. "What is Rim doing here in the palace?"

Kaida hesitated. Why should she have any loyalty to Rim-Sin?

He had done nothing for her. Perhaps this was a way to finally be free. But would Qurdi let her live if she talked?

"I will tell you," she said with a boldness she did not feel, "if you will do something for me."

Qurdi laughed. It was a dry, hollow sound. The knife moved away from her finger. "What would you have from me, little girl?"

Kaida slid her hand back and put it in her lap. She needed time to think of a plan. "I want clean clothes to wear," she said. The tunic she wore was muddy and torn from her struggle with Qurdi's slaves, so her request was not completely absurd.

Qurdi laughed again. "Women and their vanity. Very well."

He went to the door and cracked it open, his eyes still on Kaida. "Bring the woman some clothing," he said and closed the door. "Now, you will answer me."

Kaida tried to smile. "Must we talk of this before the clothing arrives?"

Qurdi's face twisted into a snarl, and he brought the knife out again. "I have waited long enough."

Peter fought his panic. He had to find another set of steps to get to the lower level. He was certain the treasury must be there. He could not go all the way back to the other side of the palace. The guards or slaves who chased him would surely find him. The upper level of the palace was here a confusing grid, constructed around the courtyards and throne room. There were no windows in the corridors, and he soon lost his bearings.

Shouts came down from the hallway.

"There he is!" Bare-chested men pushed each other to be the first to reach him. Bare chests meant slaves, not guards. Qurdi's men. At least the king did not yet know of his arrival. Hopefully.

One more corridor, he thought, taking a quick right. If he was correct about his location, this one should be running over the top of the corridor between the first and second courtyards below.

Steps!

The door of the room where Qurdi held Kaida opened again, and the slave entered with clothes. It had only been a minute since Qurdi's request. *He must have gotten them from across the hall,* Kaida thought. She'd been hoping for more time to think.

"There are your clothes," Qurdi said, throwing them at her.

"Thank you." She smiled again. "You will give me privacy while I change."

Once again, Qurdi smiled in amusement. Kaida went to an alcove in the room and tore off the ruined tunic. Even in the dim light, she could see that her new clothes were beautiful. She would look more like Ilushu than herself. She smoothed down the white fabric embroidered with tiny beads, enjoying the feel of it in spite of the situation. How could she escape? The request for clothing was only a stall. She had no plan.

She glanced around the small space. A table held a woman's cosmetics—mussel shells holding kohl for lining the eyes, cockle shells filled with white, yellow, and red pigments. Beside the kohl lay a carved ivory pin for applying it. It was small, but it was sharp. She placed the pin in the palm of her hand and turned the corner, wearing her most captivating smile.

Peter reached the main level and breathed his relief when he discovered another set of steps that led directly down. Once again he descended below the palace, passing the torches that sputtered to relieve the blackness. The slaves who chased him seemed to scatter at the main level. Probably searching the palace exits.

When he had finally reached the bottom, Peter grabbed the last torch out of its wall socket and moved forward. These steps had not been those that he and Kaida had taken before, so he was unsure of how to proceed. The prison had been down here, and the storerooms. But would the palace treasury lie underground?

He kept the torch high and slightly forward as he ran, trying to get a sense of what was before him and where he was in relation to the main level. The prison, he thought, must be under the second courtyard. He shouldn't be far from it now. Where would the treasury be?

The Hanging Gardens. They rose from the third level, but what was below them? The Gardens had been built on the north side of the palace. There must be something holding it up. Something hidden from view outside the palace by the wall of the Processional Way.

As he ran through rooms, he attempted to choose a northerly route. He burst through the doorway of yet another storeroom and entered a wide, lofty hall that stopped him short.

It was eerie, this huge, columned hall underground. Two enormous archways towered above him, side by side. Passages led deeper into darkness. Which one should he take? He chose right, simply from the habit of driving his car on the right side of the highway, and proceeded to the next chamber.

The mud floors of the storerooms had been replaced by baked brick here. His sandals echoed in the chamber. It was not that large, he realized quickly. Perhaps thirty feet by thirty. But it led to another chamber, its exact duplicate. Before Peter entered the second he could see that his own torchlight would not be the only light source in the chamber. More torches were already burning in the walls. He tiptoed in. The familiar blue and yellow glazes covered bas-relief sculptures on the walls. He must be getting close.

In the center of the next archway stood a uniformed soldier.

Qurdi seemed amused at Kaida's attempt, but she did not give up. She had to get closer to him without that knife waving around.

She glided over to the chair again, sliding herself into it and leaning forward. "Tell me about your work in the temple," she said. "It must be terribly fascinating." The ivory pin felt hot in her hand.

Qurdi leaned back with an insincere smile to match her own. "Perhaps I will," he said, and then brought his face close to hers again. "After you tell me what I want to know."

She only had one chance at this. She had better make it work.

The soldier in the archway stared straight ahead, his face expressionless. He reminded Peter of the guards at Buckingham Palace. He must have seen Peter, but he showed no sign. Peter approached him, trying to look casual. Would the soldier recognize him? Let him pass?

Peter raised his head and frowned. "Do you know who I am?"

An almost imperceptible nod from the guard. Good. Peter decided not to ask permission. He moved straight toward the guard, as if expecting him to get out of the way. He did.

Peter found himself inside another vaulted room. Torches blazed all around the perimeter, and Peter could see into several more rooms besides this one. He put his own torch in an empty socket. These rooms also connected to the other passage he had not chosen on the left. It was like a giant honeycomb with arches between each section. His eyes focused through the next archway, and what he saw riveted his eyes in awe.

It was the main vault of the treasury. Had to be. Nearly everything seemed made of gold. Torchlight reflected in a thousand bowls and vases, glimmered in the surface of gold-inlaid chests, and winked at him from a myriad of bejeweled tables, benches, and stools. Peter opened a chest nearby and plunged his hands into a pirate's treasure of precious stones, glowing blood red and deepest ebony.

He had been studying the past for his entire professional career. Sometimes he had been fortunate enough to handle items of antiquity, mainly because of Hugh's friendship. But he now stood on the threshold of a room filled with every imaginable treasure of the ancient world. Stacked, piled, scattered on the floor, heaped in corners. He half-expected to see Aladdin's lamp lying around. He would remember this scene for the rest of his life.

He must find the lampstand. A chill ran through him. He was so close now. So close to going home.

Kaida twisted the ivory pin in her hand until it poked out of her clenched fist. Qurdi leaned forward, his eyes locked on hers. "Where is he?"

Kaida snapped her arm around and thrust the pin into his neck with all the strength she had in her. Qurdi's eyes bulged in surprise, and he jerked back. The pin embedded in his neck. Blood spurted from the wound.

Kaida jumped from her chair, picked it up, and slammed it against Qurdi's head. He fell. She ran to the door and flung it open. She was almost out when a sharp kick took her legs out from under her. She rolled to her back.

Qurdi stood over her, his foot on her midsection as he yanked the pin from his neck. His face was twisted with pain and hatred.

She pushed at the foot holding her to the floor, but it would not be moved.

He threw the pin to the floor and dragged Kaida to the chair again. He laid his knife on her hand once more, his other hand covering the wound on his neck. Blood trickled through his fingers. "Where is Rim-Sin!"

The door opened, and another woman was pushed into the room. Kaida's eyes widened at the red-haired beauty. Ilushu!

"What do you want with me, Qurdi?"

Qurdi didn't move, didn't take the knife away from Kaida's hand. "You have been with Rim-Sin," he said. "What is he after?"

Ilushu rolled her eyes, apparently bored. "All this fuss over a Jewish lampstand? Why don't you just take the stupid thing and be done with it?"

Qurdi smiled and looked at Kaida.

"Perhaps we shall."

There it was. Propped against a wall in a section apart from other items. The marvelous lampstand from the night he'd appeared in Babylon. These items must have been new treasures brought from Israel, still to be catalogued. Had the king appointed someone to replace Reuben yet? He wrapped his hand around the gold center shaft of the stand.

The stand was hammered out of one solid piece of gold. Three branches extended from each side of the center shaft and curved upward so that seven lamps could be placed on the ends of the branches. More than twenty golden cups shaped like almond blossoms adorned the branches.

He lifted it and laid it across both his palms. It was quite heavy. He walked back out through the treasury, taking time to drink in the wealth accumulated here. How he wished he could bring some of these things home with him. Wouldn't Hugh go crazy if he could see this? He'd especially flip over these Jewish artifacts. Hugh took the Old Testament so seriously.

A gold box caught his attention, and he lowered the lampstand to the floor to run his hands over it. It was engraved like an intricate carving with symbols he didn't recognize. The years would wear away these symbols. If this piece were ever found, the engraving would have vanished. He traced the lines with his finger, wishing for a camera. What knowledge was in this room that would never be uncovered?

He should leave. There was still the problem of getting past that guard with this heavy thing—not to mention getting out of the palace with it. And there was Kaida. He would have to find her. He felt another stab of guilt at leaving her, but if he had given himself to Qurdi, neither of them would have had a chance.

He left the treasures behind and carried the lampstand to the entrance. The soldier still guarded the entryway, immovable. Peter didn't think he could talk his way past him with the lampstand. When no other options came to mind, he stood the lampstand against the wall, grabbed a gold, long-necked vase, and swung it like a bat, cracking the center of the vase against the back of the soldier's neck. The man fell like a sack of gold coins.

Peter picked up the lampstand. He would have to somehow carry it with one hand so he could hold his torch in the other. He stepped over the soldier. Movement on the other side of the chamber made him snap his head in that direction.

Qurdi-Marduk-lamur dragged a terrified Kaida into the vaulted chamber. A bruise swelled over one of his eyes, and blood oozed from his neck and onto his robes. At his back stood three slaves, holding torches high.

Qurdi laughed. "I see you have already found what I have come for, Rim-Sin."

Peter lowered the lampstand to the floor but kept his torch. "Let her go, Qurdi."

He laughed again. "Oh, I plan to let her go. You will see." He nodded to the slaves, and they ran to Peter's side. One took his torch and shoved it into a wall socket; then he and another grabbed Peter's arms. The third picked up the lampstand.

Qurdi whirled, still holding Kaida, and walked out of the chamber. Peter's captors followed, dragging him.

Where were they going? Qurdi led them past the underground vaults and then to the right through a long corridor. The corridor ended in a small room. An odd whirring sound echoed from the other side.

Qurdi went to the far wall. No, it was not a wall, Peter realized. The floor dropped off before the back wall. It was a shaft. A rope and pulley system drew sloshing buckets up from below them and carried them up and out of sight. To the left of the climbing buckets another rope went the other way, lowering empty buckets to whatever lay below. It was the hydraulic lifting system that watered the Hanging Gardens.

Qurdi dangled Kaida off balance out over the edge of the opening. Her toes bicycled empty space. "Tell me, Rim, what did you intend to do with the lampstand?"

Peter didn't take his eyes from Kaida. What could he say? *I was going to send it back to Jerusalem so I can travel back to the twenty-first century, Qurdi. Anything else?* All he could think of to say was, "I'm not sure."

Qurdi looked at Kaida. "I have tried several times to use this girl to force you to cooperate with me. I thought I remembered that she was very important to you. But I must have been wrong. And so she is of no use to me."

Qurdi let her go.

"No!" Peter strained against the slaves' grip, but it was too late. Kaida fell into the shaft without a sound.

"Now," Qurdi continued. "I am giving you one last chance to save your own life. Tell me what power this lampstand holds."

Peter breathed slowly through his nose, wanting to dive over the side to Kaida. "I don't know!"

Qurdi leaned backward and studied him. "Tell me, Rim-Sin."

"I am not Rim-Sin!" Peter shouted. "I don't know where he is, and I don't know why he wanted the lampstand! I just want to go home!" *And Kaida. I want Kaida.* There was no rational thought now, no strategy. Peter had exhausted every resource he had, and all that remained was an empty desperation.

Qurdi ran a hand up and down the length of the lampstand's shaft. "The diviner has lost his mind," he said to his slaves. "But it matters not. We have the key, and the goddess will tell us what to do with it." He turned to Peter. "Hold him over the hole."

The slaves dragged Peter to the edge.

This was worse than the bridge. At least there he could see what was below. Peter did not want to fall. He grabbed the biceps of the slaves, but they peeled his fingers from their arms. When they held him by only his wrists, his back to the shaft, Qurdi stepped in front of him.

"I had plans for you and your concubine, Rim-Sin. The king had already given permission. But now she is dead, and you will die, too. I will have to think of a fitting explanation for your disappearance. Perhaps I will say your grief over offending the king was so great that you took your own life. Would you like that, Rim? Would you like me to preserve your memory that way?" His faced hardened. "Or perhaps I will say you chose the way of the coward."

Peter drew back as the priest laid a gentle hand on his face, smiling his dead smile. Qurdi cupped his hand under Peter's chin and brought his face close to Peter's. Peter could feel the priest's hot breath on his face. He could feel the oppression again. This time it did not appear that Qurdi had been replaced by another presence. Instead, the two were merged, united in their hatred of him. He closed his eyes.

"Too long you have resisted me, Rim-Sin. Where is your power now?"

Qurdi's hand fell away. A sharp pain cracked into the back of Peter's skull. The slaves released their grip, and Peter felt the empty blackness swallow him.

Chapter 17

WHAT HAD HE done?

When Akkad had accused Abigail of impropriety in the throne room, he had watched the representative's face go from ashen white to angry red. Before the day had been out, word had spread through the palace that Abigail had been pursuing one of the wise men. Given their clandestine meetings, which had been witnessed by many, it was not hard to believe.

Now, Akkad leaned over the wall atop Etemenanki. Why had he come here when it was only dusk? There was nothing to be done, no stars to study yet. Instead, he watched the flow of people in and out of the palace.

He was alone with his thoughts, though he would have preferred not to be. Akkad set his shoulders and tried to ignore the raging emotions.

His anger toward Abigail had cooled as the palace had erupted in rumors about her, and now the old doubts were returning, along with increasing guilt.

What had he done?

Did hours pass? Was it days? Peter awoke in total darkness. Was he dead? No, not dead. His head hurt too much for that. It throbbed with the pain of a million drumbeats in his brain. He felt his surroundings with numb fingers. The upper half of his body lay in mud. The lower half was submerged in water. If he had fallen a foot farther to the right, he would have fallen unconscious into the water and certainly drowned. He couldn't tell how far he had fallen from the underground level of the treasury. But it must not have been too far or he'd be dead.

Had Kaida been so lucky?

"Kaida," he moaned into the darkness. Nothing. "Kaida!" She didn't answer.

He managed to climb out of the water and get to his knees. His right wrist felt as if it were on fire. He made a small effort to move it. Badly sprained, but probably not broken. He climbed to his feet. The wet ground sucked at his feet.

Beside him, he could hear the pulley system whir, splashing buckets into a waterway and lifting them again. He looked up. The shaft seemed miles high. Would sunlight from the Gardens filter down to this level if it was morning?

Where was Kaida? It was so dark he couldn't make out the surface of the floor at his feet. He shuffled around hoping to bump into her, calling her name.

Please be alive. Please be alive. I need you.

He loved her. The knowledge surprised him like ice water on his face. She was beautiful and intelligent and frustrating, and he loved her. And if he could find her, he would tell her.

Akkad went to the throne room for the evening court session. He knew he was in trouble the moment he saw Qurdi. The priest looked terrible. His eyes were blackened with insanity and hatred. One of them seemed blackened as well by a bruise. And there was a bloody bandage around his neck. Did the same voices that whispered to Akkad in the night speak to Qurdi as well? Akkad had tried to silence them. What were they telling Qurdi?

As the wise men took their accustomed places before the king, Akkad watched Qurdi approach in an attempt to gain audience.

"Yes, Qurdi?" Nabu-kudurri-usur asked. "What has happened to you?"

"It is nothing, O King. But I am saddened to report that another of your own has shown you disloyalty."

"What is it this time, Qurdi?" The king sounded exasperated. Had he grown weary of the infighting that had become such a part of the *kasdim*?

"It is Akkad, O King."

Akkad's back straightened as the king turned toward him. What was this?

"It seems if it is not the Jews, it is you, Akkad," the king said.

"O King, they are tied together more than you know," Qurdi said.

The king's eyebrows knitted.

"I have been speaking to some in his circle, O King. It would appear that Akkad's involvement with your Jewish wife has not been as he described it."

"Oh?"

"He has pursued her, not the other way around. He has pressed his affections upon her in spite of her loyalty to you."

Akkad watched the king's eyes, trying to read them. Anger? No. Closer to annoyance.

"Who is it of his circle that accuses him?" the king asked. "Let that one speak to me directly."

Nadin-Aku stepped forward from the cluster in the back of the throne room. "I accuse him, O King." Shamash took a step forward to stand beside Nadin. "And I accuse him, O King."

Akkad's anger burned. He turned back to the king.

"What do you say to these accusations, Akkad?"

Peter's feet kicked something soft. He fell to the floor, searching with his hands. Fabric. An arm. A face.

"Kaida." He stroked her face. She stirred.

"Rim?" Her voice was groggy. "What happened?"

"Qurdi threw us down the shaft. We are at the bottom where the buckets lower into the water."

"Are you hurt?" she asked.

She would still ask him that after he'd left her with Qurdi? "My wrist is sprained. What about you?"

She didn't answer for a moment.

"I think I'm all right," she said, "but bruised. I fell in the water, but crawled out."

They listened to the buckets sloshing and dripping in their endless parade. The darkness hid them from each other.

He sensed Kaida move to a sitting position beside him.

"What are we going to do?" she asked.

"I don't know. And right now I don't care." He reached for her, wrapped his good arm around her shoulders, and pulled her close. She lowered her head into him and relaxed against his chest. "Kaida." He swallowed hard. "When I thought you were—dead—I—"

He felt the gentle pressure of her fingers against his lips. He circled his hand around hers and kissed her fingertips.

"Rim, don't."

"Don't make me stop, Kaida."

She pulled her hand away. "It's not possible, Rim."

"Kaida, please."

She shifted away from him. "It's not possible."

Akkad was tired. Tired of trying to make Abigail love him, tired of hiding his love for her, tired of aching over how he had denounced her. He was tired of listening to the voices and tired of trying to quiet them. As the eyes of everyone in the throne room fell on him, the truth tumbled from his heart.

"I love her, O King. It is true. I love her. And everything she says about her God, I fear it may be true. What if we worship only false images we have created for ourselves? What if the true God waits for us to turn to Him? To see past His creation and to truly see Him?"

The king stood, his face unreadable. "Have you attempted to make my wife love you, Akkad?" he asked simply.

Akkad hung his head. "Yes."

"Then what your fellow wise men accuse you of is true?"

Akkad turned toward his circle, and some of the old anger returned. Their accusations were to silence him, he knew. To silence his questions and doubts, because both were dangerous. In a world in which wisdom and knowledge were the key to power, no one could admit doubts.

Akkad turned back to the king. "They accuse me because they fear me, O King."

The king smiled in apparent amusement. "Fear you, Akkad?"

"Yes. They fear that I speak the truth. They have these doubts themselves. They do not have all the answers. And when they fear the answers will not please you, they change them. As they did with the birth charts for the king's new son."

The throne room grew even more silent, as though Akkad had threatened to let loose a caged animal. All eyes watched the king.

Nabu-kudurri-usur cocked his head, studying first Akkad and then the wise men in the back of the room. His eyes returned to Akkad. "I cannot allow any of my staff to show me disrespect as you have, Akkad. My wives belong to me, and those that betray me as you and Abigail have must suffer."

"Abigail is innocent, O King. She has resisted me from the beginning."

The king shook his head. "That is not what the palace eyes and ears have observed. You and Abigail have wanted to be together. And so you shall." He jerked his head toward the guards at the side of the throne room. "You will die together."

Time passed. Peter and Kaida decided they would wait for morning and hope for light enough to find a way out. The night lengthened around them.

"I'm thirsty," Kaida said.

Peter nodded. His eyes had adjusted enough to see that they were in a cavern or chamber beside a narrow channel that seemed to run off in both directions. The walls of this cool place were close to the channel on either side, giving them just enough room to stay dry. He dragged himself to the edge of the canal and lay on his stomach, his upper body jutting over the water. It was only about six feet wide, more like a storm drain than a waterway. Would the water be safe to drink?

He scooped some in his hand and touched his lips to it. It seemed OK. "Come and drink," he said to Kaida. She crawled over.

They flopped at the water's edge in silence when they were finished, not caring anymore how muddy they were.

"Why is it impossible, Kaida? Why could you and I not...? Only because I am not Jewish?"

"Not only that," she said. "It is because I worship... because I worship the one true God. You only worship yourself."

Peter felt like telling her that where he came from that would be considered an insult. Perhaps she meant it that way. He sat up and hugged his knees.

Reality is that which you create for yourself. You have the power to make your life into anything you want it to be.

"Yes, I can accept that I worship myself, I think. I believe I am as worthy of worship as anything. But so are you, and so is everyone."

Kaida nodded. "Even Qurdi-Marduk-lamur?"

Peter hesitated. He could only say yes. It was the only consistent answer. "Qurdi has not yet begun to realize the divinity inside him. No doubt his next life will be a difficult one."

"And you are basing that on what standard?"

Peter closed his eyes. It kept coming back to that, didn't it? No standard, no absolute. It meant that everything else he argued was nonsense. How could this woman even think about philosophy after what she'd been through? Strange, strange, wonderful Kaida.

"Rim," she said, "there is so much in your philosophy that doesn't fit. You believe there is no absolute, yet you believe that statement absolutely. You claim that everything is god and therefore there is no good or evil, yet you insist on personal responsibility and apply a standard of right and wrong—and you resist evil as strongly as I do. You say you have turned your back on the created gods of wood and stone, yet rather than turn to the true God, you have created a god out of man. A god in man's image." She paused. "When all you have is an impersonal consciousness that does not dictate morality, you rely only on yourself for all the answers."

These sounded like modern arguments. He'd heard them all before—in the twenty-first century. How had this ancient peasant girl hit upon them? "What's wrong with relying on myself for answers?"

She smiled. "Do you really want to be left with only yourself?"

"Perhaps. Once I have completed my journey toward transformation. Once I have fully realized my own potential, it will be enough."

"And what is stopping you, Rim? Why have you not transformed?"

How could he explain that to her? He thought of the anger that always waited below the surface. Why *wasn't* he transforming? But so many of the things that blocked the realization of one's own divinity were part of his twenty-first-century society. The effects of a poisoned environment, corporate dominance, processed food, addictive chemicals, dogmatic religion. Yet even as he thought it, the logic failed him. If the current state of society in the twenty-first century was at fault for blocking people's self-realization, why had they not transformed in one of their past lives when things were better? Or why had he not changed here, when none of those things was present?

"What will it take, Rim?" Kaida asked. "More education? How much? When will it be enough?"

Peter was tired. "I don't want to talk about it."

She persisted. "Have you ever met anyone who had fully realized their own divinity? Someone who was on the verge of merging back into the oneness, Rim? It seems as though you would be meeting people like that all the time, people who were no longer searching, who had reached perfection. And if that is how it happens, why is the number of people in the world growing rather than shrinking?"

"I don't know, Kaida. I don't know."

"Your religion costs you nothing, Rim. You can talk about it, but there is no danger of it doing anything to you. There is nothing to fear, nothing to obey. It is a coward's religion."

He should have been angry, but her words struck home.

"The God I worship, Rim, speaks from history and revelation, not from your intellectual speculation or from the fuzzy mysticism of these people. He has revealed Himself as other and separate from us, with a standard that is inviolable. To serve Him is to be reconciled to Him, not absorbed by Him. It comes down to only this, Rim: will you have faith in yourself and your own divinity, or faith in a personal God who is other than yourself? One who offers you atonement—a way that He Himself has provided?"

Peter suddenly saw himself as being offered a choice. He knew he had been holding something at arm's length, shutting it out. And now he was being given this free choice to open his arms in welcome or turn his back. He felt the approach of something—or Some*one*—he did not want to face.

It was not a pleasant feeling.

Chapter 18

AKKAD KNEW THE way. As the guards dragged him through the underground storerooms where he had crept to find Belteshazzar, his mind refused to acknowledge his reversal of fortune.

Not until the guards had shoved him to his knees on the floor of the dank cell did he admit that this was the end. Very few returned to their place after spending time here. Belteshazzar's God had delivered him from the king's wrath. Would Akkad's gods be so kind?

Akkad remained on his knees until the guards had gone, leaving one of their own at the door. The room was as repulsive as it had been when he had last been here, but at that time it had not bothered him. He was only a visitor—or an intended assassin. Now his surroundings took on new horrors as he wondered how long he would be here.

How long he stayed on his knees, he did not know. But as his eyes adjusted to the dim light, a figure in the corner sharpened into focus.

"What has happened, Akkad?" a voice asked from the corner.

"Abigail?"

"Yes."

"Abigail!"

Akkad crawled over and leaned against the wall as she did. The tiny oil light in a hollow in the center of the wall barely illuminated her features. She seemed so small there in the darkness, as though it would dissolve her into itself. "Abigail." He could think of nothing else to say.

"What has happened?" she asked again.

"The truth. I have been accused of pursuing one of the king's wives and trying to win her for myself."

Abigail lowered her head in shame. "I am sorry, Akkad."

Akkad managed a quiet laugh. "Sorry? Do you know why you are here?"

"I know it was you who told the king of my feelings for you," she said.

It was Akkad's turn for shame. "I was angry."

"But why?"

"Why? Because you rejected me, because you preferred him."

"Preferred whom?" she asked.

"The king!"

Silent tears fell from Abigail's eyes. They sparkled like jewels in the lamplight. He wiped her cheeks with the back of his muddy hand.

Abigail shook her head. "I tried so hard to forget you," she said. "Tried to ignore you, to force you to leave me alone. But nothing worked. It is right that I am here. That is why God did not allow me to escape with the diviner Rim-Sin. This is what I deserve. I was married to one man, but I loved another."

The anger Akkad had felt toward her melted away. Why should he condemn her for fulfilling her duty as a wife to the king? That was what she was, and not by her own choice. It was not Akkad that she had betrayed. He was the one who had asked her to be disloyal.

"I am sorry, too, Abigail. Sorry for all of it."

She lifted a weak smile to him and laid her head against his shoulder. "In the end, I was never a true wife to him, you know. Not in that way. He only ever wanted to talk with me."

"But you said—"

"Only to keep you away."

Akkad exhaled and touched her hair.

"What will happen to us now, Akkad?"

He closed his eyes, not wanting to end the moment, but knowing the truth must be spoken.

"We are to be executed."

Kaida's intellectual arguments had ceased for the moment. She seemed spent. They listened to the buckets' rhythmic sounds.

At last Peter heard Kaida sigh. "If you decide that there must be a God," she said, "you will have to discover for yourself who He is. I cannot tell you that."

"You suddenly have no answers? I haven't seen that before!" She laughed. "Kaida," he said, "I want to know why I should choose your God and not another. Why not Ishtar? Or Marduk?"

"I have answers, but they will not become yours until you see them for yourself."

Peter needed time to think all of it over. But here on a clay floor hundreds of feet from daylight was not the place. His wrist had swollen, and it throbbed painfully.

The dawn had come while they argued and dozed, but it wasn't until midday that the sun had risen sufficiently over the city to reach feeble rays into the shaft. Their light-starved eyes made the most of what they were given. Peter could see the waterway—a man-made canal that flowed to their left.

"It's time to follow the water," he said.

Peter crawled to the edge of the canal again, this time easing his body into the water. He held the bank with his good hand, and Kaida gripped his arm. His feet hit the bottom. The water came only to his chest.

"I think you can stand here, Kaida. We will have to go out this way."

Kaida lowered herself into the water beside him. The water came almost to her chin. "I can swim if I have to."

Peter peered into the half-light, trying to decide which way to go. Something coiled itself around his leg. He reached down and pulled it off, lifting it above the surface of the water. Snakes.

Kaida screamed and started splashing.

"Swim, Kaida!" Peter said. "Keep moving."

"I *am* moving!"

"No," he said, grabbing her flailing arm and pulling her along. "I mean swim."

They swam to their left, which Peter hoped was away from the Processional Way and toward the river. If they could reach the river, they could swim to safety.

The water was shallower in parts so they half-ran, half-swam for several hundred feet. Peter felt some kind of bugs crawling on his arms, but he didn't mention it to Kaida. They had long since left the light behind in their underground crypt. They moved in darkness with the current of cold water. Occasionally the side of the canal bumped them, sending them back into the center. As they traveled downstream the walls grew tighter. Peter worried that the canal was flowing downstream toward the river. Wouldn't all the canals run away from the river? Were they going in the wrong direction? From the position of the shaft, he was certain they weren't.

A stone wall smacked Peter in the forehead.

"Stop, Kaida."

His fingers groped the stone above his head. He reached as high as he could and to both sides. The wall completely blocked their path. He could see nothing. "The water passes through some kind of tunnel here."

"Can we get through?" Kaida asked.

Peter measured the distance from the surface of the water to the ceiling of the stone tunnel.

"Only if we swim underwater."

"How far does the tunnel go?"

"I have no idea." They both knew what that meant. They could hold their breath for only so long. If they ran out of air before they reached the other end, there would be no chance to go back.

"Let me try first," Peter said. "I'll only go a little way and then come back if I don't find the other side."

"What if you can't swim back against the current?"

He took a moment to evaluate the current pushing past him. It was steady but not too strong. "I think I'll be OK."

Her hand found his under the water. "Be careful."

Peter took a deep breath and dipped below the surface, holding his hands above his head as he walked in a crouch. He kept going until he figured he'd used about half his oxygen, and then turned and swam quickly back.

"Did you reach the other side?"

"No. I'm going to try again. I can go farther if I swim hard and then stand up, rather than walking."

He plunged under the inky water again. When he stood a few moments later, his head bumped stone. But his mouth was out of the water. The ceiling must be a little higher here. He gulped air and swam back.

"Well?" Kaida said.

"I didn't reach the end, but there was room enough to breathe. I went a good distance, though. Do you think you can swim that far?"

He could hear her chuckle in the darkness. "Are you forgetting our jump into the river?"

No need to remind him.

"Let's go." He dove first, swimming as far as he could, then standing. He gulped air again, waiting for Kaida to surface. He heard a little splash much farther down the canal. She had the stronger lungs.

"Can you breathe there?" he said.

"Yes! What are you doing all the way back there?"

Very funny. He swam along the surface to catch up to her.

"Look, Rim," she pointed. "Doesn't it look lighter up ahead?"

It did. They both swam hard. They had apparently left the snakes behind. When they stood again, their stone tunnel had opened up. The light ahead was stronger. They swam again. Daylight shone ahead.

The current sucked harder at them as they moved, until they gave up swimming altogether and let it carry them.

Too late they saw that the canal seemed to end in mid-air. Peter heard the crashing of water far below just before they flew over the edge of the waterfall.

Water droplets shimmered in the sunlight, surrounded and joined him in his flight through the mighty spray. Moments of weightlessness, and then the canal below rushed up to meet his feet. He hit the water with a jolt, plunged like a dropped anchor into the depths, and felt the mucky canal floor beneath him. He beat his arms against the current, trying to find the surface. His lungs screamed. Just as he despaired of finding air, his head broke into sunlight.

He was a good distance downstream from the waterfall already. Ahead of him the canal ran past the citadel, the last remaining building between him and the river. He twisted in the water, trying to find Kaida. He spotted her at the edge of the canal. She had made it to the bank, but she did not look conscious.

He threw himself on the bank beside her, checking for

breathing. No sign of it. He thanked whatever higher power cared to hear him for the CPR course he had taken. A few thrusts, a few breaths, and Kaida was choking out canal water.

She tried to rise.

"Lie still," he said. He leaned over her, worried. Belatedly he noticed that she wasn't wearing the slave's tunic he'd always seen her in. Instead she wore a fine, beaded dress very much like something he'd seen the harem women wearing in the palace. Where had that come from? Even wet, it looked beautiful on her.

She lay back on the grass and looked up at him. "I can't believe we're alive."

"I know," Peter laughed.

Kaida smiled. "I have never heard you laugh," she said. "I like it." She looked into his eyes.

Why couldn't they stay here like this forever? Did he really have to go home? What was there to go back to? His classes? His research? He loved them, but not like he loved this amazing Jewish girl from Babylon.

"Now where?" Kaida sighed.

Peter pitied her. She was dirty, tired, and full of canal water. "You go home to Rebekah," he said, wondering if Cosam had been executed.

Kaida pushed the wet hair from her eyes. "Where will you go?"

"To the Temple of Ishtar."

Chapter 19

THERE WAS CELEBRATING in the Jewish districts of Babylon. The God of Israel had done a mighty miracle, sparing Hananiah, Azariah, and Mishael from the furnace and causing Nebuchadnezzar to recognize His authority. At least now the king would add the Most High to his list of powerful gods. It was not repentance, but it was something.

Cosam pulled Mishael aside at the first opportunity. "Praise be to God for your deliverance, brother!"

Mishael's eyes shone. "It was a thing no words can describe. I still cannot believe what happened."

"When your feet touch the ground again I must tell you all that the wise man Daniel taught me of the Messiah!"

An outsider approached, and Cosam paused.

Mishael turned to the man. "Faram-Enlil. Welcome."

The *rab alani* bowed once.

"Is there something you need, Faram?" Mishael asked.

Faram eyed Cosam. "I am searching for information."

"We will tell you what we can."

"The diviner Rim-Sin. Have you heard that he escaped prison?"

Cosam flinched. Rim-Sin had escaped?

His reaction was obviously not lost on Faram, who turned to him. "I still would like to see him face justice for killing Reuben."

Mishael nodded. "As would we. But I am afraid we cannot help you find him, if that is what you were hoping."

Faram's attention was still on Cosam. "I am told you are the brother of his concubine."

"That is true. But I do not know where he is."

Faram folded his arms and scowled. "I would hate to think the Jews were hiding someone who had killed one of their own."

Cosam said nothing, but Mishael touched Faram's arm. "You know us better than that, Faram."

The *rab alani* turned to Mishael, and his face softened into resignation. "Yes. You are right, Mishael. I do."

The streets were crowded today. Peter pushed his way through the throng, wondering how much time he had lost while in his cell. He stopped a young woman who carried a basket of brown fruit he didn't recognize. "How long until the New Year Festival begins?"

She laughed and looked at the sky. "Find a magician to tell you how many hours until the sun sets. I don't know."

Today? It started today? *Not good.*

Peter ran through the streets, avoiding the Processional Way, hoping he was taking the most direct route. He had seen the temple twice during all his exploits around Babylon. His wrist throbbed all the way down to his fingertips.

He had to double back a few times. But then, there it was. Several temple prostitutes meandered around the courtyard. There was no sign of Qurdi. Peter made his way through the women, watching for the priest.

He entered the antechamber. There was no one around. Was Ishtar neglected? Where had everyone gone? Some noise in a room off the antechamber sent him into the chapel to avoid notice. He barely glanced at the statue of Ishtar that stared at him from the center of the back wall.

Qurdi was not here either. But where was the lampstand? A table on the side of the room drew his attention, but then he wished he hadn't looked. The innards of some animal were spread on the table, with a bloody knife lying beside them. The high priest must be have been looking for knowledge in the entrails. Peter picked up the knife with his left hand and held it against his leg. Could he use it? The memory of Kerkuk bothered him.

Then suddenly Qurdi stood in the doorway, the lampstand gripped in one hand.

Peter straightened. "I want the lampstand, Qurdi."

The high priest laughed. "You will not die, will you, Rim-Sin?"

Daniel's words came back to him unbidden. *You must defeat the powers arrayed against you.* What more was there to do, besides getting the lampstand? He was no match for the power here.

He had the feeling this was going to get ugly. The knife in his hand felt good, but he wished his sprained wrist didn't prevent him from using his right hand.

Qurdi leaned the lampstand against the wall and approached. Peter held the knife in front of him. "Do not come any closer, Qurdi."

"Would you dare to harm Ishtar's favored one, Rim-Sin? In her own temple? Before the gaze of the goddess herself?"

"I'll kill you if I have to."

"Will you?" Qurdi's eyes drilled into his own, piercing him, holding him, as though they could lay his soul bare. "Will you?" he repeated, his eyes still fixed. "Or will you give the knife to me and leave the temple?"

Peter felt odd. Part of him really wanted to give the knife to Qurdi. He shook his head. What kind of sorcery was this? "No." It took effort to bring the word out.

Qurdi took a step closer, and Peter took a step backward. His thoughts were clearer now, but he really didn't want to kill this man.

Daniel's words came to him again. *You must submit to God to defeat the powers arrayed against you.*

He didn't care about defeating. He just wanted to go home. They stood face-to-face for a long moment, and then Qurdi lunged. He grabbed at Peter's left wrist and tried to wrench the knife from his hand.

Peter twisted away from him, slashing at empty air. Where was Qurdi? The priest had somehow moved to the other side of him. Peter spun, knife held out.

They circled like two prizefighters waiting for an opportunity. When it came, it was on Qurdi's side. He kicked at Peter's feet, knocking him off balance. Peter fell, and Qurdi landed a sharp kick to his stomach. Peter lay on his back and slashed again at the air above him.

Qurdi was behind him. Peter jumped to his feet and circled again. The priest seemed to be everywhere, a formidable opponent even without a weapon. His black cloak flapped around him like bat's wings.

Qurdi lunged again, this time grabbing Peter's right wrist and sending shooting sparks up his arm. Peter felt faint for a moment, long enough for Qurdi to twist the knife from his grasp. Peter fell back. Now he was unarmed.

"It is time to die, Rim-Sin."

Peter was backed against the wall, but he shook his head. "Not yet, Qurdi."

Qurdi charged at him, and Peter grabbed the only thing nearby—a small gold statue of a palace courtier. He expected it to be heavy, but it must have been wood overlaid with gold. He hefted it above his head as protection as Qurdi's knife crashed down. The priest's eyes bulged as the knife dug into the soft gold. Peter almost laughed.

The sacrilege only seemed to make Qurdi angrier. He hacked and sliced as Peter continued to ward off the blows with the statue. Peter pulled away from the wall, trying to gain a better position.

When he had a chance, Peter slid his hands to the bottom of the statue. He could wield it better this way, like a baseball bat. His right wrist throbbed.

It was like an outrageous fencing match, with Qurdi brandishing a kitchen knife and Peter a statue.

They circled. Peter saw fear flicker across Qurdi's eyes. Why? Something behind Peter. He stepped to his right to get a better view. Ah, the statue of Ishtar.

With a laugh, Peter put his hand on the statue. It rocked slightly at his touch.

"No!" Qurdi screamed and rushed forward.

Peter shoved, and the statue toppled to the ground and rolled.

"Goddess! Goddess!" The priest was shrieking now, bending over the statue.

Peter ran to the corner for the lampstand and sprinted out of the chapel with it.

The afternoon was waning. There was still so much to do. He was almost across the courtyard when a tackle from behind sent him sprawling. The lampstand flew from his grasp and landed in the stones a few feet away. He rolled to his back in time to see Qurdi over him, both hands wrapped around the hilt of the knife blade raised above Peter's chest.

Peter closed his eyes as the knife swung down in slow motion.

He felt nothing, but he heard a sickening crunch. He opened his eyes. Qurdi lay on the ground, the knife beside him. Over them both stood a grinning Cosam, the lampstand in his hand like a bludgeon.

"Kaida told me you had come here," he said. "I thought you might need help."

"Cosam!"

What could he ever do to repay this man who had saved his life more than once? Cosam held out a hand, and the big man pulled him to his feet and handed him the lampstand.

"Cosam, I'm so glad to see you alive." Peter looked at Qurdi, unconscious on the ground, but not dead. "Cosam, I need your help!"

Cosam nodded as if he understood. They jogged out of the courtyard and into the street.

He saw Kaida running toward them. "Rim," she said as she reached him, panting. "You've got the lampstand."

"I need both of you," Peter said. "I can't explain, and I don't have much time. But I have to find a way to send this lampstand to Jerusalem."

Cosam eyebrows shot up. "It is from the temple!" He touched a hand to the delicate work. "Oh! I used it as a weapon!"

"Yahweh will forgive you," Peter said. "You've got to help me. Daniel has told me that to return it, I must follow the way of your forefather Joseph, but from the end to the beginning. Do you understand what that means?"

Cosam tore his eyes from the lampstand and glanced back toward the temple. "I believe we should move elsewhere to discuss this."

Peter agreed. The three ran toward the residential section of the city for several minutes. At length they ducked into an alley between rows of houses.

Kaida touched Peter's arm, panting. "I have been thinking. About Joseph."

Peter nodded, encouraging her to continue.

"He was a free man, and then he was taken to Egypt to be a slave. Perhaps you are to send a slave to Egypt to become free."

"How did Joseph get to Egypt?"

"His brothers sold him to traders, who took him with them."

Peter gazed at the sun, sinking lower in the sky. "Could we pay traders to take someone with them? Someone who would guard the lampstand and take it to Jerusalem?"

Cosam nodded. "Traders on their way to Egypt would be a safe way of travel for someone going to Israel. But what if this is not what Daniel meant?"

Peter looked at the two of them. "It has to be! I don't have time for anything else. Cosam, you must take it back to Jerusalem."

Cosam shook his head. "I will not leave my family," he said. He looked at Kaida. "And it would not be safe to send a woman alone."

Peter slapped a hand against his thigh and turned a circle in the street. He was running out of time. Whom did he know that would be willing to leave Babylon for a chance to go to Israel?

Kaida thought of the slave at the same moment Peter did. They looked at each other and said his name together.

"Elam."

There was so little time now. Peter tried not to think about the fact that, if all went well, he would soon be leaving Kaida far behind. By the time he took his first new breath in the twenty-first century her bones would long ago have turned to dust. Better to focus on the task at hand.

Peter had tried to send Cosam and Kaida home, but they were determined to see this thing through with him. They found Elam in Rim-Sin's kitchen. A hurried explanation left the slave baffled.

"Go to . . . Jerusalem? But I— You're . . . ? I'm your slave. What does—? No! I will be killed if I am found. An escaped slave is always executed immediately."

Cosam put a hand on Peter's shoulder. "Set him free, Rim."

"How?"

"The local judge. He will perform the ceremony."

Peter looked at Elam. "Will you do it? If I set you free, will you take the lampstand back?"

Elam searched the three faces before him, and then nodded. "I will return home." He touched the lampstand that Peter still clutched. "And I will bring the symbol of our nation with me."

Peter breathed out in relief. "We will need money, Elam. Get me all the money I have."

Minutes later, they ran from Rim-Sin's house, taking care in case Qurdi stalked the streets. Peter wondered briefly if he was supposed to have killed Qurdi, if that was the thing he was leaving undone. But there was no time now. The New Year Festival would begin at dusk, within the hour.

The local judge heard testimony in a small courtyard. Proceedings were winding down when the four hurtled into the area. Peter slowed and handed the lampstand to Cosam. "Stay here."

He pulled Elam and Kaida forward.

"Rim-Sin!" the judge seemed surprised to see him. "I had heard that you were imprisoned for—certain indiscretions."

"A misunderstanding. The king has released me. And I wish to free this slave." Peter pushed Elam forward.

In their race to the judge, Peter had made another decision. If this worked and he got back to his life in the twenty-first century, it might mean that the real Rim-Sin would suddenly appear back in his own skin here in Babylon. Wouldn't that be a shock to the people who had come to know the new Rim-Sin? So, if the real Rim-Sin were returning, he knew he had to protect Kaida. He pulled her to his side. "And I also wish to free my concubine."

She looked at him in disbelief.

Peter looked at the judge. "Tell me the words to recite." He said the words as the judge instructed him, repeating the phrase for both Elam and Kaida. "You have been my faithful slave. I honor you now with freedom. Let no man enslave you again."

The judge put his seal into two small clay tablets. They were free.

Peter handed the tablets to them, and they headed for the main part of the city. As they walked, Cosam tore the bottom part of his tunic away and wrapped the still-wet clay tablet proving Elam's freedom in the fabric. Peter watched Elam place it carefully in the bag he carried, next to a half-finished carving of a wooden horse.

It took only minutes to find a group of traders moving through the clogged streets. Cosam asked if they were leaving the city heading for Egypt by way of Israel. They were not. As they searched, Peter purchased a bolt of cloth and wrapped the lampstand, securing it with a strip torn from the bottom of the fabric. The group pressed on, stopping more foreigners with loaded carts and donkeys. Finally they found a group whose destination was Egypt. Peter pressed all of the money they had retrieved from Rim-Sin's house into the palm of one bearded, dark-skinned man.

"Give him safe passage to Israel," he said.

The trader shrugged. "He will be as safe as we are."

Peter placed the lampstand on the wagon loaded with Babylonian goods and turned to grip Elam's shoulders. The older man still seemed stunned by the events of the day. "You can do this, Elam. You are going home."

The former slave nodded and wrapped his hands around Peter's forearms, returning his grip. "Thank you, Rim-Sin."

The traders moved on toward the city gate, disappearing into the crowds, with Elam in tow. Peter watched for a few moments, Cosam and Kaida at his side, then turned to go. He was barely conscious of the other two now. He ran for Cosam's house.

The vase still sat on the storeroom ledge, as he had hoped beyond imagining that it would. Cosam and Kaida followed him in. No one spoke, and Peter knew the two must be completely baffled by his bizarre actions.

"I must go," he said. He held Kaida with his eyes, trying to say good-bye somehow. "Kaida, if I... if I start acting, you know, the old way—like I used to—treating you unkindly, just stay far away from me, do you understand? You're free now. I want... you deserve a happy life."

Cosam clapped Peter on the back. "I do not know why you act so strangely, Rim, but may the blessing of the Most High be upon you."

Kaida grabbed at Peter's sleeve. "What's happening? Where are you going?"

Peter pulled away from her. "I have to. I'm sorry."

He ran from the room.

Outside, the heat of the day had dropped away. The sun was low on the horizon, the New Year Festival was so close now. Everyone was outside, making their way to the main part of the city.

"Rim-Sin!"

Peter turned to Kaida's shout.

She ran to him. "Don't leave me!"

Peter held the vase with his left hand and wrapped his right arm around the girl, pulling her toward himself. It was reckless and pointless, but he kissed her right there in the street. He kissed her passionately and wished with everything in him that he could take her with him. But she was not a souvenir. She belonged here. He had to say good-bye.

He felt her respond to his kiss. He prolonged it a moment more, then pulled away. The sun was almost gone. "You are free now, Kaida. Remember, stay as far away from Rim-Sin as you can." He kissed her again. "Good-bye."

He ran, leaving her behind, tears blurring his eyes.

Kaida watched Rim run toward the city. She touched her lips, too shocked for words.

Cosam joined her a moment later. He had seen. "I don't know what's happening with that man."

"Neither do I."

"I pray that God works in his heart, though."

Kaida smiled weakly at Cosam and nodded, but her heart had shattered.

She walked with Cosam back to his home in silence. The New Year Festival was beginning, and the residential streets had emptied. Even in the twilight, the heat was unrelenting. Kaida wondered if she would ever get used to the desert climate. She ran the back of her hand across her forehead.

Boston was never this hot.

Peter had done all he needed to do. Now he just had to get to the Hanging Gardens. The crowds made the running easy: they were all headed the same direction. He dashed through the streets, head down, until he reached the palace. The biggest celebration of the year was about to begin, and no one was looking for one escaped diviner. He slipped into the palace carrying the vase in his uninjured hand and took the wide staircase up to the Gardens.

If you do not defeat the powers arrayed against you, you will leave something very important unfinished. Take the object that brought you here. Cleanse yourself. Ask the God of Israel to return you to your home.

Peter ascended the seven huge tiers of the Hanging Gardens. He stopped at the point where the buckets of water were released into the irrigation system. He filled the vase from a spilling bucket, then turned and looked out over the city.

Standing here at the highest point in the Gardens, it was like looking down from a mountaintop. Across from him, flames surged upward on the Platform of Etemenanki. Slaves and priests were lighting the torches for the evening's celebration. Too bad they would not have their star attraction. Peter would not be there. He would not perform the sacrifice that Rim-Sin was required to perform.

Nor would he be there to face trial and execution for his actions with Ilushu.

He would not be there to watch Cosam and Rebekah raise their two children and the newly adopted Isaac.

He would not be there to love Kaida, to grow old with her, to debate religion with her, to prove to her that he could love her honorably.

Peter watched the sun dip below at the edge of the desert. As the final rays disappeared, he lifted the vase above him and poured the water over his head, cleansing himself of the dust of Babylon.

And then, for the first time in his life, Peter prayed.

Chapter 20

AM I BACK? Dear God, am I back?

The same blinding headache. The same odd taste of sulfur.

The coolness of the room enveloped him, offering blessed relief from the omnipresent heat.

He still held the blue glazed terra-cotta vase in his hand. He was alone in the museum's back room. Alone.

He bent to the vase, knowing the truth, but still unwilling to believe it.

Underneath. I must look underneath.

There it was. The simple outline of the university's logo scratched into the bottom. Hugh had called the find "unbelievable." No wonder.

Shaking, he returned the vase to the table and backed away.

Kaida. Oh, Kaida. I'm so sorry. I had no choice. If I could have made you understand, you would have agreed. I had no choice.

Peter burst out of the museum into the darkened city. A fresh coating of snow clung to the few cars left on the street, and the clouds hung heavy with an unfamiliar dampness. The subway shook the asphalt under Peter's feet, jolting him with a reminder of how far he had just traveled himself. His head still felt like it was splitting, but his wrist seemed completely healed. The swelling was gone, and he had no pain in it at all. He looked around. Was he really home? He checked his watch: 6:40. He could make the 6:45 subway if he hurried.

He ran the block to the subway entrance, stumbled down the stairs, paid his fare with the change in his tuxedo pocket, and jumped through the sliding door. He fell onto a bench and stared out the window.

Had it been real? Had it been a dream? He raked his hands through his hair, and they shook as he remembered the blue glazed vase he had left in the museum. The too familiar design around the edge. He remembered working on it with Kaida in Cosam's storeroom. He remembered where Kaida had been sitting.

Peter's heart pounded. It was so impossible he couldn't even imagine it. The ancient vase had been unearthed in some dig halfway across the world a few weeks ago. But it was his vase!

He looked at his watch again. He couldn't seem to make his foggy brain give meaning to the numbers and letters he saw there.

March 20! Time had not stood still here. Five weeks had passed!

The subway screeched to a stop. Peter got off.

Fifteen minutes later Peter reached his apartment on the third floor of the Regency Building. His keys were in his pocket, and he unlocked the door with shaky hands, noticing again that his right wrist no longer ached.

A soft throat clearing alerted him to his neighbor's presence. Peter turned.

"Mr. Allenby—"

The man held up a hand, his lips pinched. "Don't worry; I won't be bothering you."

"You're not bothering me," Peter said. "I'm sure you've been wondering where I've been—"

"I don't keep tabs on my neighbors, Dr. Thornton. You made it clear last night that you expect to be left alone. I only wanted to know if you've seen Sassy."

Peter frowned. "Sassy?" Mr. Allenby's cat often greeted Peter in the hallway with a sullen hiss. But not tonight.

"No, I'm sorry, Mr. Allenby. I—"

The man backed away. "It's OK. Sorry to bother you then. I'll leave you alone."

Peter nodded and watched the man back away. Last night? What had Peter said to Allenby last night? Last night he'd been in Babylon.

He swung his apartment door open and flicked the light switch.

The apartment looked the same. Decorated in browns and grays, with antiques and collectibles reposing on shelves and strategically snoozing on end tables. After the color of Babylon, the room was as dull as a morgue.

He wandered into the kitchen, trying to readjust. His eyes caught sight of a jar of peanut butter lying on its side on the counter, a knife smeared with the stuff beside it. Peter hated peanut butter. He never bought it, much less ate it.

What else? What other changes? In his bedroom, several books he hadn't read in years lay on the bed. The bathroom was a mess. He never left it like that.

Five minutes later he flopped down on his fuzzy brown couch. There was no doubt in his mind: while he had been spending the last five weeks living Rim-Sin's life, Rim-Sin had been living his.

The doorbell rang, and Peter roused himself to answer it.

Hugh stood in the doorway. His colleague looked dour.

"Hey, Hugh!" Peter said. "Come in. Do I have a tale for you."

"No thank you, Peter." Hugh's manner was unfriendly. "I

just came by to let you know that the board meeting will be on Thursday night."

"Board meeting?"

Hugh shook his head, irritated. "Yes, Peter, the board meeting. I told you about it yesterday, remember?"

"Can you tell me again, Hugh?" Peter rubbed his eyes. "I'm—not feeling quite right."

"You haven't been yourself for weeks, Peter."

"Yeah, you got that right."

Hugh rolled his eyes. "The Board of Trustees is meeting to determine whether to demand your resignation."

"Resignation!" Peter rubbed at his temples. Had he been named president while he was gone? Resign? "Have I botched being president that badly already, Hugh?"

Hugh snorted. "What are you talking about? You know the board named Allan Washburn president after your debacle with the accreditation team. The only reason you're still teaching is because of your tenure. But that's looking pretty shaky right now, too. Gross misconduct, they're saying."

Peter stumbled backward and sank into the ratty couch. "Allan Washburn is president?"

Hugh shook his head and reached for the doorknob. "A few weeks ago I felt sorry for you, Peter, for whatever crisis you're going through. But I'm way past pity now." He opened the door and stepped into the hallway. "If you don't get it together, Peter, you're going to have nothing left."

Allan Washburn is president.

He couldn't get over the thought. Thirty minutes after Hugh's departure Peter was still on the couch repeating the horrible news, reopening the wound again and again. *I knew Washburn wanted it, but* I *was their first choice.*

It was gone. Everything he had worked for destroyed in just a few weeks by one crazy pagan. He'd lost the presidency, maybe his teaching career. Hugh's friendship. Who knew what else?

Shock gave way to anger. He was still trying to figure out what his whole trip to Babylon was about, but now did he have to fix what had gotten messed up here? It was too much.

He finally realized he couldn't do anything until the meeting Thursday, when he would grovel before the board for his job. So he immersed himself in cleaning therapy, hoping to purge Rim-Sin from his apartment if he could not purge him from his life. He consoled himself with the thought that if Rim-Sin truly had switched back with him and was in Babylon again, he was now discovering that Peter had done a lot to mess up his little world, too. It gave him a grim smile.

He used about a gallon of Mr. Clean in the kitchen and bathroom, and then moved on to his bedroom. An unusual item in the corner caught his attention, and he took a closer look. An electric shoe buffer? It was the third such new item he had found. Where did all this stuff come from? Suddenly remembering the Sharper Image catalog on his coffee table, Peter grabbed his Visa card out of his wallet and called the 800 number to check his balance. When he heard the figure, blood pounded in his head. Could he report the card stolen? That would be a hard one to explain. He tossed the Visa card on the living room end table and went back to the bedroom.

Several books littered the floor near his bed. He retrieved them, pitching them onto the bed and flopping next to them. What would Rim-Sin find interesting reading material? The first two books Peter didn't recognize at all. *The Art of Magic* and *200 Magic Tricks Anyone Can Do.* More purchases? No, these were library books. Rim-Sin had certainly been a busy guy. No doubt he amazed them all in the palace throne room when he returned. Peter could see him pulling rabbits out of hats and coins out of people's ears. Peter looked at the date on the card in the back of the book. Overdue. Of course. A current issue of *Magician's Monthly* lay next to the books.

The next book was one he remembered from his own shelf. *Pagans and Christians* by Robin Lane Fox. This was a little more intriguing. What had Rim-Sin's goal been here? Peter flipped through the pages, surprised to see passages underlined. He read all the marked sections he found. They followed one thought: the rise of Christianity and subsequent decline of idol worship.

It would appear that Rim-Sin did as much reading as Peter did. Why was he surprised? He was a "wise man," after all. What would Rim-Sin do in the past with the knowledge that Christianity had eradicated the worship of pagan gods?

After the bedroom, Peter moved into his study, which also doubled as his pottery-making space. His mahogany desk and bookshelves occupied one side of the room, and in the other corner he had set up his wheel. He had put an arc of vinyl flooring in this section to save the carpet. One wall held floor-to-ceiling shelves and boasted several valuable pottery pieces, as well as a few of his own he felt were worthy to occupy the lower shelves. He did a quick inventory to make sure everything was still there. Nothing was missing. But then, why would Rim-Sin care about old pottery? He was older than all of it.

His life still felt foreign to him, as if he were still following Rim-Sin, stepping into places the diviner had already been.

We are all part of the divine consciousness; all of us are one. Any boundaries that we feel between ourselves do not exist. They have been artificially created.

Peter certainly didn't feel that way.

The study seemed largely untouched, though something had obviously spilled on his pottery wheel. Wine, maybe. Was Rim-Sin in here getting drunk and making pottery? In spite of himself, Peter laughed aloud.

He was headed out of the room when he realized there was an unusual odor in the room. What was it? He circled the room, sniffing like a bloodhound. The smell was worse in the pottery corner. There wasn't much there, besides the bin where Peter threw his scraps. What had Rim-Sin tossed away?

A white kitchen trash bag lay in the bin. He pulled it out and knew immediately that the odor originated from inside the bag. Dreading what he might find, Peter untied the knot and looked inside.

Blood, fur, and internal organs jumbled together in a greasy mess. He snapped the bag shut, but then forced himself to take a closer look. What was it? He jiggled the bag around a little, trying to glimpse something identifiable. And then it became obvious. Sassy had taken his final catnap.

Peter tied the bag closed again, glancing at the wine stains on the pottery wheel. Not wine, he realized. Rim-Sin had performed a sacrifice and spread the entrails out to read. Sheep were hard to come by in the city. Cats—not so hard. Poor Sassy.

Peter took the bag to the incinerator chute. He didn't want Mr. Allenby to see Sassy this way. The thought crossed his mind that he ought to say a prayer or something, but he dismissed it. He would have to think of a gentle way to break the news to the cat's owner.

When the housecleaning was finished and he'd exhausted a can of Lysol in the corner of the study, Peter slumped onto the couch again and laid his head back. While he had been purging the apartment he had not allowed himself to think about Kaida. To think about her would be to admit that she had been dead for centuries. But now thoughts of her came flooding back unbidden. He knew that whatever had happened had been over and done with for millennia. So why did he still feel a living connection with Kaida, Cosam, Ilushu, and even Daniel?

He fell into an achy half-sleep on the couch and awoke at

dawn feeling like his head was in a vise.

He wished it were the weekend, but—if his memory could be trusted—he had a ten o'clock class on Wednesdays. And he wasn't going to give the board any more ammunition before the meeting tomorrow night.

The last time he'd seen his car was in the hotel parking garage at the fund-raising banquet. He had no idea where it was now, so it had to be public transportation again this morning.

Peter dropped off the rented tuxedo on his way to the subway. As he laid the tux on the counter, he fastened on his most apologetic smile for the approaching cashier. "I'm so sorry, but I completely forgot to return this tux I rented last month. I put it in my closet and just forgot!"

The cashier, a young gum-chewing girl with dangly earrings, wrinkled her nose. "Aren't you Dr. Thornton?"

"Yes, that's right."

"You were here yesterday picking this up."

Peter blinked. "Say what?"

"The last time you rented from us you brought it back real late, remember? You never brought it back until we called you. That's why my boss made me tell you to pay in full yesterday."

Peter nodded, still smiling. "Yes, yes, of course. I'm sorry. I've been a little—unwell."

The girl shrugged. "Whatever." She took the tuxedo and turned her back on him. He left before he made himself look any more foolish.

He tossed the new information around in his mind as he waited for the subway. So Rim had returned the last tux late, after a phone call from the rental store. And then he'd rented a tux again yesterday before Peter came home. Why? Peter tried to remember if he had any engagements scheduled for yesterday. But would Rim know about them anyway?

It all suddenly clicked. When Peter had come home, he had

assumed at first that no time had passed because he was in the same place, dressed in the same way. But time *had* passed. Did that mean that Rim-Sin had come to the museum last night, dressed in a tux? If it did, it could only mean that he was trying to return to Babylon, trying to re-create the conditions that he found himself in when he arrived.

Why was Rim-Sin trying to return?

It was unknowable. Besides, it was over. What difference did any of it make anymore?

Riding the subway to school reminded him of his early days as a graduate assistant, before he had been able to afford an apartment uptown and his own car. He was still reminiscing when he pushed open the double doors into Wells Hall where his office was squeezed into a corner of the second floor. He wandered up there, feeling as if he had been gone for years instead of weeks. The halls, the offices, they all seemed so unfamiliar. He entered his office and was not surprised to find it disorganized. What had Rim been looking for in here?

The secretary of the department leaned her head in tentatively. "Dr. Thornton?"

"Yes, Susan, come in."

"Really?" She seemed reluctant.

"Yes. Come in. Sit. What have you been doing the past few weeks?"

Susan clearly thought he was the nutty professor. "I wanted to give you this." She handed him a copy of *Newsweek*.

"Why do I need this?"

Confusion again. "You told me to bring it to you as soon as it arrives."

"Yes, of course."

Susan retreated, and Peter skimmed the magazine. What had the diviner been looking for in *Newsweek*?

World events? Something to take back to Babylon? But these

events would be so far into the future, what use could they be to Rim?

An article toward the back caught his eye. Something about peace talks in the Middle East. Was that it? Had Rim been tracking the activities of the Jewish nation?

He glanced at his watch. It was time to get to class. His first class of the day on Wednesdays was one of his favorites: Comparative Religion, filled mostly with freshmen. They were still so eager to learn, yet unsure of what to think. Peter had always been a favorite professor in this building. He used his acceptance to open their minds to new possibilities.

As he trotted down the hall with his briefcase, a thought jolted him. Since his conversations with Kaida, he was not so certain anymore of the things he had once taught in that room. Could he go in there and insist that all roads of religion lead to one summit? Why had he never asked himself what that summit was? If anyone had asked, he would have told them it was the ultimate goal of religion. But now that answer sounded meaningless. Religion led to the goal of religion? Empty words. He realized that what he had really been saying was that all religion leads to nothing.

Well, he could live with that. Or could he? What if all the roads of religions *did* lead to the same place—and that place was destruction?

As he entered the room, the students quieted immediately and leaped to their seats, facing forward like lines of Babylonian soldiers. He'd never had that effect before. Maybe one positive thing had come out of Rim's interference in his life.

"Good morning," he greeted them.

As one, they chanted back, "Good morning, Chief."

Chief? As in chief of magicians? This guy was unbelievable. "Who can tell me where we left off last week?"

One student raised her hand. "Outside." The rest smiled.

"Outside?" he repeated.

"Yes, we were outside, worshiping the goddess."

It was worse than he had expected.

Between classes Peter microwaved some lunch and hid in his office, trying to readjust, trying to evaluate his experience. It had been a life-changing event, that was certain. He wondered if he were now the foremost expert on Babylonian history. Not that he could do anything about it. What group of scholars would believe some nut claiming to have been there? Perhaps he should apply himself to unsolved aspects of Babylonian culture and offer plausible explanations to current theories, without mentioning his experience.

Peter put the plastic tray from his Hungry-Man dinner into the trash and went to his computer. He had to get up again to retrieve his glasses from his briefcase. Five weeks of not needing them had turned into a habit, and he kept forgetting to put them on. A minute later he was searching online for research on Babylon, sixth century BCE.

It was fascinating to read about places he had now seen firsthand. He wondered about Qurdi-Marduk-lamur and his gods. He typed "Ishtar" into his search engine and hit Enter.

There were a few sites that looked research-oriented, but he was surprised to find titles of sites that implied a current religion. His curiosity led him on.

An hour later he leaned back from his desk, rubbing the muscles in the back of his neck. His eyes hurt, and the chair had become as uncomfortable as his thoughts. It appeared that worship of the goddess was alive and well and thriving on the Internet.

A whole new generation of pagans had sprung up, priding themselves on the name and accepting everyone and everything into their circle. Almost everything. Apparently they claimed to be tolerant of Christians along with everyone else, but anyone who insisted that their way was the only true way was not welcome. That left out Christians, of course, but the pagan community contended it was Christianity's intolerance that disqualified them.

So who were the Neo-Pagans? They celebrated life. They were not concerned with which religion you held to, only what kind of person your religion helped you to become. There was nothing right and nothing wrong.

"If there is nothing right and nothing wrong, then there is nothing."

Had he just said that aloud?

To his mind now it seemed it would be better to pick one road and stick to it, forgetting all other roads. But such thinking was dangerous. It could lead a man to belief in God. What would Kaida say to that?

Oh, Kaida. How could I have left you behind?

Chapter 21

PETER ESCAPED THE university by three in the afternoon, trying to get away from his thoughts. Thoughts of Kaida's face. Cosam's laugh. Little Hannah and her doll. He felt as if he had left his friends in another time. The hours until tomorrow's board meeting were dragging.

At home he found two messages on his machine, one from a towing company asking him if he was coming to retrieve his car. It had been towed out of the city last night.

The second was an angry message from his sister, Debra. Apparently Rim had done some damage there as well. Tired as he was, he called her number.

Though Debra sounded upset and wasn't happy about the late notice, he managed to get an invitation to dinner for tonight. He was confident he could smooth everything over, although she would probably be harder to make peace with than the university board or his students. At least he could assume that Rim-Sin hadn't damaged his relationship with his parents. He didn't even know where Mother and Father were at the moment. A cruise, maybe. Or in the Mediterranean.

He picked up the car on the way to Debra's. His Buick didn't look quite like he remembered. Apparently Rim-Sin hadn't taken the time to attend driver's education while he was living Peter's life. The front headlight had been smashed out, the back fender was dented, and there was an angry scratch across the driver's side door. Hopefully no other cars had been involved. Peter would hate to see what Rim-Sin might have done to someone who had jumped out of their car screaming at him.

When he rang Debra's doorbell at five o'clock, he was thrilled to be greeted by little Kate, the only child on the planet who was not afraid of him. She jumped into his arms.

"Uncle Peter!"

Children were so forgiving.

He could see Debra in the kitchen. "Come in, Peter," she said.

"Hello, Debra." Peter went into the kitchen and kissed his sister on the forehead, something he didn't do very often. She pulled back in surprise. "Hello, Peter."

"It smells wonderful."

"Spaghetti."

"My favorite."

She was warming up a little, he could tell. Nothing worked on Debra like complimenting her cooking.

"Can I help with anything?"

"Like pressing buttons on the microwave?"

Peter laughed. "I can do that!"

"Put some ice in the glasses. Rick will be home in a minute, and then we can eat."

Peter filled the glasses and went into the living room with Kate. She was playing with one of her glamorous little dolls, changing her clothes from beachwear to evening attire.

Kate came to sit on Peter's lap with her doll. He stroked her hair. Things had changed very little in three thousand years. Little girls and their dolls.

"Do you know my doll's name, Uncle Peter?"

He looked at the curvaceous plastic blonde. He knew what she was called, but the only name that came to mind was "Ishtar." And Kate was her young slave—dressing her, feeding her. She was all about beauty and sex. She even had her own estate—a house, a sports car, a consort.

Was he losing his mind, comparing this doll to the temple worship of the goddess? Or was he finally seeing clearly? Had society removed the carved images but kept the ideas? The culture worshiped fertility, beauty, and sex. People paid their dues to the goddess in the movie tickets they bought, in the diet pills they consumed, in the hair salons and fitness centers they belonged to. The gods had disappeared, but into their place had stepped the professional athlete—the modern-day Hercules and the blond bombshell actresses who stood for lust and indulgence.

OK, so it was a little over the top to associate little Kate's doll with Ishtar. Kate wasn't thinking about all that. But still, was society really so different than it had been twenty-six centuries ago?

"Peter, you're like yourself again tonight," Debra commented by dessert. Just the words Peter had been hoping to hear.

"I don't know what's been going on with me, Debra. Midlife crisis, I guess. I'm sorry if I've done anything to upset you."

Debra shrugged. "I hope the end of your crisis means the end of that girl in your apartment."

Peter straightened. Girl? Had Rim-Sin led a more interesting social life than Peter? Where was this girl now? "Uh, yeah. I think so."

"She was very strange, Peter."

"How so?"

Debra shook her head. "I don't know. Just something not right about her. Even Kate noticed."

"Her name was like mine," Kate said. "Only different."

When dessert and coffee were finished, Peter excused himself to head home. He didn't have the energy for after-dinner conversation tonight.

His confidence in the superiority of modern culture had begun to be shredded today. The world had not changed at all. He saw it so clearly. The gods and goddesses lived on television and in the toy stores. The universities had become modern-day temples, complete with their own sacred symbols. The people sought the favor of the powerful ones with their university endowments and campaign contributions. His own title of "Doctor" around his university-temple had been hard-won, but respect was his. He was a temple diviner. Not the chief of magicians yet. No, he'd lost his chance when Washburn had been named university president.

It was all the same. He could no longer rest in the fact that his postmodern culture had evolved and discovered a new way, a better way. There was no better way. There was only the same way as there had always been: people trying to better their position in life in any way they could while indulging themselves in whatever they could get away with. He just didn't know what to think anymore.

There was only one thing Peter hated worse than being wrong. Uncertainty.

Peter drove home on autopilot, stewing over the mess his life had become. He parked his car in the off-street garage and took the elevator to his third-floor apartment. When the elevator doors opened, he stood facing Hugh Rohner.

"Hey," Peter said. "What have I done now?"

Hugh frowned. "I came to get that book you took from my office last week. I forgot to get it last night. I need it for tomorrow's class."

"Come in." Peter unlocked the door and motioned Hugh into

his apartment. Hugh stepped across the threshold and waited inside the door.

Peter didn't even try to fake it. "What book was it, Hugh?"

Hugh raised an eyebrow. "The one on Koldewey's digs in Babylon."

Right. Peter retrieved the book from the stash in his bedroom.

Hugh took it from him and hesitated. "Peter, I just want you to know that if you need to talk, I'm willing."

"Talk about what, Hugh? Why I should become a Christian?"

Hugh inhaled. "Never mind."

Peter grabbed his arm before he could get out the door. "No, you brought it up. Finish the thought."

"I know you think Christianity is fast becoming a dead religion, Peter. But there—"

"Actually," Peter interrupted, "you don't know what I think, Hugh." Peter turned away and threw himself into a dining room chair. He crossed his arms. "The multitude of religions proves that none of them are right, that there is no god at all, only ourselves."

"Oh, you want to debate, huh?" Hugh said. He closed the door. "All right, let's debate. You say that having multiple religions proves there is no God. But that doesn't make sense, Peter. Isn't it more logical to believe that there *must* be a God and He must communicate with men, since so many cultures—all cultures that have ever walked the earth—have always believed it?"

Peter pounded a fist on the table. "Exactly! Do you know how many gods have been worshiped throughout history?"

Hugh leaned back against the door. "Peter, the question is not how to find the one true religion among a thousand. The question is, where has religion reached its true maturity? If pagan religions contained hints of the ultimate truth, where have all the hints of paganism been fulfilled?" He yanked out a chair across from Peter and sat, leaning his elbows on the cherrywood table. "I've watched you develop a cynicism toward polytheism over the years, Peter. And yet your own beliefs are so close to it, without your even realizing it!"

"That's insane. I've never believed in any ancient god!" He couldn't help remembering the personified powers he'd felt warring against each other in the dungeon and how the Hebrew God's power had prevailed. But he didn't feel like mentioning that at the moment.

"All the mythological gods ever dreamed up hinted at the truth. They spoke of a god who was other than man. And yet they didn't deliver what mankind really needed. They promised wealth, fertility, riches. But where was the god who could give them what they really needed, things like love, acceptance, a purpose in life, fulfillment, eternal existence? The centuries went by, and the gods disappeared. Next instead of worshiping the *god* of the sun and the *god* of the moon, mankind decided that the sun and the moon *themselves* were divine, along with all of creation. And that would have to include mankind. Man became god. Polytheism gave us a god who didn't deliver what people truly needed. Now we're promised what we need, but from a god who can't deliver. The god of self."

"So," Peter said, "in Christianity, all other myths and religions supposedly find their fulfillment?"

"Yes," Hugh nodded. "Everything before Christ was a preparation for Him, and everything after has been an imitation of Him."

Peter sat back against the wooden chair and studied the window. "What about Judaism?"

"Christianity is fulfilled Judaism," Hugh said. "God set apart one nation of people to work with directly. These He taught that there was one God. To this people He gave the Law to show that He was holy and to prove how they couldn't live up to it by their own power. So when Jesus came to the Jews, it was God presenting the Messiah to a people who could fully understand their sinfulness, their inadequacy, their need for a Savior. They had been prepared for Christianity by Judaism. But He was to be the Savior of every people, and the Jewish nation was to be a lampstand for the other nations."

Peter's breath caught. A lampstand!

"Jesus' death was a substitute for ours, paying our debt, making it possible to be reconciled with God. This is grace, Peter," Hugh said, "and we would never have invented it. We would never have dreamed up a God who would stoop to offer us grace, a free gift. We would have created religion and works, something to earn. And we did. What other system of belief offers a Savior and salvation by grace? None. Examples, yes. Teachers, plenty. But no saviors. No religious teacher offers *forgiveness* for sin."

This was feeling uncannily like a debate with Kaida. "And what does the Christian God require of men, Hugh?"

"What do you have that He might want, Peter?"

Peter stood and pushed his chair against the table in disgust. "Nothing."

Hugh watched him carefully. "Exactly. There is no climbing to reach this God, Peter. There is only letting go."

Peter all but kicked Hugh out, not caring what his friend thought of him tonight.

Against his better judgment he went to his bookshelf. There it was: an old Bible he'd gotten as a gift years ago. It wasn't as dusty as he'd expected. Hugh had asked him to read Isaiah 29:16 as they had parted. He checked the table of contents and eventually found the verse.

It read, "You turn things upside down, as if the potter were thought to be like the clay! Shall what is formed say to him who formed it, 'He did not make me'? Can the pot say of the potter, 'He knows nothing'?"

Peter snapped the Bible shut, stunned. How did Hugh know? How could he know that only days ago Peter had said he was both the potter and the clay? He ran his hand over the leather binding. Did he have the power to transform himself, or didn't he? Could he pull himself up by his own bootstraps, or would it take a power outside of himself? What else did this book say?

He settled into his couch and turned on a lamp. Where to begin? His conversations with Hugh and his experience in Babylon had left him feeling fairly comfortable with Old Testament history. Might as well start in the New Testament. He wanted to find out more about this Jesus. He remembered Christmas services at church. Wasn't it always from the Book of Luke that the preacher would read the Christmas story?

He checked the table of contents again and turned to the Book of Luke. It started out talking about some woman named Elizabeth, and Peter thought he might have the wrong place, but he scanned for a page or two until it mentioned Mary and Jesus. He read through the birth of Jesus, His early life, the beginning of His public life.

The story bogged down in the third chapter with a section that the notes explained was the genealogy of Jesus' mother, Mary. Peter plowed through the unfamiliar names, barely paying attention. But when he turned the page, he was shocked to see a verse underlined on it. Who would have done that? He never recalled having opened this Bible.

He read the verse, number 28. It was a continuation of the genealogy. "The son of Melki, the son of Addi, the son of Cosam, the son of Elmadam..."

A chill shot up his spine. *Cosam.* Addi. In the line of Jesus?

The verse underlined. Only Rim-Sin could have marked this verse. Rim-Sin, who hated Jews, who read *Newsweek*, who knew Jesus and Christianity had wiped out the gods.

And who was back in Babylon right now.

The doorbell interrupted his thoughts.

Chapter 22

Peter looked at his watch. 6:45. Had Hugh come back to try to pound the paganism out of him again?

He swung open the door and found a clean-cut kid, maybe around twenty, standing in the hall. He wore a dark cable-knit sweater, khakis, and an enthusiastic smile. "Ready, Dr. Thornton?"

Peter ran a hand through his hair. "Um... no."

He tried to close the door, but the kid thrust a hand out.

"Come on, sir. We're going to be late!"

Peter was finished acting like he had a clue what Rim-Sin had done to his life. "Where are we going?"

The kid's forehead wrinkled. "To the vernal equinox assembly. It starts in forty-five minutes."

Peter tried to close the door again. "I can't make it, son. Sorry."

This time the kid's hand was on Peter's arm, the fingers tightening. The smile disappeared. "No one's ever been moved up the ranks as quickly as you have, Dr. Thornton." He squeezed harder. "The council members would not be pleased to hear that you were too busy to attend."

A funny sensation was traveling up Peter's arm, originating with the kid's fingers. He pulled away from his grasp and rubbed his still-tingling arm. The slight heaviness on his chest concerned him. He thought briefly that his symptoms could be that of a heart attack, but realized that was wishful thinking.

The odd sensation was one he remembered all too well. He and the boy were not alone. Some other presence had joined them.

"What's your name?" he asked.

The boy didn't seem surprised at the question. Instead he watched Peter, wary. "Kevin," he said. "And it's time to go."

Peter wasn't sure if it was curiosity or fear that led him out of his apartment in Kevin's wake. The kid led him to a blue Taurus parked in the nearby garage. They navigated toward the expressway and headed across the city.

"Tell me about the meeting, Kevin."

"It will be much the same as last week. Several people will speak from the front. There will be a chance for others to share the ways they've connected to the goddess's power this week."

Peter watched through the passenger window as the city's towering skyscrapers flew past them, lights glittering all the way to the top. "The goddess?"

Kevin looked sideways at him. "Are you doubting your calling, Dr. Thornton?"

Calling. He hadn't heard that word since Daniel had used it on the muddy floor of a prison cell, thousands of years ago.

"The goddess isn't real, Kevin. It's only a symbol of the universal consciousness. The divine power in all of us." He glanced at Kevin.

The boy scowled, his jaw working in silent tension. "The elders thought you held promise, Dr. Thornton. Thought perhaps you were the one to lead us into the bright future the goddess has spoken of. But you sound like every other ignorant mystic, believing all that impersonal nonsense."

Kevin swerved sharply, exiting the expressway to the left. Peter's head banged against his window. They finished the ride in silence and pulled into a hotel parking lot a few minutes later.

Peter considered parting ways right here, but two of Kevin's friends materialized from another car.

"Dr. Thornton's having doubts," Kevin said. His emphasis on *doubts* took on a sinister tone, especially when the three young men surrounded him and moved him toward the hotel.

The heaviness returned, an odd foreboding, as though his body warned him to leave. And yet he allowed himself to be pulled in, feeling repulsed and drawn at the same time.

If he expected a candlelit circle of pagans around an animal sacrifice, he was disappointed. The hotel meeting room held about a hundred ordinary-looking people chatting at round tables and nibbling hors d'oeuvres.

There were nods of recognition for Peter. The three young men who'd escorted him deposited him at a table. An elderly man rose in the front of the room, and there was instant silence.

"Thank you for coming, friends. There is much to accomplish, and the goddess asks for our dedication to the cause. But our numbers grow every day. Tonight, the meeting will be opened by one of our newest and most enthusiastic members, Dr. Peter Thornton."

The room erupted in applause. Peter felt as though the walls were closing in. He turned to Kevin next to him. "What does he want me to do?"

Kevin jerked his head toward the front. "Get up there. Open the meeting."

Peter shook his head. "I'm not—feeling well. Have someone else do it."

The applause died. The man up front coughed pointedly. "Dr. Thornton, please lead us in a prayer." The man's eyes seemed to bore into Peter's, even from across the room. Peter tried to look away and could not. His breath shortened. Words simmered to his lips, threatened to spill out. Words he never wanted to utter again.

O heroic one, Ishtar; the immaculate one of the goddesses...

It was the incantation he'd uttered before scaling the Tower of Babel. When he'd said it, the voices had begun. But the voices had ceased, had been silent for days. He didn't want them back.

A hundred pairs of eyes were trained on him expectantly. Peter felt the urge to retch. His blood pounded in his ears. He pushed away from his table, stood on unsteady feet. The room was silent except for the drumming of his heart.

He turned and ran.

The stars were dim and unfamiliar tonight. Peter breathed great gulps of cold air, air polluted with the fumes of a thousand cars and trucks in the city below him. He stood on the rooftop of his apartment building, trying vainly to escape the claustrophobia of his mind by getting closer to the open sky.

He was seriously freaked out.

From Hugh's challenge to the discovery of Cosam's and Addi's names in the New Testament, to the Ishtar-fest at the Marriott and his frenzied getaway from Kevin and his friends, he was having trouble with rational thought. He struggled to put the pieces together.

When the pagan gods had faded to myth, the people had no higher authority to answer to but themselves. As ultimate authority, man himself must be god. But there must be an explanation for why man did not feel like a god, did not feel happy, did not have everything he wanted. That answer was self-transformation, self-enlightenment, self-actualization. Whatever you called it, it meant that man needed to *change* in order to be truly happy, and since there was no one else to do it, he would have to change himself. Thus began every man's long journey down the road of self-transformation. Peter had yet to meet anyone who claimed he had reached the end—or even gotten near it. Now, dissatisfied with their inability to transform, some were taking a logical next step: bringing back the old gods to help them on their journey. And there was real power there. But where did it originate? Did it matter?

You are mine.

Ignore that. Ignore it. You're imagining things now.

If Rim-Sin had learned that Addi was a forefather of Jesus and that Christianity had wiped out the worship of the ancient gods, would he try to harm Addi? Was that why he'd gone back to his life in ancient Babylon? But all that was in the past. Christianity *had* come. The recent conversation with Hugh had proved it. So Rim-Sin must have failed, and Addi must have been fine. Or was this some kind of quantum contingency in which all of what Peter knew of this reality was dependent on him doing something with this knowledge now? If he did nothing with it, would Addi's existence evaporate—and all of Christianity with it? It made his head hurt to think of it. And what could he do? Could he travel back again and fix it?

You can do nothing.

Stop. There is no one there. Never has been. Just a voice in your head.

In your head... in your heart... you are mine.

"Stop!"

An unnatural laughter filled his ears. The voice was audible now. "You could not command me then, and you cannot now. You have no power."

Peter breathed heavily, gripped the handrail at the edge of the roof. Was he losing his mind? He shouted into the night, "What do you want with me?"

"Surrender. You will never lead."

The stars themselves seemed to mock Peter, watching him with half-closed lids, their light dimmed by the city's competition.

Tears sprung to Peter's eyes. Regret. Shame. "I don't want to lead! Why would I?"

"Because you have seen the truth. The end is coming. The people believe they harness the power of the gods. We will allow them their delusion. And then we will chew them up and spit them out in the face of their Creator. It has only begun. But no one can stop us."

Peter could hardly breathe now, the pressure on his chest like bony fingers squeezing the air from his lungs. "I don't care," he gasped. "I don't care."

"That is right," the voice said. "There is nothing to care about."

Peter leaned out over the edge of the rooftop as though an unseen hand pulled him toward the abyss. The voice whispered one more word.

Jump.

Peter couldn't say how he found himself in his apartment again. He didn't remember resisting the voice. Only that something had muted it, had loosened the hold on him, and he was free, if only for a time.

He stood now in the dark with his back against the inside of his apartment door. A red light blinked at him from the kitchen counter. He stumbled to the answering machine and hit Play, hoping the routine task would bring normalcy with it.

A female voice, low and soft, whispered through the dark kitchen. "Hello? I—I don't know if you are there." The voice paused. "I . . . I'm so afraid you've left me here. You never came last night." The voice grew teary. "I don't know what I'll do if you've left without me. I . . . want to go back. Even with you." Another pause. "I have the books you wanted. I'll be at the entrance where you told me to meet you last night. Please. Please come and get me."

The machine beeped and went silent. Peter listened to the message again.

Who was she? The girl Debra and Kate had mentioned? What did she mean that she wanted to go back, even with him?

A slow suspicion burned its way across his mind. He grabbed his car keys and flew out the door.

Thirty minutes later, he burst into Debra's house. She was washing dishes in the kitchen.

"Peter!"

Kate sat at the white laminate table in her pink pajamas, finishing a mug of hot chocolate.

He grabbed his sister's arms, the dishcloth dripping on his feet. "Debra, the woman you met in my apartment a few days ago. Do you remember her name?"

Debra looked from Peter to Kate, her eyes wide. "What's wrong, Peter?"

Kate tugged at his sleeve. "Uncle Peter!"

He looked down.

"I remember," she said. "Hers was the same as mine, only different."

"The same as yours?"

She nodded. "Mmm-hmm. It was like 'Kate,' but a little more."

Kaida.

He knelt to the little girl. "Kaida, honey? Was her name Kaida?"

"That's right!" Her smile was adoring. "You're so smart, Uncle Peter!"

He pulled onto the highway and tried to collect his scattered thoughts.

On that day five weeks ago he had touched the vase, and everything had changed. Rim-Sin's house. Rueben dead on the floor. The lampstand burning hot in his hand. And Kaida. Backing away from him, confusion and terror in her eyes.

When Rim-Sin had been catapulted forward into the twenty-first century, had he taken his concubine with him? Peter had stepped back into Rim's place. They had switched places. So if Rim-Sin's concubine had come to the present, too, then *someone else* must've been yanked back into the concubine's body and life. The woman he'd come to love was not Kaida at all!

Who was she?

So many things made sense now. Her unfamiliarity with the city. Her insistence that she didn't know what had happened to Reuben. Her defiant attitude in spite of her slave status. Her understanding of world religions. Her modern arguments. Even her American crawl swimming stroke!

The woman on the answering machine—she was the real Kaida! When Peter had come home from Babylon, he had done it alone, leaving the woman he loved stranded in the past. And Rim-Sin's concubine, the real Kaida, had been left in this time and was waiting to meet him right now.

I have the books. Be at the entrance.

She had books. Did that mean she was at a bookstore? If so, which one? What about the library?

Peter raced across the city to the university library, his best guess. The streets were nearly empty. The library wouldn't close until 10:00, though. He screeched to a stop at the curb outside the south entrance.

A shadow moved in the vestibule beside the entrance. A shadow, then a face at the glass door.

Peter's heart leaped to his throat. Long, dark hair. Dark eyes in olive skin. She was so like the Kaida he knew. Yet different. And she looked vaguely familiar.

He thrust a leg from his car and stood, signaling her over the top of the car. She took a tentative step from the vestibule, books clutched to her chest.

"Kaida!"

She looked both ways on the sidewalk, then hurried across to his car. He watched her walk, his heart aching for the woman he'd left behind. She slipped into the car and closed the door. He faced her, studied her features. She was afraid.

"I thought you'd left me," she said. "Last night. I was afraid you were so desperate to get back for the New Year Festival that you would leave without me."

Peter took a deep breath. "He did."

Confusion furrowed her brow.

"Rim-Sin is gone, Kaida. He's gone back to Babylon. I am—from this time. I'm Peter, the one he switched places with. I've been back in your time and have only just gotten back where I belong."

Her eyes filled with tears, and she looked away. "Then I am alone."

"I think I may know how to get you home."

Her eyes widened. "To Israel?"

Peter nearly cried for the girl. "No, I'm sorry. Back to Babylon."

She nodded. "That is better than—than this place. My brother lives there."

Peter smiled. "Yes, I know. Cosam. A very good man." He touched her arm. "Pray to Yahweh, Kaida. Pray this works."

Peter unlocked the side entrance to the museum and led Kaida through. He climbed the steps two at a time. Kaida struggled to keep up.

The third floor was deserted. Peter led Kaida to Hugh's back room, unlocked it, and flicked the switch. The harsh light made them both squint.

Where was the vase? There, on a back shelf.

He pointed. "The vase, Kaida. That is all I can think of. It took me back there once and brought Rim-Sin here. Perhaps it will take you back." And bring *her* here.

The girl hesitated, searched his eyes. "What should I do?"

He looked at the vase, the blue glazed design that Kaida had helped him paint mocking him now. "Just lay your hands on it. And pray."

She took a deep breath and crossed the room.

"One more thing, Kaida," he said. "You should know that I've set you free. I mean, that Rim-Sin has set you free back in Babylon. You can leave him. Go to Cosam's and hide. Maybe go back to Jerusalem."

It was clear she didn't understand everything he was telling her. But she straightened her shoulders and laid both hands across the rim of the vase.

Nothing.

She looked back at Peter.

Pray, girl. Pray.

Her eyes closed. Her lips moved.

Nothing.

Peter pounded a fist into his other hand. "It has to work. It has to!" He paced the room. "What were you doing just before you came here?"

"I was in your—in Rim-Sin's house. Reuben came for the lampstand. I think—I think that Rim-Sin was going to kill him."

Peter rubbed at his face. That didn't help at all.

Kaida turned away from the vase. "Maybe it only works for you," she said quietly.

Peter leaned his hip against the rickety table cluttered with pottery. *Maybe you're right.*

It took only moments to decide. His Kaida was stranded in the past. She didn't belong there any more than he had. If he could find a way to retrieve her, he had to try, even if it meant neither of them could get back. He thought briefly of tomorrow's board meeting, then let it go.

If he held on to this Kaida's hand while touching the vase, would they both go back? Would his Kaida switch places and return here with Rim-Sin? Then *he* would be there by himself.

He scrawled a note on a scrap of paper, wrote her name across the top in large, block letters, and placed it on the shelf next to the vase.

"Come on," he said to the real Kaida, wrapping an arm around her, "let's try something." Peter reached across and touched the vase.

It was both darker and hotter at the same time. Peter opened his eyes, wincing at the shooting pain in his head. Stars pierced the ebony sky above him. A fierce wind blew against him, threatening to sweep him away. Beside him, the tower rose. He could see torches blazing far above. He stood in the courtyard of the Platform of Etemenanki beside a stone table. He had done it! He was back in ancient Babylon.

He realized that Kaida was no longer with him. Then he noticed that in his right hand he held a knife.

Something moved on the altar. No, not something. Someone.

Chapter 23

"And so we wait," Abigail finished.

The waiting she spoke of was not about how she and Akkad were waiting together in this cell for their execution. In the days she and Akkad had spent waiting for *that*, they had rejoiced that the king had thrown them here together. Abigail had spent the time patiently instructing Akkad in everything she had been taught since childhood about the God of Israel, the Law, and the promised Messiah. Now, as Akkad learned of the Redeemer who would come for them, his heart opened yet a little more to the truth that Abigail poured out.

"And when He comes...?" Abigail said, urging him to answer.

"He will reconcile all people to God."

Her smile was brilliant. "Yes!"

Akkad sat back against the wall, realizing that he had been leaning forward in his intensity to hear more.

The past days had been the happiest of his life, despite the darkness and the fact that he was awaiting his execution. His doubts and questions had fled from him one by one as he'd learned from Abigail in the wet clay of their cell. Guards had come and gone bringing food, but the two had barely noticed. It was as if time stood still for them here as Akkad learned of Yahweh and they both learned of each other.

Now that they knew they were to be executed, the constraints of obligation had fallen away. They were free to be honest with each other about their love, and Akkad reveled in the knowledge that Abigail loved him alone.

Akkad was formulating another question about the Messiah when the door opened and a figure in flowing robes slipped in quietly.

"So the wise man is taught by the captive?" the man said. He laughed, but not unkindly.

"Daniel!" Abigail jumped to her feet, embracing her fellow Hebrew. Then she pulled away as though embarrassed by her impropriety.

Daniel held out a hand to her, smiling.

"What news do you bring us, Daniel?" Akkad asked.

The Jewish man's face registered surprise at Akkad's use of his Hebrew name. "I wish I could report that the king's anger toward you wanes, but it does not. I have tried to speak with him about you two, but there is not much I can do to alter the facts."

The two prisoners studied the floor.

"The king still intends to execute you," Daniel said, "but he is loath to be entered into the annals as the king who sent his captive wife to her death. So he has devised another plan to avoid that report. He will have his marriage to Abigail annulled. The history of his reign will show no mention of her, and it will be as if they were never married at all."

"But how—? Why—? I don't understand," Akkad said. "Why does he not divorce her?"

"A divorce would be recorded," Daniel said, "but because their marriage was not consummated, it can be annulled."

Akkad looked to Abigail for a contradiction of this fact, but her face was shining.

"I am so pleased," she said. "I would rather die unknown and unrecorded than to be remembered as the wife of the king of Babylon."

Peter took a deep breath and looked down at the altar. The knife in his hand glinted in the torchlight.

Below him, a bundle of rags squirmed. He used his other hand to move the rags.

An infant lay on the altar. It was *Addi.* Son of Cosam, son of Elmadam. A direct link to Jesus Christ.

The knife still hovered above his head.

He watched it, disconnected from it somehow.

Do it. Do it.

A moaning arrested his attention. He lowered the knife and looked across the courtyard.

There was Kaida. She was bound and gagged and tied to a pole used to hold torches. One look in her eyes told him that she was *his* Kaida. But her eyes were filled with hate, burning with a rage that scalded his heart. He'd told her to stay away from Rim-Sin! Why hadn't she?

And they were not alone. Others ringed the courtyard, all eyes on him. Purple robes, embroidered with golden stars. Tightly wrapped turbans.

Of course! It was the second day of the Festival. The New Year sacrifice must be performed. This child's death would appease the gods and bring prosperity on the city for another year. Yes, it must be accomplished.

The certainty faltered for a moment. What was he doing?

Do it. Do it.

Yes, he wanted to do it. Needed to do it.

You are mine.

Daniel's words came to him, competing with the other voices in his head. "You must defeat the powers arrayed against you."

You are mine.

A voice rang in his head again, but these were fresh words,

words Daniel had never said to him. "Submit to Me, Peter . . . and you can be *Mine.*"

Peter felt the cosmic tug-of-war and knew the torture of his soul being torn apart.

The circle waited. Kaida still moaned, shaking her head, tears coursing down her face.

Peter forced his stiff legs to take him across the sand to Kaida. He brought the knife to her wrists. Her eyes widened in terror. He flicked the knife through the rope that held her.

"Kaida, listen to me—"

The circle of diviners watched, as though uncertain if this was part of the ritual.

He leaned in close to her. "I'm not—"

She ripped the gag from her mouth and beat her fists against his chest. "Don't you touch him!" she screamed. "Don't you dare touch that baby!"

Peter felt the stares of the diviners. He dragged Kaida to the altar. She tried to break his grasp. He held her firmly. He turned his back to the diviners and whispered harshly into her ear. "Take the baby, Kaida! Take the baby and run!"

She glanced up at him in confusion.

"I am not Rim-Sin," he said.

Her eyes widened. "What?"

Peter took Addi from the altar and gave him to her. Then he pushed her toward the edge of the courtyard.

In the same movement he raised his arms above his head and faced the circle. "My brothers!"

They watched him, their faces a mixture of confusion and distrust.

"The gods demand a different sacrifice this year. One who is not so helpless, so easy to conquer!"

A shout from the edge of the circle. "That is why the king has demanded that your concubine be offered!"

Another diviner, to his left, joined in. "You are the one who insisted that this child be added to your offering this year. And now you mock the gods by sending them both away!"

Someone to his right stepped toward him. "He does not intend to fulfill his responsibility! Return him to his cell, and let the gods and the king deal harshly with him!"

The circle closed in on him. Palace guards appeared behind the diviners.

Peter turned and fled.

Shouting all around him.

The people of the city waited at the outside of the courtyard, waited for the sacrifice they believed would assure their city's future for another year. At the sight of Peter flying toward them, a cheer rose up. Perhaps they thought the sacrifice was already finished.

Behind him he could hear the diviners and guards screaming curses on his head. But the people were too loud to hear them. He didn't dare look back. The guards must be nearly on top of him.

He was panting when he reached the gate of the courtyard, and he fell into the crowd. The shouts behind him merged with the chanting of the city. They reached out to him, grabbing at his clothes, pushing him through the crowd like a piece of driftwood bobbing in the surf. He felt the throng close around him, behind him, cutting him off from the guards. He tore himself from the hands that clutched at him and pushed through, forcing his way to the edge of the crowd. He feared the people would follow him, but when he finally broke free, they turned their attention to whatever the next spectacle might be.

Peter broke into a dead run headed straight for Cosam's house.

The voices that had warred for his soul in the courtyard of the tower still rang in his mind as he ran.

You are mine!

Then the other voice: "But you can become Mine."

It was all a big cheat. His whole philosophy was like a sheet of white satin laid over the pit of a stinking cesspool. Had he been deluded all this time? Assured and reassured that he had the divine within himself already, that he needed only to uncover it? What would he uncover if he really looked at his soul? Divinity? No, *he* was the cesspool, disguised by the white satin of his well-constructed arguments. He had accomplished many moments of feeling oneness, of awareness, moments of transformation, but in the end they proved to be counterfeit because he always ended up exactly where he started. He had never received any *truth* during these moments, only an assurance that he was on the right path to healing. A path that never went anywhere. Climbing and climbing but never arriving.

It was all false. All his foolish arguments. Kaida's arguments rang in his head, and Hugh's, and even Daniel's. Like ducks at the carnival when he was seven years old, all his fine theories were shot down, one by one, until there was none left. All these years thinking he'd been looking inside himself for answers, he'd really been climbing. Climbing and reaching. They all had, since the very beginning. They'd taken away the carved images and left everything else. There was no "new age." There was no new thought. It was all the same lies. The very same lies told in the Garden of Eden. "You will not surely die. You will be like God." The new ultimate consciousness he had thought was about to envelop the world had been there since the very beginning, clawing at the throne of God, enlisting any and all who would help. How had he been such a fool? Had he truly looked inside himself and believed he was divine? The overwhelming arrogance of the self-delusion shamed him. The poverty of his spirit gripped him. The helplessness and hopelessness of all his efforts toward transformation left him weak with futility.

He reached Cosam's house with his soul stripped bare.

He threw himself into Cosam's courtyard. Cosam was there. He turned to Peter, his wife behind him holding Addi. With one quick step, Cosam threw his entire bulky frame behind the power of his fist. The punch landed on Peter's jaw and knocked him flat.

He lay on his back, panting. His jaw seared with pain, and he thought he might pass out. Cosam stood over him, murder in his eyes.

"Cosam, listen." Peter held his hands in front of him but did not get up. "Listen. I am not Rim-Sin. And Kaida is not your real sister."

"He's insane!" Rebekah said.

"I know you think I've lost my senses. But the Kaida and Rim you have known for these past few weeks have not been the two you once knew, isn't that true?

Cosam frowned.

"It was Rim-Sin who tried to kill Addi tonight, but he is gone again and I am here. You must believe me when I say that your true sister—and the real Rim—may return. You are still in danger from that Rim. You and your son."

"This is foolishness," Cosam said. "I should kill you right now."

"Cosam, you have been a friend to me. Look in my eyes. I have been gone one day, but now I am back."

Cosam studied his face, then looked back at Rebekah, who clutched Addi to her heart. "What do you want with Addi?"

"Not me, Cosam. Rim-Sin. I know I look like him to you, but I'm not. We have...we have temporarily switched bodies. I can't explain it now. But you must hear me: Rim has knowledge about you that makes him want to take Addi's life."

"What knowledge?"

Peter hesitated only a moment. "Cosam, the Messiah will be born of your line."

Cosam's jaw dropped. "The Messiah?"

"Yes, through Addi. Many generations from now."

Rebekah came to his shoulder. "Cosam? What does he mean?"

Peter pulled himself to sitting and put a hand to his bruised jaw. "Keep Addi safe, Cosam. Evil seeks to destroy you both."

Cosam took a step backward, his face still registering shock.

"Where is Kaida, Cosam?"

The big man shook his head. If he knew, he was not going to say. Peter didn't blame him. She must have been here, though, because Addi was here. Had she left again?

He stood. "Rescue your sister from him, Cosam. From Rim-Sin. She can still be saved."

He wanted to do more, but what?

Somewhere in this city that wanted him dead, the woman he loved also ran in fear.

Since the day she had arrived in this place and people had begun calling her "Kaida," she had thought of nothing but escape. How could she possibly serve this ancient, foreign man as his concubine? And yet, how could she do anything else? He had involved her in his mission to find answers but had never explained why. She had not dared to ask. To reveal her identity could mean execution.

So she'd played along, hoping to escape, but knowing her only real chance to go home was somehow tied to Rim-Sin. She had tried not to let herself get to know him. It hadn't worked. In spite of his ridiculous beliefs that would persist into the twenty-first century, she had grown to care for him more than she wanted to admit. And then, yesterday, everything had changed. He'd said good-bye in the street after freeing her and saying those cryptic words. Then, hours later, he'd returned to Cosam's house and roughly dragged her to his own house. She went with him, thinking it was an act for the benefit of watching eyes. But when he shoved her into his bedroom, four years of triathlon training kicked in and she left him. In her mind she could still hear him screaming curses as she outran him.

She had the tablet that proved she was free. It had meant nothing to the palace guards who had grabbed her in the streets. The New Year Festival, they said. The king's decree. *She* was to be the sacrifice.

When Rim-Sin had cut her bonds and given Addi to her, she had been shocked. And in that instant when their eyes met, she saw the old emotions in his look and had almost stayed with him. But it was too much of a chance to take. Was he some kind of split personality? She had taken Addi and fled.

After returning Addi to Rebekah, she'd left, hoping to blend into the city. As she ran, his last words pounded through her mind.

I am not Rim-Sin.

Chapter 24

BABYLON LOVED THE New Year Festival. Her people raised their level of drunkenness and gluttony to new heights. The gods were worshiped, and sacrifices were made. Eleven days of frenzied ecstasy dedicated to fertility and pleasure.

The second day was one of her favorites. The Sacred Marriage of king and goddess, and the ritual sacrifice of someone close to the heart of the one who held the knife. The obedience was an attitude she cultivated all through the year, and during these eleven days her people assured her that she had been successful.

Daniel returned once more to the cell where the two prisoners were learning to love each other more with each day that passed.

"It is done," Daniel said simply after he had greeted the captives. "Abigail's marriage contract has been annulled."

"Now what happens?" Akkad asked.

Daniel's face fell. "Now we wait for the order of execution."

"Why has the king not yet given it?" Abigail said.

"I have a plan," Daniel said. "In the meantime, thank the Lord in heaven for each day that you have."

Peter prowled through the velvet darkness of the celebrating city. The New Year Festival. The spring equinox marked the new year. He had returned to the very event he had been avoiding.

Musicians spun melodies from the corners of the streets. The smell of roasting meat drifted from homes. His mouth watered at the thought of a juicy, flame-broiled steak.

Peter let himself be pulled into the revelers. They danced and chanted toward the center of the city. The people were celebrating Marduk's annual blessing on the city. It was the most important religious event of the year.

Peter searched the crowd for Kaida.

The crowd was reaching a feverish pitch now. It seemed everyone was drunk or at least drinking. Musicians twisted through the press of flesh banging their tambourines and cymbals. All around him men and women alike tore off their clothing to honor Ishtar. The noisy festivity climbed above the city, offered to the gods.

Peter reached the great courtyard of Esagila where the statues of Marduk, Nabu, and other gods had been brought from their temples. They were dressed in their sacred garments and adorned with golden pectorals and crowns.

The people danced and jumped, sang and shook as Nebuchadnezzar's horse-drawn chariot rolled into the torch-lit courtyard of the temple. The king raised his arm in greeting, and the people shouted with joy.

The gods were loaded onto chariots themselves. The chariot of the gods pulled away from the temple, and the king followed in his own chariot. The entire city followed in the procession, dancing and shouting. Peter followed at a safe distance, watching for Kaida or Qurdi, knowing he would never find them in the crush of thousands of people.

The pageant snaked up the Processional Way, past the palace, and out through the massive arches of the Ishtar Gate. Outside the city the people surrounded the Akitu House, a chapel set in the midst of gardens.

The king shouted from his chariot to the people. "The king has taken the hand of Marduk." Cheers from the people. The king continued. "The Sacred Marriage will be performed. Ishtar will honor Babylon once again with fertility. Her fruit trees will bear fruit, her flocks will be fertile." More cheers.

The high priest of Marduk stood beside the king. "The king represents Marduk in the Sacred Marriage," he shouted. "High Priestess Warad-Sin represents Ishtar!"

More screaming, more chanting. The music grew louder. Warad-Sin and the king joined hands. People grabbed anyone close to them in passionate embraces, kicking and flailing each other at the same time. Peter jammed his elbow into the chest of a man who tried to embrace him.

Nebuchadnezzar and Warad-Sin entered the Akitu House. The people were wild with excitement. Peter was disgusted.

Hands wrapped around his chest. "Rim-Sin!"

Ilushu. Her red hair flowing around her head like flames.

"Rim-Sin!" she panted again, pulling his head down toward hers. He yanked away. She shrugged and laughed, dancing off to find someone else.

When the king and Warad-Sin emerged from the Akitu House, the city's fertility was assured. The people followed the procession back to the temple, screaming their frenzied rituals of joy.

Another shove from behind caused Peter to swivel sharply. Two hooded figures had been pushed against him. Now they stared at him as though they had been caught. The eyes that peered out from under one of the hoods reflected fear.

"Rim-Sin," the man said.

It was Akkad, Rim's young protégé who had tried to kill Daniel. Peter said nothing, taking in the other character, a woman trying unsuccessfully to pose as a man. Abigail.

"We—we are joining the Festival," Akkad said.

Through the crowd, another person pushed his way to the three.

"Daniel!" Peter said.

Daniel nodded briefly, as though distracted. "Rim-Sin. You have seen through our deception."

Deception? "What's happening?"

"Please, Rim-Sin," Akkad said. "Don't tell the king you've seen us."

Abigail reached out a hand from under her robes and clung to Akkad.

Daniel spoke to the two. "Do you have provisions for the journey, Akkad?"

The crowd pressed around them, but the little group tightened.

"Yes," Akkad said. "We are ready."

Daniel looked at Peter. "I took advantage of the Festival's distractions to release Akkad and Abigail from prison. They have been married and are fleeing Babylon today, in search of a better life."

"We go to Olympia," Akkad said, "where the Greeks do not care what race or country you come from nor what gods you worship. It is a safe place for those who do not belong."

There were quick embraces all around, as though they were all family.

Daniel gripped Akkad's arms. "There are donkeys waiting at the Western Gate. I have paid a trader to take you through the desert. From there, you will have to find Olympia on your own."

Moments later, they were gone. Peter was surprised at the gratification he felt when one of the most famous men of the Judeo-Christian world patted his shoulder in appreciation. He turned to speak to him again, but Daniel was gone.

The celebration of the Sacred Marriage was winding down, and Peter was no closer to finding Kaida. People danced away to continue their revelry all around the city.

He looked across at the tower. Being back here after a day at home made the experience even more incredible. The Tower of Babel. Man's very first effort to be god. The seven lofty tiers reached above the city, their steep stairs assuring the citizens who climbed them that they could find the gods if they ascended to the highest platform, where even tonight men stood searching the stars for answers. The tower had never been finished. Its bricks stood in mute testimony that one could never reach God.

Above him, slaves touched torches around the High Temple with flames that shot to life. He moved in that direction, hoping to remain unseen. There would be some sort of ceremony there tonight in honor of the New Year. But how was he to find Kaida?

And then he saw her.

One glimpse was all he had before the people closed in on her again. But she had been there, watching him, her dark hair hanging around her shoulders, her white robe glowing in the night.

He pushed forward. The crowd opened up again. She watched him still. He reached for her. She took a step backward, as though to run. He stopped.

Their eyes connected. The crowds at the edge of his vision blurred and then faded, their chants and cries muted. There was nothing but him and Kaida under the Babylonian stars. He dared not move for fear she would disappear.

Peter placed one hand over his heart, and held the other hand, palm up, out to her. He didn't let her eyes go.

Come, Kaida, he said with his eyes. *Come to me.*

Her expression faltered. Confusion, uncertainty. He watched her shoulders begin to shake, but couldn't hear the sobbing. *Come, Kaida.*

She walked slowly toward his outstretched arm. The crowds closed in on them again, but they were together. She was close enough to take his hand. He pulled her to him and wrapped both arms around her waist. Her eyes still held fear.

"You said—you said you're not Rim-Sin."

He held her face in his hands. "I'm not."

Her voice was a whisper. "But you are. You tried to kill me."

"No! Rim-Sin has been here this last day, but now I'm back. I am the man you have known these weeks."

Silent tears still washed her face, sparkling in the moonlight. Peter wiped her tears with his fingers. "I know you're from the future."

Again that wide-eyed look of astonishment. "You...you *know?*"

He smiled into her eyes. "Yes. I finally figured it out when I went back there yesterday without you."

Her eyes showed amazement. "You— You, too?" Then she shut her eyes tight and wrapped her arms around him. He held her to his chest and felt the tension leave her in great, heaving sobs. She pulled away moments later and looked up into his face. "What is—"

The crowd jostled them suddenly, and Kaida lost her footing.

A flash of black blurred Peter's vision. He heard Kaida scream. He shoved someone out of his way.

Ten feet from him he spotted Kaida. Qurdi-Marduk-lamur stood behind her, both arms wrapped around her and his chin on her shoulder, as though she were his own.

"She must die, Rim," he said. He brought his shaved head closer to hers, rubbed his cheek against Kaida's. "Whether you have the stomach for it or not. The goddess demands it."

And then the crowd closed in, and they were gone.

"No!" Peter's scream disappeared into the crowd with Kaida and Qurdi. He threw himself in their direction.

His yell turned people in the crowd toward him.

"Rim-Sin!" someone shouted.

"It is Rim-Sin!"

Rough hands grabbed at him, slowing him down. "Take him to the king!"

"He is wanted by the king!"

A fat man with a dirt-stained tunic grabbed his arm and leaned close. "You must perform the sacrifice, Rim-Sin!" His foul breath made Peter recoil.

"Let me go!" Peter thrashed and kicked at the crowd, clearing a path with his fists.

The tower several hundred yards away rose above the city. Peter fought through the people, swatting them away like disease-carrying insects.

He reached the tower courtyard in minutes. It was filled with people, as the streets had been. Peter ran for the altar where he had found himself leaning over Addi not long ago.

The altar was empty.

Several diviners milled in the area. Peter stopped one, clutched his arm, and shouted over the noise. "Where is Qurdi-Marduk-lamur?"

The diviner raised his eyebrows, then pointed skyward. "Preparing the sacrifice," he said. "*Your* sacrifice."

Peter looked up the tower steps. A black-cloaked man ascended quickly, a bare-chested slave following him, with a woman in white slung over his back like a sack of new wheat.

Peter raced up the stairs.

He reached the Platform only moments after Qurdi. The slave had lowered the unconscious Kaida onto the altar and moved aside. Qurdi's back was to Peter.

Peter spent half a second wishing for a weapon, then ran across the Platform.

Qurdi sensed his presence and whirled before Peter reached

him. In a movement as smooth as liquid he swept his arms upward, palms facing Peter.

Peter was stopped short, but not by Qurdi's arms. An unseen force surrounded the priest. Peter felt the heavy presence of darkness. The torches flickered. Some went out.

Evil. Evil so powerful Peter could feel it and taste it and smell it. He was no match for this. From across the Platform, someone screamed.

"Have you not learned, Rim-Sin?" It was the voice he had grown to recognize: half Qurdi, half Ishtar. "We will not be defeated. We will not be stopped."

The darkness swirled around Peter. He swayed with the wind, listless and sleepy. "Let her go," he managed to say. Behind Qurdi, Kaida stirred on the stone altar.

"Lay yourself in her place, then," Qurdi said.

Peter's feet were rooted to the Platform.

Qurdi stepped toward Peter. "Or perhaps we will have you both."

Peter waited, unmoving, for his destruction.

"No!" Kaida slipped from the altar behind Qurdi. "In the name of the one true God, no!"

The barrier around Qurdi seemed to dissolve. Peter's legs found freedom. He charged at the priest and rammed Qurdi's chest with his head.

The air *whooshed* from Qurdi's lungs. Peter pulled away from the doubled-over priest and smashed his fist to the back of Qurdi's neck. He fell to the ground. Kaida rushed into his arms. Peter pulled her toward the steps. "Come!"

But four slaves moved into position in front of the steps. They were trapped.

Peter turned back toward the altar. Qurdi struggled to his feet. Peter moved Kaida behind him.

Qurdi raised a clenched fist. "Listen to us, human." His voice was not Qurdi's at all now. "You are nothing. We will destroy you."

Qurdi rushed at him. Peter raised his arms, ready.

Ready to fight a man, perhaps, but not whatever force had taken control of Qurdi. The priest rained down blows on Peter's head. He fought back, felt his fists connect. It did no good. There was more at work here than the physical.

Peter felt his strength draining. From far away, he heard Kaida screaming. He wished for a chance to tell her he loved her.

The thought propelled him backward, away from the killing blows of the priest. He scrambled away, until he felt stone at his back.

The wall around the Platform. Waist high and a foot wide.

He became aware of the crowd below. Cheers rose up to meet him. The people watched. Watched and waited for a sacrifice. They didn't care who it was. Qurdi or Rim or someone else, it didn't matter. Nothing fired the blood like death.

Qurdi's eyes glowed with an unnatural fire. He pushed up against Peter. The sharp edge of the wall cut against Peter's lower back. Qurdi smiled. Then, laughing, Qurdi pushed him over the edge.

Peter grasped the ledge as he fell. He hung by the fingers of one hand off the edge of the tower. He swung the other arm upward, grasped the wall with his hand. Qurdi's shaved head appeared above him, and Peter waited for the blow that would loosen his hold.

Instead, there was a flash of white and Qurdi disappeared. Kaida. She was trying to buy him time to climb back up.

He brushed his feet across the face of the tower searching for a toehold, the tiniest ledge to give him the leverage he would need. There was nothing. His arms trembled. His fingers were slipping. He didn't have long.

Time slowed down. He saw the years behind him—in images, not thoughts. Years of climbing, of searching for *something*. He saw his choice laid out before him.

And as he hung there, suspended from the Tower of Babel, he realized that this was what it all came down to. All the arguments, the sermons, the conversations, books, and tapes boiled down to one question: was he, Peter Thornton, part of the divine consciousness, a god unto himself, able to transform himself into ultimate reality, or was God *other* and *separate* from him? Everything he had ever wanted in his deepest soul was promised from both sides.

Was Peter Thornton god, or was he not?

Would he continue to climb, to pull himself upward and keep his heart closed to the truth of his own inadequacy and the redemption offered by Jesus, or would he finally give up control?

The crowd cheered far beneath him, chanting and dancing beneath his swinging feet. With a shout of surrender to the God who had pursued him over two thousand years of history, Peter let go.

Faram-Enlil hated the New Year Festival. In truth, with each passing year he found he hated everything Babylonian with increasing passion. These Jews and their one God had worked on his heart and his mind until he wondered if one could become a Jew simply by thinking like one.

Tonight, the second night of the Festival, when the all-important sacrifice would be performed, Babylon sickened him.

Rim-Sin had killed the Jew Reuben, but had yet to face justice. But get in trouble with one of the king's wives—that was enough to get a diviner executed. Now it seemed the diviner had eluded the king once again, and perhaps he would not even pay for that.

Faram pushed his way through the celebration, wanting to be

at the tower in spite of the disgusting act that was about to take place. If Rim-Sin had been found, he would be brought here to fulfill his obligation. And Faram would be ready when it was over. Ready to assure that justice was done.

And if Rim-Sin were still free, then Faram prayed to whatever god might hear that he would be the one to find the diviner at last.

On the Platform, she had surprised Qurdi by attacking him at the wall. Now she leaped onto his back and dug her fingers into his face. Qurdi flailed backward and tried to remove her hands. She inched her fingers upward, digging into his eyes. Qurdi screamed, an unearthly howl that turned her stomach.

Her hold on him didn't last long. He tossed her off like a fouled piece of clothing. She fell to the ground, jarring her hip.

Qurdi turned back to the edge where Rim-Sin might still be clinging to the wall.

She heard Rim-Sin shout. *Rim-Sin* was how she thought of him, though surely that wasn't his name if he was from the future, even as *Kaida* was not hers. His words were lost to the wind. She saw his hands disappear from the ledge.

Qurdi saw as well and turned back to her. A sickening delight spread across his features. He motioned to a slave. "The knife."

The tattooed slave of Ishtar brought a silver blade, long and slim, and laid it across Qurdi's palm.

Qurdi jerked his head at her. "Tie her up."

Peter fell.

Not all the way to the city floor, thankfully, but a good twenty feet to the next tier of the tower and into the waiting arms of the people of Babylon. They had flung themselves up the tower steps, spread over the lower levels, waiting for the gods to finally decide which diviner was more favored.

Now they passed Peter's prone body over their heads, like the crowd at some frenzied rock concert. Peter felt their hands, but his eyes were turned upward, drinking in the beauty of the night sky. He remembered something Kaida had said once, about praying to the stars instead of the Maker of the stars. No longer. *Thank You, God.*

You must submit to God.... You must defeat the powers arrayed against you.

It was time.

Peter's senses returned with an acrid sharpness. He struggled from the grasp of the people. They lowered him to the ground. Peter found the steps leading to the Platform and ran up them. He kept his eyes trained upward as he climbed, a holy fury building. The image of Qurdi holding a knife to Kaida's throat burned in his mind.

Qurdi's slaves stood with their backs to the steps, blocking any chance of Kaida escaping. Peter knocked them out of his way. One reached for him, but Peter turned on him. The heat flash from his eyes was hot enough to send the slave staggering backward.

Something was happening inside Peter Thornton. Something unexpected and yet somehow destined since that odd dream here in Babylon.

He turned back to the altar. Another slave fought the struggling Kaida, trying to tie her up. Qurdi stood nearby, a knife clutched in the hand held to his side.

Peter felt a shout begin in his chest, rise to his throat, then explode across the Platform and echo into the night. "Qurdi-Marduk-lamur!"

Qurdi turned slowly, saw Peter, and for the first time, showed a flicker of fear in his eyes. "I have hurled you from a bridge, dropped you into a shaft, and pushed you from the tower. How many times must the gods throw you down before you give up, Rim-Sin?"

"I have long resisted, Qurdi. It wasn't until I had fallen from Babel that I learned what it meant to be free."

The priest's teeth bared. "You will never be free."

Peter drew back and stared into Qurdi's eyes. The words that came from Peter's mouth were not his own. He felt his lips pour forth with the words of a prophet. "Your rebellion will not be tolerated forever, Ishtar! There will come a day, a time, a place, where you will be defeated for all eternity."

Qurdi raised his knife hand, but to Peter it was as if he held nothing but a child's toy.

"There is but one God, demon! And He is not threatened by you!"

Peter watched a struggle in Qurdi's eyes, and he also saw what was unseen. Ishtar battled for Qurdi's body, urged him forward, shouted at him to attack Peter. But Qurdi was a weak vessel, and Ishtar's power was draining before the word of the Lord.

The moment seemed suspended, with all the powers of darkness rushing from the abyss piling up against the unseen yet glowing circle of protection that now surrounded Peter. They beat themselves against the circle, threw themselves at it in fury. Peter watched, awed by the God who protected him from the onslaught. His trust in God deepened even in that moment. He settled further into His loving embrace. The circle blazed brighter, like a flare that would incinerate them all. A screeching filled Peter's ears and mind and heart.

And then silence. The evil departed, burning away into the night sky, leaving Peter in the center of the gently ebbing circle of light.

Something had left Qurdi. His eyes were more vacant, deader

than Peter had ever seen. He was a shell, hollowed out by Ishtar and left to collapse inward on himself.

The priest held the knife outward from his waist and began to run toward Peter.

Faram-Enlil reached the base of the tower just as someone had fallen to the second tier. He couldn't tell who the man was, but something was going on, and he wanted to get a closer look. He began the long climb up the central stairs. Word spread quickly down the tower that Rim-Sin and Qurdi battled on the Platform. Faram quickened his pace.

Peter saw Qurdi approach him, saw the knife in the priest's hand, but felt no fear. Today was the day he accepted his calling. It was not the day to die.

He simply reached out and grabbed Qurdi's wrist. The priest slammed up against him as a wave breaks against a rocky cliff—angry yet futile.

Peter bent the man's wrist backward until the knife dropped. He thrust Qurdi away from him and picked up the knife. Kaida moved in from behind Qurdi, and Peter smiled at her.

Qurdi glanced back and forth between the two of them, panting and snarling like a rabid beast.

"It's over, Qurdi," Peter said. "You have long wanted to see whom the gods favored. Now you know. There is only one God, and He has spoken."

With a fierce shriek, the priest hurled himself at Peter.

Peter barely moved, only raised the knife in his hand to point toward Qurdi, waiting.

The point slipped silently between Qurdi's ribs, divided flesh from bone, and came to rest buried to its hilt. Peter yanked it backward and saw the blood-covered blade catch the reflection of the torchlight.

Qurdi's eyes widened, their last remaining flicker of life fading as Peter watched. The priest fell at Peter's feet, his blood pooling on the stones beneath him.

Kaida came to Peter. He swept her into his arms and buried his face in her hair, holding the knife away from her. "My name is Peter," he whispered.

She smiled up at him through tears. "Lauren."

Lauren.

"Nice to meet you, Lauren."

She laughed weakly. "Nice to meet you, too, Peter."

Movement on the side of the Platform caught his eye. The slaves had long disappeared, but another figure leaped from the steps.

Faram-Enlil was face-to-face with the diviner Rim-Sin at last. It took only a moment to see that Qurdi-Marduk-lamur was dead at Rim-Sin's feet, that Rim-Sin held a bloody knife aloft, and that he held the Jewish girl in his grasp. All the love Faram had long denied for this captive people surged up from somewhere inside him. He pulled his own knife from its sheath at his waist and charged forward. Justice would finally be satisfied.

Peter saw the man at the steps, took in his official uniform. He watched the man's features turn to anger and realized that he still held the knife. He dropped it quickly, but it was too late. The man had his own knife and was running at them both. Peter tried to push Kaida away from him, but she clutched at his arm.

He turned to face the unknown man just as the knife buried

itself in his chest. He saw it but didn't feel it. The Platform faded from sight, like a memory that couldn't be grasped.

Babylon wouldn't miss the outsiders. She wondered at the Power that had taken them from her, but she quickly shifted her attention to those they'd left behind.

She had much to accomplish still, and many years ahead in which to do it. She would live forever, she was certain. She would draw all people into herself, making them one with her. Eventually she would let them release the carved images of the gods and goddesses. In their place she would encourage them to see themselves as gods, urging them to keep climbing until they realized their own human potential. After all, that was how it all began.

When man had first gathered on her sandy plain to build a tower.

Chapter 25

Pain. Not his chest. His head. Darkness gave way to light. Incandescent light. A bare light bulb.

Peter's eyes flickered closed, then open. Best to keep them closed. Both hands held tightly to something.

He opened his eyes. In his right hand, he clutched the now familiar vase. In his left hand, he held the woman he loved.

She blinked at him. Then a jolt like an electric shock sparked through both of them. Her hand was on the vase, too. They jerked away from it.

The vase fell to the floor and shattered into a thousand terra-cotta fragments.

He looked at the pieces spinning on the floor, then turned from them and pulled the woman close. "Lauren."

She laughed, the sound muffled in his chest, but still a warm, healing laugh. "Peter."

It felt strange to hold her there, dressed in jeans and a sweater, in a back room of a museum. Strange, but very, very good. "Thank you," he whispered.

"For what?"

"For pushing me to think beyond my comfortable nonsense and to see the truth."

"The truth?"

"The shocking truth that I am not a god!"

She smiled and touched his face.

"Who are you?" he asked.

She shrugged. "A graduate student. In archeological studies."

Peter frowned. "Then you're young."

"Twenty-four."

"I'm almost old enough to be your father," Peter said.

She laughed again. "I don't care. Besides, you're in fairly good shape."

"Me? What about you—all that running and swimming! Are you some kind of athlete?"

She grinned and shrugged again. "Triathlon. Believe me, more than once I was wishing for a bike." She reached to the shelf beside them and touched a scrap of paper. His hastily scribbled note.

Wait for me.

He smiled. "I didn't know if we'd get back here together."

Lauren folded the paper and slipped it into the front pocket of her jeans. She pulled her hair away from her face. "Do I look different?" she asked.

"A little. Even more beautiful. I'm sorry I don't look much different."

She kissed him, to prove a point.

"How did you—get to Babylon?" Peter asked.

She looked at their feet. "The vase. I came to see it. I sneaked away from a fund-raising banquet before the speaker could bore me to death, and I came up here. I had such a strange feeling when I saw the vase."

Peter smiled and nodded, remembering his own reaction.

"It was the same feeling I'd had earlier," she said. "Someone asked me a question, and, Peter, I would swear that I answered in Aramaic!"

Peter held her hands to his chest. "*Têtê malkuthach. Nehwê tzevjânach.* 'Your kingdom come. Your will be done.'"

They studied each other in silence.

Something she had already said worked its way into Peter's

mind. A graduate student. Archeological studies. And that slightly familiar face. He held her away from him, staring at her eyes. Could it be? "Are you—are you Hugh's daughter?"

Her eyes widened. "Do you know my father?"

"He's one of my only friends! Or at least he was until I went crazy the past couple months when Rim-Sin was me." Lauren. Of course. Braces and giggles. Oh, Hugh was going to kill him. "I haven't seen you in years!"

"Who are *you?*" Lauren asked.

"Peter Thornton."

"Dr. Thornton! Wait a minute, you're the speaker who was going to bore me to death?"

"Guilty, I'm afraid."

"Wow, you *are* old!"

He watched her eyes, but she was laughing.

There was nothing left to do, then, but hold her close and kiss her thoroughly. It was a kiss to erase the past, a kiss that promised the future.

A kiss interrupted by the present.

The storeroom door burst open. Peter and Lauren pulled apart reluctantly and turned to the open door.

Peter had never seen a look quite like the shock on the face of Hugh Rohner.

Epilogue

PETER ADJUSTED HIS glasses and stepped to the microphone with his notes, tilting it up a bit.

It wouldn't be a speech accepting the presidency, but at least he'd held on to his teaching job. And it was a speech that would come from his heart.

"Ladies and gentleman, my study of ancient religions has recently taken me on a . . . a journey. I have been to the top of the mountain, the summit I believed all the roads of religion led to. There was nothing there, my friends. It was a barren wasteland, and I was alone with myself. I saw the weak, pathetic god that I had created out of myself, and it mocked me.

"The study of ancient mythology has taught us one thing: that all myth is essentially the same. There is a certain oneness that unifies it. I used to say that this fact meant we could not know truth. But that is not so. Now I realize that all myth is similar because it has pointed us, in some way, to what would one day become fact.

"I once thought that if I could climb high enough and lift myself courageously enough, I would find what I sought. But I have been to the place where man has reached the highest . . ."

He stared across the audience, his mind far away. Images and memories played across his thoughts.

"Ladies and gentlemen, I have been to that place where man reached highest, and I can tell you with confidence that it is not in climbing that God is to be found. Instead, it is in surrendering. God reaches down to us with redemption. And we must only let go."

His speech finished, Peter mingled with the audience and was pulled into a conversation with Angela-somebody, an obviously affluent businesswoman.

"Your speech intrigued me, Dr. Thornton, but I would have to disagree with your premise."

Peter tried to concentrate, but his mind was on the past few weeks. His calling burned hot in his veins. Speeches were not enough. There was much to be done to fight the growing evil. The old gods were indeed rising—but Peter would stand against them, for he had changed. He had tasted evil, had learned what it took to fight it, and had realized that he was not God. And he had felt the true God's power enlivening him.

There had been one more change. One he had given up on long ago.

He saw her before she saw him. Standing at the doorway, dressed in white, with a white lily tucked in her hair. She saw him then, and her smile was like the sun breaking through dark clouds.

He lost track of what his companion was saying. Lauren joined them, smiled at Angela, and listened intently to the woman.

He and Lauren would fight together, he knew. They both understood the power of the dark "gods" and the greater power of the God of the Bible. But would the two of them be enough? Who would stand with them?

"There will be others," Angela said.

Peter focused on her again. "What did you say?"

"Elthétô hê basileía sou. Genethétô tò thélêmá sou."

Peter and Lauren looked at each other, then back at Angela. "Was that Greek?"

The woman backed away from them, her face a mixture of confusion and fear. "I—I don't know." She looked around at the crowd, then back to them. "I have to go."

They watched as she ran from the room, as though pursued by something strange and terrible.

Peter took Lauren's hand in his own and nodded at her. They recognized the Greek and knew what it meant. Where would Angela be sent back to? What would it take for her to understand?

There *would* be others. The fight would go on. And when Angela returned, perhaps she would join their cause.

The one true God had called him, and Peter realized that he had finally been granted what he'd always wanted... to lead an important work. But this calling was more than he had ever imagined. He lifted his eyes to the ceiling and smiled.

He was ready.